HO

A DISTANT PLANET

FROM THEN ON, Alfven was able to work at his materializer without the sense of impending doom. Now they were sure that they would live until Christmas—at least that most of them would live, and there was a good chance even for the more severely injured among the invalids.

Contact kept sending turkeys which it managed to squeeze into a crowded materialization schedule, and soon they had enough for two Christmas dinners. The one on Christmas Eve wasn't bad, but none the less, the celebration was rather tame. Contact had been inspired enough to try to send a couple of bottles of ethanolic stimulant, but these had broken in transit, and their contents spilled somewhere over a distance of a hundred light-years . . .

—From "Stars Over Santa Claus"

**Plus many more
fantastic tales of
Yuletide fantasy and science fiction!**

EDITED BY
DAVID G. HARTWELL

CHRISTMAS STARS

A TOM DOHERTY ASSOCIATES BOOK
NEW YORK

CHRISTMAS STARS

Cover art by Nick Jainschigg

A Tor Book
Published by Tom Doherty Associates, Inc.
175 Fifth Avenue
New York, NY 10010

Tor ® is a registered trademark of Tom Doherty Associates, Inc.

ISBN: 0-812-52286-9

First edition: November 1992

Printed in the United States of America

0 9 8 7 6 5 4 3 2

COPYRIGHT ACKNOWLEDGMENTS

To Tom Doherty, who likes Christmas stories,
and to the SMP sales force, who asked for some.

ACKNOWLEDGMENTS

I would like to thank a number of people who helped make this book better. Thanks go to Frank Robinson, for open access to his pulps and speedy response to requests for favors; to Gardner Dozois, for his good memory and good taste; to George Scithers, ditto; to Stan Schmidt, Tina Lee and Ian at Analog, for more of the same; to Connie Willis for being a list-maker; to Robert Legault for unsolicited correspondence; to Sheila Williams, Audrey Ferman, Donald G. Keller, Patrick Nielsen Hayden, Virginia Kidd, and Maggie Flinn for a variety of reasons.

CONTENTS

ADESTE FIDELES
Frederik Pohl

A CHRISTMAS WAS only an abstraction on Mars, even for Henry Steegman. The calendars didn't match; Earth's winter solstice had nothing to do with Martian timekeeping. But they kept to the twelve familiar months, to make it easier to count up how long before they could leave for the slow-orbit return trip. As the calendar crept past November and Thanksgiving and crawled toward the holiday, Steegman thought more and more about wrapping paper and Christmas cards and, above all, Christmas trees.

The Christmas before the community had pulled itself together and made an effort. Most of them were still alive then, and even fairly healthy; so they flanged together something tree-shaped—sort of tree-shaped—out of foam plastic and transparent piping. After it was sprayed, it did at least look green. It didn't smell like a tree. But once they had hung it with bright red and green micromatrices from the spare-parts bins and festooned it with instrument lights, it did cheer up the common room. They went further than that, too. They had even made a Santa Claus suit out of somebody's red flannel long johns, stuffed with somebody else's sweaters and bearded with some other body's curly wig. It made Santa Claus's beard platinum blond rather than white, but that was the least of the incongruities. Santa Claus had very few gifts to give them. For most of them, not even the gift of survival.

Henry Steegman was not an important member of his community of Mars explorers. He was neither a xenoanthropologist nor a xenobiologist, nor did he have any of the special skills that made the lives of the survivors fairly tolerable—or almost—like food chemist, power technician, or medic. Steegman was a construction engineer. That is, he drove tractors. He drove interesting kinds of tractors: a nuclear one that crawled through the Martian rock and melted out tunnels, as well as two or three solar-powered ones that leveled and shaped the surface of the planet, twenty meters up from where they lived. He didn't usually drive any of them in person. The places where his tractors went were not very hospitable to human beings. When his services were needed, which was less and less often, as the captain and the council decided that there was really no more need ever to build new domes and explore new anomalies the gravitometers pointed out for them, he sat before a television screen and commanded his tractors by remote control.

That was more or less Christmassy too. It was like having the world's biggest—anyway, Mars' biggest—set of electric trains to play with.

It was about that useful, too, for a community of thirty-eight, once two hundred and four, mostly sick human beings.

Since there was no necessity for much activity of any kind anymore, Steegman was encouraged to play with his toys whenever he wanted to. It kept him out of the way, and it cost nothing. It didn't cost the community valuable working time, because there wasn't a whole lot Steegman was able to do. Radiation sickness in his case had attacked the nerves. He was likely to spasm when he tried anything very demanding. Since the diggers were nine-tenths automatic he couldn't do much harm there. But he couldn't be trusted with anything as delicate as, say, changing bedpans for the dying. And it certainly didn't cost any more than they could afford in power. As long as the photovolatic cascades were given plenty of time to recharge, they provided plenty of power for the surface tractors. For the tunneler there were stocks far beyond any reasonable expectation of need of fuel rods, salvaged from the wreck of the slave rocket. The instrumentation it bore was all mangled, but there's not much you can do to stubby, heavily clad rods of radio-nuclides. There was also plenty of food, water, heat, and light.

The community was really only short of three things. People. Purpose. And hope.

Hope had gone for most of them, along with purpose, when the slave rocket crashed. The expedition was there to conduct scientific investigations. When the drone toppled off its axis of thrust, it split open, blew its fuel tanks, wrecked every delicate part of the instruments, which was most of their parts, and drenched the surface with radionuclides. The misguidance of the rocket wasn't the only thing that went wrong. Someone, unforgivably, in the frantic rush to salvage what they could, had brought hot piping down into the cavern; someone else had hooked it into the water recirculators; it had simmered there, seeping powdery fission products into their drinking water for more than a day before someone else thought to put a dosimeter to his coffee cup.

By then, of course, it was all contaminated. They couldn't live without water. They drank it, glumly watching the dosimeters go into the black. As soon as they could, they began to melt water out of the permafrost under the Martian polar ice cap, only a dozen kilometers away; but by then the people began to get sick. The dosage was not terribly high. Just enough to kill, but not very quickly.

There was one other bad effect.

NASA's vast and powerful public relations machine fought for them most courageously, but the odds were too much. No matter how many tearjerker TV interviews NASA ran with weeping wives and children, no matter what presidential proclamations and prayers, the public image of the expedition was robust against propaganda. *Bunch of clowns*, the public thought. *Busted their rocket ship. Ruined their equipment. Got themselves killed.*

Fortunately for the American spirit, there was a new black American tennis player who won the Wimbledon that year, and a TV star who actually wrestled grizzly bears in his spare time.

The public found new heroes.

And thought rarely, if at all, about the spoiled heroes on Mars.

So on what the calendars said was the twenty-first of December Henry Steegman got out of his bunk, felt his gums to see if they were bleeding, and went to the common room for a leisurely breakfast. He peered in first to make sure Captain Seerseller wasn't up unusually early. He wasn't. The only other person there was Sharon bas Ramirez, the biochemist, and when Henry had picked his almost-hash out of the freezer and passed it through the microwave, he joined her. Sharon bas Ramirez was one of the few survivors who treated Steegman like a worthwhile human being, no doubt because it was Steegman who had brought back samples of organic-contaminated rock for her. "Life on Mars!" their dispatch had read, and they had hoped for a wonderful rebirth of excitement back home. But it wasn't really anything alive, only chemicals that might once have been. And besides, that day the movie star had wrestled a female grizzly with cubs.

"Henry," said Sharon bas Ramirez, "do me a favor, will you? See if you can bring back some better samples."

She was looking very tired. He ate his almost-hash slowly, studying her: black patches under her eyes, fatigue in the set of her jaw.

"What kind of samples?" he asked.

She shrugged wearily. "You cook them with the heat of the drill," she complained, "so the structure gets degraded."

"I tried cold rock drills, Sharon! I even went out myself! I even swiped some blasting powder and a detonator and—"

"Don't get excited, Henry," she said sharply, reaching over to wipe some spilled hash off his coverall. He muttered an apology, calming himself down. "Maybe you can find a fissure somewhere," she said. "Try, anyway? Because I'm a biochemist, not a candy striper, and I get real tired of feeding the sick ones because I don't have anything more important to do."

"I'll try," he promised, and thought hard about how he could keep that promise, all the way to his handler room.

He took the deep tunneler this time, pondering how he could oblige Sharon bas Ramirez. He pushed it through deep Martian rock, twenty kilometers north of the camp. He was not paying strict attention to what he was doing. He was humming "Adeste Fideles," part of his mind thinking about Sharon bas Ramirez, part of it worrying about the latest one to begin to lose blood rapidly—sickly, pale little Terry Kaplan—when the instruments revealed a temperature surge before the nose of the borer.

He shut the machine down at once and palped the rock ahead with sonic probes. The dials showed it was very thin. The sonar scan showed a lumpy, mostly ball-shaped patch, quite large, filled with white-traced, shadowy shapes.

Henry Steegman grinned. A cavern! Even better than a fissure in the rock! He could break in at one end, let it cool, bring the borer back home, get in it himself, and ride back to collect all the samples Sharon could want, uncooked. He started the drill again on low power and gentled the tunneler another meter along its course.

The instruments told him that he had broken through.

Steegman shut the tunneler down and thought for a minute.

Good practice required that he let the rock cool for half an hour before opening the shutters over the delicate and rarely used optical system. He could do that. Or he could start it back without looking and then go in person, which would take two or three hours anyway.

He shrugged and stretched and leaned back, waiting for time to pass, with a smile on his face. Sharon was going to be real pleased! Especially if there turned out to be anything organic in the rock of the cavern—though of course, he cautioned himself, that wasn't guaranteed. Was pretty damn rare, actually. The crust of the planet Mars was very cold and very lifeless; it was only in a few places, where a vagrant stirring of deep-down heat made a patch minutely warmer than what was around it, that you could say it was anything capable of supporting a microbe, anyway. Still, they were well under the polar cap with the digger now. There would at least be residual water, here and there. . . .

When the time was up he looked, and in the searchlight beam, he saw that the cavern was there, all right, but it wasn't exactly empty. It wasn't natural, either. It was a great bubble laced with what might have been catwalks and what looked like balconies, and all about it were what seemed to be shelves and what could be called tables. Some of them had things on them.

Henry Steegman didn't know what it was he had found, but it had a funnily suggestive look to it. He didn't make the connection for nearly twenty minutes, though. By then his yells had brought others into the control room.

They began to yell, too. Captain Seerseller ordered Henry back out of the way because they were all afraid, naturally, that he would get too excited and knock something over or push the wrong button, but he could catch glimpses of what was on the screen and hear what everyone was shouting to each other. He heard perfectly when Marty Lawless yelled, "You know what it is? It's a Martian Macy's!"

By the time Steegman had painfully inched his drill out of the way, he was almost alone at the base. Not quite alone. The walking sick, Terry Kaplan and Bruce DeAngelis and one or two others who were well enough to look but far from well enough to make the trip to the cavern, were wheezing and gasping behind him, but everyone else was gone.

The tunnel from the base camp to the "department store" was thirty-three kilometers and a bit, the last five still unlined. Wheeled vehicles couldn't go down the unlined part, but no one was willing to wait for lining. So the first two parties drove, six or eight at a time in the big-wheeled tunnel buggies, as far as the surfaced section of the tunnel went. Then they walked, in air masks and backpacks, because the department store was by light-years the most astonishing discovery the expedition had made on Mars, and therefore the thing that most nearly justified the loss of nearly all their lives.

They *almost* all went, all but the ones too sick ... and Henry Steegman. The discoverer of the department store was not allowed to enter it.

It wasn't just that he was needed to get the big borer out of the tunnel so people could clamber through. Captain Seerseller's last order had made that clear. It was, "You stay here, Steegman, you understand? No matter what."

So for the first ten minutes Steegman and his hovering casualties saw nothing on the screen but the sonar scan, reporting on what sorts of rock the drill tractor was nibbling through. Then Steegman turned it off and switched channels to the portable cameras in the first buggy. "Is that it?" little Terry Kaplan asked, hoarding breath to speak. "It looks ... looks"—she took a deep breath—"looks different."

"It's only the tunnel," Steegman said absently, watching as the field of view swung dizzyingly around. Then the first party was inside, and whoever was carrying that camera was glad to set it down on automatic scan. So Steegman watched jealously as the others piled into the wonderland he had found for them, each one more excited than the other. Marty Lawless, six feet six and fifty years old, pulled his spidery body in and out of prism-shaped structures inside the great hollow bubble and cried, "It really is a store! Kind of a store! Like an enclosed market! Like a great big shopping mall, where you can find almost anything."

"It could be a warehouse," objected Manuel Andrew Applegate, senior surviving archaeologist, annoyed at the presumption of someone who actually was a communications engineer.

"There's nothing on most of the shelves, Manny-Anny." Captain Seerseller pointed out.

Lawless answered that one, too. "The perishables have perished, of course," he cried. "God knows how old this is! But it's a store, all right. A suq. A bazaar!"

And back in the control booth Terry Kaplan whispered to Steegman with what sounded like the last of her breath, "It really is a Macy's, Henry. Oh, how Morton is going to love this!"

And no one answered, because Terry was a widow. Morton Kaplan had died more than three months before.

And so the expedition began to live again—as much as it could with most of its people already buried under the Martian soil. Pictures, samples, diagrams, data of all kinds—everyone wanted to put his specialty to work at once, no, not after the archaeological team made its inventories, but now, me first! Not only were they thrilled at what they had found, they were actually getting signs of real interest from Earth, for the first time in many months.

It didn't happen right away. The round-trip travel time for talking to NASA Command was less than thirty minutes, but no one at NASA Command was paying attention when the first excited messages came in. Hours later, some no-doubt-bored comm specialist decided he might, after all, earn his day's pay by looking over the last batch of accumulated tapes. And did. And boredom vanished.

It was a good time for Earth to take an interest in Mars again. The movie star had lost his last bout with a grizzly, terminally; and there was a new Czechoslovakian kid burning up the tennis courts. So the network news carried the pictures, and there were special half-hour reports every night after the late news, and NASA's P.R. people were in heaven. Send us more, they begged. Not just some crummy old archaeological drawings and photographs. Personalities! *Interviews!*

Interviews with, most of all, that one hero of the expedition, whoever he was, who had first discovered the Martian Macy's.

Since the captain was well and truly NASA trained, he saw his duty and did it. They co-opted Sharon bas Ramirez away from her delightful duties of studying moldering samples of definitely organic substances from the store and put her to work patching Henry Steegman's old tunic; the one surviving surgeon was taken off the wards of the dying to cut Henry's hair and shave him; and they put him in front of the TV camera.

Captain Seerseller, of course, did the interview himself—he remembered *all* of his training. They found the two best-looking chairs in the colony and planted them before a camera, with a table containing a bizarre sort of unrusted metal implement between them. It was the most spectacular piece the archaeologists had so far allowed them to bring in.

Then the captain gestured the camera to himself. When it was on, he smiled directly into the lens. "Hello, my friends," he said. "Mars reporting. Under my leadership the expedition has continued to survey this old planet, on its surface and under, and we have just made the most wonderful discovery in human history. Under my direction Henry Steegman was extending our network of exploratory tunnels. He broke through into a sealed underground chamber of approximately twenty thousand cubic meters volume. It is divided into five levels. All levels are built over with triangular prism-shaped structures. Each triangular 'booth' contains a different kind of item. Our specialists have made a preliminary inspection, on my orders, and have reached the tentative conclusion that the objects are merchandise and that the cavern itself was the equivalent of a Martian department store. This object," he said, picking up the gleaming thing, "was perhaps a scientific instrument or possibly even a household utensil. Of course, most of the contents of this 'store' are rusted, decayed, or simply vanished—they have been there for a long, long time. So I have ordered our archaeologists to exercise extreme care in their handling so that no valuable data might be lost."

The camera focus had pulled back to show the stand the object had come from, and also Henry Steegman, digging into one ear with a finger while he was listening in fascination to the captain. Steegman was not at all sure what he was supposed to be doing. His instructions had been, Just relax. But it was hard to relax with the captain's occasional frosty, sidelong looks. He was feeling that funny, buzzy sensation that meant his ruined nervous system was being overstimulated again; he closed his eyes and breathed deeply.

"Now," said the captain, with an edge in his voice, "I want to introduce to you the man who, carrying out my directions, made the first penetration of this Martian marvel, Henry Steegman."

Steegman jerked his eyes open and blinked at the camera. He didn't like having it look at him; his eyes wavered away but only onto the monitor, which was worse. He could see that he was shaking. He tried to control it, which made it worse. "Henry," said the captain, "tell us how you felt when you broke through into the cavern."

Steegman thought for a moment and then said uncertainly, "Real good?"

"Real good! Well, we all did that, Henry," said the captain with audible forbearance. "But when you completed this task I had assigned you and saw for the first time proof that there had once been life on Mars—even civilized life!—were you surprised? Excited? Happy? Did it make you want to laugh? Or cry? Or both at once?"

"Oh, I see what you mean," Henry said, pondering. "Pretty much that kind of thing, I guess."

"And did it make you realize that all the great sacrifices of blood and treasure—the lives of so many of us, and the wonderful support the people have given in making this venture possible—did it make you think it was all worthwhile?"

Henry had figured out a safe response. He said promptly, "I don't exactly remember that, Captain."

The captain swallowed a sigh and motioned to Mina Wandwater, the best looking of the surviving women, who came forward into camera range with a champagne bottle and a glass. "This is for you, Henry," said the captain, leaning forward to stay in range of the camera as Mina poured. "It's your just reward for carrying out my instructions so successfully!"

Henry held the glass carefully while Mina filled it, curtsied prettily to him and the captain, and withdrew. He looked at the captain for instructions.

The captain said tightly, "Drink it!"

"Right, Captain," Henry said. He stared at the glass, then suddenly jerked it to his lips. He slobbered half the contents over himself and the floor. Then—because the bottle was champagne but the contents weren't; they were something bubbly the chemists had cooked up to refill the empty— Steegman sputtered and choked. He twitched and dropped the glass and then sat there, gaping dumbly into the television camera.

It was not only a lot of trouble to keep up the morale back home, it sometimes didn't work at all. The captain gave the camera a great smile and said, "That concludes our interview with Henry Steegman, who under my—what is it, Henry?" he asked irritably. Steegman had stopped dabbing at the mess on his tunic long enough to wave frantically at the captain.

"I just wanted to say one more thing," he pleaded. "You folks at home? I know it's a little early, but—Merry Christmas!"

They made Steegman take another physical after that, which kept him in the ward overnight, among the immobile and the dying. The surgeon studied his tests and plates and told Henry matter-of-factly, "You're going, I'm afraid. A few more weeks. Your myelin sheaths are rotted away. It's going to get worse pretty soon—that's a nice haircut, though, isn't it?"

When Henry went to the captain's office, the captain wasn't there. Neither was the surgeon, but his report had already come over the net, and the executive officer was studying it on her screen.

"You want what, Henry?" she asked. "You want to go into the *cavern*? Good lord, no! Captain Seerseller would never permit it. The surgeon's report makes it very clear, your motor reflexes are too untrustworthy, that's very delicate stuff in there, and we don't want it wrecked."

"I wouldn't hurt anything," he protested, but she wasn't listening anymore. She just waved him out.

Nobody else wanted to listen, either, though some of them

tried to make it more palatable. "You wouldn't want to spoil your own discovery, would you?" Mina Wandwater asked.

"I wouldn't hurt anything," Steegman pleaded.

"Of course you wouldn't *mean* to. No," she said kindly, "you just stay out of there, okay? We just can't afford any more accidents on our record, you know."

She was gone before Steegman remembered to point out that he wasn't the one who had crashed the instrument rocket or let the fission products into the water. Sharon bas Ramirez was kinder but also busier. She looked up from the tubes of samples long enough to say, "I really can't talk to you now, Henry, but don't worry. They'll let you in sooner or later, you know."

But if it weren't sooner, it couldn't be later. Steegman said absently, "You know it's Christmas Eve?"

"Oh. So it is. Merry Christmas, Henry," she said, turning back to her lab bench.

Steegman limped back to his control booth and activated his tunneler. Then he sat moping before the screen without sending it forward. Sometimes he got pleasure out of executing circles and figure eights under the surface of Mars, drilling the old planet hollow, lacing it with wormholes and channels the likes of which it had never known. Would never know again, most likely, but would also never forget. The Martian crust was too thick and too old and too cold to squeeze itself seamless again. The arteries Steegman gouged would stay there forever.

He turned it off and thought about the surface tractors. But he didn't like working on surface much. Oh, in those first weeks after landing—in spite of the deaths and the doom that hung over most of the survivors—what a thrill it had been! He had delighted in bulldozing ageless, eternally untrodden Martian sand and gravel into flat bases for the huge dish transmitter that sent their signals back to Earth, or in roaming out fifty or a hundred kilometers to pick up samples and bring them back for testing. Just seeing the dwarfed, distant sun was a thrill. The tiny points of hot light that were the stars were a delight. The queerly close horizon was an astonishment—they were marvels, all of them, all the time. Over every hummock there was the mystery of what Mars was all about. What would they find? A city? An oasis? A ... *Martian*?

Or, as hopes for any of those dwindled, a tree?

Or a bush?

Or a thin patch of moss on a rock?

And they had found none of them. There was nothing. There was always nothing except the same sterile sand and rock or sandy ice at the beginning of the cap. Even the tiny sun and the white-hot stars weren't exciting anymore.

Steegman kicked against the rock wall under his control desk.

Then he brightened.

It was, after all, Christmas Eve!

So Henry Steegman made the long trek back to the captain's office again, pausing on the way in his own chamber. The Santa Claus suit was still there in the locker under his cot! He pulled out a knapsack, stuffed the suit in, and hurried down the corridor. Captain Seerseller was not there, and Lieutenant Tesca was not encouraging. "He's at Macy's," she said, "and really very busy, and so am I—I'm going there myself. What, a Christmas party? No, no, I can't authorize that—really, Henry," she said fairly patiently. "I don't think you understand what finding this means to us. We just don't have time for nonsense right now."

But she let Steegman hitch a ride with her. The big-wheeled buggy slid smoothly down the tunnel until they reached the unlined part; then the executive officer jumped out and left rapidly for the last few kilometers. Steegman toiled patiently behind. His gait was getting worse all the time, he knew. His knees were wobbly—not painful, just sort of loosely put together, so that he was never sure his legs would support him at any stride—and his calves were beginning to ache from the unaccustomed strain on the muscles caused by his awkward foot placement. It took him an hour,

but by the time he passed the side shaft where he had left the
tunneler, he could already hear voices up ahead.

The loudest voice was Captain Seerseller's. He was argu-
ing with Manuel Andrew Applegate at the entrance to the
cavern. Beyond them Steegman could see the interior of the
cavern as he had never seen it before. A score of bright lights
had been put in place all around it, throwing shadows, illumi-
nating bright colors and pastels, clusters of long-rusted-away
metal things and heaps of heaven knew what, rotted into
black grit. When the captain caught sight of Steegman he
turned and blazed, "What are you doing here? I've told you
to stay out of this place!"

"I wasn't coming in, Captain," Henry said humbly. "I just
wanted to ask if we were going to have a Christmas party this
year."

"Christmas?" the captain repeated, and Applegate next to
him said, "What about Christmas? We don't have time for
that, Henry. Everybody's too busy!"

"I'm not too busy, Manny-Anny," Steegman said, and the
captain snorted, "Then get busy! Dig something useful!"

"I've already dug six of everything we could ever use."

"Then make some of the things bigger."

"But I've already—" Steegman began, shifting position to
back away from the captain—and in the process sliding on
the rubble of loose talus from where the drill had broken
through. He lurched against the captain.

"Oh, sorry," he said, "but nothing needs enlarging. Not
even the grave-yards."

"*Go,*" snarled the captain. And Steegman went. He hesitated at the tunnel buggy, casting a look at the captain. But
the captain was once again deep in argument with Manny-
Anny Applegate.

Steegman sighed and started the long, limping walk back
to the dome. He could not, after all, just take the buggy and
leave those people marooned.

But a dozen meters down the tunnel his face brightened,
his stride quickened, and he turned off into the shaft where he
had left the digger. He could drive himself home! Not in that

tunnel, of course. But there was nothing to stop him from making a new one.

Steegman pressed against the scarred metal of the tunneler, just where it rounded into the straight flank. He found the recessed catch. It had rock chips in it, of course; but he patiently worked them free, opened the hatch, climbed in, and made his way to the driver's seat.

The quarters were cramped, and the cabin was still uncomfortably hot from the last spate of digging. But it was his own. He pulled the Santa Claus suit out of his knapsack and rolled it up behind his head. Then he leaned back and closed his eyes.

He didn't sleep.

After a while he sat up straight, turned the idling circuits on, checked his instruments. The tunneler had communications as well as control circuits to the campsite, and Steegman considered calling back to let anyone who might care know where he was. He thought he might leave a message about how he felt, too, because in fact he was beginning to feel very peculiar.

Since very few persons would really care, Steegman decided against it. He cut the communications system out entirely. Then he advanced the control for the drills and engaged the tractor motors.

There was a racketing roar of noise. The cab, and the whole tunneler, shook in short, sharp shocks. It began to move forward, down into virgin Martian rock.

Twenty minutes later Steegman began to throw up for the first time. Fortunately, he was expecting it. The pounding motion of the tunneler was enough to make anyone queasy, even if he hadn't been drinking the colony's water; and Steegman had found a receptacle—actually, it was a case for one of the fuel rods—to throw up in. When he was through he was sweating and light-headed, but peaceful.

He advanced the speed of the tunneler a bit and bored on.

He had no particular objective in mind except to go on. He liked having no objectives. It was how you found unexpected things. At the head of the borer, where the immense, terribly hard, tough teeth ground into the rock, where two flush-mounted poppers. Every second each of them emitted a shattering pistol crack of sound, the frequencies just different enough from each other, and sufficiently unlike any of the spectrum of noises the chewing of the borer itself produced, to be distinguishable by the sonar receivers inside the shell. Every second they reached out and felt for flaws or faults or soft spots and displayed the results on the screen before Steegman. Steegman didn't have a windshield, of course. There was no glass strong enough to fit the shell of the tunneler, and generally nothing to see if there had been. But the screen was as good.

Steegman leaned back, watching the patterns change before him. What he was looking for, mostly, were soft spots in the rock ahead—an intrusion of lighter rock, maybe, or a lens of clathrate, the ice-and-solids mix that was the principal Martian source of liquid water.

Or—perhaps!—another cavern. . . .

It was a pity, Steegman reflected, that he was going to die soon.

It was not a horror. The first shock of that sort of realization had long worn calloused. He had known for a year that his life would be short and had been certain almost that long that he would not survive to the liftoff, much less through the endless return to low Earth orbit and home. So there were pleasures he would never have again. Item, he would never see clouds in a blue sky. Item, he would never swim. Item, he would never get a chance to see the marvels he had not got around to—Niagara Falls, Stonehenge, the Great Wall of China. Never again a full moon or a rainbow or a thunderstorm; never hail a taxi on a city street; never walk into a movie theater with a pretty woman; never—

Never any of those things. On the other hand, he comforted himself, there was hardly anyone who would ever see the things he had seen on Mars!

Even what he was seeing now on the screen, why, it was wonderful! He was kilometers beyond the "department store" now, far under the thin smear of dry ice and water ice that was the North polar cap. The false-color images on the screen formed pretty patterns, constantly changing as the tunneler moved forward and the sonars got better information on what was before them. If there was any tectonic activity at all on Mars, it lay not far from here, where echo sounders had indicated an occasional plume of warmer, lighter, softer matter—even liquid water in a few sparse, small places. Peter Braganza, the head geologist, had likened some of them to the white smoke/black smoke fountains at the bottom of some of the earth's seas, slow upwellings of warmth from the tiny residual core heat of the old planet.

It was from plumes like those that Steegman had brought back the samples that thrilled Sharon bas Ramirez. Organics! It was almost certainly organic matter, she thought, at least— but the heat of the tunneler had boiled the water out of the minerals and had cooked the carbon compounds as well. If they had just had some of the instruments they should have had, the nuclear magnetic resonance scanner in particular, she could have been sure ... but the NMR equipment had been on the crashed rocket.

Steegman leaned forward, peering at the screen.

A gray blob on the lower right-hand corner had changed to pale blue as the sonars got a better reading on it. Clathrate? Not exactly. Liquid water? Perhaps. Steegman couldn't get a temperature reading that meant anything while the drills were going, but things did warm up a little as one approached the plumes. It was quite possible that water could be liquid here. He was humming "Silent Night" to himself as he studied the screen.

It was unusually pretty now. It was almost a hologram, or at least it gave the illusion of depth. What the poppers scanned, the sonar computers examined and analyzed and sculpted into the scene before him.

What they displayed was almost always more intricate and beautiful than anything he would have seen drilling through the crust of the earth. Even the most homogeneous of earthly rock shows differences of texture and density. On Mars, where the crust had been almost all cold for almost forever, there were countless splits and cracks and fault lines to make a pleasing tracery of color streaks and blobs.

It was funny, Steegman thought, that they didn't look really random.

He had to pause for another seizure of vomiting, holding the canister close to his lips against the cruelly sharp lurches of the tunneler. When he was through he put it aside, still staring at the screen. He tried to make sense of what he was seeing.

Almost ahead, a little below the level he was drilling through, there was a prism-shaped tubular structure that was displayed in golden yellow. Not clathrate! Not even liquid water. It stretched off to the left and away as far as the sound probe could reach in one direction. In the other, for a hundred meters or so back toward the "department store" he had long ago passed, until it came up against a hard new—geologically new—intrusion.

Smiling to himself in pleasure, Steegman inched the nose of the borer down and around to intersect it.

When it was huge before him, there was a lurch, and the cutting nose spun madly.

That was a surprise! There were not many caverns under the Martian surface. Steegman quickly shut the blades off. On the tractor treads alone, dead slow, the tunneler shoved its way through a few crumbling edges of rock. When it was free, he turned everything off and paused to consider the situation.

He was really very tired, he realized. Although he was glad that the painful jolting of the tunneler had stopped, he was still very queasy. He cautiously allowed himself a few sips of water from the tunneler's supplies. When he did not immediately throw them up again, he felt more cheerful.

He thought for a moment of opening the communications link again to report his find. The geologists would surely want to investigate this unusual structure. . . .

But Steegman wanted to investigate it himself.

He pulled on his air mask and, with less strength than he

had expected, was finally able to force the front hatch open against the gravel that had accumulated outside it. It was hot.

When he stepped cautiously out onto the talus, it burned his feet. He hopped back into the tunneler, rubbing one foot and looking around for what he needed. Lights. There was a shoulder pack of batteries and a hand lamp. Clothing, too, because apart from the rock that had been heated by the drill the tunnel was quite cold.

He grinned to himself, took the garments from the back of the seat, and pulled them on, even the platinum-blond beard.

He engaged the tractor treads and inched forward, past the rubble where he had broken through, as far as he could until the motionless drill teeth crunched against the far wall.

Then he stepped out onto the smooth, flat floor of the tunnel, which was no geologic feature at all.

Although his vision was blurring and his breathing had become painful, Steegman was sure of that. The tunnel was as much an artifact as the "department store." Crystalline walls, undimmed by the millennia, bounced back the light of his hand lamp. The cross section of the tunnel was triangular, with rounded corners. Natural formations did not come in such shapes.

What price Niagara Falls now! Steegman laughed out loud in triumph. His duty was clear. He should jump back in the tunneler and tell the rest of the expedition what he had found. They would want to come rushing, to explore this tunnel, to see what it led to—

But so did he.

Without looking back he turned left, settled the battery pack better on his shoulder straps, and began limping down the tunnel. When he had his next spasm of vomiting he had no handy canister to fill. (On the other hand, there was not much left in him to throw up, so the mess was minimal.) When at last he could walk no longer he sat down, his fingers fumbling with crumbled bits of what might have been broken porcelain or might have been some kind of stone.

He closed his eyes, perfectly happy.

It was a long time before he opened them again, and he

wouldn't have, except that he felt as though his old dog were nuzzling at his fingers.

When he woke, the sensation remained. Something was nuzzling at his hand. It wasn't a dog. When he stirred, it flinched away from the light, but with the last of his vision he got a good look at it. More than anything else, it looked like one of those baby harp seals the fur hunters clubbed, only with skinny, stiltlike legs. "Merry Christmas," Henry Steegman whispered, and died.

When at last anyone noticed that Steegman was missing, the captain ordered Manuel Andrew Applegate to follow the new tunnel and retrieve the borer itself, at least—whether Steegman were retrieved or not, he declared, he didn't at all care.

When Applegate reached the borer and saw what it had broken into, his almost incoherent message back brought half the colony there on as close to a run as they could manage.

When finally they saw the dimming glow of Steegman's hand lamp, far down the corridor, and hurried toward it, they saw that Steegman was not alone.

He was dead, propped against the wall in his Santa Claus suit. Even under the fake beard they could see he was smiling; and around him, whistling in distress as they tried to avoid the harsh glare of the approaching lights, were eight unbelievably, wholly unexpectedly, unarguably living and breathing Martians.

And when at last the few survivors of the expedition came home to a presidential reception and a New York ticker-tape parade, Broadway was not renamed Captain Seerseller Avenue for the occasion. It was called Henry Steegman Boulevard.

Yes, Virginia, there'll always be a Santa.

THE SANTA CLAUS
COMPROMISE
Thomas M. Disch

THE FIRST REVELATIONS hit the headlines the day after Thanksgiving, less than a year from the Supreme Court's epochal decision to extend full civil liberties to five-year-olds. After centuries of servitude and repression the last minority was finally free. Free to get married. Free to vote and hold office. Free to go to bed at any hour they wanted. Free to spend their allowances on whatever they liked.

For those services geared to the newly liberated young it was a period of heady expansion. A typical example was Lord & Taylor's department stores, which had gone deeply into the red in the two previous years, due to the popularity of thermal body-paints. Lord & Taylor changed its name to Dumb Dresses and Silly Shoes, and its profits soared to record heights in the second quarter of '79. In the field of entertainment, the Broadway musical *I See London, I See France* scored a similar success with audiences and critics alike. "I think it shows," wrote *Our Own Times* Drama Critic Sandy Myers, "how kids are really on the ball today. I think everyone who likes singing and dancing and things like that should go and see it. But prudes should be warned that some of the humor is pretty spicy."

It was the same newspaper's team of investigative reporters, Bobby Boyd and Michelle Ginsberg, who broke the Santa Claus story one memorable November morning. Under a banner headline that proclaimed: "THERE IS NO SANTA CLAUS!" Bobby told how, months before, rummaging through various trunks and boxes in his parents' home in Westchester, he had discovered a costume identical in every respect with that worn by the "Santa Claus" who had visited the Boyd household on the previous Christmas Eve. "My soul was torn," wrote the young Pulitzer Prize winner, "between feelings of outrage and fear. The thought of all the years of imposture and deceit that had been practiced on me and my brothers and sisters around the world made me furious. Then, when I foresaw all that I'd be up against, a shiver of dread went through me. If I'd known that the trail of guilt would lead me to the door of my father's bedroom, I can't be sure that I'd have followed it. I had my suspicions, of course."

But suspicions, however strong, weren't enough for Bobby and Michelle. They wanted evidence. Months of back-breaking and heart-breaking labor produced nothing but hearsay, innuendo, and conflicting allegations. Then, in mid-November, as the stores were already beginning to fill with Christmas displays, Michelle met the mysterious Clayton E. Forster. Forster claimed that he had repeatedly assumed the character and name of Santa Claus, and that this imposture had been financed from funds set aside for this purpose by a number of prominent New York businesses. When asked if he had ever met or spoken to the real Santa Claus, Forster declared outright that *there wasn't any!* Though prevented from confirming Forster's allegations from his own lips by the municipal authorities (Forster had been sent to prison on a vagrancy charge), reporters were able to listen to Michelle's tape recording of the interview, on which the self-styled soldier-of-fortune could be heard to say: "Santa Claus? Santa's just a pile of (expletive deleted), kid! Get wise—there ain't no (expletive deleted), and there never was one. It's nothing but your (expletive deleted) mother and father!"

The clincher, however, was Bobby's publication of a number of BankAmericard receipts, charging Mr. Oscar T. Boyd for, among much else, "2 rooty-toot-toots and 3 rummy-tum-tums." These purchases had been made in early December of the previous year and coincided *in all respects* with the Christmas presents that the Boyd children subsequently received, presumably from Santa Claus. "You could call it circumstantial evidence, sure," admitted *Our Own Times'* Senior Editor Barry "Beaver" Collins, "but we felt we'd reached the point when we had to let the public know."

The public reacted at first with sheer, blank incomprehension. Only slowly did the significance and extent of the alleged fraud sink in. A Gallup poll, taken on December 1, asked voters aged five through eight: "Do you believe in Santa Claus?" The results: Yes, 26%; No, 38%; Not sure, 36%. Older children were even more skeptical. A Harris poll taken at the same time seemed to show a more widespread faith in Santa: 84% of all younger voters replied "Yes" when asked if they expected Santa to leave presents for them on Christmas morning. Only the grownup-oriented media saw fit to point out that a Santa who didn't exist could not very well leave presents.

On December 12, an estimated 300,000 children converged on the Boyd residence in Westchester from every part of the city and the state. Chanting "Poop on the big fat hypocrites," they solemnly burned no less than 128 effigies of Santa Claus in the Boyds' front yard. Equivalent protests took place in every major city.

The height of the scandal—and of the protests—came the following day, when the two young reporters revealed that Dorothy Biddle, personnel director of the vast Macy's Toy Store, had ordered the contents of three personnel department files shredded and burned on the very day the *Times'* story had broken. The employee who had carried out this task, Miss Charlotte Olson, contacted Bobby and Michelle after hearing Baby Jesus sing "Jingle Bells" in a vision. Though

Miss Olson claimed not to have examined the documents she shredded, the implication was irresistible that these were the employment records of the "False Santas" spoken of by Clayton Forster. Director Biddle would neither confirm nor deny the *Times*' sensational charges, insisting that whether or not they were true, the *real* Santa Claus might nevertheless exist. For many young people, however, this argument was no longer persuasive. As Bobby later wrote, looking back on those momentous days, "It had become something bigger than just Santa Claus. We began to question everything our daddies and mommies told us. It was scary. You know?"

The real long-range consequences of the scandal did not become apparent for much longer, since they lay rather in what wasn't done than in what was. People were acting as though not only Santa but Christmas itself had been called in question. Log-jams of unsold merchandise piled up in stockrooms and warehouses, and the streets filled up with forests of brittle evergreens.

Any number of public figures tried, unavailingly, to reverse this portentous state of affairs. The Congress appropriated $3 million to decorate the Capitol and the White House with giant figures of Santa and his reindeer, and the Lincoln Memorial temporarily became the Santa Claus Memorial. Reverend Billy Graham announced that he was a personal friend of both Santa Claus and his wife, and had often led prayer meetings at Santa's workshop at the North Pole. But nothing served to restore the public's confidence. By December 18, one week before Christmas, the Dow-Jones industrial average had fallen to an all-time low.

In response to appeals from businessmen all over the country, a national emergency was declared and Christmas was pushed back one month, to the 25th of January, on which date it continues to be celebrated. An effort was made by the National Association of Manufacturers to substitute their own Grandma America for the disgraced Santa Claus. Grandma America had a distinct advantage over her predecessor, in that she was invisible and could walk through walls, thereby eliminating the age-old problem of how children living in chim-

neyless houses get their presents. There appeared to be hope
that this campaign would succeed, until a rival group of businesses which had been excluded from the Grandma America
franchise introduced Aloysius the Magic Snowman, and the
Disney Corporation premiered their new nightly TV series,
Uncle Scrooge and the Spirit of Christmas Presents.

The predictable result of the mutual recriminations of the
various franchise-holders was an even greater dubiety on the
part of both children and grownups. "I used to be a really
convinced believer in Santa," declared Bobby's mother in an
exclusive interview with her son, "but now with all this
fufaraw over Grandma America and the rest of them, I just
don't know. It seems sordid, somehow. As for Christmas itself, I think we may just sit this one out."

"Bobby and I, we just felt *terrible*," pretty little (3'11")
Michelle Ginsberg said, recalling those dark mid-January
days at the Pulitzer Prize ceremony. "We'd reported what we
honestly believed were the facts. We never considered that it
could lead to a recession or anything so awful. I remember
one Christmas morning—what *used* to be Christmas, that is—
sitting there with my empty pantyhose hanging from the fireplace and just crying my heart out. It was probably the single
most painful moment of my life."

Then, on January 21, *Our Own Times* received a telephone
call from the President of the United States, who invited its
two reporters, Billy and Michelle, to come with him on the
Presidential jet, *Spirit of '76*, on a special surprise visit to the
North Pole!

What they saw there, and whom they met, the whole nation
learned on the night of January 24, the new Christmas Eve,
during the President's momentous press conference. After
Billy showed his Polaroid snapshots of the elves at work in
their workshop, of himself shaking Santa's hand and sitting
beside him in the sleigh, and of everyone—Billy, Michelle,
Santa Claus and Mrs. Santa, the President and the First
Lady—sitting down to a big turkey dinner, Michelle read a
list of all the presents that she and Billy had received. Their

estimated retail value: $18,599.95. As Michelle bluntly put it: "My father just doesn't make that kind of money."

"So would you say, Michelle," the President asked with a twinkle in his eye, "that you do believe in Santa Claus?"

"Oh, absolutely, there's no question."

"And you, Billy?"

Billy looked at the tips of his new cowboy boots and smiled. "Oh, sure. And not just 'cause he gave us such swell presents. His beard, for instance. I gave it quite a yank. I'd take my oath that the beard was real."

The President put his arms around the two children and gave them a big warm squeeze. Then, becoming suddenly more serious, he looked right at the TV camera and said: "Billy, Michelle—your friends who told you that there is no Santa Claus were wrong. They have been affected by the skepticism of a skeptical age. They do not believe except they see. They think that nothing can be which is not comprehensible by their little minds. But all minds, Virginia—uh, that is to say, Billy and Michelle—whether they be men's or children's, are little. In this great universe of ours, man is a mere *insect*, an ant, in his intellect, as compared with the boundless world about him, as measured by the intelligence capable of grasping the *whole* of truth and knowledge.

"Not believe in Santa Claus? You might as well not believe in fairies. No Santa Claus! Thank God he lives, and he lives forever. A thousand years from now—nay, ten times ten thousand years from now, he will continue to make glad the hearts of childhood."

Then, with a friendly wink, and laying his finger aside of his nose, he added, "In conclusion, I would like to say—to Billy and Michelle and to my fellow Americans of every age—Merry Christmas to all, and to all a good night!"

Your shopping days are numbered.

MIRACLE
Connie Willis

THERE WAS A Christmas tree in the lobby when Lauren got to work, and the receptionist was sitting with her chin in her hand, watching the security monitor. Lauren set her shopping bag down and looked curiously at the screen. On it, Jimmy Stewart was dancing the Charleston with Donna Reed.

"The Personnel Morale Special Committee had cable piped in for Christmas," the receptionist explained, handing Lauren her messages. "I love *It's a Wonderful Life*, don't you?"

Lauren stuck her messages in the top of her shopping bag and went up to her department. Red and green crepe paper hung in streamers from the ceiling, and there was a big red crepe paper bow tied around Lauren's desk.

"The Personnel Morale Special Committee did it," Cassie said, coming over with the catalogue she'd been reading. "They're decorating the whole building, and they want us and Document Control to go caroling this afternoon. Don't you think PMS is getting out of hand with this Christmas spirit thing? I mean, who wants to spend Christmas Eve at an office party?"

"I do," Lauren said. She set her shopping bag down on the desk, sat down, and began taking off her boots.

"Can I borrow your stapler?" Cassie asked. "I've lost mine again. I'm ordering my mother the Water of the Month, and I need to staple my check to the order form."

"The water of the month?" Lauren said, opening her desk drawer and taking out her stapler.

"You know, they send you bottles of a different one every month. Perrier, Evian, Calistoga." She peered in Lauren's shopping bag. "Do you have Christmas presents in there? I hate people who have their shopping done four weeks before Christmas."

"It's four *days* till Christmas," Lauren said, "and I don't have it all done. I still don't have anything for my sister. But I've got all my friends, including you, done." She reached in the shopping bag and pulled out her pumps. "*And* I found a dress for the office party."

"Did you buy it?"

"No." She put on one of her shoes. "I'm going to try it on during my lunch hour."

"If it's still there," Cassie said gloomily. "I had this echidna toothpick holder all picked out for my brother, and when I went back to buy it, they were all gone."

"I asked them to hold the dress for me," Lauren said. She put on her other shoe. "It's gorgeous. Black off-the-shoulder. Sequined."

"Still trying to get Scott Buckley to notice you, huh? I don't do things like that anymore. Nineties women don't use sexist tricks to attract men. Besides, I decided he was too cute to ever notice somebody like me." She sat down on the edge of Lauren's desk and started leafing through the catalogue. "Here's something your sister might like. The Vegetable of the Month. February's okra."

"She lives in Southern California," Lauren said, shoving her boots under the desk.

"Oh. How about the Sunscreen of the Month?"

"No," Lauren said. "She's into New Age stuff. Channeling

and stuff. Last year she sent me a crystal pyramid mate selector for Christmas."

"The Eastern philosophy of the month," Cassie said. "Zen, sufism, tai chi—"

"I'd like to get her something she'd really like," Lauren mused. "I always have a terrible time figuring out what to get people for Christmas. So this year, I decided things were going to be different. I wasn't going to be tearing around the mall the day before Christmas, buying things no one would want and wondering what on earth I was going to wear to the office party. I started doing my shopping in September, I wrapped my presents as soon as I bought them, I have all my Christmas cards done and ready to mail—"

"You're disgusting," Cassie said. "Oh, here, I almost forgot." She pulled a folded slip of paper out of her catalogue and handed it to Lauren. "It's your name for the Secret Santa gift exchange. PMS says you're supposed to bring your present for it by Friday so it won't interfere with the presents Santa Claus hands out at the office party."

Lauren unfolded the paper, and Cassie leaned over to read it. "Who'd you get? Wait, don't tell me. Scott Buckley."

"No. Fred Hatch. And I know just what to get him."

"Fred? The fat guy in Documentation? What is it, the Diet of the Month?"

"This is supposed to be the season of love and charity, not the season when you make mean remarks about someone just because he's overweight," Lauren said sternly. "I'm going to get him a videotape of *Miracle on 34th Street.*"

Cassie looked uncomprehending.

"It's Fred's favorite movie. We had a wonderful talk about it at the office party last year."

"I never heard of it."

"It's about Macy's Santa Claus. He starts telling people they can get their kids' toys cheaper at Gimbel's, and then the store psychiatrist decides he's crazy—"

"Why don't you get him *It's a Wonderful Life?* That's *my* favorite Christmas movie."

"Yours and everybody else's. I think Fred and I are the

only two people in the world who like *Miracle on 34th Street* better. See, Edmund Gwenn, he's Santa Claus, gets committed to Bellevue because he thinks he's Santa Claus, and since there isn't any Santa Claus, he has to be crazy, but he *is* Santa Claus, and Fred Gailey, that's John Payne, he's a lawyer in the movie, he decides to have a court hearing to prove it, and—"

"I watch *It's a Wonderful Life* every Christmas. I love the part where Jimmy Stewart and Donna Reed fall into the swimming pool," Cassie said. "What happened to the stapler?"

They had the dress and it fit, but there was an enormous jam-up at the cash register, and then they couldn't find a hanging bag for it.

"Just put it in a shopping bag," Lauren said, looking anxiously at her watch.

"It'll wrinkle," the clerk said ominously and continued to search for a hanging bag. By the time Lauren convinced her a shopping bag would work, it was already twelve-fifteen. She had hoped she'd have time to look for a present for her sister, but there wasn't going to be time. She still had to run the dress home and mail the Christmas cards.

I can pick up Fred's video, she thought, fighting her way onto the escalator. That wouldn't take much time since she knew what she wanted, and maybe they'd have something with Shirley Maclaine in it she could get her sister. Ten minutes to buy the video, she thought, tops.

It took her nearly half an hour. There was only one copy, which the clerk couldn't find.

"Are you sure you wouldn't rather have *It's a Wonderful Life*?" she asked Lauren. "It's my favorite movie."

"I want *Miracle on 34th Street*," Lauren said patiently. "With Edmund Gwenn and Natalie Wood."

The clerk picked up a copy of *It's a Wonderful Life* off a huge display. "See, Jimmy Stewart's in trouble and he wishes he'd never been born, and this angel grants him his wish—"

"I know," Lauren said. "I don't care. I want *Miracle on 34th Street.*"

"Okay!" the clerk said, and wandered off to look for it, muttering, "Some people don't have any Christmas spirit."

She finally found it, in the M's of all places, and then insisted on giftwrapping it.

By the time Lauren made it back to her apartment, it was a quarter to one. She would have to forget lunch and mailing the Christmas cards, but she could at least take them with her, buy the stamps, and put the stamps on at work.

She took the video out of the shopping bag and set it on the coffee table next to her purse, picked up the bag and started for the bedroom.

Someone knocked on the door.

"I don't have time for this," she muttered, and opened the door, still holding the shopping bag.

It was a young man wearing a "Save the Whales" T-shirt and khaki pants. He had shoulder-length blond hair and a vague expression that made her think of Southern California.

"Yes? What is it?" she asked.

"I'm here to give you a Christmas present," he said.

"Thank you, I'm not interested in whatever you're selling," she said, and shut the door.

He knocked again immediately. "I'm not selling anything," he said through the door. "Really."

I don't have *time* for this, she thought, but she opened the door again.

"I'm not a salesguy," he said. "Have you ever heard of the Maharishi Ram Dras?"

A religious nut.

"I don't have time to talk to you." She started to say, "I'm late for work," and then remembered you weren't supposed to tell strangers your apartment was going to be empty. "I'm very busy," she said and shut the door, more firmly this time.

The knocking commenced again, but she ignored it. She started into the bedroom with the shopping bag, came back and pushed the deadbolt across and put the chain on, and then went in to hang up her dress. By the time she'd extricated it from the tissue paper and found a hanger, the knocking had stopped. She hung up the dress, which looked just as deadly now that she had it home, and went back in the living room.

The young man was sitting on the couch, messing with her TV remote. "So, what do you want for Christmas? A yacht? A pony?" He punched buttons on the remote, frowning. "A new TV?"

"How did you get in here?" Lauren said squeakily. She looked at the door. The deadbolt and chain were both still on.

"I'm a spirit," he said, putting the remote down. The TV suddenly blared on. "The Spirit of Christmas Present."

"Oh," Lauren said, edging toward the phone. "Like in *A Christmas Carol*."

"No," he said, flipping through the channels. She looked at the remote. It was still on the coffee table. "Not Christmas Present. Christmas *Present*. You *know*, Barbie dolls, ugly ties, cheese logs, the stuff people give you for Christmas."

"Oh, Christmas *Present*. I see," Lauren said, carefully picking up the phone.

"People *always* get me confused with him, which is really insulting. I mean, the guy obviously has a really high cholesterol level. Anyway, I'm the Spirit of Christmas Present, and your sister sent me to—"

Lauren had dialed nine one. She stopped, her finger poised over the second one. "My sister?"

"Yeah," he said, staring at the TV. Jimmy Stewart was sitting in the guard's room wrapped in a blanket. "Oh, wow! *It's a Wonderful Life*."

My sister sent you, Lauren thought. It explained everything. He was not a Moonie or a serial killer. He was this year's version of the crystal pyramid mate selector. "How do you know my sister?"

"She channeled me," he said, leaning back against the sofa. "The Maharishi Ram Dras was instructing her in trance-meditation, and she accidentally channeled my spirit out of the astral plane." He pointed at the screen. "I love this part where the angel is trying to convince Jimmy Stewart he's dead."

"I'm not dead, am I?"

"No. I'm not an angel. I'm a spirit. The Spirit of Christmas Present. You can call me Chris for short. Your sister sent me to give you what you really want for Christmas. You know, your heart's desire. So what is it?"

For my sister not to send me any more presents, she thought. "Look, I'm really in a hurry right now. Why don't you come back tomorrow and we can talk about it then?"

"I hope it's not a fur coat," he said as if he hadn't heard her. "I'm opposed to the killing of endangered species." He picked up Fred's present. "What's this?"

"It's a videotape of *Miracle on 34th Street*. I really have to go."

"Who's it for?"

"Fred Hatch. I'm his Secret Santa."

"Fred Hatch." He turned the package over. "You had it gift-wrapped at the store, didn't you?"

"Yes. If we could just talk about this later—"

"This is a great part, too," he said, leaning forward to watch the TV. The angel was explaining to Jimmy Stewart how he hadn't gotten his wings yet.

"I *have* to go. I'm on my lunch hour, and I need to mail my Christmas cards, and I have to get back to work—" She glanced at her watch, "—oh my God, fifteen minutes ago."

He put down the package and stood up. "Gift-wrapped presents," he said, making a "tsk"-ing noise. "Everybody rushing around spending money, rushing to parties, never stopping to have some eggnog or watch a movie. Christmas is an endangered species." He looked longingly back at the screen, where the angel was trying to convince Jimmy Stewart he'd never been alive, and then wandered into the kitchen. "You got any Evian water?"

"No," Lauren said desperately. She hurried after him. "Look, I really have to get to work."

He had stopped at the kitchen table and was holding one of the Christmas cards. "Computer-addressed," he said reprovingly. He tore it open.

"Don't—" Lauren said.

"Printed Christmas cards," he said. "No letter, no quick note, not even a handwritten signature. That's exactly what I'm talking about. An endangered species."

"I didn't have time," Lauren said defensively. "And I don't have time to discuss this or anything else with you. I have to get to work."

"No time to write a few words on a card, no time to think about what you want for Christmas." He slid the card back into the envelope. "Not even on recycled paper," he said sadly. "Do you know how many trees are chopped down every year to send Christmas cards?"

"I am *late* for—" Lauren said, and he wasn't there anymore.

He didn't vanish like in the movies, or fade out slowly. He simply wasn't there.

"—work," Lauren said. She went and looked in the living room. The TV was still on, but he wasn't there, or in the bedroom. She went in the bathroom and pulled the shower curtain back, but he wasn't there either.

"It was an hallucination," she said out loud, "brought on by stress." She looked at her watch, hoping it had been part of the hallucination, but it still read one-fifteen. "I will figure this out later," she said. "I *have* to get back to work."

She went back in the living room. The TV was off. She went into the kitchen. He wasn't there. Neither were her Christmas cards, exactly.

"You! Spirit!" she shouted. "You come back here this minute!"

"You're late," Cassie said, filling out a catalogue form. "You will not believe who was just here. Scott Buckley. God, he is so cute." She looked up. "What happened?" she said. "Didn't they hold the dress?"

"Do you know anything about magic?" Lauren said.

"What *happened*?"

"My sister sent me her Christmas present," Lauren said grimly. "I need to talk to someone who knows something about magic."

"Fat . . . I mean Fred Hatch is a magician. What did your sister send you?"

Lauren started down the hall to Documentation at a half-run.

"I told Scott you'd be back any minute," Cassie said. "He said he wanted to talk to you."

Lauren opened the door to Documentation and started looking over partitions into the maze of cubicles. They were all empty.

"Anybody here?" Lauren called. "Hello?"

A middle-aged woman emerged from the maze, carrying five rolls of wrapping paper and a large pair of scissors. "You don't have any Scotch tape, do you?" she asked Lauren.

"Do you know where Fred Hatch is?" Lauren asked.

The woman pointed toward the interior of the maze with a roll of reindeer-covered paper. "Over there. Doesn't *anyone* have any tape? I'm going to have to staple my Christmas presents."

Lauren worked her way toward where the woman had pointed, looking over partitions as she went. Fred was in the center one, leaning back in a chair, his hands folded over his ample stomach, staring at a screen covered with yellow numbers.

"Excuse me," Lauren said, and Fred immediately sat forward and stood up.

"I need to talk to you," she said. "Is there somewhere we can talk privately?"

"Right here," Fred said. "My assistant's on the 800 line in my office placing a catalogue order, and everyone else is next door in Graphic Design at a Tupperware party." He pushed a key, and the computer screen went blank. "What did you want to talk to me about?"

"Cassie said you're a magician," she said.

He looked embarrassed. "Not really. The PMS Committee put me in charge of the magic show for the office party last year, and I came up with an act. This year, luckily, they assigned me to play Santa Claus." He smiled and patted his stomach. "I'm the right shape for the part, and I don't have to worry about the tricks not working."

"Oh, dear," Lauren said. "I hoped . . . do you know any magicians?"

"The guy at the novelty shop," he said, looking worried. "What's the matter? Did PMS assign you the magic show this year?"

"No." She sat down on the edge of his desk. "My sister is into New Age stuff, and she sent me this spirit—"

"Spirit," he said. "A ghost, you mean?"

"No. A person. I mean he looks like a person. He says he's the Spirit of Christmas Present, as in Gift, not Here and Now."

"And you're sure he's not a person? I mean, tricks can sometimes really look like magic."

"There's a Christmas tree in my kitchen," she said.

"Christmas tree?" he said warily.

"Yes. The spirit was upset because my Christmas cards weren't on recycled paper, he asked me if I knew how many trees were chopped down to send Christmas cards, then he disappeared, and when I went back in the kitchen there was this Christmas tree in my kitchen."

"And there's no way he could have gotten into your apartment earlier and put it there?"

"It's *growing* out of the floor. Besides, it wasn't there when we were in the kitchen five minutes before. See, he was watching *It's a Wonderful Life* on TV, which, by the way, he turned on without using the remote, and he asked me if I had any Evian water, and he went into the kitchen and . . . this is ridiculous. You have to think I'm crazy. *I* think I'm crazy just listening to myself tell this ridiculous story. Evian water!" She folded her arms. "People have a lot of nervous breakdowns around Christmas time. Do you think I could be having one?"

The woman with the wrapping paper rolls peered over the cubicle wall. "Have you got a tape dispenser?"

Fred shook his head.

"How about a stapler?"

Fred handed her his stapler, and she left.

"Well," Lauren said when she was sure the woman was gone, "do you think I'm having a nervous breakdown?"

"That depends," he said.

"On what?"

"On whether there's really a tree growing out of your kitchen floor. You said he got angry because your Christmas cards weren't on recycled paper. Do you think he's dangerous?"

"I don't know. He says he's here to give me whatever I want for Christmas. Except a fur coat. He's opposed to the killing of endangered species."

"A spirit who's an animal rights activist!" Fred said delightedly. "Where did your sister get him from?"

"The astral plane," Lauren said. "She was trance-channeling or something. I don't care where he came from. I just want to get rid of him before he decides my Christmas presents are recyclable, too."

"Okay," he said, hitting a key on the computer. The screen lit up. "The first thing we need to do is find out what he is and how he got here. I want you to call your sister. Maybe she knows some New Age spell for getting rid of the spirit." He began to type rapidly. "I'll get on the networks and see if I can find someone who knows something about magic."

He swiveled around to face her. "You're sure you want to get rid of him?"

"I have a *tree* growing out of my kitchen floor!"

"But what if he's telling the truth? What if he really can get you what you want for Christmas?"

"What I *wanted* was to mail my Christmas cards, which are now shedding needles on the kitchen tile. Who knows what he'll do next?"

"Yeah," he said. "Listen, whether he's dangerous or not, I think I should go home with you after work, in case he shows up again, but I've got a PMS meeting for the office party—"

"That's okay. He's an animal rights activist. He's not dangerous."

"That doesn't necessarily follow," Fred said. "I'll come

over as soon as my meeting's over, and meanwhile I'll check the networks. Okay?"

"Okay," she said. She started out of the cubicle and then stopped. "I really appreciate your believing me, or at least not saying you don't believe me."

He smiled at her. "I don't have any choice. You're the only other person in the world who likes *Miracle on 34th Street* better than *It's a Wonderful Life.* And Fred Gailey believed Macy's Santa Claus was really Santa Claus, didn't he?"

"Yeah," she said. "I don't think this guy is Santa Claus. He was wearing Birkenstocks."

"I'll meet you at your front door," he said. He sat down at the computer and began typing.

Lauren went through the maze of cubicles and into the hall.

"*There* you are!" Scott said. "I've been looking for you all over." He smiled meltingly. "I'm in charge of buying gifts for the office party, and I need your help."

"My help?"

"Yeah. Picking them out. I hoped maybe I could talk you into going shopping with me after work tonight."

"Tonight?" she said. "I can't. I've got—" A Christmas tree growing in my kitchen. "Could we do it tomorrow after work?"

He shook his head. "I've got a date. What about later on tonight? The stores are open till nine. It shouldn't take more than a couple of hours to do the shopping, and then we could go have a late supper somewhere. What say I pick you up at your apartment at six-thirty?"

And have the spirit lying on the couch, drinking Evian water and watching TV? "I can't," she said regretfully.

Even his frown was cute. "Oh, well," he said, and shrugged. "Too bad. I guess I'll have to get somebody else." He gave her another adorable smile and went off down the hall to ask somebody else.

I hate you, Spirit of Christmas Present, Lauren thought, standing there watching his handsome back recede. You'd better not be there when I get home.

A woman came down the hall, carrying a basket of candy

canes. "Compliments of the Personnel Morale Special Committee," she said, offering one to Lauren. "You look like you could use a little Christmas spirit."

"No, thanks, I've already got one," Lauren said.

The door to her apartment was locked, which didn't mean much since the chain and the deadbolt had both been on when he got in before. But he wasn't in the living room, and the TV was off.

He had been there, though. There was an empty Evian water bottle on the coffee table. She picked it up and took it into the kitchen. The tree was still there, too. She pushed one of the branches aside so she could get to the wastebasket and throw the bottle away.

"Don't you know plastic bottles are nonbiodegradable?" the spirit said. He was standing on the other side of the tree, hanging things on the branches. He was dressed in khaki shorts and a "Save the Rain Forest" T-shirt, and had a red bandana tied around his head. "You should recycle your bottles."

"It's your bottle," Lauren said. "What are you doing here, Spirit?"

"Chris," he corrected her. "These are organic ornaments," he said. He held one of the brown things out to her. "Handmade by the Yanomamo Indians. Each one is made of natural by-products found in the Brazilian rain forest." He hung the brown thing on the tree. "Have you decided what you want for Christmas?"

"Yes," she said. "I want you to go away."

He looked surprised. "I can't do that. Not until I give you your heart's desire."

"That is my heart's desire. I want you to go away and take this tree and your Yanomamo ornaments with you."

"You know the biggest problem I have as the Spirit of Christmas Present?" he said. He reached in the back pocket of his shorts and pulled out a brown garland of what looked like coffee beans. "My biggest problem is that people don't know what they want."

"I know what I want," Lauren said. "I don't want to have to write my Christmas cards all over again—"

"You didn't write them," he said, draping the garland over the branches. "They were printed. Do you know that the inks used on those cards contain harmful chemicals?"

"I don't want to be lectured on environmental issues, I don't want to have to fight my way through a forest to get to the refrigerator, and I don't want to have to turn down dates because I have a spirit in my apartment. I want a nice, quiet Christmas with no hassles. I want to exchange a few presents with my friends and go to the office Christmas party and . . ." And dazzle Scott Buckley in my off-the-shoulder black dress, she thought, but she decided she'd better not say that. The spirit might decide Scott's clothes weren't made of natural fibers or something and turn him into a Yanomamo Indian.

" . . . and have a nice, quiet Christmas," she finished lamely.

"Take *It's a Wonderful Life*," the spirit said, squinting at the tree. "I watched it this afternoon while you were at work. Jimmy Stewart didn't know what he wanted."

He reached into his pocket again and pulled out a crooked star made of Brazil nuts and twine. "He thought he wanted to go to college and travel and get rich, but what he *really* wanted was right there in front of him the whole time."

He did something, and the top of the tree lopped over in front of him. He tied the star on with the twine, and did something else. The tree straightened up. "You only think you want me to leave," he said.

Someone knocked on the door.

"You're right," Lauren said. "I don't want you to leave. I want you to stay right there." She ran into the living room.

The spirit followed her into the living room. "Luckily, being a spirit, I know what you really want," he said, and disappeared.

She opened the door to Fred. "He was just here," she said. "He disappeared when I opened the door, which is what all the crazies say, isn't it?"

"Yeah," Fred said. "Or else, 'He's right there. Can't you

see him?' " He looked curiously around the room. "Where was he?"

"In the kitchen," she said, shutting the door. "Decorating a tree which probably isn't there either." She led him into the kitchen.

The tree was still there, and there were large brownish cards stuck all over it.

"You really do have a tree growing in your kitchen," Fred said, squatting down to look at the roots. "I wonder if the people downstairs have roots sticking out of their ceiling." He stood up. "What are these?" he said, pointing at the brownish cards.

"Christmas cards." She pulled one off. "I told him I wanted mine back." She read the card aloud. " 'In the time it takes you to read this Christmas card, eighty-two harp seals will have been clubbed to death for their fur.' " She opened it up. " 'Happy Holidays.' "

"Cheery," Fred said. He took the card from her and turned it over. " 'This card is printed on recycled paper with vegetable inks and can be safely used as compost.' "

"Did anyone in the networks know how to club a spirit to death?" she asked.

"No. Didn't your sister have any ideas?"

"She didn't know how she got him in the first place. She and her Maharishi were channeling an Egyptian nobleman and he suddenly appeared, wearing a "Save the Dolphins" T-shirt. I got the idea the Maharishi was as surprised as she was." She sat down at the kitchen table. "I tried to get him to go away this afternoon, but he said he has to give me my heart's desire first." She looked up at Fred, who was cautiously sniffing one of the organic ornaments. "Didn't you find out anything on the networks?"

"I found out there are a lot of loonies with computers. What *are* these?"

"By-products of the Brazilian rain forest." She stood up. "I told him my heart's desire was for him to leave, and he said I didn't know what I really wanted."

"Which is what?"

"I don't know," she said. "I went into the living room to answer the door, and he said that luckily he knew what I wanted because he was a spirit, and I told him to stay right where he was, and he disappeared."

"Show me," he said.

She took him into the living room and pointed at where he'd been standing, and Fred squatted down again and peered at the carpet.

"How does he disappear?"

"I don't know. He just . . . isn't there."

Fred stood up. "Has he changed anything else? Besides the tree?"

"Not that I know of. He turned the TV on without the remote," she said, looking around the room. The shopping bags were still on the coffee table. She looked through them and pulled out the video. "Here. I'm your Secret Santa. I'm not supposed to give it to you till Christmas Eve, but maybe you'd better take it before he turns it into a snowy owl or something."

She handed it to him. "Go ahead. Open it."

He unwrapped it. "Oh," he said without enthusiasm. "Thanks."

"I remember last year at the party we talked about it, and I was afraid you might already have a copy. You don't, do you?"

"No," he said, still in that flat voice.

"Oh, good. I had a hard time finding it. You were right when you said we were the only two people in the world who liked *Miracle on 34th Street*. Everybody else I know thinks *It's a Wonderful Life* is—"

"You bought me *Miracle on 34th Street*?" he said, frowning.

"It's the original black-and-white version. I hate those colorized things, don't you? Everyone has gray teeth."

"Lauren." He held the box out to her so she could read the front. "I think your friend's been fixing things again."

She took the box from him. On the cover was a picture of Jimmy Stewart and Donna Reed dancing the Charleston.

"Oh, no! That little rat!" she said. "He must have changed it when he was looking at it. He told me *It's a Wonderful Life* was his favorite movie."

"*Et tu, Brute?*" Fred said, shaking his head.

"Do you suppose he changed all my other Christmas presents?"

"We'd better check."

"If he has . . ." she said. She dropped to her knees and started rummaging through them.

"Do you think they look the same?" Fred asked, squatting down beside her.

"*Your* present looked the same." She grabbed a package wrapped in red-and-gold paper and began feeling it. "Cassie's present is okay, I think."

"What is it?"

"A stapler. She's always losing hers. I put her name on it in Magic Marker." She handed it to him to feel.

"It feels like a stapler, all right," he said.

"I think we'd better open it and make sure."

Fred tore off the paper. "It's still a stapler," he said, looking at it. "What a great idea for a Christmas present! Everybody in Documentation's always losing their staplers. I think PMS steals them to use on their Christmas decorations." He handed it back to her. "Now you'll have to wrap it again."

"That's okay," Lauren said. "At least it wasn't a Yanomamo ornament."

"But it might be any minute," Fred said, straightening up. "There's no telling what he might take a notion to transform next. I think you'd better call your sister again, and ask her to ask the Maharishi if *he* knows how to send spirits back to the astral plane, and I'll go see what I can find out from the networks."

"Okay," Lauren said, following him to the door. "Don't take the videotape with you. Maybe I can get him to change it back."

"Maybe," Fred said, frowning. "You're sure he said he was here to give you your heart's desire?"

"I'm sure."

"Then why would he change my videotape?" he said thoughtfully. "It's too bad your sister couldn't have conjured up a nice, straightforward spirit."

"Like Santa Claus," Lauren said.

Her sister wasn't home. Lauren tried her off and on all evening, and when she finally got her, she couldn't talk. "The Maharishi and I are going to Barbados. They're having a harmonic divergence there on Christmas Eve, so don't worry about getting my present here by Christmas because I won't be back till the day after New Year's," she said and hung up.

"I don't even have her Christmas present bought yet," Lauren said to the couch, "and it's all your fault."

She went in the kitchen and glared at the tree. "I don't even dare go shopping because you might turn the couch into a humpbacked whale while I'm gone," she said, and then clapped her hand over her mouth.

She peered cautiously into the living room and then made a careful circuit of the whole apartment, looking for endangered species. There were no signs of any, and no sign of the spirit. She went back into the living room and turned on the TV. Jimmy Stewart was dancing the Charleston with Donna Reed. She picked up the remote and hit the channel button. Now he was singing, "Buffalo Gals, Won't You Come Out Tonight?"

She hit the automatic channel changer. Jimmy Stewart was on every channel except one. The Ghost of Christmas Present was on that one, telling Scrooge to change his ways. She watched the rest of *A Christmas Carol*. When it reached the part where the Cratchits were sitting down to their Christmas dinner, she remembered she hadn't had any supper and went in the kitchen.

The tree was completely blocking the cupboards, but by mightily pushing several branches aside she was able to get to the refrigerator. The eggnog was gone. So were the Stouffer's frozen entrees. The only thing in the refrigerator was a half-empty bottle of Evian water.

She shoved her way out of the kitchen and sat back down

on the couch. Fred had told her to call if anything happened, but it was after eleven o'clock, and she had a feeling the eggnog had been gone for some time.

A Christmas Carol was over, and the opening credits were starting. "Frank Capra's It's a Wonderful Life. Starring Jimmy Stewart and Donna Reed."

She must have fallen asleep. When she woke up, Miracle on 34th Street was on, and the store manager was giving Edmund Gwenn as Macy's Santa Claus a list of toys he was supposed to push if Macy's didn't have what the children asked Santa for.

"Finally," Lauren said, watching Edmund Gwenn tear the list into pieces, "something good to watch," and promptly fell asleep. When she woke up again, John Payne and Maureen O'Hara were kissing and someone was knocking on the door.

I don't remember anyone knocking on the door, she thought groggily. John Payne told Maureen O'Hara how he'd convinced the State of New York Edmund Gwenn was Santa Claus, and then they both stared disbelievingly at a cane standing in the corner. "The End" came on the screen.

The knocking continued.

"Oh," Lauren said, and answered the door.

It was Fred, carrying a McDonald's sack.

"What time is it?" Lauren said, blinking at him.

"Seven o'clock. I brought you an Egg McMuffin and some orange juice."

"Oh, you wonderful person!" she said. She grabbed the sack and took it over to the coffee table. "You don't know what he did." She reached into the sack and pulled out the sandwich. "He transformed the food in my refrigerator into Evian water."

He was looking curiously at her. "Didn't you go to bed last night? He didn't come back, did he?"

"No, I waited for him, and I guess I fell asleep." She took a huge bite of the sandwich.

Fred sat down beside her. "What's that?" He pointed to a pile of dollar bills on the coffee table.

"I don't know," Lauren said.

Fred picked up the bills. Under them was a handful of change and a pink piece of paper. " 'Returned three boxes of Christmas cards for refund,' " Lauren said, reading it. " '$22.18.' "

"That's what's here," Fred said, counting the money. "He didn't turn your Christmas cards into a Douglas fir after all. He took them back and got a refund."

"Then that means the tree isn't in the kitchen!" she said, jumping up and running to look. "No, it doesn't." She came back and sat down on the couch.

"But at least you got your money back," Fred said. "And it fits in with what I learned from the networks last night. They think he's a friendly spirit, probably some sort of manifestation of the seasonal spirit. Apparently these are fairly common, variations of Santa Claus being the most familiar, but there are other ones, too. All benign. They think he's probably telling the truth about wanting to give you your heart's desire."

"Do they know how to get rid of him?" she asked, and took a bite.

"No. Apparently no one's ever wanted to exorcise one." He pulled a piece of paper out of his pocket. "I got a list of exorcism books to try, though, and this one guy, Clarence, said the most important thing in an exorcism is to know exactly what kind of spirit it is."

"How do we do that?" Lauren asked with her mouth full.

"By their actions, Clarence said. He said appearance doesn't mean anything because seasonal spirits are frequently in disguise. He said we need to write down everything the spirit's said and done, so I want you to tell me exactly what he did." He took a pen and a notebook out of his jacket pocket. "Everything from the first time you saw him."

"Just a minute." She finished the last bite of sandwich and took a drink of the orange juice. "Okay. He knocked on the door, and when I answered it, he told me he was here to give me a Christmas present, and I told him I wasn't interested and I shut the door and started into the bedroom to hang up my dress and—my dress!" she gasped and went tearing into the bedroom.

"What's the matter?" Fred said, following her.

She flung the closet door open and began pushing clothes madly along the bar. "If he's transformed this—" She stopped pushing hangers. "I'll kill him," she said and lifted out a brownish collection of feathers and dried leaves. "Benign?!" she said. "Do you call that benign?!"

Fred gingerly touched a brown feather. "What was it?"

"A dress," she said. "My beautiful black, off-the-shoulder, drop-dead dress."

"Really?" he said doubtfully. He lifted up some of the brownish leaves. "I think it still is a dress," he said. "Sort of."

She crumpled the leaves and feathers against her and sank down on the bed. "All I wanted was to go to the office party!"

"Don't you have anything else you can wear to the office party? What about that pretty red thing you wore last year?"

She shook her head emphatically. "Scott didn't even notice it!"

"And that's your heart's desire?" Fred said after a moment. "To have Scott Buckley notice you at the office party?"

"Yes, and he would have, too! It had sequins on it, and it fit perfectly!" She held out what might have been a sleeve. Greenish-brown pods dangled from brownish strips of bamboo. "And now he's ruined it!"

She flung the dress on the floor and stood up. "I don't care what this Clarence person says. He is not benign! And he is not trying to get me what I want for Christmas. He is trying to ruin my life!"

She saw the expression on Fred's face and stopped. "I'm sorry," she said. "None of this is your fault. You've been try-ing to help me."

"And I've been doing about as well as your spirit," he said. "Look, there has to be some way to get rid of him. Or at least get the dress back. Clarence said he knew some transformation spells. I'll go to work and see what I can find out."

He went out to the living room and over to the door. "Maybe you can go back to the store and see if they have another dress like it." He opened the door.

"Okay." Lauren nodded. "I'm sorry if I yelled at you. And you have been a lot of help."

"Right," he said glumly, and went out.

"Where'd you get that dress?" Jimmy Stewart said to Donna Reed.

Lauren whirled around. The TV was on. Donna Reed was showing Jimmy Stewart her new dress.

"Where are you?" Lauren demanded, looking at the couch. "I want you to change that dress back right now!"

"Don't you like it?" the spirit said from the bedroom. "It's completely biodegradable."

She stomped into the bedroom. He was putting the dress on the hanger and making little "tsk"-ing noises. "You have to be careful with natural fibers," he said reprovingly.

"Change it back the way it was. This instant."

"It was handmade by the Yanomamo Indians," he said, smoothing down what might be the skirt. "Do you realize that their natural habitat is being destroyed at the rate of seven hundred and fifty acres a day?"

"I don't care. I want my dress back."

He carried the dress on its hanger over to the chest. "It's so interesting. Donna Reed knew right away she was in love with Jimmy Stewart, but he was so busy thinking about college and his new suitcase, he didn't even know she existed." He hung up the dress. "He practically had to be hit over the head."

"I'll hit you over the head if you don't change that dress back this instant, Spirit," she said, looking around for something hard.

"Call me Chris," he said. "Did you know sequins are made from nonrenewable resources?" and disappeared as she swung the lamp.

"And good riddance!" she shouted to the air.

❉   ❉   ❉

They had the dress in a size three. Lauren put herself through the indignity of trying to get into it and then went to work. The receptionist was watching Jimmy Stewart standing on the bridge in the snow, and weeping into a Kleenex. She handed Lauren her messages.

There were two memos from the PMS Committee—they were having a sleigh ride after work, and she was supposed to bring cheese puffs to the office party. There wasn't a message from Fred.

"Oh!" the receptionist wailed. "This is so sad!"

"I hate *It's a Wonderful Life*," Lauren said, and went up to her desk. "I hate Christmas," she said to Cassie.

"It's normal to hate Christmas," Cassie said, looking up from the book she was reading. "This book, it's called *Let's Forget Christmas*, says it's because everyone has these unrealistic expectations. When they get presents, they—"

"Oh, that reminds me," Lauren said. She rummaged in her bag and brought out Cassie's present, fingering it quickly to make sure it was still a stapler. It seemed to be. She held it out to Cassie. "Merry Christmas."

"I don't have yours wrapped yet," Cassie said. "I don't even have my wrapping paper bought yet. The books says I'm suffering from an avoidance complex." She picked up the package. "Do I have to open it now? I know it will be something I love, and you won't like what I got you half as well, and I'll feel incredibly guilty and inadequate."

"You don't have to open it now," Lauren said. "I just thought I'd better give it to you before—" She picked her messages up off her desk and started looking through them. "Before I forgot. There haven't been any messages from Fred, have there?"

"Yeah. He was here about fifteen minutes ago looking for you. He said to tell you the networks hadn't been any help, and he was going to try the library." She looked sadly at the present. "It's even wrapped great," she said gloomily. "I went shopping for a dress for the office party last night, and do you think I could find anything off-the-shoulder or with sequins? I couldn't even find anything I'd be caught dead in. Did you know the rate of stress-related illness at Christmas is seven times higher than the rest of the year?"

"I can relate to that," Lauren said.

"No, you can't. You didn't end up buying some awful gray thing with gold chains hanging all over it. At least Scott will notice me. He'll say, 'Hi, Cassie, are you dressed as Marley's ghost?' And there you'll be, looking fabulous in black sequins—"

"No, I won't," Lauren said.

"Why? Didn't they hold it for you?"

"It was ... defective. Did Fred want to talk to me?"

"I don't know. He was on his way out. He had to pick up his Santa Claus suit. Oh, my God," her voice dropped to a whisper. "It's Scott Buckley."

"Hi," Scott said to Lauren. "I was wondering if you could go shopping with me tonight." Lauren stared at him, so taken aback she couldn't speak.

"When you couldn't go last night, I decided to cancel my date."

"Uh ... I ..." she said.

"I thought we could buy the presents and then have some dinner."

She nodded.

"Great," Scott said. "I'll come over to your apartment around six-thirty."

"No!" Lauren said. "I mean, why don't we go straight from work?"

"Good idea. I'll come up here and get you." He smiled meltingly and left.

"I think I'll kill myself," Cassie said. "Did you know the rate of suicides at Christmas is four times higher than the rest of the year? He is so cute," she said, looking longingly down the hall after him. "There's Fred."

Lauren looked up. Fred was coming toward her desk with a Santa Claus costume and a stack of books. Lauren hurried across to him.

"This is everything the library had on exorcisms and the

occult," Fred said, transferring half of the books to her arms. "I thought we could both go through them today, and then get together tonight and compare notes."

"Oh, I can't," Lauren said. "I promised Scott I'd help him pick out the presents for the office party tonight. I'm sorry. I could tell him I can't."

"Your heart's desire? Are you kidding?" He started awkwardly piling the books back on his load. "You go shopping. I'll go through the books and let you know if I come up with anything."

"Are you sure?" she said guiltily. "I mean, you shouldn't have to do all the work."

"It's my pleasure," he said. He started to walk away and then stopped. "You didn't tell the spirit Scott was your heart's desire, did you?"

"Of course not. Why?"

"I was just wondering . . . nothing. Never mind." He walked off down the hall. Lauren went back to her desk.

"Did you know the rate of depression at Christmas is sixteen times higher than the rest of the year?" Cassie said. She handed Lauren a package.

"What's this?"

"It's from your Secret Santa."

Lauren opened it. It was a large book entitled, *It's a Wonderful Life: The Photo Album.* On the cover, Jimmy Stewart was looking depressed.

"I figure it'll take a half hour or so to pick out the presents," Scott said, leading her past two inflatable palm trees into The Upscale Oasis. "And then we can have some supper and get acquainted." He lay down on a massage couch. "What do you think about this?"

"How many presents do we have to buy?" Lauren asked, looking around the store. There were a lot of inflatable palm trees, and a jukebox, and several life-size cardboard cutouts of Malcolm Forbes and Leona Helmsley. Against the far wall were two high-rise aquariums and a bank of televisions with neon-outlined screens.

"Seventy-two." He got up off the massage couch, handed her the list of employees and went over to a display of brown boxes tied with twine. "What about these? They're handmade Yanomamo Christmas ornaments."

"No," Lauren said. "How much money do we have to spend?"

"The PMS Committee budgeted six thousand, and there was five hundred left in the Sunshine fund. We can spend . . ." He picked up a pocket calculator in the shape of Donald Trump and punched several buttons. "Ninety dollars per person, including tax. How about pet costume jewelry?" He held up a pair of rhinestone earrings for German shepherds.

"We got those last year," Lauren said. She picked up a digital umbrella and put it back down.

"How about a car fax?" Scott said. "No, wait. This, this is it!"

Lauren turned around. Scott was holding up what looked like a gold cordless phone. "It's an investment pager," he said, punching keys. "See, it gives you the Dow Jones, treasury bonds, interest rates. Isn't it perfect?"

"Well," Lauren said.

"See, this is the hostile takeover alarm, and every time the Federal Reserve adjusts the interest rate it beeps."

Lauren read the tag. " 'Portable Plutocrat. $74.99.' "

"Great," Scott said. "We'll have money left over."

"To invest," Lauren said.

He went off to see if they had seventy-two of them, and Lauren wandered over to the bank of televisions.

There was a videotape of *Miracle on 34th Street* lying on top of the VCR/shower massage. Lauren looked around to see if anyone was watching and then popped the *Wonderful Life* tape out and stuck in *Miracle*.

A dozen Edmund Gwenns dressed as Macy's Santa Clauses appeared on the screens, listening to twelve store managers tell them which overstocked toys to push.

Scott came over, lugging four shopping bags. "They come gift wrapped," he said happily, showing her a Portable Plutocrat wrapped in green paper with gold dollar signs. "Which gives us a free evening."

"That's what I've been fighting against for years," a dozen Edmund Gwenns said, tearing a dozen lists to bits, "the way they commercialize Christmas."

"What I thought," Scott said when they got in the car, "was that instead of going out for supper, we'd take these over to your apartment and order in."

"Order in?" Lauren said, clutching the bag of Portable Plutocrats on her lap to her.

"I know a great Italian place that delivers. Angel hair pasta, wine, everything. Or, if you'd rather, we could run by the grocery store and pick up some stuff to cook."

"Actually, my kitchen's kind of a mess," she said. There is a Christmas tree in it, she thought, with organic byproducts hanging on it.

He pulled up outside her apartment building. "Then Italian it is." He got out of the car and began unloading shopping bags. "You like prosciutto? They have a great melon and prosciutto."

"Actually, the whole apartment's kind of a disaster," Lauren said, following him up the stairs. "You know, wrapping presents and everything. There are ribbons and tags and paper all over the floor—"

"Great," he said, stopping in front of her door. "We have to put tags on the presents, anyway."

"They don't need tags, do they?" Lauren said desperately. "I mean, they're all exactly alike."

"It personalizes them," he said, "it shows the gift was chosen especially for them." He looked expectantly at the key in her hand and then at the door.

She couldn't hear the TV, which was a good sign. And every time Fred had come over, the spirit had disappeared. So all I have to do is keep him out of the kitchen, she thought.

She opened the door and Scott pushed past her and dumped the shopping bags on the coffee table. "Sorry," he said. "Those were really heavy." He straightened up and looked around the living room. There was no sign of the spirit, but there were three Evian water bottles on the coffee table. "This doesn't look too messy. You should see my apartment. I'll bet your kitchen's neater than mine, too."

Lauren walked swiftly over to the kitchen and pulled the door shut. "I wouldn't bet on it. Aren't there still some more presents to bring up?"

"Yeah. I'll go get them. Shall I call the Italian place first?"

"No," Lauren said, standing with her back against the kitchen door. "Why don't you bring the bags up first?"

"Okay," he said, smiling meltingly, and went out.

Lauren leaped to the door, put the deadbolt and the chain on, and then ran back to the kitchen and opened the door. The tree was still there. She pulled the door hastily to and walked rapidly into the bedroom. He wasn't there, or in the bathroom. "Thank you," she breathed, looking heavenward, and went back in the living room.

The TV was on. Edmund Gwenn was shouting at the store psychiatrist.

"You know, you were right," the spirit said. He was stretched out on the couch, wearing a "Save the Black-Footed Ferret" T-shirt and jeans. "It's not a bad movie. Of course, it's not as good as *It's a Wonderful Life*, but I like the way everything works out at the end."

"What are you doing here?" she demanded, glancing anxiously at the door.

"Watching *Miracle on 34th Street*," he said, pointing at the screen. Edmund Gwenn was brandishing his cane at the store psychiatrist. "I like the part where Edmund Gwenn asks Natalie Wood what she wants for Christmas, and she shows him the picture of the house."

Lauren picked up Fred's video and brandished it at him. "Fine. Then you can change Fred's video back."

"Okay," he said and did something. She looked at Fred's video. It showed Edmund Gwenn hugging Natalie Wood in front of a yellow moon with Santa Claus's sleigh and reindeer flying across it. Lauren put the video hastily down on the coffee table.

"Thank you," she said. "And my dress."

"Natalie Wood doesn't really want a house, of course. What she really wants is for Maureen O'Hara to marry John Payne. The house is just a symbol for what she really wants."

On the TV Edmund Gwenn rapped the store psychiatrist smartly on the forehead with his cane.

There was a knock on the door. "It's me," Scott said.

"I also like the part where Edmund Gwenn yells at the store manager for pushing merchandise nobody wants. Christmas presents should be something the person wants. Aren't you going to answer the door?"

"Aren't you going to disappear?" she whispered.

"Disappear?" he said incredulously. "The movie isn't over. And besides, I still haven't gotten you what you want for Christmas." He did something, and a bowl of trail mix appeared on his stomach.

Scott knocked again.

Lauren went over to the door and opened it two inches.

"It's me," Scott said. "Why do you have the chain on?"

"I ..." She looked hopefully at Chris. He was eating trail mix and watching Maureen O'Hara bending over the store psychiatrist, trying to wake him up.

"Scott, I'm sorry, but I think I'd better take a rain check on supper."

He looked bewildered. And cute. "But I thought ..." he said.

So did I, she thought. But I have a spirit on my couch who's perfectly capable of turning you into a Yanomamo byproduct.

"The Italian take-out sounds great," she said, "but it's kind of late, and we've both got to go to work tomorrow."

"Tomorrow's Saturday."

"Uh ... I meant go to work on wrapping presents. Tomorrow's Christmas Eve, and I haven't even started my wrapping. And I have to make cheese puffs for the office party and wash my hair and ..."

"Okay, okay, I get the message," he said. "I'll just bring in the presents and then leave."

She thought of telling him to leave them in the hall, and then closed the door a little and took the chain off the door.

Go *away*! she thought at the spirit, who was eating trail mix.

She opened the door far enough so she could slide out, and pulled it to behind her. "Thanks for a great evening," she said, taking the shopping bags from Scott. "Good night."

"Good night," he said, still looking bewildered. He started down the hall. At the stairs he turned and smiled meltingly.

I'm going to kill him, Lauren thought, waving back, and took the shopping bags inside.

The spirit wasn't there. The trail mix was still on the couch, and the TV was still on.

"Come back here!" she shouted. "You little rat! You have ruined my dress and my date, and you're not going to ruin anything else! You're going to change back my dress and my Christmas cards, and you are going to get that tree out of my kitchen right *now*!"

Her voice hung in the air. She sat down on the couch, still holding the shopping bags. On the TV, Edmund Gwenn was sitting in Bellevue, staring at the wall.

"At least Scott finally noticed me," she said, and set the shopping bags down on the coffee table. They rattled.

"Oh, no!" she said. "Not the plutocrats!"

"The problem is," Fred said, closing the last of the books on the occult, "that we can't exorcise him if we don't know which seasonal spirit he is, and he doesn't fit the profiles of any of these. He must be in disguise."

"I don't want to exorcise him," Lauren said. "I want to kill him."

"Even if we did manage to exorcise him, there'd be no guarantee that the things he's changed would go back to their original state."

"And I'd be stuck with explaining what happened to six thousand dollars' worth of Christmas presents."

"Those portable plutocrats cost six thousand dollars?"

"$5895.36."

Fred gave a low whistle. "Did your spirit say why he didn't like them? Other than the obvious, I mean. That they were nonbiodegradable or something?"

"No. He didn't even notice them. He was watching *Miracle on 34th Street*, and he was talking about how he liked the way things worked out at the end and the part about the house."

"Nothing about Christmas presents?"

"I don't remember." She sank down on the couch. "Yes, I do. He said he liked the part where Edmund Gwenn yelled at the store manager for talking people into buying things they didn't want. He said Christmas presents should be something the person wanted."

"Well, that explains why he transformed the plutocrats then," Fred said. "It probably also means there's no way you can talk him into changing them back. And I've got to have something to pass out at the office party, or you'll be in trouble. So we'll just have to come up with replacement presents."

"Replacement presents?" Lauren said. "How? It's ten o'clock, the office party's tomorrow night, and how do we know he won't transform the replacement presents once we've got them?"

"We'll buy people what they want. Was six thousand all the money you and Scott had?"

"No," Lauren said, rummaging through one of the shopping bags. "PMS budgeted sixty-five hundred."

"How much have you got left?"

She pulled out a sheaf of papers. "He didn't transform the purchase orders or the receipt," she said, looking at them. "The investment pagers cost $5895.36. We have $604.64 left." She handed him the papers. "That's eight dollars and thirty-nine cents apiece."

He looked at the receipt speculatively and then into the shopping bag. "I don't suppose we could take these back and get a refund from the Upscale Oasis?"

"They're not going to give us $5895.36 for seventy-two 'Save the Ozone Layer' buttons," Lauren said. "And there's nothing we can buy for eight dollars that will convince PMS it cost sixty-five hundred. And where am I going to get the money to pay back the difference?"

"I don't think you'll have to. Remember when the spirit changed your Christmas cards into the tree? He didn't really. He returned them somehow to the store and got a refund. Maybe he's done the same thing with the Plutocrats and the money will turn up on your coffee table tomorrow morning."

"And if it doesn't?"

"We'll worry about that tomorrow. Right now we've got to come up with presents to pass out at the party."

"Like what?"

"Staplers."

"Staplers?"

"Like the one you got Cassie. Everybody in my department's always losing their staplers, too. And their tape dispensers. It's an office party. We'll buy everybody something they want for the office."

"But how will we know what that is? There are seventy-two people on this list."

"We'll call the department heads and ask them, and then we'll go shopping." He stood up. "Where's your phone book?"

"Next to the tree." She followed him into the kitchen. "How are we going to go shopping? It's ten o'clock at night."

"Bizmart's open till eleven," he said, opening the phone book, "and the grocery store's open all night. We'll get as many of the presents as we can tonight and the rest tomorrow morning, and that still gives us all afternoon to get them wrapped. How much wrapping paper do you have?"

"Lots. I bought it half-price last year when I decided this Christmas was going to be different. A stapler doesn't seem like much of a present."

"It does if it's what you wanted." He reached for the phone.

It rang. Fred picked up the receiver and handed it to Lauren.

"Oh, Lauren," Cassie's voice said. "I just opened your present, and I *love* it! It's exactly what I wanted!"

"Really?" Lauren said.

"It's perfect! I was so depressed about Christmas and the office party and still not having my shopping done. I wasn't even going to open it, but in *Let's Forget Christmas* it said you should open your presents early so they wouldn't ruin Christmas morning, and I did, and it's wonderful! I don't even care whether Scott notices me or not! Thank you!"

"You're welcome," Lauren said, but Cassie had already hung up. She looked at Fred. "That was Cassie. You were right about people liking staplers." She handed him the phone. "You call the department heads. I'll get my coat."

He took the phone and began to punch in numbers, and then put it down. "What exactly did the spirit say about the ending of *Miracle on 34th Street*?"

"He said he liked the way everything worked out at the end. Why?"

He looked thoughtful. "Maybe we're going about this all wrong."

"What do you mean?"

"What if the spirit really does want to give you your heart's desire, and all this transforming stuff is some round-about way of doing it? Like the angel in *It's a Wonderful Life*. He's supposed to save Jimmy Stewart from committing suicide, and instead of doing something logical, like talking him out of it or grabbing him, he jumps in the river so Jimmy Stewart has to save *him*."

"You're saying he turned seventy-two Portable Plutocrats into 'Save the Ozone Layer' buttons to help me?"

"I don't know. All I'm saying is that maybe you should tell him you want to go to the office party in a black sequined dress with Scott Buckley and see what happens."

"See what happens? After what he did to my dress? If he knew I wanted Scott, he'd probably turn him into a Brazilian rainforest by-product." She put on her coat. "Well, are we going to call the department heads or not?"

❄   ❄   ❄

The Graphic Design department wanted staplers, and so did Accounts Payable. Accounts Receivable, which was having an outbreak of stress-related Christmas colds, wanted Puffs Plus and cough drops. Document Control wanted scissors.

Fred looked at the list, checking off Systems and the other departments they'd called. "All we've got left is the PMS Committee," he said.

"I know what to get them," Lauren said. "Copies of *Let's Forget Christmas*."

They got some of the things before Bizmart closed, and Fred was back at nine Saturday morning to do the rest of it. At the bookstore they ran into the woman who had been stapling presents together the day Lauren enlisted Fred's help.

"I completely forgot my husband's first wife," she said, looking desperate, "and I don't have any idea of what to get her."

Fred handed her the videotape of *It's a Wonderful Life* they were giving the receptionist. "How about one of these?" he said.

"Do you think she'll like it?"

"*Everybody* likes it," Fred said.

"Especially the part where the bad guy steals the money, and Jimmy Stewart races around town trying to replace it," Lauren said.

It took them most of the morning to get the rest of the presents and forever to wrap them. By four they weren't even half done.

"What's next?" Fred asked, tying the bow on the last of the staplers. He stood up and stretched.

"Cough drops," Lauren said, cutting a length of red paper with Santa Clauses on it.

He sat back down. "Ah, yes. Accounts Receivable's heart's desire."

"What's your heart's desire?" Lauren asked, folding the paper over the top of the cough drops and taping it. "What would you ask for if the spirit inflicted himself on you?"

Fred unreeled a length of ribbon. "Well, not to go to an office party, that's for sure. The only year I even had a remotely good time was last year, talking to you."

"I'm serious," Lauren said. She taped the sides and handed the package to Fred. "What do you really want for Christmas?"

"When I was eight, I asked for a computer for Christmas. Home computers were new then and they were pretty expensive, and I wasn't sure I'd get it. I was a lot like Natalie Wood in *Miracle on 34th Street*. I didn't really believe in Santa Claus, and I didn't believe in miracles, but I really wanted it."

He cut off the length of ribbon, wrapped it around the package, and tied it in a knot.

"Did you get the computer?"

"No," he said, cutting off shorter lengths of ribbon. "Christmas morning I came downstairs, and there was a note telling me to look in the garage." He opened the scissors and pulled the ribbon across the blade, making it curl. "It was a puppy. The thing was, a computer was too expensive, but there was an outside chance I'd get it, or I wouldn't have asked for it. Kids don't ask for stuff they *know* is impossible."

"And you hadn't asked for a puppy because you knew you couldn't have one?"

"No, you don't understand. There are things you don't ask for because you know you can't have them, and then there are things so far outside the realm of possibility, it would never even occur to you to want them." He made the curled ribbon into a bow and fastened it to the package.

"So what you're saying is your heart's desire is something so far outside the realm of possibility you don't even know what it is?"

"I didn't say that," he said. He stood up again. "Do you want some eggnog?"

"Yes, thanks. If it's still there."

He went in the kitchen. She could hear forest-thrashing noises and the refrigerator opening. "It's still here," he said.

"It's funny Chris hasn't been back," she called to Fred. "I keep worrying he must be up to something."

"Chris?" Fred said. He came back into the living room with two glasses of eggnog.

"The spirit. He told me to call him that," she said. "It's short for Spirit of Christmas Present." Fred was frowning. "What's wrong?" Lauren asked.

"I wonder . . . nothing. Never mind." He went over to the TV. "I don't suppose *Miracle on 34th Street*'s on TV this afternoon?"

"No, but I made him change your video back." She pointed. "It's there, on top of the TV."

He turned on the TV, inserted the video, and hit play. He came and sat down beside Lauren. She handed him the wrapped box of cough drops, but he didn't take it. He was watching the TV. Lauren looked up. On the screen, Jimmy Stewart was walking past Donna Reed's house, racketing a stick along the picket fence.

"That isn't *Miracle*," Lauren said. "He told me he changed it back." She snatched up the box. It still showed Edmund Gwenn hugging Natalie Wood. "That little sneak! He only changed the box!"

She glared at the TV. On the screen Jimmy Stewart was glaring at Donna Reed.

"It's all right," Fred said, taking the package and reaching for the ribbon. "It's not a bad movie. The ending's too sentimental, and it doesn't really make sense. I mean, one minute everything's hopeless, and Jimmy Stewart's ready to kill himself, and then the angel convinces him he had a wonderful life, and suddenly everything's okay." He looked around the table, patting the spread-out wrapping paper. "But it has its moments. Have you seen the scissors?"

Lauren handed him one of the pairs they'd bought. "We'll wrap them last."

On the TV Jimmy was sitting in Donna Reed's living room, looking awkward. "What I have trouble with is Jimmy Stewart's being so self-sacrificing," she said, cutting a length of red paper with Santa Clauses on it. "I mean, he gives up college so his brother can go, and then when his brother has a chance at a good job, he gives up college *again*. He even gives up committing suicide to save Clarence. There's such a thing as being too self-sacrificing, you know."

"Maybe he gives up things because he thinks he doesn't deserve them."

"Why wouldn't he?"

"He's never gone to college, he's poor, he's deaf in one ear. Sometimes when people are handicapped or overweight they just assume they can't have the things other people have."

The telephone rang. Lauren reached for it and then realized it was on TV.

"Oh, hello, Sam," Donna Reed said, looking at Jimmy Stewart.

"Can you help me with this ribbon?" Fred said.

"Sure," Lauren said. She scooted closer to him and put her finger on the crossed ribbon to hold it taut.

Jimmy Stewart and Donna Reed were standing very close together, listening to the telephone. The voice on the phone was saying something about soybeans.

Fred still hadn't tied the knot. Lauren glanced at him. He was looking at the TV, too.

Jimmy Stewart was looking at Donna Reed, his face nearly touching her hair. Donna Reed looked at him and then away. The voice from the phone was saying something about the chance of a lifetime, but it was obvious neither of them were hearing a word. Donna Reed looked up at him. His lips almost touched her forehead. They didn't seem to be breathing.

Lauren realized she wasn't either. She looked at Fred. He was holding the two ends of ribbon, one in each hand, and looking down at her.

"The knot," she said. "You haven't tied it."

"Oh," he said. "Sorry."

Jimmy Stewart dropped the phone with a clatter and grabbed Donna Reed by both arms. He began shaking her, yelling at her, and then suddenly she was wrapped in his arms, and he was smothering her with kisses.

"The knot," Fred said. "You have to pull your finger out."

She looked blankly at him and then down at the package. He had tied the knot over her finger, which was still pressing against the wrapping paper.

"Oh. Sorry," she said, and pulled her finger free. "You were right. It does have its moments."

He yanked the knot tight. "Yeah," he said. He reached for the spool of ribbon and began chopping off lengths for the bow. On the screen Donna Reed and Jimmy Stewart were being pelted with rice.

"No. You were right," he said. "He is too self-sacrificing." He waved the scissors at the screen. "In a minute he's going to give up his honeymoon to save the building and loan. It's a wonder he ever asked Donna Reed to marry him. It's a wonder he didn't try to fix her up with that guy on the phone."

The phone rang. Lauren looked at the screen, thinking it must be in the movie, but Jimmy Stewart was kissing Donna Reed in a taxicab.

"It's the phone," Fred said.

Lauren scrambled up and reached for it.

"Hi," Scott said.

"Oh, hello, Scott," Lauren said, looking at Fred.

"I was wondering about the office party tonight," Scott said. "Would you like to go with me? I could come get you and we could take the presents over together."

"Uh . . . I . . ." Lauren said. She put her hand over the receiver. "It's Scott. What am I going to tell him about the presents?"

Fred motioned for her to give him the phone. "Scott," he said. "Hi. It's Fred Hatch. Yeah, Santa Claus. Listen, we ran into a problem with the presents."

Lauren closed her eyes.

"We got a call from the Upscale Oasis that investment pagers were being recalled by the Federal Safety Commission."

Lauren opened her eyes. Fred smiled at her. "Yeah. For excessive cupidity."

Lauren grinned.

"But there's nothing to worry about," Fred said. "We replaced them. We're wrapping them right now. No, it was no trouble. I was happy to help. Yeah, I'll tell her." He hung up. "Scott will be here to take you to the office party at seven-thirty," he said. "It looks like you're going to get your heart's desire after all."

"Yeah," Lauren said, looking at the TV. On the screen, the building and loan was going under.

They finished wrapping the last pair of scissors at six-thirty, and Fred went back to his apartment to change clothes and get his Santa Claus costume. Lauren packed the presents in three of the Upscale Oasis shopping bags, said sternly, "Don't you dare touch these," to the empty couch, and went to get ready.

She showered and did her hair, and then went into the bedroom to see if the spirt had biodegraded her red dress, or, by some miracle, brought the black off-the-shoulder one back. He hadn't.

She put on the red dress and went back in the living room. It was only a little after seven. She turned on the TV and put Fred's video in the VCR. She hit play. Edmund Gwenn was giving the doctor the X-ray machine he'd always wanted.

Lauren picked up one of the shopping bags and felt the top pair of scissors to make sure they weren't Yanomamo ornaments. There was an envelope stuck between two of the packages. Inside was a check for $5895.36. It was made out to the Children's Hospital fund.

She shook her head, smiling, and put the check back in the envelope.

On TV Maureen O'Hara and John Payne were watching Natalie Wood run through an empty house and out the back door to look for her swing. They looked seriously at each other. Lauren held her breath. John Payne moved forward and kissed Maureen O'Hara.

Someone knocked on the door. "That's Scott," Lauren said to John Payne, and waited till Maureen O'Hara had finished telling him she loved him before she went to open the door.

It was Fred, carrying a foil-covered plate. He was wearing the same sweater and pants he'd worn to wrap the presents. "Cheese puffs," he said. "I figured you couldn't get to your stove." He looked seriously at her. "I wouldn't worry about not having your black dress to dazzle Scott with."

He went over and set the cheese puffs on the coffee table. "You need to take the foil off and heat them in a microwave for two minutes on high. Tell PMS to put the presents in Santa's bag, and I'll be there at eleven-thirty."

"Aren't you going to the party?"

"Office parties are your idea of fun, not mine," he said. "Besides, *Miracle on 34th Street*'s on at eight. It may be the only chance I have to watch it."

"But I wanted you—"

There was a knock on the door. "That's Scott," Lauren said.

"Well," Fred said, "if the spirit doesn't do something in the next fifteen seconds, you'll have your heart's desire in spite of him." He opened the door. "Come on in," he said. "Lauren and the presents are all ready." He handed two of the shopping bags to Scott.

"I really appreciate your helping Lauren and me with all this," Scott said.

Fred handed the other shopping bag to Lauren. "It was my pleasure."

"I wish you were coming with us," she said.

"And give up a chance of seeing the real Santa Claus?" He held the door open. "You two had better get going before something happens."

"What do you mean?" Scott said, alarmed. "Do you think these presents might be recalled, too?"

Lauren looked hopefully at the couch and then the TV. On the screen Jimmy Stewart was standing on the bridge in the snow, getting ready to kill himself.

"Afraid not," Fred said.

It was snowing by the time they pulled into the parking lot at work. "It was really selfless of Fred to help you wrap all those presents," Scott said, holding the lobby door open for Lauren. "He's a nice guy."

"Yes," Lauren said. "He is."

"Hey, look at that!" Scott said. He pointed at the security monitor. "*It's a Wonderful Life*. My favorite movie!"

On the monitor Jimmy Stewart was running through the snow, shouting, "Merry Christmas!"

"Scott," Lauren said, "I can't go to the party with you."

"Just a minute, okay?" Scott said, staring at the screen. "This is my favorite part." He set the shopping bags down on the receptionist's desk and leaned his elbows on it. "This is the part where Jimmy Stewart finds out what a wonderful life he's had."

"You have to take me home," Lauren said.

There was a gust of cold air and snow. Lauren turned around.

"You forgot your cheese puffs," Fred said, holding out the foil-covered plate to Lauren.

"There's such a thing as being too self-sacrificing, you know," Lauren said.

He held the plate out to her. "That's what the spirit said."

"He came back?" She shot a glance at the shopping bags.

"Yeah. Right after you left. Don't worry about the presents. He said he thought the staplers were a great idea. He also said not to worry about getting a Christmas present for your sister."

"My sister!" Lauren said, clapping her hand to her mouth. "I completely forgot about her."

"He said since you didn't like it, he sent her the Yanomamo dress."

"She'll love it," Lauren said.

"He also said it was a wonder Jimmy Stewart ever got Donna Reed, he was so busy giving everybody else what they wanted," he said, looking seriously at her.

"He's right," Lauren said. "Did he also tell you Jimmy Stewart was incredibly stupid for wanting to go off to college when Donna Reed was right there in front of him?"

"He mentioned it."

"What a great movie!" Scott said, turning to Lauren. "Ready to go up?"

"No," Lauren said. "I'm going with Fred to see a movie." She took the cheese puffs from Fred and handed them to Scott.

"What am I supposed to do with these?"

"Take the foil off," Fred said, "and put them in a microwave for two minutes."

"But you're my date," Scott said. "Who am I supposed to go with?"

There was a gust of cold air and snow. Everyone turned around.

"How do I look?" Cassie said, taking off her coat.

"Wow!" Scott said. "You look terrific!"

Cassie spun around, her shoulders bare, the sequins glittering on her black dress. "Lauren gave it to me for Christmas," she said happily. "I love Christmas, don't you?"

"I *love* that dress," Scott said.

"He also told me," Fred said, "that his favorite thing in *Miracle on 34th Street* was Santa Claus's being in disguise—"

"He wasn't in disguise," Lauren said. "Edmund Gwenn told everybody he was Santa Claus."

Fred held up a correcting finger. "He told everyone his name was Kris Kringle."

"Chris," Lauren said.

"Oh, I love this part," Cassie said.

Lauren looked at her. She was standing next to Scott, watching Jimmy Stewart standing next to Donna Reed and singing "Auld Lang Syne."

"He makes all sorts of trouble for everyone," Fred said. "He turns Christmas upside down—"

"Completely disrupts Maureen O'Hara's life," Lauren said.

"But by the end, everything's worked out, the doctor has his X-ray machine, Natalie Wood has her house—"

"Maureen O'Hara has Fred—"

"And no one's quite sure how he did it, or if he did anything."

"Or if he had the whole thing planned from the beginning." She looked seriously at Fred. "He told me I only thought I knew what I wanted for Christmas."

Fred moved toward her. "He told me just because something seems impossible doesn't mean a miracle can't happen."

"What a great ending!" Cassie said, sniffling. "*It's a Wonderful Life* is my favorite movie."

"Mine, too," Scott said. "Do you know how to heat up cheese puffs?" He turned to Lauren and Fred. "Cut that out, you two, we'll be late for the party."

"We're not going," Fred said, taking Lauren's arm. They started for the door. "*Miracle*'s on at eight."

"But you can't leave," Scott said. "What about all these presents? Who's going to pass them out?"

There was a gust of cold air and snow. "Ho ho ho," Santa Claus said.

"Isn't that your costume, Fred?" Lauren said.

"Yes. It has to be back at the rental place by Monday morning," he said to Santa Claus. "And no changing it into rainforest by-products."

"*Merry* Christmas!" Santa Claus said.

"I like the way things worked out at the end," Lauren said.

"All we need is a cane standing in the corner," Fred said.

"I have no idea what you're talking about," Santa Claus said. "Where are all these presents I'm supposed to pass out?"

"Right here," Scott said. He handed one of the shopping bags to Santa Claus.

"Plastic shopping bags," Santa Claus said, making a "tsk"-ing sound. "You should be using recycled paper."

"Sorry," Scott said. He handed the cheese puffs to Cassie and picked up the other two shopping bags. "Ready, Cassie?"

"We can't go yet," Cassie said, gazing at the security monitor. "Look, *It's a Wonderful Life* is just starting." On the screen Jimmy Stewart's brother was falling through the ice. "This is my favorite part," she said.

"Mine, too," Scott said, and went over to stand next to her.

Santa Claus squinted curiously at the monitor for a moment and then shook his head. "*Miracle on 34th Street*'s a much better movie, you know," he said reprovingly. "More realistic."

There's no place like home in the sky
for the holidays.

THE CHRISTMAS COUNT
Henry Melton

FRED JERRET SQUINTED his eyes against the light. The sun was
a white band of light stretching high across the sky. The
checkerboard fields of the farms he knew to be on the other
side of the sky were washed out in the glare. There was
no change. Winter should have come by now—it was past
four P.M.

"Fred," his wife, Dot, called across the field to him, as she
stood at the back porch of their gray stone farm house. "Fred,
I need the list."

"Okay! I'm coming." Reluctantly, he stepped from furrow
to furrow in the caked black earth until he reached the wide
patch of grass he kept as a backyard for the kids to play in.

Waiting out in the field wouldn't make winter happen any
faster. He had been a farmer for too many years to try to
second-guess the climate control computer. The *Piedmont
Herald* would publish the day, but no one knew the exact moment. The weather in their farming world was at the mercy of
a real-time computer system far too concerned with solar

flares and the heat balance of their self-contained space colony to give out predictions.

Fred had a couple of bucks down in the 4:15-4:20 spot in the betting pool that the boys at the general store were keeping. He had wanted four P.M., but that spot had been taken. *Just as well,* he thought. *Maybe I'll win anyway.*

Dot had vanished back into the house, and he slowed his pace a trifle. He was born a farmer, and today he needed to be outside, soaking up the peace he knew was always there in his fields.

Joey had been gone all day, vanished at first sunlight. He had not asked to leave. It was a deliberate escape from the chores he knew he was responsible for. Fred thought of the scolding he would give the boy. There was a sick anger in his stomach. He had said those words before, when Tim, his oldest, was sixteen.

A distant metallic rumble, like the legendary pre-space locomotives on rails, stopped Fred in his tracks. It was difficult to see through the hazy sky that clouded the center of this cylindrical world, but he knew it was the sun shutters. Three great metal gates had moved on their courses, restricting and channeling the sunlight that entered the world of Piedmont, shifting the energy balance. For the next few weeks, more heat would be radiated from the back side of this enclosed world than would be let through the great mirrors. It would get colder. Winter had begun.

Fred looked at his watch and shook his head. Missed it by three minutes.

Inside, Dot looked up as he entered. "Winter's come," he informed her. "Here's the list." He handed the clipboard to her. "I thought we had finished with the kitchen."

Dot gave him a twisted little grin. "Well . . . I have to reduce the roach count." She pushed the selector button on the clipboard a few times until the roach count appeared on the display plate. She subtracted two from the count and then gave it back to Fred.

He shook his head. "Dot, this is not the day to kill roaches.

This is Christmas Eve. Today we count the beasties, not try to wipe them out."

She curled her lower lip. "But they asked for it. I had my pumpkin pies cooling on the cabinet and those two came after them. I wasn't about to let them get on my pies!"

Fred tried to hide a smile. "Pumpkin, hmmm. Well, if it was pumpkin, I won't turn you in. But don't tell David about it. He will take it as approval to go hunting the rats in the woodpile again."

Dot nodded, then looked out the kitchen window to the fields and the woods beyond. "Where are Kim and David? Haven't they finished yet? With winter here, dark will come sooner."

"Maybe I had better go looking for them. I've got all the livestock counted and I keyed in the changes in the acreages for the insect estimates." He sniffed the kitchen air. "How soon is food?"

"Maybe another hour. By the way, are you sure we won't have any guests for Christmas dinner tomorrow?"

He shrugged. "I guess not. I made the invitations, but everyone was taken." He was not terribly surprised. After all there were three farming families for every one of the city folk. Dot had come from Galvin, a manufacturing world that circled the Point in the same lazy orbit as Piedmont. The world she had grown up in was nothing but one big city. Even after all these years as his wife, living on the soil, she still tended to think of that city as a big place, rather than the handful of support and maintenance people it actually was.

He continued. "I thought Charlie from river maintenance might come, but his wife had already made other arrangements." Maybe it would be better with just family this year. If there was company coming, Dot would work herself to exhaustion to get the house spotlessly clean.

Outside, the air was already getting cooler. Fred looked over his fields, freshly planted and waiting for the winter to make its appearance, and then leave for the long growing season.

Fred expected the winter to be colder than usual this year.

The ant infestation down by Southport had hurt a dozen farmers. A good solid freeze or two would wipe out the nests.

Spot came bounding across the fields to meet him. Fred clapped his hands together and the dog jumped high to snap the imaginary treat out of the air. Spot knew there was nothing there, but he liked to play the game. Sometimes Fred would fool him with the real thing.

Off to the east, a neighbor's dog barked. Spot lost interest in Fred and raced off, voicing his challenge. Fred could just spot the tiny figures in the next farm over. The curve of the ground rose enough to show a man building his Christmas fire. Fred glanced at his watch and hurried on.

The strip of woods that bordered the Jerret farm was partly on his property, so he was responsible for it in the count. It was the kids' job to help him with that.

The high-pitched shout of five-year-old David helped him locate them quickly. Kim and David were having a leaf fight. Fred adjusted his path slightly so he kept out of sight behind a stand of oak as he approached. Just yesterday, ten-year-old Kim had gotten a scolding from her mother about getting leaves in her hair. Fred waited until the last moment, then stepped out from behind a tree just as David was dumping a double handful of leaves onto his older sister's head.

"David!" Fred used his stern-father voice. Both kids jumped. David spilled most of the leaves off to the side of his target. He guiltily brushed his hands against his trousers.

"Yes, Daddy?" he asked timidly.

Fred let a moment of silence grow. But he had no intention of doing anything about the leaves. The kids would get the necessary dusting from their mother. It was her restriction, she would enforce it. Personally, Fred had nice memories of playing in the leaves when he was younger.

"David, you are going to have to help me with the fire. Have you two finished your counts?"

David pouted. "Why do I have to help with the fire? That is Joey's job."

"Joey is not back yet." His voice showed a little impatience. "Now did you finish your counts?"

Kim gave a warning glance at her brother. Now was not the time to complain about chores, not with Joey being out late again. Daddy was likely going to be in a bad mood until he came home.

She spoke up. "Yes. We counted twenty-two squirrels, and nine rabbits. The mice didn't seem to be as bad this year, there were only ten in the sample square. I didn't spot the badger, but there were fresh signs."

Fred tapped in the numbers on the clipboard. "Are you sure all of these were on our side of the boundary line? We are not supposed to count the animals on any other property."

She nodded. "I'm sure. I think the rabbits moved their hole down by the gully since the last count."

"How about the birds?"

"I didn't see any crows, but I saw five orioles. David claims to have seen a cowbird, but I didn't."

Fred nodded. "If David saw it, we count it. The climate computer needs to know everything we see, so it can plan the right amount of rain to make and plan how many days of winter we need."

"And summer?" asked David.

Fred smiled. "Yes, and summer. That's why we have four counts: the Christmas Count, the Easter Count, the Earthday Count, and the Harvest Count. We have a small, special world here in Piedmont and the counts are one of the ways we take care of our home."

David's attention had already wandered off to something in the sky by the time Fred had finished saying that. But Kim was older, and this time the words seemed to make some kind of impression on her.

David pointed. "Daddy, look."

Up high, halfway to the patchwork of fields on the other side of the sky, was a tiny speck moving south. A man-shape and a set of wings. It was too high for them to hear the sputtering of the tiny engine.

"A flier," Fred said, "trying to make the run to Southport. He'd better hurry." He looked at his watch. "And we had better run. Dark will come in five minutes."

❄   ❄   ❄

Darkness, when it came, closed down over Piedmont like the lid on a large cedar chest. The distant rumble of the shutters followed as the sound hurried to catch up with the shadow, like black thunder chasing the stroke of darkness. With only the light leak around the sun shutters to provide a pale imitation of moonlight, they had to step carefully as they made their way back to the house.

David shouted, "Hey look! Lights in the sky!"

And there were. First a dozen yellow lights scattered across the far side of the sky, then more, as farmers all through Piedmont lit the traditional Christmas Eve fire. Dot came out of the house, rubbing her hands on the towel at her waist. She, too, stared up at the sight.

"Hurry and help me, David," Fred said to his youngest. "We have to get our fire going."

"Aww. Why do I have to . . ."

"None of that!" Fred spoke sharply. "Santa is coming in just a few hours. This is not the time to act up."

"Yes, Davie," taunted his sister. "If you're naughty, Santa won't give you anything."

"Kim," commanded Dot, "come on and help me set the fireside table." Kim's face twisted as she realized she had trapped herself into helping her mother.

As the door closed, David heard his mother's voice rise sharply. "Kim Jerret, what is that in your hair?"

David giggled.

David was not really strong enough to help much with the firebuilding, but his father believed in chores for the children, even if it meant more work for him. They had the stack of wood placed in the firepit, ready for lighting by the time the dinner was served.

"Can I light it now, Daddy?" David asked. Fred shook his head.

Dot looked up at her husband with a question in her eyes. He turned away, looking briefly at the road that led past the front of their property. Joey had been late getting home several times before. But it was Christmas Eve! He shook off a rising flood of anger and frustration. He couldn't let Christmas be spoiled for the other kids.

He said, "Let's just sit here for a little bit and enjoy the lights."

Dot insisted they eat while the food was still hot. Helplessly, Fred felt the liquid trickle of an old hurt as they watched the lights flickering above. Empty places at the family table again.

Joey was at a difficult age. His older brother had been the same—staying out later and later with his friends. The role and restrictions of being a child were too much for him to bear. The harder his father fought to keep control, the more Joey managed to slip away.

His brother Tim had vanished one day, leaving a note saying that he had left to apprentice as a shuttle pilot. That had been two years ago. Christmas that first year had been hard, with that vacant chair as a constant reminder of a part of them that was gone.

The second year Tim sent Christmas presents for the kids, and a letter for his parents. They wrote back, but it was clear that their son had left for good. He was a regular pilot, with a regular run among the different orbital worlds. He had a life of his own, and it did not include Piedmont. Fred's boy would never be a farmer like his father.

"Why do we light a fire on Christmas Eve, Daddy?" Kim asked.

His little girl was growing up, too. He smiled at her as she stared up at the display above.

"There are a couple of reasons. When I was a boy, my father told me that Piedmont had started the Christmas fires to remind us of the stars in the night sky of Earth."

"What is the other reason?"

Fred went over to the storage shed and picked up a bag of powder from the shelf. He set it down on the bench before the kids. "This is seeding powder. We put it on the fire and it helps the formation of raindrops. Piedmont is a special world and we have to take care of it in a lot of little ways."

David asked, as he stuck his finger in the grayish powder "Does it make snow, too?"

Fred laughed. "Yes, it helps make snow, too."

"Good, let's light it!" David grabbed the bag and headed over to the fire.

Fred was quick on his feet and grabbed the bag before the boy had dumped it. "Okay. But we have to sprinkle the powder over the fire carefully."

Kim wanted to help, but Fred ruled that since David had helped build the fire, he ought to be the one to start it. They soon had a blazing fire and he showed David the proper way to toss the little scoops of powder over the fire.

In the yellow light, Fred noticed tears in Dot's eyes. He moved to her side. Christmas was a time for extremes. If you didn't feel wonderful, you felt horrible. He held her hand as they watched the flames.

He tried to smile, to feel as happy as his two little ones. But it was so hard. He squeezed Dot's hand. She squeezed back.

"Hey!" Kim pointed. "Here comes Joey!"

And sure enough, the bouncy white light of a bicycle on a dirt road was visible in the night. They all watched it as it pulled up and Joey walked up to the fireside.

He came right up to the flames and rubbed his hands. "This feels good. It's getting cold."

"Where have you been?" Fred tried to keep his voice level. There would be nothing good in having another shouting match like last time he returned home late.

Joey looked at his father's face and then looked back to the fire. "Mr. Grey, the scout troop leader, he asked me to help. Troop Two was supposed to handle the count on the Common." He shrugged, carefully watching the flames. "It took longer than we thought."

Fred nodded. He had heard it before. He sighed. "Dot, could you heat up something for Joey?" To Joey, he said, "David had to do your chores today. He gets your allowance, too."

David squealed in delight. Joey started to protest, then thought better of it.

It took an hour or more for the fire to die down to a red piping bed of coals. With Dot leading, they sang Christmas carols.

David asked, "How can Santa get to every house in one night?"

Kim eagerly explained. "He has a magic flier so he can land and take off real quick. He comes in a red shuttle and visits all the worlds in the circuit all in one night."

Fred always held his breath when the little ones asked about Santa. He dreaded the moment when they would ask if Santa was real. For David, at least, the moment had not yet come. He was just a little too young to guess at such a great conspiracy. At least his older ones were firmly coached not to give away the secret to the younger ones, at least not on purpose.

Across the landscape, like a metallic rolling thunder, the clank of the great doors of the Northport docking hangar clanked shut.

Kim and David started shouting, "Santa's here! Santa's ship is here!"

Distant voices, far too distant to resolve into anything more than the sound of humanity, told of all the world's children cheering the coming of Santa.

Dot said, "Okay. Bedtime, kids." She hustled them off to bed, giving David his medicine and getting Kim to wash her hair. Bedtime was never quick and easy with kids, not even on Christmas Eve.

It was much later that Dot came back to join Fred as he tended the bed of coals. *Woooo!* It's cold." She rubbed her hands together before the warmth of the coals, then sat down on the bench next to him. He put his arm around her.

Quiet moments, and a spot of warmth on a cold night—that and love can drain the stress of the day. They sat and breathed the frosty air, and enjoyed the moment.

"Oh," Fred asked, "did you upload the clipboard file?"

"Mmm. I plugged it into house storage. The midnight poll will upload it to central." She leaned her head against his shoulder and laughed. "Did you see Kim's hair? She must have rolled in the leaves!"

"No," he contradicted. "David dumped those on her. I caught them at it in the woods."

"Why didn't you tell me? I gave her quite a scold."

"If she didn't snitch on him, why should I? Besides, I would have liked to play in the leaves, too, if they would have let me."

She poked him in the ribs. "Impossible. Farm kids! And you're the worst of the lot."

Fred nodded. "Good kids," he said quietly.

"All of them," she agreed.

Then, a touch of wetness on her cheek turned Dot's eyes to the sky above them. "Snow! It's starting to snow."

Drifting down in lazy swirls, large snowflakes were suddenly filling the air. Minute by minute, the white stuff increased, until it became clear that they had to get up and go inside or get wet from all the snow melting on them.

"It will be a good snow this year," Fred said, getting to his feet and helping his wife up. "Good for snowmen."

"And don't forget Santa."

Almost on cue, they heard a strange sound faintly through the snow-muffled air. The sound of a flier. But no one would be flying on a night like this! And the sound was becoming louder, as if the flier was coming down.

Neither of them spoke. Her hand gripped his tighter when the flier flickered into view at the edge of the field. The wings tilted up, the sputtering died. A man in a heavy suit, carrying a large bag over his shoulder, set the flier back on its struts. He walked toward them.

"Tim?" Dot spoke.

"Son?" Fred asked.

The young man's face, dimly lit by the rosy glow of the coals, was one big smile. "Mom, Dad. Sorry I'm late." Then words were lost in a joyous round of bear hugs and happy tears.

"I couldn't get here any sooner," he explained. "Northpole control had me delay docking so that I could be Santa's ship this year. I'm sorry I didn't warn you I was coming. It took some fancy last-minute schedule swapping with the regular pilot to get me here. And then I almost got lost in the snow." He shook his head in embarrassment. "I had forgotten about the snow."

"Just so you are here." His mother gave him another hug. "All my children are here."

"Dot!" said Fred, as the thought struck him. "Go correct the count, quickly before the midnight upload. Our family is six—our Christmas Count tonight."

The mystery of Christmas is deepened
far out in time and space.

THE STAR
Arthur C. Clarke

IT IS THREE thousand light-years to the Vatican. Once, I believed that space could have no power over faith, just as I believed that the heavens declared the glory of God's handiwork. Now I have seen that handiwork, and my faith is sorely troubled. I stare at the crucifix that hangs on the cabin wall above the Mark VI Computer, and for the first time in my life I wonder if it is no more than an empty symbol.

I have told no one yet, but the truth cannot be concealed. The facts are there for all to read, recorded on the countless miles of magnetic tape and the thousands of photographs we are carrying back to Earth. Other scientists can interpret them as easily as I can, and I am not one who would condone that tampering with the truth which often gave my order a bad name in the olden days.

The crew are already sufficiently depressed: I wonder how they will take this ultimate irony. Few of them have any religious faith, yet they will not relish using this final weapon in their campaign against me—that private, good-natured, but fundamentally serious, war which lasted all the way from

Earth. It amused them to have a Jesuit as chief astrophysicist: Dr. Chandler, for instance, could never get over it (why are medical men such notorious atheists?). Sometimes he would meet me on the observation deck, where the lights are always low so that the stars shine with undiminished glory. He would come up to me in the gloom and stand staring out of the great oval port, while the heavens crawled slowly around us as the ship turned end over end with the residual spin we had never bothered to correct.

"Well, Father," he would say at last, "it goes on forever and forever, and perhaps *Something* made it. But how you can believe that Something has a special interest in us and our miserable little world—that just beats me." Then the argument would start, while the stars and nebulae would swing around us in silent, endless arcs beyond the flawlessly clear plastic of the observation port.

It was, I think, the apparent incongruity of my position that caused most amusement to the crew. In vain I would point to my three papers in the *Astrophysical Journal*, my five in the *Monthly Notices of the Royal Astronomical Society*. I would remind them that my order has long been famous for its scientific works. We may be few now, but ever since the eighteenth century we have made contributions to astronomy and geophysics out of all proportion to our numbers. Will my report on the Phoenix Nebula end our thousand years of history? It will end, I fear, much more than that.

I do not know who gave the nebula its name, which seems to me a very bad one. If it contains a prophecy, it is one that cannot be verified for several billion years. Even the word nebula is misleading: this is a far smaller object than those stupendous clouds of mist—the stuff of unborn stars—that are scattered throughout the length of the Milky Way. On the cosmic scale, indeed, the Phoenix Nebula is a tiny thing—a tenuous shell of gas surrounding a single star.

Or what is left of a star . . .

The Rubens engraving of Loyola seems to mock me as it hangs there above the spectrophotometer tracings. What would *you*, Father, have made of this knowledge that has come into my keeping, so far from the little world that was all the universe you knew? Would your faith have risen to the challenge, as mine has failed to do?

You gaze into the distance, Father, but I have traveled a distance beyond any that you could have imagined when you founded our order a thousand years ago. No other survey ship has been so far from Earth: we are at the very frontiers of the explored universe. We set out to reach the Phoenix Nebula, we succeeded, and we are homeward bound with our burden of knowledge. I wish I could lift that burden from my shoulders, but I call to you in vain across the centuries and the light-years that lie between us.

On the book you are holding the words are plain to read. AD MAIOREM DEI GLORIAM, the message runs, but it is a message I can no longer believe. Would you still believe it, if you could see what we have found?

We knew, of course, what the Phoenix Nebula was. Every year, in our galaxy alone, more than a hundred stars explode, blazing for a few hours or days with thousands of times their normal brilliance before they sink back into death and obscurity. Such are the ordinary novae—the commonplace disasters of the universe. I have recorded the spectrograms and light curves of dozens since I started working at the Lunar Observatory.

But three or four times in every thousand years occurs something beside which even a nova pales into total insignificance.

When a star becomes a *supernova*, it may for a little while outshine all the massed suns of the galaxy. The Chinese astronomers watched this happen in A.D 1054, not knowing what it was they saw. Five centuries later, in 1572, a supernova blazed in Cassiopeia so brilliantly that it was visible in the daylight sky. There have been three more in the thousand years that have passed since then.

Our mission was to visit the remnants of such a catastrophe, to reconstruct the events that led up to it, and, if possible, to learn its cause. We came slowly in through the concentric shells of gas that had been blasted out six thousand years before, yet were expanding still. They were immensely hot, radiating even now with a fierce violet light, but were far too tenuous to do us any damage. When the star had exploded, its outer layers had been driven upward with such speed that they had escaped completely from its gravitational field. Now they formed a hollow shell large enough to engulf a thousand solar systems, and at its center burned the tiny, fantastic object which the star had now become—a White Dwarf, smaller than the Earth, yet weighing a million times as much.

The glowing gas shells were all around us, banishing the normal night of interstellar space. We were flying into the center of a cosmic bomb that had detonated millennia ago and whose incandescent fragments were still hurtling apart. The immense scale of the explosion, and the fact that the debris already covered a volume of space many billions of miles across, robbed the scene of any visible movement. It would take decades before the unaided eye could detect any motion in these tortured wisps and eddies of gas, yet the sense of turbulent expansion was overwhelming.

We had checked our primary drive hours before, and were drifting slowly toward the fierce little star ahead. Once it had been a sun like our own, but it had squandered in a few hours the energy that should have kept it shining for a million years. Now it was a shrunken miser, hoarding its resources as if trying to make amends for its prodigal youth.

No one seriously expected to find planets. If there had been any before the explosion, they would have been boiled into puffs of vapor, and their substance lost in the greater wreckage of the star itself. But we made the automatic search, as we always do when approaching an unknown sun, and presently we found a single small world circling the star at an immense distance. It must have been the Pluto of this vanished solar system, orbiting on the frontiers of the night. Too far from the central sun ever to have known life, its remoteness had saved it from the fate of all its lost companions.

The passing fires had seared its rocks and burned away the

mantle of frozen gas that must have covered it in the days before the disaster. We landed, and we found the Vault.

Its builders had made sure that we should. The monolithic
marker that stood above the entrance was now a fused stump,
but even the first long-range photographs told us that here
was the work of intelligence. A little later we detected the
continent-wide pattern of radio-activity that had been buried
in the rock. Even if the pylon above the Vault had been destroyed, this would have remained, an immovable and all but
eternal beacon calling to the stars. Our ship fell toward this
gigantic bull's-eye like an arrow into its target.

The pylon must have been a mile high when it was built,
but now it looked like a candle that had melted down into a
puddle of wax. It took us a week to drill through the fused
rock, since we did not have the proper tools for a task like
this. We were astronomers, not archaeologists, but we could
improvise. Our original purpose was forgotten: this lonely
monument, reared with such labor at the greatest possible distance from the doomed sun, could have only one meaning. A
civilization that knew it was about to die had made its last
bid for immortality.

It will take us generations to examine all the treasures that
were placed in the Vault. They had plenty of time to prepare,
for their sun must have given its first warnings many years
before the final detonation. Everything that they wished to
preserve, all the fruit of their genius, they brought here to this
distant world in the days before the end, hoping that some
other race would find it and that they would not be utterly
forgotten. Would we have done as well, or would we have
been too lost in our own misery to give thought to a future
we could never see or share?

If only they had had a little more time! They could travel
freely enough between the planets of their own sun, but they
had not yet learned to cross the interstellar gulfs, and the
nearest solar system was a hundred light-years away. Yet
even had they possessed the secret of the Transfinite Drive,
no more than a few millions could have been saved. Perhaps
it was better thus.

Even if they had not been so disturbingly human as their sculpture shows, we could not have helped admiring them and grieving for their fate. They left thousands of visual records and the machines for projecting them, together with elaborate pictorial instructions from which it will not be difficult to learn their written language. We have examined many of these records, and brought to life for the first time in six thousand years the warmth and beauty of a civilization that in many ways must have been superior to our own. Perhaps they only showed us the best, and one can hardly blame them. But their worlds were very lovely, and their cities were built with a grace that matches anything of man's. We have watched them at work and play, and listened to their musical speech sounding across the centuries. One scene is still before my eyes—a group of children on a beach of strange blue sand, playing in the waves as children play on Earth. Curious whiplike trees line the shore, and some very large animal is wading in the shadows yet attracting no attention at all.

And sinking into the sea, still warm and friendly and lifegiving, is the sun that will soon turn traitor and obliterate all this innocent happiness.

Perhaps if we had not been so far from home and so vulnerable to loneliness, we should not have been so deeply moved. Many of us had seen the ruins of ancient civilizations on other worlds, but they had never affected us so profoundly. This tragedy was unique. It is one thing for a race to fail and die, as nations and cultures have done on Earth. But to be destroyed so completely in the full flower of its achievement, leaving no survivors—how could that be reconciled with the mercy of God?

My colleagues have asked me that, and I have given what answers I can. Perhaps you could have done better, Father Loyola, but I have found nothing in the *Exercitia Spiritualia* that helps me here. They were not an evil people: I do not know what gods they worshiped, if indeed they worshiped any. But I have looked back at them across the centuries, and have watched while the loveliness they used their last strength to preserve was brought forth again into the light of their shrunken sun. They could have taught us much: why were they destroyed?

I know the answers that my colleagues will give when they get back to Earth. They will say that the universe has no purpose and no plan, that since a hundred suns explode every year in our galaxy, at this very moment some race is dying in the depths of space. Whether that race has done good or evil during its lifetime will make no difference in the end: there is no divine justice, for there is no God.

Yet, of course, what we have seen proves nothing of the sort. Anyone who argues thus is being swayed by emotion, not logic. God has no need to justify His actions to man. He who built the universe can destroy it when He chooses. It is arrogance—it is perilously near blasphemy—for us to say what He may or may not do.

This I could have accepted, hard though it is to look upon whole worlds and peoples thrown into the furnace. But there comes a point when even the deepest faith must falter, and now, as I look at the calculations lying before me, I know I have reached that point at last.

We could not tell, before we reached the nebula, how long ago the explosion took place. Now, from the astronomical evidence and the record in the rocks of that one surviving planet, I have been able to date it very exactly. I know in what year the light of this colossal conflagration reached our Earth. I know how brilliantly the supernova whose corpse now dwindles behind our speeding ship once shone in terrestrial skies. I know how it must have blazed low in the east before sunrise, like a beacon in that oriental dawn.

. There can be no reasonable doubt: the ancient mystery is solved at last. Yet, oh God, there were so many stars you could have used. What was the need to give these people to the fire, that the symbol of their passing might shine above Bethlehem?

You better watch out ... he's coming again!

When Jesus Comes
Down the Chimney
Ian Watson

Now, Jamie, if you don't go to bed when your Daddy tells
you to, Jesus won't come down the chimney!

Oh, so you can't even *imagine* sleeping yet?

Saints! Tell you the whole story of Jesus—and of Santa
Claus too? Why, that would take till nine.

Well, maybe ... (No, I am *not* spoiling the boy!)

You just snuggle up in your chair by the fire there, Jamie,
and listen to me. And I'll be carrying you upstairs before
you've heard the half of it!

We'd better start with Santa Claus.

We all know how Santa was born in a humble stable
amongst the chickens and goats. Most of his countryfolk were
poor, and Santa's parents were no exception. No shoes on
their feet, no fine cakes in the larder. No larders, often! A lot
of those people lived in tents, and it got pretty cold in the
winter. Three magicians had hiked a thousand miles to be
present when Santa was born. They followed a bright comet
in the sky, and brought a magic sack as a gift. You could take
whatever you wished for out of this sack. Santa's mother

didn't want to stir up jealousy amongst her neighbors, so she hid the sack away. Anyway, her country was being occupied by the Roman army. If the Romans heard of the magic sack she feared they'd take it away for their wild, greedy emperor.

When Santa grew to manhood his mother gave him the magicians' gift and explained all about it. Santa decided then and there that he would like to shower presents on his countryfolk, though he swore that he would never pull anything out of the sack for himself.

So Santa tramped around the land with the sack over his shoulder, giving people whatever their hearts most desired, or what they needed most. He kept his vow about giving nothing to himself. Even so, one widow woman requested a fine red coat trimmed with angora wool and then insisted that Santa should wear it, not she. A leper whose feet were rotted and crippled asked for a pair of stout black boots, and forced these on Santa.

That wasn't all. Such a number of grateful people pressed bread and cheese on Santa, from out of their meagre stocks, not to mention fish and fruit and meat and milk and wine—which he couldn't decently refuse—that within a few years he grew positively stout!

Well, the Roman soldiers finally arrested him. All of those free gifts that poured from Santa's sack were destabilizing a marginal economy. They were weakening the currency. They were causing job refusal in the colonial labour market.

The Romans tied the magic sack over Santa's head. They marched him up to the top of a hill and nailed him to a wooden cross, then jabbed their spears through the sack a couple of times to blind him.

When they took Santa down dead at last they bundled his corpse into the sack, tied it tight, and set an official seal on it. They debated tossing him into the nearby river, but eventually their captain allowed Santa's friends to carry him away to a tomb.

That night the tomb was broken into by robbers who hoped to steal the magic sack . . . and they found the sack lying there empty. It was as if that burlap bag had digested Santa

Claus! As if it had spirited him away to the dimension where all free gifts came from.

The robbers were filled with wonder, and didn't want to steal ever again. Instead, they made a pact to spread the word about Santa all over the world and to carry the sack (or snippets from it) wherever they went, as proof. The sack was first carried to Roma, then later to Torino, where most of it remains to this very day.

In later years the descendants of those original robbers promised that one day when everybody in the world had heard of Santa and loved him, the sack would begin to distribute free gifts again. That's why, every Easter, we all receive presents wrapped in sack-cloth, in memory of Santa. Jesus? Oh, yes, I'm coming to him. Of course I am, Jamie! It's Jesus who's important tonight.

Jesus was the leader of those thieves who broke into Santa's tomb. (There's something symmetrical, don't you think, between gifts and robbery? Robbery is the product of a society where there aren't enough gifts to go round—or where there are too many gifts for too few people. What's that? Sym-met-ric-al. It means ... oh, it doesn't really matter, Jamie darling. Honest!)

Jesus was the ex-thief who carried the sack to Roma where the hysterical greedy emperor lived, guarded by his soldiers with their spears.

When Jesus arrived in Roma he went straight to the Forum. That's a sort of meeting place, like a Senate, but for the common people.

Jesus stood up on a marble block and waved the empty sack and called out—with the help of a translator, from Aramaic into Latin, "Plebeians of Roma, I bring you gifts!" (A plebeian was someone unemployed, living on free bread and enjoying free entry into circuses.)

At first the plebeians who thronged the Forum stared at the sack as eagerly as if they were looking up a girl's skirt.

When they saw that the sack was empty, many of them hooted and jeered. Others lost their temper and chucked pebbles.

But Jesus cried out, "The gifts I bring you are dialectical!" (This was a term which Jesus borrowed from the Greek philosophers.) "Your desires are the thesis. This sack is the antithesis. The synthesis is that you should empty yourselves of false goals, vain dreams, the products of a diseased society. Just you empty all of that false consciousness of yours into this sack! It will hold everything, and reduce everything that is contradictory. In its place you'll discover that gifts ought to be given according to one's needs, not one's desires—but society at present is based on legalized theft, on the alienation of persons from their soil, from their work, even from their own bodies and sexuality."

With daily repetition, Jesus' message began to sink in. Soon a few of the plebeians believed him—and stepped into the sack and out again, as a symbol of their change of heart. Then many.

At last the emperor's curiosity was piqued; for the circus seats remained empty, and the elephants and the trained apes which rode them wept. Also there was growing unrest among his soldiers at the prospect of yet another colonial war.

The emperor in person led a party of trusted guards to the Forum, intending to spear this Jesus. On the way there the emperor . . . now, we must tell the truth: he was a hysteric but he also cunningly sensed his own political and economic infrastructure ebbing away . . . the emperor experienced a visionary fit. He saw a sack in the sky which swallowed the sun. (Actually, we believe this was a total eclipse.) When he reached the Forum he dismounted from his horse—and stepped into the sack. Soon the empire had totally changed . . . into a republic.

Ah, now you're nodding off.

Let's go quietly, mm? Up up up to bed.

Tonight, night of nights, Jesus will climb down the chimney and take away whatever you think is most precious to you. Will it be your rocking horse? Or your toy bear? Or just your tin whistle?

Tush. How else could other deserving little children receive fine gifts at Easter time?

Hush. He'll take something from us all. Not just you, you dobbin. Maybe I'll lose my spinning wheel tonight. Maybe it'll be my purple velvet dress.

Jesus'll redistribute all our wealth. That's why he's called "the good thief." He brings Santa's empty sack with him down all the chimneys in the whole wide world, and fills it full from every house.

Here we are now, darling. Tuck up tight, and shut those eyes. No peeping, or he mightn't come.

Who would want to do in a jolly old elf?

THE PLOT AGAINST
SANTA CLAUS
James Powell

RORY BIGTOES, SANTA'S Security Chief, was tall for an elf,
measuring almost seven inches from the curly tips of his
shoes to the top of his fedora. But he had to stride to keep
abreast of Garth Hardnoggin, the quick little Director General
of the Toyworks, as they hurried, beards streaming back over
their shoulders, through the racket and bustle of Shop
Number 5, one of the many vaulted caverns honeycombing
the undiscovered island beneath the Polar icecap.

Director General Hardnoggin wasn't pleased. He slapped
his megaphone, the symbol of his office (for as a member of
the Board he spoke directly to Santa Claus), against his thigh.
"A bomb in the Board Room on Christmas Eve!" he muttered
with angry disbelief.

"I'll admit that Security doesn't look good," said Bigtoes.

Hardnoggin gave a snort and stopped at a construction site
for Dick and Jane Doll dollhouses. Elf carpenters and painters
were hard at work, pipes in their jaws and beards tucked into
their belts. A foreman darted over to show Hardnoggin the
wallpaper samples for the dining room.

"See this unit, Bigtoes?" said Hardnoggin. "Split-level ranch type. Wall-to-wall carpeting. Breakfast nook. Your choice of Early American or French Provincial furnishings. They said I couldn't build it for the price. But I did. And how did I do it?"

"Cardboard," said a passing elf, an old carpenter with a plank over his shoulder.

"And what's wrong with cardboard? Good substantial cardboard for the interior walls!" shouted the Director General striding off again. "Let them bellyache, Bigtoes. I'm not out to win any popularity contests. But I do my job. Let's see you do yours. Find Dirk Crouchback and find him fast."

At the automotive section the new Lazaretto sports cars (1/32 scale) were coming off the assembly line. Hardnoggin stopped to slam one of the car doors. "You left out the *kachunk*," he told an elf engineer in white cover-alls.

"Nobody gets a tin door to go *kachunk*," said the engineer.

"Detroit does. So can we," said Hardnoggin, moving on. "You think I don't miss the good old days, Bigtoes?" he said. "I was a spinner. And a damn good one. Nobody made a top that could spin as long and smooth as Garth Hardnoggin's."

"I was a jacksmith myself," said Bigtoes. Satisfying work, building each jack-in-the-box from the ground up, carpentering the box, rigging the spring mechanism, making the funny head, spreading each careful coat of paint.

"How many could you make in a week?" asked Director General Hardnoggin.

"Three, with overtime," said Security Chief Bigtoes.

Hardnoggin nodded. "And how many children had empty stockings on Christmas morning because we couldn't handcraft enough stuff to go around? That's where your Ghengis Khans, your Hitlers, and your Stalins come from, Bigtoes—children who through no fault of their own didn't get any toys for Christmas. So Santa had to make a policy decision: quality or quantity? He opted for quantity.

Crouchback, at that time one of Santa's right-hand elves, had blamed the decision on Hardnoggin's sinister influence.

By way of protest he had placed a bomb in the new plastic machine. The explosion had coated three elves with a thick layer of plastic which had to be chipped off with hammers and chisels. Of course they lost their beards. Santa, who was particularly sensitive about beards, sentenced Crouchback to two years in the cooler, as the elves called it. This meant he was assigned to a refrigerator (one in Ottawa, Canada, as it happened) with the responsibility of turning the light on and off as the door was opened or closed.

But after a month Crouchback had failed to answer the daily roll call which Security made by means of a two-way intercom system. He had fled the refrigerator and become a renegade elf. Then suddenly, three years later, Crouchback had reappeared at the North Pole, a shadowy fugitive figure, editor of a clandestine newspaper, *The Midnight Elf*, which made violent attacks on Director General Hardnoggin and his policies. More recently, Crouchback had become the leader of SHAFT—Santa's Helpers Against Flimsy Toys—an organization of dissident groups including the Anti-Plastic League, the Sons and Daughters of the Good Old Days, the Ban the Toy-Bomb people and the Hippie Elves for Peace . . .

"Santa opted for quantity," repeated Hardnoggin. "And I carried out his decision. Just between the two of us it hasn't always been easy." Hardnoggin waved his megaphone at the Pacification and Rehabilitation section where thousands of toy bacteriological warfare kits (JiffyPox) were being converted to civilian use (The Freckle Machine). After years of pondering Santa had finally ordered a halt to war-toy production. His decision was considered a victory for SHAFT and a defeat for Hardnoggin.

"Unilateral disarmament is a mistake, Bigtoes," said Hardnoggin grimly as they passed through a door marked *Santa's Executive Helpers Only* and into the carpeted world of the front office. "Mark my words, right now the tanks and planes are rolling off the assembly lines at Acme Toy and into the department stores." (Acme Toy, the international consortium of toymakers, was the elves' greatest bugbear.) "So the rich kids will have war toys, while the poor kids won't even have a popgun. That's not democratic."

Bigtoes stopped at a door marked *Security*. Hardnoggin strode on without slackening his pace. "Sticks-and-Stones session at five o'clock," he said over his shoulder. "Don't be late. And do your job. Find Crouchback!"

Dejected, Bigtoes slumped down at his desk, receiving a sympathetic smile from Charity Nosegay, his little blonde blue-eyed secretary. Charity was a recent acquisition and Bigtoes had intended to make a play for her once the Sticks-and-Stones paperwork was out of the way. (Security had to prepare a report for Santa on each alleged naughty boy and girl.) Now that play would have to wait.

Bigtoes sighed. Security looked bad. Bigtoes had even been warned. The night before, a battered and broken elf had crawled into his office, gasped, "He's going to kill Santa," and died. It was Darby Shortribs who had once been a brilliant doll designer. But then one day he had decided that if war toys encouraged little boys to become soldiers when they grew up, then dolls encouraged little girls to become mothers, contributing to overpopulation. So Shortribs had joined SHAFT and risen to membership on its Central Committee.

The trail of Shortribs' blood had led to the Quality Control lab and the Endurance Machine which simulated the brutal punishment, the bashing, crushing, and kicking that a toy receives at the hands of a four-year-old (or two two-year-olds). A hell of a way for an elf to die!

After Shortribs' warning, Bigtoes had alerted his Security elves and sent a flying squad after Crouchback. But the SHAFT leader had disappeared. The next morning a bomb had exploded in the Board Room.

On the top of Bigtoes' desk were the remains of that bomb. Small enough to fit into an elf's briefcase, it had been placed under the Board Room table, just at Santa's feet. If Owen Brassbottom, Santa's Traffic Manager, hadn't chosen just that moment to usher the jolly old man into the Map Room to pinpoint the spot where, with the permission and blessing of the Strategic Air Command, Santa's sleigh and reindeer were to penetrate the DEW Line, there wouldn't have been much left of Santa from the waist down. Seconds before the bomb went off, Director General Hardnoggin had been called from the room to take a private phone call. Fergus Bandylegs, Vice-President of Santa Enterprises, Inc., had just gone down to the other end of the table to discuss something with Tom Thumbskin, Santa's Creative Head, and escaped the blast. But Thumbskin had to be sent to the hospital with a concussion when his chair—the elves sat on high chairs with ladders up the side like those used by lifeguards—was knocked over backward by the explosion.

All this was important, for the room had been searched before the meeting and found safe. So the bomb must have been brought in by a member of the Board. It certainly hadn't been Traffic Manager Brassbottom who had saved Santa, and probably not Thumbskin. That left Director General Hardnoggin and Vice-President Bandylegs ...

"Any luck checking out that personal phone call Hardnoggin received just before the bomb went off?" asked Bigtoes.

Charity shook her golden locks. "The switchboard operator fainted right after she took the call. She's still out cold."

Leaving the Toyworks, Bigtoes walked quickly down a corridor lined with expensive boutiques and fashionable restaurants. On one wall of Mademoiselle Fanny's Salon of Haute Couture some SHAFT elf had written: *Santa, Si! Hardnoggin, No!* On one wall of the Hotel St. Nicholas some Hardnoggin backer had written: *Support Your Local Director General!* Bigtoes was no philosopher and the social unrest that was racking the North Pole confused him. Once, in disguise, he had attended a SHAFT rally in The Underwood, that vast and forbidding cavern of phosphorescent stinkhorn and hanging roots. Gathered beneath an immense picture of Santa were hippie elves with their beards tied in outlandish knots, matron-lady elves in sensible shoes, tweedy elves and green-collar elves.

Crouchback himself had made a surprise appearance, coming out of hiding to deliver his now famous "Plastic Lives!" speech. "Hardnoggin says plastic is inanimate. But I say that plastic lives! Plastic infects all it touches and spreads like crab grass in the innocent souls of little children. Plastic toys make plastic girls and boys!" Crouchback drew himself up to his full six inches. "I say: quality—quality now!" The crowd roared his words back at him. The meeting closed with all the elves joining hands and singing "We Shall Overcome." It had been a moving experience ...

As he expected, Bigtoes found Bandylegs at the Hotel St. Nicholas bar, staring morosely down into a thimble-mug of ale. Fergus Bandylegs was a dapper, fast-talking elf with a chestnut beard which he scented with lavender. As Vice-President of Santa Enterprises, Inc., he was in charge of financing the entire Toyworks operation by arranging for Santa to appear in advertising campaigns, by collecting royalties on the use of the jolly old man's name, and by leasing Santa suits to department stores.

Bandylegs ordered a drink for the Security Chief. Their friendship went back to Rory Bigtoes' jacksmith days when Bandylegs had been a master sledwright. "These are topsy-turvy times, Rory," said Bandylegs. "First there's that bomb and now Santa's turned down the Jolly Roger cigarette account. For years now they've had this ad campaign showing Santa slipping a carton of Jolly Rogers into Christmas stockings. But not any more. 'Smoking may be hazardous to your health,' says Santa."

"Santa knows best," said Bigtoes.

"Granted," said Bandylegs. "But counting television residuals, that's a cool two million sugar plums thrown out the window." (At the current rate of exchange there are 4.27 sugar plums to the U.S. dollar.) "Hardnoggin's already on my back to make up the loss. Nothing must interfere with his grand plan for automating the Toyworks. So it's off to Madison Avenue again. Sure I'll stay at the Plaza and eat at the Chambord, but I'll still get homesick."

The Vice-President smiled sadly. "Do you know what I

used to do? There's this guy who stands outside Grand Central Station selling those little mechanical men you wind up and they march around. I used to march around with them. It made me feel better somehow. But now they remind me of Hardnoggin. He's a machine, Rory, and he wants to make all of us into machines."

"What about the bomb?" asked Bigtoes.

Bandylegs shrugged. "Acme Toy, I suppose."

Bigtoes shook his head. Acme Toy hadn't slipped an elf spy into the North Pole for months. "What about Crouchback?"

"No," said Bandylegs firmly. "I'll level with you, Rory. I had a get-together with Crouchback just last week. He wanted to get my thoughts on the quality-versus-quantity question and on the future of the Toyworks. Maybe I'm wrong, but I got the impression that a top-level shake-up is in the works with Crouchback slated to become the new Director General. In any event I found him a very perceptive and understanding elf."

Bandylegs smiled and went on, "Darby Shortribs was there, prattling on against dolls. As I left, Crouchback shook my hand and whispered, 'Every movement needs its lunatic fringe, Bandylegs. Shortribs is ours.' " Bandylegs lowered his voice. "I'm tired of the grown-up ratrace, Rory. I want to get back to the sled shed and make Blue Streaks and High Flyers again. I'll never get there with Hardnoggin and his modern ideas at the helm."

Bigtoes pulled at his beard. It was common knowledge that Crouchback had an elf spy on the Board. The reports on the meetings in *The Midnight Elf* were just too complete. Was it his friend Bandylegs? But would Bandylegs try to kill Santa?

That brought Bigtoes back to Hardnoggin again. But cautiously. As Security Chief, Bigtoes had to be objective. Yet he yearned to prove Hardnoggin the villain. This, as he knew, was because of the beautiful Carlotta Peachfuzz, beloved by children all around the world. As the voice of the Peachy Pippin Doll, Carlotta was the most envied female at the North Pole, next to Mrs Santa. Girl elves followed her glamorous exploits in the press. Male elves had Peachy Pippin Dolls propped beside their beds so they could fall asleep with Carlotta's sultry voice saying: "Hello, I'm your talking Peachy Pippin Doll. I love you. I love you. I love you . . ."

But once it had just been Rory and Carlotta, Carlotta and Rory—until the day Bigtoes had introduced her to Hardnoggin. "You have a beautiful voice, Miss Peachfuzz," the Director General had said. "Have you ever considered being in the talkies?" So Carlotta had dropped Bigtoes for Hardnoggin and risen to stardom in the talking-doll industry. But her liaison with Director General Hardnoggin had become so notorious that a dutiful Santa—with Mrs. Santa present—had had to read the riot act about executive hanky-panky. Hardnoggin had broken off the relationship. Disgruntled, Carlotta had become active with SHAFT, only to leave after a violent argument with Shortribs over his anti-doll position.

Today Bigtoes couldn't care less about Carlotta. But he still had that old score to settle with the Director General.

Leaving the fashionable section behind, Bigtoes turned down Apple Alley, a residential corridor of modest, old-fashioned houses with thatched roofs and carved beams. Here the mushrooms were in full bloom—the stropharia, inocybe, and chanterelle—dotting the corridor with indigo, vermilion, and many yellows. Elf householders were out troweling in their gardens. Elf wives gossiped over hedges of gypsy pholiota. Somewhere an old elf was singing one of the ancient work songs, accompanying himself on a concertina. Until Director General Hardnoggin discovered that it slowed down production, the elves had always sung while they worked, beating out the time with their hammers; now the foremen passed out song sheets and led them in song twice a day. But it wasn't the same thing.

Elf gardeners looked up, took their pipes from their mouths, and watched Bigtoes pass. They regarded all front-office people with suspicion—even this big elf with the candy-stripe rosette of the Order of Santa, First Class, in his buttonhole.

Bigtoes had won the decoration many years ago when he was a young Security elf, still wet behind his pointed ears. Somehow on that fateful day, Billy Roy Scoggins, President of Acme Toy, had found the secret entrance to the North Pole and appeared suddenly in parka and snowshoes, demanding to see Santa Claus. Santa arrived, jolly and smiling, surrounded by Bigtoes and the other Security elves. Scoggins announced he had a proposition "from one hardheaded businessman to another."

Pointing out the foolishness of competition, the intruder had offered Santa a king's ransom to come in with Acme Toy. "Ho, ho, ho," boomed Santa with jovial firmness, "that isn't Santa's way." Scoggins—perhaps it was the "ho, ho, ho" that did it—turned purple and threw a punch that floored the jolly old man. Security sprang into action.

Four elves had died as Scoggins flayed at them, a snowshoe in one hand and a rolled up copy of *The Wall Street Journal* in the other. But Bigtoes had crawled up the outside of Scoggins' pantleg. It had taken him twelve karate chops to break the intruder's kneecap and send him crashing to the ground like a stricken tree. To this day the President of Acme Toy walks with a cane and curses Rory Bigtoes whenever it rains.

As Bigtoes passed a tavern—The Bowling Green, with a huge horse mushroom shading the door—someone inside banged down a thimble-mug and shouted the famous elf toast: "My Santa, right or wrong! May he always be right, but right or wrong, my Santa!" Bigtoes sighed. Life should be so simple for elves. They all loved Santa—what did it matter that he used blueing when he washed his beard, or liked to sleep late, or hit the martinis a bit too hard—and they all wanted to do what was best for good little girls and boys. But here the agreement ended. Here the split between Hardnoggin and Crouchback—between the Establishment and the revolutionary—took over.

Beyond the tavern was a crossroads, the left corridor leading to the immense storage areas for completed toys, the right corridor to The Underwood. Bigtoes continued straight and was soon entering that intersection of corridors called Pumpkin Corners, the North Pole's bohemian quarter. Here, until his disappearance, the SHAFT leader Crouchback had lived with relative impunity, protected by the inhabitants. For this was SHAFT country. A special edition of *The Midnight Elf* was already on the streets denying that SHAFT was involved in the assassination attempt on Santa. A love-bead vendor, his beard tied in a sheepshank, had *Hardnoggin Is a Dwarf* written across the side of his pushcart. *Make love, not plastic* declared the wall of The Electric Carrot, a popular discotheque and hippie hangout.

The Electric Carrot was crowded with elves dancing the latest craze, the Scalywag. Until recently, dancing hadn't been popular with elves. They kept stepping on their beards. The hippie knots effectively eliminated that stumbling block.

Buck Withers, leader of the Hippie Elves for Peace, was sitting in a corner wearing a *Santa Is Love* button. Bigtoes had once dropped a first-offense drug charge against Withers and three other elves caught nibbling on morning-glory seeds. "Where's Crouchback, Buck?" said Bigtoes.

"Like who's asking?" said Withers. "The head of Hardnoggin's Gestapo?"

"A friend," said Bigtoes.

"Friend, like when the news broke about Shortribs, he says 'I'm next, Buck.' Better fled than dead, and he split for parts unknown."

"It looks bad, Buck."

"Listen, friend," said Withers, "SHAFT's the wave of the future. Like Santa's already come over to our side on the disarmament thing. What do we need with bombs? That's a bad scene, friend. Violence isn't SHAFT's bag."

As Bigtoes left The Electric Carrot a voice said, "I wonder, my dear sir, if you could help an unfortunate elf." Bigtoes turned to find a tattered derelict in a filthy button-down shirt and greasy gray-flannel suit. His beard was matted with twigs and straw.

"Hello, Baldwin," said Bigtoes. Baldwin Redpate had once been the head of Santa's Shipping Department. Then came the Slugger Nolan Official Baseball Mitt Scandal. The mitt had been a big item one year, much requested in letters to Santa. Through some gigantic snafu in Shipping, thousands of inflatable rubber ducks had been sent out instead. For months afterward, Santa received letters from indignant little boys, and though each one cut him like a knife he never reproached Redpate. But Redpate knew he had failed Santa. He brooded, had attacks of silent crying, and finally took to drink, falling so much under the spell of bee wine that Hardnoggin had to insist he resign.

"Rory, you're just the elf I'm looking for," said Redpate. "Have you ever seen an elf skulking? Well, I have."

Bigtoes was interested. Elves were straightforward creatures. They didn't skulk.

"Last night I woke up in a cold sweat and saw strange things, Rory," said Redpate. "Comings and goings, lights, skulking." Large tears rolled down Redpate's cheeks. "You see, I get these nightmares, Rory. Thousands of inflatable rubber ducks come marching across my body and their eyes are Santa's eyes when someone's let him down." He leaned toward Bigtoes confidentially. "I may be a washout. Occasionally I may even drink too much. But I don't skulk!" Redpate began to cry again.

His tears looked endless. Bigtoes was due at the Sticks-and-Stones session. He slipped Redpate ten sugar plums. "Got to go, Baldwin."

Redpate dabbed at the tears with the dusty end of his beard. "When you see Santa, ask him to think kindly of old Baldy Redpate," he sniffed and headed straight for The Good Gray Goose, the tavern across the street—making a beeline for the bee wine, as the elves would say. But then he turned. "Strange goings-on," he called. "Storeroom Number 14, Unit 24, Row 58. Skulking."

"Hardnoggin's phone call was from Carlotta Peachfuzz," said Charity, looking lovelier than ever. "The switchboard operator is a big Carlotta fan. She fainted when she recognized her voice. The thrill was just too much."

Interesting. In spite of Santa's orders, were Carlotta and Hardnoggin back together on the sly? If so, had they conspired on the bomb attempt? Or had it really been Carlotta's voice? Carlotta Peachfuzz impersonations were a dime a dozen.

"Get me the switchboard operator," said Bigtoes and returned to stuffing Sticks-and-Stones reports into his briefcase.

"No luck," said Charity, putting down the phone. "She just took another call and fainted again."

Vice-President Bandylegs looked quite pleased with himself and threw Bigtoes a wink. "Don't be surprised when I cut out of Sticks-and-Stones early, Rory," he smiled. "An affair of the heart. All of a sudden the old Bandylegs charm has come through again." He nodded down the hall at Hardnoggin, waiting impatiently at the Projection Room door. "When the cat's away, the mice will play."

The Projection Room was built like a movie theater. "Come over here beside Santa, Rory, my boy," boomed the jolly old man. So Bigtoes scrambled up into a tiny seat hooked over the back of the seat on Santa's left. On Bigtoes' left sat Traffic Manager Brassbottom, Vice-President Bandylegs, and Director General Hardnoggin. In this way Mrs. Santa, at the portable bar against the wall, could send Santa's martinis to him down an assembly line of elves.

Confident that no one would dare to try anything with Santa's Security Chief present, Bigtoes listened to the Traffic Manager, a red-lipped elf with a straw-colored beard, talk enthusiastically about the television coverage planned for Santa's trip. This year, live and in color via satellite, the North Pole would see Santa's arrival at each stop on his journey. Santa's first martini was passed from Hardnoggin to Bandylegs to Brassbottom to Bigtoes. The Security Chief grasped the stem of the glass in both hands and, avoiding the heady gin fumes as best he could, passed it to Santa.

"All right," said Santa, taking his first sip, "let's roll 'em, starting with the worst."

The lights dimmed. A film appeared on the screen. "Waldo Rogers, age five," said Bigtoes. "Mistreatment of pets, eight demerits." (The film showed a smirking little boy pulling a cat's tail.) "Not coming when he's called, ten demerits." (The film showed Waldo's mother at the screen door, shouting.) "Also, as an indication of his general bad behavior, he gets his mother to buy Sugar Gizmos but he won't eat them. He just wants the boxtops." (The camera panned a pantry shelf crowded with opened Sugar Gizmo boxes.) The elves clucked disapprovingly.

"Waldo Rogers certainly isn't Santa's idea of a nice little boy," said Santa. "What do you think, Mother?" Mrs. Santa agreed.

"Sticks-and-stones then?" asked Hardnoggin hopefully.

But the jolly old man hesitated. "Santa always likes to check the list twice before deciding," he said.

Hardnoggin groaned. Santa was always bollixing up his production schedules by going easy on bad little girls and boys.

A new film began. "Next on the list," said Bigtoes, "is Nancy Ruth Ashley, age four and a half ..."

Two hours and seven martinis later, Santa's jolly laughter and Mrs. Santa's giggles filled the room. "She's a little dickens, that one," chuckled Santa as they watched a six-year-old fill her father's custom-made shoes with molasses, "but Santa will find a little something for her." Hardnoggin groaned. That was the end of the list and so far no one had been given sticks-and-stones. They rolled the film on Waldo Rogers again. "Santa understands some cats like having their tails pulled," chuckled Santa as he drained his glass. "And what the heck are Sugar Gizmos?"

Bandylegs, who had just excused himself from the meeting, paused on his way up the aisle. "They're a delicious blend of toasted oats and corn," he shouted, "With an energy-packed coating of sparkling sugar. As a matter of fact, Santa, the Gizmo people are thinking of featuring you in their new advertising campaign. It would be a great selling point if I could say that Santa had given a little boy sticks-and-stones because he wouldn't eat his Sugar Gizmos."

"Here now, Fergy," said the jolly old man, "you know that isn't Santa's way."

Bandylegs left, muttering to himself.

"Santa," protested Hardnoggin as the jolly old man passed his glass down the line for a refill, "let's be realistic. If we can't draw the line at Waldo Rogers, where can we?"

Santa reflected for a moment. "Suppose Santa let you make the decision, Garth, my boy. What would little Waldo Rogers find in his stocking on Christmas morning?"

Hardnoggin hesitated. Then he said, "Sticks-and-stones."

Santa looked disappointed. "So be it," he said.

The lights dimmed again as they continued their review of the list. Santa's eighth martini came down the line from elf to elf. As Bigtoes passed it to Santa, the fumes caught him—the smell of gin and something else. Bitter almonds. He struck the glass from Santa's hand.

Silent and dimly lit, Storeroom Number 14 seemed an immense, dull suburb of split-level, ranch-type Dick and Jane Doll dollhouses. Bigtoes stepped into the paper-mâché shrubbery fronting Unit 24, Row 58 as an elf watchman on a bicycle pedaled by singing "Colossal Carlotta," a current hit song. Bigtoes hoped he hadn't made a mistake by refraining from picking Hardnoggin up.

Bandylegs had left before the cyanide was put in the glass. Mrs. Santa, of course, was above suspicion. So that left Director General Hardnoggin and Traffic Manager Brassbottom. But why would Brassbottom first save Santa from the bomb only to poison him later? So that left Hardnoggin. Bigtoes had been eager to act on this logic, perhaps too eager. He wanted no one to say that Santa's Security Chief had let personal feelings color his judgment. Bigtoes would be fair.

Hardnoggin had insisted that Crouchback was the villain. All right, he would bring Crouchback in for questioning. After all, Santa was now safe, napping under a heavy guard in preparation for his all-night trip. Hardnoggin—if *he* was the villain—could do him no harm for the present.

As Bigtoes crept up the fabric lawn on all fours, the front door of the dollhouse opened and a shadowy figure came down the walk. It paused at the street, looked this way and that, then disappeared into the darkness. Redpate had been right about the skulking. But it wasn't Crouchback—Bigtoes was sure of that.

The Security Chief climbed in through a dining-room window. In the living room were three elves, one on the couch, one in an easy chair, and, behind the bar, Dirk Crouchback, a distinguished-looking elf with a salt-and-pepper beard and graying temples. The leader of SHAFT poured himself a drink and turned. "Welcome to my little ménage-à-trois, Rory Bigtoes," he said with a surprised smile. The two other elves turned out to be Dick and Jane dolls.

"I'm taking you in, Crouchback," said the Security Chief.

The revolutionary came out from behind the bar pushing a .55mm. howitzer (⅟₃₂ scale) with his foot. "I'm sorry about this," he said. "As you know, we are opposed to the use of violence. But I'd rather not fall into Hardnoggin's hands just now. Sit over there by Jane." Bigtoes obeyed. At that short range the howitzer's plastic shell could be fatal to an elf.

Crouchback sat down on the arm of Dick's easy chair. "Yes," he said, "Hardnoggin's days are numbered. But as the incidents of last night and today illustrate, the Old Order dies hard. I'd rather not be one of its victims."

Crouchback paused and took a drink. "Look at this room, Bigtoes. This is Hardnoggin's world. Wall-to-wall carpeting. Breakfast nooks. Cheap materials. Shoddy workmanship." He picked up an end table and dropped it on the floor. Two of the legs broke. "Plastic," said Crouchback contemptuously, flinging the table through the plastic television set. "It's the whole middle-class, bourgeois, suburban scene." Crouchback put the heel of his hand on Dick's jaw and pushed the doll over. "Is this vapid plastic nonentity the kind of grownup we want little boys and girls to become?"

"No," said Bigtoes. "But what's your alternative?"

"Close down the Toyworks for a few years," said Crouchback earnestly. "Relearn our ancient heritage of handcrafted toys. We owe it to millions of little boys and girls as yet unborn!"

"All very idealistic," said Bigtoes, "but—"

"Practical, Bigtoes. And down to earth," said the SHAFT leader, tapping his head. "The plan's all here."

"But what about Acme Toy?" protested Bigtoes. "The rich kids would still get presents and the poor kids wouldn't."

Crouchback smiled. "I can't go into the details now. But my plan includes the elimination of Acme Toy."

"Suppose you could," said Bigtoes. "We still couldn't handcraft enough toys to keep pace with the population explosion."

"Not at first," said Crouchback. "But suppose population growth was not allowed to exceed our rate of toy production?" He tapped his head again.

"But good grief," said Bigtoes, "closing down the Toyworks means millions of children with empty stockings on Christmas. Who could be that cruel?"

"Cruel?" exclaimed Crouchback. "Bigtoes, do you know how a grownup cooks a live lobster? Some drop it into boiling water. But others say, 'How cruel!' They drop it in cold water and then bring the water to a boil slowly. No, Bigtoes, we have to bite the bullet. Granted there'll be no Christmas toys for a few years. But we'd fill children's stockings with literature explaining what's going on and with discussion-group outlines so they can get together and talk up the importance of sacrificing their Christmas toys today so the children of the future can have quality handcrafted toys. They'll understand."

Before Bigtoes could protest again, Crouchback got to his feet. "Now that I've given you some food for thought I have to go," he said. "That closet should hold you until I make my escape."

Bigtoes was in the closet for more than an hour. The door proved stronger than he had expected. Then he remembered

Hardnoggin's cardboard interior walls and karate-chopped his way through the back of the closet and out into the kitchen.

Security headquarters was a flurry of excitement as Bigtoes strode in the door. "They just caught Hardnoggin trying to put a bomb on Santa's sleigh," said Charity, her voice shaking.

Bigtoes passed through to the Interrogation Room where Hardnoggin, gray and haggard, sat with his wrists between his knees. The Security elves hadn't handled him gently. One eye was swollen, his beard was in disarray, and there was a dent in his megaphone. "It was a Christmas present for that little beast, Waldo Rogers," shouted Hardnoggin.

"A bomb?" said Bigtoes.

"It was supposed to be a little fire engine," shouted the Director General, "with a bell that goes clang-clang!" Hardnoggin struggled to control himself. "I just couldn't be responsible for that little monster finding nothing in his stocking but sticks-and-stones. But a busy man hasn't time for last-minute shopping. I got a—a friend to pick something out for me."

"Who?" said Bigtoes.

Hardnoggin hung his head. "I demand to be taken to Santa Claus," he said. But Santa, under guard, had already left his apartment for the formal departure ceremony.

Bigtoes ordered Hardnoggin detained and hurried to meet Santa at the elevator. He would have enjoyed shouting up at the jolly old man that Hardnoggin was the culprit. But of course that just didn't hold water. Hardnoggin was too smart to believe he could just walk up and put a bomb on Santa's sleigh. Or—now that Bigtoes thought about it—to finger himself so obviously by waiting until Bandylegs had left the Sticks-and-Stones session before poisoning Santa's glass.

The villain now seemed to be the beautiful and glamorous Carlotta Peachfuzz. Here's the way it figured: Carlotta phones Hardnoggin just before the bomb goes off in the Board Room, thus making him a prime suspect; Carlotta makes a rendezvous with Bandylegs that causes him to leave Sticks-

and-Stones, thus again making Hardnoggin Suspect Number One; then when Bigtoes fails to pick up the Director General, Carlotta talks him into giving little Waldo Rogers a present that turns out to be a bomb. Her object? To frame Hardnoggin for the murder or attempted murder of Santa. Her elf spy? Traffic Manager Brassbottom. It all worked out—or seemed to . . .

Bigtoes met Santa at the elevator surrounded by a dozen Security elves. The jolly old eyes were bloodshot, his smile slightly strained. "Easy does it, Billy," said Santa to Billy Brisket, the Security elf at the elevator controls. "Santa's a bit hungover."

Bigtoes moved to the rear of the elevator. So it was Brassbottom who had planted the bomb and then deliberately taken Santa out of the room. So it was Brassbottom who had poisoned the martini with cyanide, knowing that Bigtoes would detect the smell. And it was Carlotta who had gift-wrapped the bomb. All to frame Hardnoggin. And yet . . . Bigtoes sighed at his own confusion. And yet a dying Shortribs had said that someone was going to kill Santa.

As the elevator eased up into the interior of the Polar ice-cap, Bigtoes focused his mind on Shortribs. Suppose the dead elf had stumbled on your well-laid plan to kill Santa. Suppose you botched Shortribs's murder and therefore knew that Security had been alerted. What would you do? Stage three fake attempts on Santa's life to provide Security with a culprit, hoping to get Security to drop its guard? Possibly. But the bomb in the Board Room could have killed Santa. Why not just do it that way?

The elevator reached the surface and the first floor of the Control Tower building which was ingeniously camouflaged as an icy crag. But suppose, thought Bigtoes, it was important that you kill Santa in a certain way—say, with half the North Pole looking on?

More Security elves were waiting when the elevator doors opened. Bigtoes moved quickly among them, urging the utmost vigilance. Then Santa and his party stepped out onto the frozen runway to be greeted by thousands of cheering elves.

Hippie elves from Pumpkin Corners, green-collar elves from the Toyworks, young elves and old had all gathered there to wish the jolly old man godspeed.

Santa's smile broadened and he waved to the crowd. Then everybody stood at attention and doffed their hats as the massed bands of the Mushroom Fanciers Association, Wade Snoot conducting, broke into "Santa Claus Is Coming to Town." When the music reached its stirring conclusion, Santa, escorted by a flying wedge of Security elves, made his way through the exuberant crowd and toward his sleigh.

Bigtoes' eyes kept darting everywhere, searching for a happy face that might mask a homicidal intent. His heart almost stopped when Santa paused to accept a bouquet from an elf child who stuttered through a tribute in verse to the jolly old man. It almost stopped again when Santa leaned over the Security cordon to speak to some elf in the crowd. A pat on the head from Santa and even Roger Chinwhiskers, leader of the Sons and Daughters of the Good Old Days, grinned and admitted that perhaps the world wasn't going to hell in a handbasket. A kind word from Santa and Baldwin Redpate tearfully announced—as he did every year at that time—that he was off the bee wine for good.

After what seemed an eternity to Bigtoes, they reached the sleigh. Santa got on board, gave one last wave to the crowd, and called to his eight tiny reindeer, one by one, by name. The reindeer leaned against the harness and the sleigh, with Security elves trotting alongside, and slid forward on the ice. Then four of the reindeer were airborne. Then the other four. At last the sleigh itself left the ground. Santa gained altitude, circled the runway once, and was gone. But they heard him exclaim, ere he drove out of sight: "Happy Christmas to all and to all a good night!"

The crowd dispersed quickly. Only Bigtoes remained on the wind-swept runway. He walked back and forth, head down, kicking at the snow. Santa's departure had gone off without a hitch. Had the Security Chief been wrong about the frame-up? Had Hardnoggin been trying to kill Santa after all?

Bigtoes went over the three attempts again. The bomb in the Board Room. The poison. The bomb on the sleigh.

Suddenly Bigtoes broke into a run.

He had remembered Brassbottom's pretext for taking Santa into the Map Room.

Taking the steps three at a time, Bigtoes burst into the Control Room. Crouchback was standing over the remains of the radio equipment with a monkey wrench in his hand. "Too late, Bigtoes," he said triumphantly. "Santa's as good as dead."

Bigtoes grabbed the phone and ordered the operator to put through an emergency call to the Strategic Air Command in Denver, Colorado. But the telephone cable had been cut. "Baby Polar bears like to teethe on it," said the operator.

Santa Claus was doomed. There was no way to call him back or to warn the Americans.

Crouchback smiled. "In eleven minutes Santa will pass over the DEW Line. But at the wrong place, thanks to Traffic Manager Brassbottom. The American ground-to-air missiles will make short work of him."

"But why?" demanded Bigtoes.

"Nothing destroys a dissident movement like a modest success or two," said Crouchback. "Ever since Santa came out for unilateral disarmament, I've felt SHAFT coming apart in my hands. So I had to act. I've nothing against Santa personally, bourgeois sentimentalist that he is. But his death will be a great step forward in our task of forming better children for a better world. What do you think will happen when Santa is shot down by American missiles?"

Bigtoes shaded his eyes. His voice was thick with emotion. "Every good little boy and girl in the world will be up in arms. A Children's Crusade against the United States."

"And with the Americans disposed of, what nation will become the dominant force in the world?" said Crouchback.

"So that's it—you're a Marxist-Leninist elf!" shouted Bigtoes.

"No!" said Crouchback sharply. "But I'll use the Russians to achieve a better world. Who else could eliminate Acme

Toy? Who else could limit world population to our rate of toy production? And they have agreed to that in writing, Bigtoes. Oh, I know the Russians are grownups too and just as corrupt as the rest of the grownups. But once the kids have had the plastic flushed out of their systems and are back on quality hand-crafted toys, I, Dirk Crouchback, the New Santa Claus, with the beautiful and beloved Carlotta Peachfuzz at my side as the New Mrs. Santa, will handle the Russians."

"What about Brassbottom?" asked Bigtoes contemptuously.

"Brassbottom will be Assistant New Santa," said Crouchback quickly, annoyed at the interruption. "Yes," he continued, "the New Santa Claus will speak to the children of the world and tell them one thing: Don't trust anyone over thirty inches tall. And that will be the dawning of a new era full of happy laughing children, where grownups will be irrelevant and just wither away!"

"You're mad, Crouchback. I'm taking you in," said Bigtoes.

"I'll offer no resistance," said Crouchback. "But five minutes after Santa fails to appear at his first pit stop, a special edition of *The Midnight Elf* will hit the streets announcing that he has been the victim of a conspiracy between Hardnoggin and the CIA. The same mob of angry elves that breaks into Security headquarters to tear Hardnoggin limb from limb will also free Dirk Crouchback and proclaim him their new leader. I've laid the groundwork well. A knowing smile here, an innuendo there, and now many elves inside SHAFT and out believe that on his return Santa intended to make me Director General."

Crouchback smiled. "Ironically enough, I'd never have learned to be so devious if you Security people hadn't fouled up your own plans and assigned me to a refrigerator in the Russian Embassy in Ottawa. Ever since they found a CIA listening device in their smoked sturgeon, the Russians had been keeping a sharp eye open. They nabbed me almost at once and flew me to Moscow in a diplomatic pouch. When they thought they had me brainwashed, they trained me in deviousness and other grownup revolutionary techniques. They thought they could use me, Bigtoes. But Dirk Crouchback is going to use them!"

Bigtoes wasn't listening. Crouchback had just given him an idea—one chance in a thousand of saving Santa. He dived for the phone.

"We're in luck," said Charity, handing Bigtoes a file. "His name is Colin Tanglefoot, a stuffer in the Teddy Bear Section. Sentenced to a year in the cooler for setting another stuffer's beard on fire. Assigned to a refrigerator in the DEW Line station at Moose Landing. Sparks has got him on the intercom."

Bigtoes took the microphone. "Tanglefoot, this is Bigtoes," he said.

"Big deal," said a grumpy voice with a head cold.

"Listen, Tanglefoot," said Bigtoes, "in less than seven minutes Santa will be flying right over where you are. Warn the grownups not to shoot him down."

"Tough," said Tanglefoot petulantly. "You know, old Santa gave yours truly a pretty raw deal."

"Six minutes, Tanglefoot."

"Listen," said Tanglefoot. "Old Valentine Woody is ho-ho-hoing around with that 'jollier than thou' attitude of his, see? So as a joke I tamp my pipe with the tip of his beard. It went up like a Christmas tree."

"Tanglefoot—"

"Yours truly threw the bucket of water that saved his life," said Tanglefoot. "I should have got a medal."

"You'll get your medal!" shouted Bigtoes. "Just save Santa."

Tanglefoot sneezed four times. "Okay," he said at last. "Do or die for Santa. I know the guy on duty—Myron Smith. He's always in here raiding the cold cuts. But he's not the kind that would believe a six-inch elf with a head cold."

"Let me talk to him then," said Bigtoes. "But move—you've got only four minutes."

Tanglefoot signed off. Would the tiny elf win his race against the clock and avoid the fate of most elves who revealed themselves to grownups—being flattened with the first object that came to hand? And if he did, what would Bigtoes say to Smith? Grownups—suspicious, short of imagination, afraid—grownups were difficult enough to reason with under ideal circumstances. But what could you say to a grownup with his head stuck in a refrigerator?

An enormous squawk came out of the intercom, toppling Sparks over backward in his chair. "Hello there, Myron," said Bigtoes as calmly as he could. "My name is Rory Bigtoes. I'm one of Santa's little helpers."

Silence. The hostile silence of a grownup thinking. "Yeah? Yeah?" said Smith at last. "How do I know this isn't some Commie trick? You bug our icebox, you plant a little pinko squirt to feed me some garbage about Santa coming over and then, whammo, you slip the big one by us, nuclear warhead and all, winging its way into Heartland, U.S.A."

"Myron," pleaded Bigtoes. "We're talking about Santa Claus, the one who always brought you and the other good little boys and girls toys at Christmas."

"What's he done for me lately?" said Smith unpleasantly. "And hey! I wrote him once asking for a Slugger Nolan Official Baseball Mitt. Do you know what I got?"

"An inflatable rubber duck," said Bigtoes quickly.

Silence. The profound silence of a thunderstruck grownup. Smith's voice had an amazed belief in it. "Yeah," he said. "Yeah."

Pit Stop Number One. A December cornfield in Iowa blazing with landing lights. As thousands of elfin eyes watched on their television screens, crews of elves in cover-alls changed the runners on Santa's sleigh, packed fresh toys aboard, and chipped the ice from the reindeer antlers. The camera panned to one side where Santa stood out of the wind, sipping on a hot buttered rum. As the camera dollied in on him, the jolly old man, his beard and eyebrows caked with frost, his cheeks as red as apples, broke into a ho-ho-ho and raised his glass in a toast.

Sitting before the television at Security headquarters, a

smiling Director General Hardnoggin raised his thimble-mug of ale. "My Santa, right or wrong," he said.

Security Chief Bigtoes raised his glass. He wanted to think of a new toast. Crouchback was under guard and Carlotta and Brassbottom had fled to the Underwood. But he wanted to remind the Director General that SHAFT and the desire for something better still remained. Was automation the answer? Would machines finally free the elves to handcraft toys again? Bigtoes didn't know. He did know that times were changing. They would never be the same. He raised his glass, but the right words escaped him and he missed his turn.

Charity Nosegay raised her glass. "Yes, Virginia," she said, using the popular abbreviation for another elf toast; "yes, Virginia, there is a Santa Claus."

Hardnoggin turned and looked at her with a smile. "You have a beautiful voice, Miss Nosegay," he said. "Have you ever considered being in the talkies?"

He knows if you've been bad or good.

SANITY CLAUSE
Edward Wellen

HO HO HO.

They said he used to come down the chimney. But of course these days there were no more chimneys. They said he used to travel in an eight-reindeer-power sleigh. But of course these days there were no more reindeer.

The fact was that he traveled in an ordinary aircar and came in through the ordinary iris door.

But he did have on a red suit with white furry trim, and he did carry a bundle of toys, the way they said he did in the old old days. And here he came.

His aircar parked itself on the roof of the Winterdream condom, and he worked his way down through the housing complex. The Winterdream condom's 400 extended families, according to his list, had an allotment of nine children under seven.

The first eight were all sanes and did not take up more than two minutes of his time apiece. The ninth would be Cathy Lesser, three.

Like the others, the Clements and the Lessers had been

awaiting his yearly visit in fearful hope. The door of the Clement-Lesser apartment irised open before he had a chance to establish his presence. He bounced in.

He read in its eyes how the family huddle saw him. His eyes how they twinkled! His dimples how merry! His cheeks were like roses, his nose like a cherry! His droll little mouth was drawn up like a bow, and the beard of his chin was as white as the snow. The stump of a pipe he held tight in his teeth, and the smoke it encircled his head like a wreath. He had a broad face and a little round belly that shook when he laughed, like a bowlful of jelly.

"Ho ho ho."

He looked around for Cathy. The child was hanging back, hiding behind her mother's slacks.

"And where is Cathy?"

Her mother twisted around and pushed Cathy forward. Slowly Cathy looked up. She laughed when she saw him, in spite of herself. A wink of his eye and a twist of his head soon gave her to know she had nothing to dread.

"Ho ho ho. And how is Cathy?"

He knew as soon as he saw her eyes. He vaguely remembered them from last year, but in the meanwhile something in them had deepened.

Cathy stuck her thumb in her mouth, but her gaze locked wonderingly and hopefully on the bulging sack over his shoulder.

"Cat got Cathy's tongue?"

"She's just shy," her mother said.

"Cathy doesn't have to be shy with me." He looked at the mother and spoke softly. "Have you noticed anything . . . special about the child?"

The child's mother paled and clamped her mouth tight. But a grandmother quickly said, "No, nothing. As normal a little girl as you'd want to see."

"Yes, well, we'll see." It never paid to waste time with the relatives; he had a lot of homes to visit yet. Kindly but firmly he eased the Lessers and the Clements out of the room and into the corridor, where other irises were peeping.

Now that she was alone with him Cathy looked longingly at the closed door. Quickly he unslung his bundle of toys and set it down. Cathy's eyes fixed on the bulging sack.

"Have you been a good little girl, Cathy?"

Cathy stared at him and her lower lip trembled.

"It's all right, Cathy. I know you've been as good as any normal little girl can be, and I've brought you a nice present. Can you guess what it is?"

He visualized the beautiful doll in the lower left corner of the bag. He watched the little girl's eyes. She did not glance at the lower left corner of the bag. He visualized the swirly huge lollipop in the upper right corner of the bag. She did not glance at the upper right corner of the bag. So far so good. Cathy could not read his mind.

"No? Well, here it is."

He opened the bag and took out the doll. A realistic likeness of a girl with Cathy's coloring, it might have been the child's sibling.

"Ooo," with mouth and eyes to match.

"Yes, isn't she pretty, Cathy? Almost as pretty as you. Would you like to hold her?"

Cathy nodded.

"Well, let's see first what she can do. What do you think she can do? Any idea?"

Cathy shook her head.

Still all right. Cathy could not see ahead.

He cleared a space on the table and stood the doll facing him on the far edge. It began walking as soon as he set it down. He lifted Cathy up so she could watch. The doll walked toward them and stopped on the brink of the near edge. It looked at the girl and held out its arms and said, "Take me."

He lowered Cathy to the floor, and the doll's eyes followed her pleadingly. Cathy gazed up at the doll. It stood within her sight but out of her reach. The girl's eyes lit up. The doll trembled back to pseudo life and jerkily stepped over the edge of the table.

He caught it before it hit the floor, though his eyes had

been on Cathy. He had got to Cathy too in the nick of time. Strong telekinesis for a three-year-old.

"Here, Cathy, hold the doll."

While she cradled the doll, he reached into a pocket and palmed his microchip injector.

"Oh, what lovely curls. Just like the dolly's." He raised the curls at the nape of Cathy's neck, baring the skin. "Do you mind if I touch them?" For some reason he always steeled himself when he planted the metallic seed under the skin, though he knew the insertion didn't hurt. At most, a slight pulling sensation, no more than if he had tugged playfully at her curls. Then a quick forgetting of the sensation. He patted the curls back in place and pocketed the injector.

"Let's play that game again, shall we, sugar plum?"

Gently he pried the doll from her and once more put it on the far edge of the table. This time it did not walk when he set it down. With one arm he lifted Cathy up and held her so she could see the doll. The fingers of his free hand hovered over studs on his broad black belt. The doll looked at the girl and held out its arms and said, "Take me."

The girl's eyes yearned across the vastness of the table. The doll suddenly trembled into pseudo life and began to walk toward them, jerkily at first, then more and more smoothly. He fingered a stud. The doll slowed. It moved sluggishly, as if bucking a high wind, but it kept coming. He fingered another stud. The doll slowed even more. In smiling agony it lifted one foot and swung it forward and set it down, tore the other free of enormous g's and swung it forward, and so kept coming. He fingered a third stud.

He sweated. He had never had to use this highest setting before. If this failed, it meant the child was incurably insane. Earth had room only for the sane. The doll had stopped. It fought to move, shuddered and stood still.

The girl stared at the doll. It remained where it was, out of reach. A tear fattened and glistened, then rolled down each cheek. It seemed to him a little something washed out of the child's eyes with the tears.

He reached out and picked up the doll and handed it to Cathy.

"She's yours to keep, Cathy, for always and always."

Automatically cradling the doll, Cathy smiled at him. He wiped away her tears and set her down. He irised the door open. "It's all right now. You can come in."

The Lessers and Clements timidly flooded back into the room.

"Is she—?"

"Cathy's as normal as any little girl around."

The worried faces regained permanent-press smoothness.

"Thank you, than you. Say thank you, Cathy."

Cathy shook her head.

"Cathy!"

"That's quite all right. I'll settle for a kiss."

He brought his face close to Cathy's. Cathy hesitated, then gave his rosy cheek a peck.

"Thank *you*, Cathy." He shouldered his toys and straightened up. "And to all a good night."

And laying a finger aside of his nose, and giving a nod, through the iris he bounded. The Clement-Lesser apartment was on the ground floor, and the corridor let him out onto a patch of lawn. He gave his aircar a whistle. It zoomed from the roof to his feet.

As he rode through the night to his next stop, an image flashed into his mind. For an instant he saw, real as real, a weeping doll. It was just this side of subliminal. For a moment he knew fear. Had he failed after all with Cathy? Had she put that weeping doll in his mind?

Impossible. It came from within. Such aberrations were the aftermath of letdown. Sometimes, as now after a trying case, he got these weird flashes, these near-experiences of a wild frighteningly free vision, but always something in his mind mercifully cut them short.

As if on cue, to take him out of himself, the horn of his aircar sounded its *Ho ho ho* as it neared the Summerdaze condom. He looked down upon the chimneyless roofs. Most likely the chimney in the Sanity Clause legend grew out of folk etymology, the word *chimney* in this context coming from a misunderstanding of an ancient chant of peace on Earth: *Ho ... Ho ... Ho Chi Minh.* His eyes twinkled, his dimples deepened. There was always the comfort of logic to explain the mysteries of life.

The aircar parked itself on the roof of the Summerdaze condom, and he shouldered his bundle of toys and worked his way down through the housing complex.

Ho ho ho

Twas the night before Christmas but the missiles were not snug in their silos.

Silent Night
Ben Bova

SHE WAS A tiny figure, skating alone in the darkness. Dow's Lake was firmly frozen this late in December. Earlier in the evening the ice had been covered with skaters in their holiday finery, the pavilion crammed with couples dancing to the heavy beat of rock music.

But this close to midnight, Kelly skated alone, bundled against the cold with a thickly quilted jacket that made her look almost like one of those ragamuffin toy dolls the stores were selling this year.

The wind keened through the empty night. The only light on the ice came from the nearly full moon grinning lopsidedly at Kelly as she spun and spiraled in time to the music in her head.

Swan Lake was playing in her stereo earplugs, the same music she had skated to when she had failed to make the Olympic team. The music's dark passion, its sense of foreboding, fitted Kelly's mood exactly. She skated alone, without audience, without judges. Without anyone.

I don't care, she told herself. It's better alone. I don't need any of them. I can enjoy myself without anybody else.

She was just starting a double axel when the beep from the communicator interrupted the music, startling her so badly that she faltered and went sprawling on her backside.

Sitting spraddle-legged on the ice, Kelly thumbed the communicator at her belt and heard:

"Angle Star, this is Robbie. We've got a crisis. All hands to their stations. Reply at once."

Kelly hated the nickname. Her mother had christened her Stella Angela, but she had grown up to be a feisty, snub-nosed, freckled little redhead, more the neighborhood's tomboy roughneck than an angelic little star. At ten she could beat up any boy in school; at thirteen she had earned a karate black belt. But she could not gain a place on the national skating team. And she could not make friends.

She was stubby, quick with her reflexes and her wits. Her figure was nonexistent, a nearly straight drop from her shoulders to her hips.

And she could not make friends, even after three months of being stationed here in Ottawa.

Picking herself off the ice, Kelly pulled off her right mitten and yanked the pinhead mike from the communicator, its hair-thin wire whirring faintly.

"Okay, Robert, I'm on my way. Seems like a damned odd night for a crisis, if you ask me."

Robbie's voice was dead serious. "We don't make 'em, we just stop 'em from blowing up. Get your little butt down here, sweetie, double quick."

Kelly skated to the dark and empty pavilion, grumbling to herself all the way. My twenty-second birthday tomorrow, she groused silently. Think they know? Think they care? But underneath the cynical veneer she hoped desperately that they did know and did care. Especially Robert.

The base was less than a mile from the pavilion, a clump of low buildings on the site of the old experimental farm. Kelly rode her electric bike along the bumpy road, man-tall banks of snow on either side, the towers of Ottawa glistening and winking off in the distance, brilliant with their holiday decorations.

Past the wire fence of the perimeter and directly into the big open doors of the main entrance she rode, paying scant attention to the motto engraved above it. Locking the bike in the rack just inside the entrance, she nodded hello to the two guards lounging by the electric heater inside their booth, perfunctorily waved her identification badge at them, then clumped in her winter boots down the ramp toward the underground monitoring center.

If there's a friggin' crisis, she thought, the dumb guards sure don't show it.

In the locker room Kelly stripped off her bulging coat and the boots. She wore the sky-blue uniform of the Peacekeepers beneath it. The silver bars on her shoulders proclaimed her to be a junior lieutenant. A silver stylized T, shaped like an extended, almost mechanical, hand, was clipped to her high collar; it identified her as a teleoperator.

Helluva night to make me come in to work, she complained to herself as she changed into her blue-gray duty fatigues. There are plenty of others who could fill in this shift. Why do they always pick on me? And why can't they make this damned cave warm enough to work in?

But then two more operators clumped in, silent and grim-faced. The men nodded to Kelly; she nodded back.

Shivering slightly against the damp chill, Kelly briefly debated bringing her coat with her into the monitoring center, then decided against it. As she pushed the door to the hall open, another three people in fatigues were hurrying past, down the cold concrete corridor toward the center: two women and a man. One of the women was still zipping her cuffs as she rushed by.

Robbie was outwardly cheerful: a six-three Adonis with a smile that could melt tungsten steel. His uniforms, even his fatigues, fit him like a second skin. He wore the four-pointed star of a captain on his shoulders.

"Sorry to roust you, tonight of all nights," he said, treating her to his smile. "We've got a bit of a mess shaping up, Angel Star."

If anyone else called her by anything but her last name, Kelly bristled. But she let handsome Robert get away with his pet name for her.

"What's going on?" she asked.

She saw that all ten monitoring consoles were occupied and working, ten men and women sitting in deeply padded chairs, headsets clamped over their ears, eyes riveted to the banks of display screens curving around them, fingers playing ceaselessly over the keyboards in front of them. Tension sizzled in the air. The room felt hot and crowded, sweaty. Images from the display screens provided the only light, flickering like flames from a fireplace, throwing nervous jittering shadows against the bare concrete walls.

Several of the pilots were lounging in the chairs off to one side, trying to look relaxed even though they knew they might be called to action at any moment. Robert was in charge of this shift, sitting in the communicator's high chair above and behind the monitors. Standing her tallest, Kelly was virtually at eye level with him.

"What *isn't* going on?" Robert replied. "You'd think tonight of all nights everybody'd be at home with their families."

He waved a hand toward the screens as the displays on them blinked back and forth, showing scenes from dozens of locations around the world.

"Got a family of mountain climbers trapped on Mt. Burgess up in the Yukon Territory. Satellite picked up their emergency signal." Kelly saw an infrared image of rugged mountainous country over the shoulder of Jan Van der Meer, one of the few monitors she knew by name.

"And some loony terrorists," Robbie went on, pointing to another console down the line, "tried to hijack one of the nuclear submarines being decommissioned by the U.S. Navy in Connecticut."

Kelly saw the submarine tied to a pier from a ground-level view. Military police in polished steel helmets were leading a ragged gaggle of men and women, their faces smeared with camouflage paint, up the gangway and into a waiting police van.

"But the crisis in Eritrea," said Robert.

"Not again," Kelly blurted. "They've been farting around there for more than a year."

Nodding tightly, Robert touched a button in the armrest of his high chair and pulled the pin mike of his headset down before his lips. "Jan, pick up the Eritrea situation, please."

Van der Meer, a languid, laconic Dutchman whose uniform always seemed too big for him, looked over his shoulder almost shyly and nodded. With his deepset eyes, hollow cheeks and bony face, he looked like a death's head beckoning. He tapped his keypad with a long slim finger, and his display screens showed ghostly images in infrared, taken from a reconnaissance satellite gliding in orbit over the Middle East.

It took Kelly a moment to identify the vague shapes and shadows. Tanks. And behind them, trucks towing artillery pieces. Threading their way in pre-dawn darkness through the mountains along the border of Eritrea.

"They're really going to attack?" Kelly asked, her voice suddenly high and squeaky, like a frightened little girl's.

"If we let them," answered Robbie, quite serious now.

"But they must know we'll throw everything we have at them!"

Robert arched his brows, making his smooth young forehead wrinkle slightly. "I guess they think they can get away with it. Maybe they think we won't be able to react fast enough, or their friends in the African Bloc will prevent Geneva from acting at all."

"We just barely did stop the mess in Sri Lanka. Maybe they don't think we've got the muscle to . . ."

"Priority One from Geneva!" called Bailey, the black woman working station three. She was an American, from Los Angeles, tall and leggy and graceful enough to make Kelly ache with jealousy over her good looks and smooth cocoa-butter skin. She had almond-shaped eyes, too, dark and exotic. Kelly's eyes were plain dumb brown.

Robert clamped a hand to his earphone. His eyes narrowed, then shifted to lock onto Kelly's.

Nodding and whispering a response, he pushed the mike up and away, then said, "This is it, kid. Everybody up!"

Kelly felt a surge of electricity tingle through her: part fear, part excitement. The other pilots stirred, too.

"I'm on my way," she said.

But Robert had already shifted his mike down again and was calling through the station's intercom. "Pilots, man your planes. All pilots, man your planes."

As Kelly dashed through the monitoring center's doors and out into the long central corridor, she thought she heard Robbie wishing her good luck. But she wasn't certain.

Doesn't matter, she told herself, knowing it was a lie.

The technicians backed away as Kelly slid into the cockpit and cast a swift professional glance at the instruments. On the screen in front of her she saw the little plane's snub nose, painted dead black, glinting in the pre-dawn starlight.

She clamped her comm set over her chopped-short red hair and listened to her mission briefing. There was no preflight checkout; the technicians did that and punched it into the flight computer. She swung the opaque canopy down and locked it shut, then took off into the darkness, getting her mission profile briefing from Geneva as she flew.

Dozens of planes were being sent against the aggressors, pilots from every available Peacekeepers' station were in their cockpits, hands on their flight controls. There were the usual delays and mixups, but Kelly suddenly felt free and happy, alone at the controls of an agile little flying machine, her every movement answered by a movement of the plane, her nerves melding with the machine's circuitry, the two of them mated more intimately than a man and a woman could ever be.

The plane was as small as it could be made and still do its job. Using the latest in stealth technology, it flew in virtual silence, its quiet Stirling engine turning the six paddle blades of the propeller so slowly that they barely made a sound. But the plane was slow, painfully slow. Built of wood and plastic for the most part, it was designed to avoid detection by radar and infrared heat-seekers, not to outrun any opposition that might find her.

To make it hard to find visually, Kelly was trained to fly the machine close to the ground, hugging the hills and tree-tops, flirting with sudden downdrafts that could slam the fragile little plane into the ground.

She thought of herself as a hunting owl, cruising silently through the night, seeking her prey. Everything she needed to know—rather, everything that Geneva could tell her—had been fed to her through her radio earphones. Now, as she flew silently through the dark and treacherous mountain passes on the border of Eritrea, she maintained radio silence.

I am an owl, Kelly told herself, a hunting owl. But there were hawks in the air, and the hunter must not allow herself to become the hunted. A modern jet fighter armed with air-to-air missiles or machine cannon that fired thousands of rounds per minute could destroy her within moments of sighting her. And the second or two delay built into her control system bothered her; a couple of seconds could be the difference between life and death.

But they've got to see me first, Kelly told herself. Be silent. Be invisible.

Despite the cold, she was perspiring now. Not from fear; it was the good kind of sweat that comes from a workout, from preparation for the kind of action that your mind and body have trained for over long grueling months.

Virtually all the plane's systems were tied to buttons on the control column's head. With the flick of her thumb Kelly could make the plane loop or roll or angle steeply up into the dark sky. Like a figure skater, she thought. You and me, machine, we'll show them some Olympic style before we're through.

She was picking up aggressor radio transmissions in her earphones now: she could not understand the language, so she flicked the rocker switch on the control board to her left that activated the language computer. It was too slow to be of much help, but it got a few words:

" . . . tank column A . . . jumpoff line . . . deploy . . ."

With her left hand she tapped out a sequence on the ECM board, just by her elbow, then activated the sequence with the barest touch of a finger on the black button set into the gray control column head.

Thousands of tiny metallic slivers poured out of a hatch just behind the cockpit, scattering into the dark night air like sparkling crystals of snow. But these flakes, monomolecular thin, floated lightly in the calm pre-dawn air. They would hover and drift for hours, wafting along on any stray air current that happened by, jamming radio communications up and down thousands of megahertz of the frequency scale.

First rule of Peacekeeper tactics: Modern warfare is heavily dependent on electronic communications. Screw up their comm system and you screw up their attack.

Leaving a long cloud of jamming chaff behind her, Kelly swooped down a rugged tree-covered valley so low that she almost felt leaves brushing the plane's underside. A river glinted in the faint light. Kelly switched her display screen to infrared and, sure enough, there was a column of tanks snaking along the road that hugged the riverbank. Gray ugly bulks with long cannons poking out like stiffened snouts.

Have fun with your radios, fellas, she called to them silently.

If the tanks reached the border and actually crossed into Sudanese territory, they would be guilty of aggression, and small, smart missiles launched from Peacekeeper command-and-control planes would greet them. But until they crossed the border, their crews were not to be endangered.

Second rule of Peacekeeper tactics: You can't counterattack until the aggressor attacks. Show enough force to convince the aggressor that his attack will be stopped, but launch no weapon until aggression actually takes place.

Corollary No. 1: It makes no difference *why* an attack is launched, or by whom. The Peacekeepers' mission is to prevent the attack from succeeding. We are police, not judges.

Kelly had seen what those smart missiles could do. Barely an arm's length in size, their warheads were nonexplosive slugs of spent uranium, so dense that they sliced through a hundred millimeters of armor like a bullet goes through butter.

Third rule of Peacekeeper tactics: Destroy the weapons, not the men—when possible.

But a tank is a rolling armory, filled with flammable fuel and explosive ammunition. Hit it with a hypervelocity slug almost anywhere and it will burst into flame or blow up like a mini volcano. The men inside have no chance to escape. And the missile, small as it is, is directed by a thumbnail-sized computer chip that will guide it to its target with the dogged accuracy of a Mach 10 assassin.

Banking slightly for a better look at the slowly moving column of tanks, Kelly found herself wishing that her chaff fouled their communications so thoroughly that they had to stop short of the border. Otherwise, most of those million-dollar tanks would be destroyed by thousand-dollar missiles. And the men in them would die. Young men foolish enough to believe that their nation had a right to invade its neighbor. Or serious enough to believe that they must obey their orders, no matter what. Young men who looked forward to life, to marriage, to families, and honored old age where they would tell their grandchildren stories about their famous battles and noble heroism.

They would die ingloriously, roasted inside their tanks, screaming with their last breath as the flames seared their lungs.

But she had other work to do.

Fourth rule of Peacekeeper tactics: A mechanized army needs fuel and ammunition. Cut off those supplies and you stop the army just as effectively as if you had killed all its troops.

Kelly's plane was a scout, not a missile platform. It was unarmed. If she was a hunting owl, she hunted for information, not victims. Somewhere in this treacherous maze of deeply scoured river valleys and arid tablelands there were supply dumps, fuel depots, ammunition magazines that provided the blood and sinew of the attacking army. Kelly's task was to find them. Quickly.

If it had been an easy assignment, she would not have gotten it. If the dumps could have been found by satellite reconnaissance, they would already be targeted for attack. But the Eritreans had worked long and patiently for this invasion of their neighbor. They had dug their supply dumps deeply underground, as protection against both the prying satellite eyes of the Peacekeepers and the inevitable pounding of missiles and long-range artillery, once the dumps had been located.

Kelly and her owl-like aircraft had to fly through those tortuous valleys hunting, seeking, scanning up and down the spectrum with sensors that could detect heat, light, magnetic fields, even odors. And she had to find the dumps before the sun got high enough to fill those valleys with lights. In daylight, her little unarmed craft would be spotted, inevitably. And once found, it would be swiftly and mercilessly destroyed.

All her sensors were alive and scanning now, as Kelly gently, deftly flew the tiny plane down one twisting valley after another. She felt tense, yet strangely at peace. She knew the stakes, and the danger, yet as long as she was at the controls of her agile little craft she was happy. Like being alone out on the ice: nothing in the world mattered except your own actions. There was no audience here, no judges. Kelly felt happy and free. And alone.

But the eastern sky was brightening, and her time was growing short.

The sensors were picking up data now, large clumps of metal buried *here*, unmistakable heat radiations emanating from *there*, molecules of human sweat and machine oil and plastic explosive wafting from that mound of freshly turned earth. She squirted the data in highly compressed bursts of laser light up to a waiting satellite, hoping that the Eritreans did not have the sophisticated comm equipment needed to detect such transmissions and home in on her plane.

There were many such planes flitting across the honeycomb of valleys, each pilot hoping that the Eritreans did not catch its transmissions, did not find it before it had completed its task and flown safely home.

Small stuff, Kelly realized as she scanned the data her screens displayed. None of the dumps she had found were terribly important. Local depots for the reserves. Where was the big stuff, the major ammo and fuel supplies for the main forces? It couldn't be farther back, deeper inside the country, she reasoned. They must have dug it in somewhere closer to the border.

The sky was bright enough now to make the stars fade, although the ground below her was still cloaked in shadow. Kelly debated asking Geneva for permission to turn around, rather than continue her route deeper into the Eritrean territory.

"Fuck it," she muttered to herself. "By the time they make up their minds it'll be broad daylight out here."

She banked the little plane on its left wingtip and started to retrace her path. Climbing above the crest of the valley, she began a weaving flight path that took her back and forth across the four major valley chains of her assigned territory.

There's got to be a major dump around here somewhere, she insisted to herself. There's got to be.

If there were not, she knew, she was in trouble. If the main supply dump was deeper inside Eritrea and she had missed it because she had failed to carry out her full assignment, she would be risking the lives not only of Eritreans and Sudanese, but Peacekeepers as well. She would be risking her own career, her own future, too.

The plane's sensors faithfully picked up all the small dumps she had found on her flight in. Even this high up, they were detectable.

She felt a jolt of panic when she noticed the shadow of her plane racing along the ground ahead of her. The sun was up over the horizon now, and she was high enough to be easily visible to anyone who happened to look up.

Gritting her teeth, she kept stubbornly on her plan, criss-crossing the valleys, back and forth, weaving a path to the frontier. She could see columns of tanks and trucks below her, some of them moving sluggishly forward, others stopped. Long ugly artillery pieces were firing now, sending shells whistling across the border into the Sudan.

The attack had started.

Far ahead, she saw columns of smoke rising black and oily into the brightening sky. Men were dying there.

Quickly she flicked her fingers across the display controls. Forward and rear observation scopes: no other aircraft in sight. So far so good, she thought. I haven't been found. Yet.

The infrared scanner showed an anomaly off to her left: a hot spot along the face of a steep rocky slope that plunged down to the riverbed. Kelly banked slightly and watched the sensor displays hopefully.

It was a cave in the face of the deeply scoured hillside. Ages of sudden rainstorms had seamed the slope like rumpled gray corduroy.

"Just a friggin' cave," Kelly muttered, disappointed. Until she noticed that a fairly broad road had been built up in a series of switchbacks from the valley floor to the lip of the cave's entrance. It was a dirt road, rough, dangerous if it rained. But this was the dry season, and a single truck was jouncing up that road at a fairly high rate of speed, spewing a rooster tail of dust from its rear tires.

Kelly coasted her plane lower, below the crest of the hills that formed the valley. Hidden down among the scruffy trees that lined the riverbank was a column of trucks, their motors running, judging from the heat emissions.

Punching her comm keypad furiously, Kelly sang into her microphone, "I've found it! Major supply dump, not more than ten klicks from the frontier!"

She knew that the monitors in Geneva—and Ottawa, for that matter—would home in on her transmission. So would the Eritreans, most likely.

It was not Robbie's voice that replied, an agonizing ten seconds later, "It *might* be a supply dump, but how can you be sure?"

"The truck convoy, dammit!" Kelly shouted back, annoyed. "They're starting up the road!"

And they were. The trucks seemed empty. They were going up the steep road to the cavern, where they would be loaded with the fuel and ammunition necessary to continue the battle.

"Even if you are right," came the voice from Geneva—tense, a slight Norse accent in it—"we have no means to get at the dump. It is too well protected."

Kelly said nothing. She knew what would come next.

"Return to your base of operations. Your mission is terminated."

Kelly bit her lip in frustration. Then a warning beep on her instrument panel told her that she was being scanned by a radar beam. Ordinarily that would not have bothered her. But in morning's brightening light, with a few hundred enemy soldiers below her, she knew she was in trouble.

By reflex, she craned her head to look above, then checked the display screens. A couple of contrails way up there. If she tried to climb out of this valley those two jet fighters would be on her like stooping hawks.

Kelly took a deep breath and weighed her options. Blowing her breath out through puffed cheeks, she said aloud, "Might as well find out for sure if I'm right."

She pushed the throttle forward and angled the little plane directly toward the mouth of the cave.

Tracers sizzled past her forward screen and her acoustic sensors picked up the sounds of many shots: small-arms fire, for the most part. The troops down there were using her for target practice. They're lousy shots, Kelly told herself. Then she added, Thank God.

Kelly dove at maximum speed, nearly as fast as a modern sports car, through a fusilade of rifle and machine-gun fire, and flew directly at the yawning cavern. It was dark inside, but the plane's sensors immediately displayed the forward view in false-color infrared.

It's their main dump, all right, Kelly told herself. She saw it all as if in freeze-frame, a bare fraction of a second yet she made out every detail.

Dozens of trucks were already inside the mammoth cave,

in the process of being loaded by troops suddenly startled to find an airplane buzzing straight at them. Some men stood frozen with wide-eyed fright, staring directly at her, while others were scattering, ducking under the trucks or racing for the cave's entrance.

The cave was crammed with stacks of fuel drums, cases of ammunition. Be nice to know who they bought all this crap from, Kelly thought. For the briefest flash of an instant she considered trying to pull up and eluding the fighters waiting for her. Maybe the cameras have picked up valuable information on who's supplying this war, she thought.

But she knew that was idle fancy. This mission was terminated. Not by Geneva, but by the gunners who would shoot the plane to pieces once she tried to make it to the border.

So she did not pull up. She leaned on the throttle, hurtling the plane directly into the cave's mouth and a massive stack of fuel drums. She neither heard nor felt the explosion.

For long seconds Kelly sat in the contoured chair of the cockpit, staring at the darkened screen. Her hands were trembling too badly to even try to unlatch the canopy. A technician lifted it open and stared down at her. Usually the techs were grinning and cracking jokes after a mission. But this one looked solemn.

"You okay?" she asked.

Kelly managed a nod. Sure, she answered silently. For a pilot who's just kamikazed, I'm fine.

Another tech, a swarthy male, appeared on the other side of the cockpit and helped Kelly to her feet. She stepped carefully over the control banks and onto the concrete floor of the Ottawa station's teleoperations chamber. Two other teleoperator cockpits were tightly closed, with teams of technicians huddled over the consoles grouped around them. The fourth cockpit was open and empty.

The captain in charge of the station's teleoperations unit strode from his desk toward Kelly, his face grim. He was a sour-faced, stocky Oriental with a vaguely menacing moustache, all formality and spit and polish.

"We lost one RPV due to ground fire," he said in a furious whisper, "and one deliberately destroyed by its operator."

"But I . . ."

"There is no need for you to defend yourself, Lieutenant Kelly. A board of review will examine the tapes of your mission and make its recommendations. Dismissed."

He turned on his polished heel and strode back to his desk.

Anger replaced Kelly's emotional exhaustion. RPV, she fumed to herself. Operator. They're *planes*, dammit. And I'm a pilot!

But she knew it was not so. They were remotely piloted vehicles, just as the captain had said. And expensive enough so that deliberately crashing one was cause for a review board to be convened. Then Kelly remembered that she had also tossed away her prescribed flight plan. The review board would not go easily, she realized.

She dragged herself tiredly down the corridor toward the locker room, longing now for her bunk and the oblivion of sleep.

Halfway there, Robbie popped out of the monitoring center, his smile dazzling.

"Hi there, Angle Star! Good job!"

Kelly forced the corners of her mouth upward a notch. From behind Robbie's tall, broad-shouldered form she saw most of the other monitors pushing through the doors and spilling out into the corridor. It can't be a shift change, she thought. Nobody else has gone in.

Robbie caught the puzzlement in her face.

"It's all over," he said brightly. "The Eritreans called it quits a few minutes ago."

"They stopped the invasion?"

"We beat them back. Clobbered the tanks in their first wave and demolished most of their supply dumps."

The rest of the monitor team headed down the corridor toward the locker room, chattering like schoolkids suddenly let loose.

"Somebody," Robbie added archly, "even knocked out their main ammo dump."

"That was me," Kelly said weakly.

Throwing an arm around her slim shoulders, Robbie laughed, "I know! We saw it on the screens. The explosion shook down half the mountain."

"Must have killed a lot of men," she heard herself say.

"Not as many as a full-fledged war would have taken."

Kelly knew the truth of it, but it was scant comfort.

"They started it," Robbie said, more softly. "It's not your fault."

"It's my responsibility. So was the plane."

Robbie broke out his dazzling grin again. "Worried about a review board? Don't be. They'll end up pinning a medal on you."

Somehow Kelly could not visualize that.

"Come on, Angel Star," Robbie said, with a one-armed hug, "don't be glum, chum. We're going out to celebrate."

"Now?"

"It's Christmas, isn't it? You didn't see a big sleigh pulled by reindeer while you were flinging around out there, did you?"

Kelly grinned. "No, I don't think so."

With his arm still around her shoulders, Robbie started for the locker room. "I'm throwing a party in my quarters. You've invited."

Kelly let him half-drag her to the locker room. Van der Meer and Bailey were already there, pulling on their heavy winter coats.

"Hello there, little sister," Bailey called to her. "Nice job."

The whole group trudged up the sloping corridor and past the guards, who still sat close to the electric heater in their little booth. If they were aware that a war had just been started and stopped within the span of the past hour or so, they gave no indication of it.

"You're quite a flier," Robbie said to her. "You'll have to give me lessons; I'd love to learn how to fly."

Kelly gulped and swallowed, glad that it was too dark for him to see the expression on her face. I've never flown a real plane, up in the air, she wanted to confess. Only simulators and teleoperations. But she kept silent, too afraid of breaking the crystal beauty of this moment.

The sky was still dark and sprinkled with stars, the air bitingly cold. As she followed along beside Robbie and the others, snow crunching under their boots, Kelly glanced over her shoulder at the sign carved above the base's entrance:

INTERNATIONAL PEACEKEEPING FORCE
NATION SHALL NOT LIFT UP SWORD AGAINST NATION

We stopped a war, she said to herself. It cost some lives, but we protected the peace. Then she remembered, It might also cost me my job.

"Don't look so down, girl," Bailey assured her. "The review board ain't gonna go hard on you."

"I hope," said Kelly.

"Don't worry about it," Bailey insisted.

Kelly trudged along, heading for the officers' dormitory across the road from the underground nerve center of the base.

Should I tell them? she asked herself. They wouldn't care. Or maybe they'd think I was just trying to call attention to myself.

But she heard herself saying, "You know, this is my birthday. Today, Christmas Day."

"Really?" said Van der Meer.

"Happy birthday, little sister," Bailey said.

Robbie pushed his coat sleeve back and peered at his wristwatch. "Not just yet, Angel Star. Got another few ticks to go . . ."

Then they heard, far off in the distance, the sound of voices singing.

"Your watch must be slow," said Bailey. "The midnight chorale's already started."

"Their clock must be fast," Robbie countered.

The whole group of them stopped in the clear night air and

listened to the children's voices, coming as if from another world. Kelly stood between tall Robert and beautiful, warm Bailey and felt as if they were singing especially to her.

"*Silent night . . .*
Holy night . . .
All is calm, all is bright . . ."

The Christmas spirit is magic.

A PROPER SANTA CLAUS
Anne McCaffrey

JEREMY WAS PAINTING. He used his fingers instead of the brush because he liked the feel of paint. Blue was soothing to the touch, red was silky, and orange had a gritty texture. Also he could tell when a color was "proper" if he mixed it with his fingers. He could hear his mother singing to herself, not quite on pitch, but it was a pleasant background noise. It went with the rhythm of his fingers stroking color onto the paper.

He shaped a cookie and put raisins on it, big, plump raisins. He attempted a sugar frosting but the white kind of disappeared into the orange of the cookie. So he globbed up chocolate brown and made an icing. Then he picked the cookie out of the paper and ate it. That left a hole in the center of the paper. It was an excellent cookie, though it made his throat very dry.

Critically he eyed the remaining unused space. Yes, there was room enough, so he painted a glass of Coke. He had trouble representing the bubbles that're supposed to bounce up from the bottom of the glass. That's why the Coke tasted flat when he drank it.

It was disappointing. He'd been able to make the cookie taste so good, why couldn't he succeed with the Coke? Maybe if he drew the bubbles in first . . . he was running out of paper.

"Momma, Momma?"

"What is it, honey?"

"Can I have more paper? Please?"

"Honest, Jeremy,, you use up more paper . . . Still, it does keep you quiet and out of my hair . . . why, whatever have you done with your paper? What are those holes?"

Jeremy pointed to the round one. "That was a cookie with raisins and choc'late icing. And that was a Coke only I couldn't make the bubbles bounce."

His mother gave him "the look," so he subsided.

"Jeremy North, you use more paper than—than a . . ."

"Newspaperman?" he suggested, grinning up at her. Momma liked happy faces best.

"Than a newspaperman."

"Can you paint on newspaper?"

His mother blinked. "I don't see why not. And there's pictures already. You can color them in." She obligingly rummaged in the trash and came up with several discarded papers. "There you are, love. Enough supplies to keep you in business a while. I hope."

Well, Jeremy hadn't planned on any business, and newsprint proved less than satisfactory. There weren't enough white spaces to draw *his* paintings on, and the newspaper soaked up his paints when he tried to follow the already-pictures. So he carefully put the paints away, washed his hands, and went outside to play.

For his sixth birthday Jeremy North got a real school-type easel with a huge pad of paper that fastened onto it at the top and could be torn off, sheet by sheet. There was a rack of holes for his poster paint pots and a rack for his crayons and chalk and eraser. It was exactly what he wanted. He nearly cried for joy. He hugged his mother, and he climbed into his father's lap and kissed him despite his prickly beard.

"Okay, okay, da Vinci," his father laughed. "Go paint us a masterpiece."

Jeremy did. But he was so eager that he couldn't wait until the paint had completely dried. It smeared and blurred, brushing against his body as he hurried to find his dad. So the effect wasn't quite what Jeremy intended.

"Say, that's pretty good," said his father, casting a judicious eye on the proffered artwork. "What's it supposed to be?"

"Just what you wanted." Jeremy couldn't keep the disappointment out of his voice.

"I guess you're beyond me, young feller me lad. I can dig Andy Warhol when he paints tomato soup, but you're in Picasso's school." His father tousled his hair affectionately and even swung him up high so that, despite his disappointment, Jeremy was obliged to giggle and squeal in delight.

Then his father told him to take his painting back to his room.

"But it's your masterpiece, Daddy. I can fix it . . ."

"No, son. You painted it. You understand it." And his father went about some Sunday errand or other.

Jeremy did understand his painting. Even with the smears he could plainly see the car, just like the Admonsens', which Daddy had admired the previous week. It *had* been a proper car. If only Daddy had *seen* it . . .

His grandmother came, around lunchtime, and brought him a set of pastel crayons with special pastel paper and a simply superior picture book of North American animals and birds.

"Of course, he'll break every one of the pastels in the next hour," he heard his grandmother saying to his mother, "but you said he wants only drawing things."

"I like the book, too, Gramma," Jeremy said politely, but his fingers closed possessively around the pastels.

Gramma glanced at him and then went right on talking. "But I think it's about time he found out what animals really look like instead of those monstrosities he's forever drawing. His teacher's going to wonder about his home life when she sees those nightmares."

"Oh, c'mon, Mother. There's nothing abnormal about Jeremy. I'd far rather he daubed himself all over with paint than ran around like the Reckoffs' kids, slinging mud and sand everywhere."

"If you'd only *make* Jeremy . . ."

"Mother, you can't *make* Jeremy do anything. He slides away from you like . . . like a squeeze of paint."

Jeremy lost interest in the adults. As usual, they ignored his presence, despite the fact that he was the subject of their conversation. He began to leaf through the book of birds and animals. The pictures weren't proper. That brown wasn't a bird-brown. And the red of the robin had too much orange, not enough gray. He kept his criticism to himself, but by the time he'd catalogued the anatomical faults in the sketch of the mustang, he was thoroughly bored with the book. His animals might *look* like nightmares, but they were proper ones for all of that. They worked.

His mother and grandmother were engrossed in discussing the fixative that would have made the pictures "permanent." Gramma said she hadn't bought it because it would be dangerous for him to breathe the fumes. They continued to ignore him. Which was as well. He picked up the pastels and began to experiment. A green horse with pink mane and tail, however anatomically perfect, would arouse considerable controversy.

He didn't break a single one of the precious pastels. He even blew away the rainbow dust from the tray. But he didn't let the horse off the pad until after Gramma and his mother had wandered into the kitchen for lunch.

"I wish . . ."

The horse was lovely.

"I *wish* I had some . . ." Jeremy said.

The horse went cantering around the room, pink tail streaming out behind him and pink mane flying.

" . . . Fixative, Green Horse!" But it didn't work. Jeremy knew it took more than just *wishing* to do it proper.

He watched regretfully as Green Horse pranced too close to a wall and brushed himself out of existence.

❆   ❆   ❆

Miss Bradley, his first-grade teacher, evidently didn't find anything untoward about his drawings, for she constantly displayed them on the bulletin boards. She had a habit of pouncing on him when he had just about finished a drawing so that after all his effort, he hadn't much chance to see if he'd done it "proper" after all. Once or twice he managed to reclaim one from the board and use it, but Miss Bradley created so much fuss about the missing artwork that he diplomatically ceased to repossess his efforts.

On the whole he liked Miss Bradley, but about the first week in October she developed the distressing habit of making him draw to order: "class assignments," she called it. Well, that was all right for the ones who never knew what to draw anyhow, but "assignments" just did not suit Jeremy. While part of him wanted to do hobgoblins, and witches, and pumpkin moons, the other part obstinately refused.

"I'd really looked forward to *your* interpretations of Hallowe'en, Jeremy," Miss Bradley said sadly when he proffered another pedantic landscape with nothing but ticky-tacky houses. "This is very beautiful, Jeremy, but it isn't the assigned project. Now, look at Cynthia's witch and Mark's hobgoblin. I'm certain you could do something just as original."

Jeremy dutifully regarded Cynthia's elongated witch on an outsized broomstick apparently made from 2 x 4s instead of broom reeds, and the hobgoblin Mark had created by splashing paint on the paper and folding, thus blotting the wet paint. Neither creation had any chance of working properly; surely Miss Bradley could see that. So he was obliged to tell her that his landscape was original, particularly if she would *look* at it properly.

"You're not getting the point, Jeremy," Miss Bradley said with unaccustomed sternness.

She wasn't either, but Jeremy thought he might better not say that. So he was the only student in the class who had no Hallowe'en picture for parents to admire on Back-to-School Night.

His parents were a bit miffed since they'd heard that Jeremy's paintings were usually prominently displayed.

"The assignment was Hallowe'en and Jeremy simply refused to produce something acceptable," Miss Bradley said with a slightly forced smile.

"Perhaps that's just as well," his mother said, a trifle sourly. "He used to draw the most frightening nightmares and say he 'saw' them."

"He's got a definite talent. Are either you or Mr. North artistically inclined?"

"Not like he is," Mr. North replied, thinking that if he himself were artistically inclined he would use Miss Bradley as a model. "Probably he's used up all his Hallowe'en inspiration."

"Probably," Miss Bradley said with a laugh.

Actually Jeremy hadn't. Although he dutifully set out trick-or-treating, he came home early. His mother made him sort out his candy, apples, and money for UNICEF, and permitted him to stay up long past his regular bedtime to answer the door for other beggars. But, once safely in his room, he dove for his easel and drew frenetically, slathering black and blue poster paint across clean paper, dashing globs of luminescence for horrific accents. The proper ones took off or crawled obscenely around the room, squeaking and groaning until he released them into the night air for such gambols and aerial maneuvers as they were capable of. Jeremy was impressed. He hung over the windowsill, cheering them on by moonlight. (Around three o'clock there was a sudden shower. All the water solubles melted into the ground.)

For a while after that, Jeremy was not tempted to approach the easel at all, either in school or at home. At first, Miss Bradley was sincerely concerned lest she had inhibited her budding artist by arbitrary assignments. But he was only busy with a chemical garden, lumps of coal and bluing and ammonia and all that. Then she got the class involved in making candles out of plastic milk cartons for Thanksgiving, and Jeremy entered into the project with such enthusiasm that she was reassured.

She ought not to have been.

Three-dimensionality and a malleable substance fascinated Jeremy. He went in search of anything remotely pliable. He started with butter (his mother had a fit about a whole pound melted on his furry rug; he'd left the creature he'd created prancing around his room, but then the heat came up in the radiators.) Then he tried mud (which set his mother screaming at him). She surrendered to the inevitable by supplying him with Play-Doh. However, now his creations thwarted him because as soon as the substance out of which the proper ones had been created hardened, they lost their mobility. He hadn't minded the ephemeral quality of his drawings, but he'd begun to count on the fact that sculpture lasted a while.

Miss Bradley introduced him to plasticine. And Christmas.

Success with three-dimensional figures, the availability of plasticine, and the sudden influx of all sorts of Christmas mail order catalogues spurred Jeremy to unusual efforts. This time he did not resist the class assignment of a centerpiece to deck the Christmas festive tables. Actually, Jeremy scarcely heard what Miss Bradley was saying past her opening words.

"Here's a chance for you to create your very own Santa Claus and reindeer, or a sleigh full of presents . . ."

Dancer, Prancer, Donner, Blitzen, and Dasher and Comet and Rudolph of the red nose, took form under his flying fingers. Santa's sack was crammed with full-color advertisements clipped from mail order wishbooks. Indeed, the sleigh threatened to crumble on its runners from paper weight. He saved Santa Claus till the last. And once he had the fat and jolly gentleman seated in his sleigh, whip in hand, ready to urge his harnessed team, Jeremy was good and ready to make them proper.

Only they weren't; they remained obdurately immobile. Disconsolate, Jeremy moped for nearly a week, examining and re-examining his handiwork for the inhibiting flaw.

Miss Bradley had been enthusiastically complimentary and the other children sullenly envious of his success when the finished group was displayed on a special table, all red and white, with Ivory Snow snow and little evergreens in proportion to the size of the figures. There was even a convenient chimney for the good Santa to descend. Only Jeremy knew that that was not *his* Santa's goal.

In fact Jeremy quite lost interest in the whole Christmas routine. He refused to visit the Santa on tap at the big shopping center, although his mother suspected that his heart had been set on the Masterpiece Oil Painting Set with its enticing assortment of brushes and every known pigment in life-long-lasting color.

Miss Bradley, too, lost all patience with him and became quite stern with his inattentiveness, to the delight of his classmates.

As so often happens when people concentrate too hard on a problem, Jeremy almost missed the solution, inadvertently provided by the pert Cynthia, now basking in Miss Bradley's favor.

"He's naked, that's what. He's naked and ugly. Everyone knows Santa is red and white. And reindeers aren't gray-yecht. They're brown and soft and have fuzzy tails."

Jeremy had, of course, meticulously detailed the clothing on Santa and the harness on the animals, but they were still plasticine. It hadn't mattered with his other creations that they were the dull gray-brown of plasticine because that's how he'd envisaged them, being products of his imagination. But Santa wasn't, or so he thought.

To conform to a necessary convention was obviously, to Jeremy, the requirement that had prevented his Santa from being a proper one. He fabricated harness of string for the reindeer. And a new sleigh of balsa wood with runners of laboriously straightened bobby pins took some time and looked real tough. A judicious coat of paint smartened both reindeer and sleigh. However, the design and manufacture of the red Santa suit proved far more difficult and occupied every spare moment of Jeremy's time. He had to do it in the privacy of his room at home because, when Cynthia saw him putting harness on the reindeer, she twitted him so unmercifully that he couldn't work in peace at school.

He had had little practice with needle and thread, so he actually had to perfect a new skill in order to complete his project. Christmas was only a few days away before he was satisfied with his Santa suit.

He raced to school so he could dress Santa and make him proper. He was just as startled as Miss Bradley when he slithered to a stop inside his classroom door, and found her tying small gifts to the branches of the class tree. They stared at each other for a long moment, and then Miss Bradley smiled. She'd been so hard on poor Jeremy lately.

"You're awfully early, Jeremy. Would you like to help me . . . Oh! How adorable!" She spotted the Santa suit which he hadn't had the presence of mind to hide from her. "And you did them yourself? Jeremy, you never cease to amaze me." She took the jacket and pants and little hat from his unresisting hand, and examined them carefully. "They are simply beautiful. Just beautiful. But honestly, Jeremy, your Santa is lovely just as he is. No need to gild the lily."

"He isn't a proper Santa without a proper Santa suit."

Miss Bradley looked at him gravely, and then put her hands on his shoulders, making him look up at her.

"A *proper* Santa Claus is the one we have in our own hearts at this time of year, Jeremy. Not the ones in the department stores or on the street corners or on TV. They're just his helpers." You never knew which of your first-graders still did believe in Santa Claus in this cynical age, Miss Bradley thought. "A proper Santa Claus is the spirit of giving and sharing, of good fellowship. Don't let anyone tell you that there isn't a Santa Claus. The proper Santa Claus belongs to all of us."

Then, pleased with her eloquence and restraint, she handed him back the Santa suit and patted his shoulder encouragingly.

Jeremy was thunderstruck. *His* Santa Claus had only been made for Jeremy. But poor Miss Bradley's words rang in his ears. Miss Bradley couldn't know that she had improperly understood Jeremy's dilemma. Once again the blight of high-minded interpretation and lady-like good intentions withered primitive magic.

The little reindeer in their shrinking coats of paint would have pulled the sleigh only to Jeremy's house so that Santa could descend only Jeremy's chimney with the little gifts all bearing Jeremy's name.

There was no one there to tell him that it's proper for little boys and girls of his age to be selfish and acquisitive, to regard Santa as an exclusive property.

Jeremy took the garments and let Miss Bradley push him gently toward the table on which his figures were displayed.

She'd put tinsel about the scene, and glitter, but they didn't shine or glisten in the dull gray light filtering through the classroom windows. They weren't proper snow and icicles anyway.

Critically, he saw only string and the silver cake ornaments instead of harness and sleigh bells. He could see the ripples now in the unbent bobby pins which wouldn't ever draw the sleigh smoothly, even over Ivory Snow snow. Dully, he reached for the figure of his Santa Claus.

Getting on the clothes, he dented the plasticine a bit, but it scarcely mattered now. After he'd clasped Santa's malleable paw around the whip, the toothpick, with a bright, thick, nylon thread attached to the top with glue, he stood back and stared.

A proper Santa Claus is the spirit of giving and sharing.

So overwhelming was Jeremy's sense of failure, so crushing his remorse for making a selfish Santa Claus instead of the one that belonged to everyone, that he couldn't imagine ever creating anything properly again.

Christmas is and will be what we make of it.

A Little Girl's
Xmas in Moderan
David R. Bunch

It was in Jingle-Bell weather that Little Sister came across the white yard, the snow between her toes all gray and packed and starting to ball up like the beginnings of two snowmen. For clothing she had nothing, her tiny rump sticking out red-cold, and blue-cold, and her little-jewel knees white almost as bones. She stuck up ten stiff fingers, and she said, "Daddy! Something is wrong at my place! Come see!" She lisped a little perhaps and did not say it all as precisely as grownups, because she was just past four.

He turned like a man in the bottom third of bad dreaming; he pointed two bored eyes at her. Damn the kid, he thought. "What the hell deal has Mox got us into now?" he said. And he sang the little rhyme that made the door come open. Then as she stepped toward him he saw the snowballs on her feet. They were melting now, making deep furrows in the green rug spread across his spacious thinking room. The tall nap, like flooded grass now along little canals bending away from her feet, was speckled white here and there with crumpled paper balls. His trial plans and formulas peeped out like golf balls.

Coming back across the iron fields of nightmare that always rose to confront him at such times, he struggled to make the present's puzzling moment into sense. Damn the kid, he thought, didn't wipe her feet. All flesh, as yet—her own—and bone and blood, and didn't wipe her feet. The snow melts!

He motioned her to him. "Little Sister," he began in that tired dull-tinny voice that was his now, and must be his, because his larynx was worked all in gold against cancer, "tell me slowly, Little Sister. Why don't you stay in your plastic place more? Why don't you use the iron Mox more? Why do you bother me at all? Tell me slowly."

"Daddy!" she cried and started to jig up and down in the fits that he hated so, "come over to my place, you old boogie. Something needs fixing."

So they went across the big white yard to her place, past Mother's place, past Little Brother's place, with her snowhurt limping and naked, and him lumbering in strange stiffjointedness, but snug in a fire-red snuggie suit of fine insulation with good black leather space high-tops. Arrived at her place he whistled at the door the three sharp notes. The door moved into the wall and Mox the iron one stood sliding the iron sections of his arms up into one another until he had only hands hanging from shoulders. It was his greeting way. He ogled with bulb eyes and flashed his greeting code.

"What would you have done," her father said, "if I had not come with you? You brought no whistle for the door." Three sharp notes sprang at him from the normal holes of her head, and the heavy door rolled softly out of the wall until it shut them in the gay red-carpeted room with a Xmas tree—the father, the naked little girl and the iron Mox. And she was impishly holding the whistle between her teeth, grinning up at him. "I had it all along," she said and dropped the whistle into the tall red grass of her room's carpet.

She wiped the waning snowballs from her feet and sidled her icy-cold rump over toward the slits where the heat came through the wall, soft and perfumed like an island summer. Her knees turned knee-color again and her rump became no longer vari-colored cold. It became the nicest of baby-pink little-girl rumps, and she stood there a health-champion of a little miss, all flesh and bone and blood—as yet—pointing at an angle toward the ceiling. "The star!" she said. "The star has fallen down." And he noticed that she was pointing toward the tree.

"What star?" he started to say, across the fog that always smelled like metal in his mind these last few years, and then he thought, Oh hell, she means the Xmas star. "You came across all that yard," he asked incredulously, "to annoy me with a thing like that, when Mox—?"

"Mox wouldn't," she broke in. "I asked him and asked him, but he wouldn't. It's been down since the fifteenth. You remember when those dumb students went home in their jets early and fast and broke the rules and shook the houses down. BOOM! and the star fell down. Just like that. Well, he'd just do silly when I asked him, like you just now saw him, just shake his arms up into his shoulders and ogle. Pretty darn dumb, if you ask me."

"But what about your mother?"

"I asked her when I was over to her place, over a week ago. But she's been too busy and tired. You know how Mama is, always having that plastic guy rubbing parts of her, that she says hurt, and jumping on the bed at any little thing. Sometimes I think that guy's in love with Mama. What's love?"

"*What?!* What's love? Should I tell you, did I know? Love is—is not an iron ceiling on a plastic . . . But—oh, never mind! *Hell!*—How's her star?"

"*Twinkle twinkle, little star, how I wonder what you are, up above the world so high, like a mama in the sky.* Heard that on the programs advertising diamonds."

"Just answer the questions. How's her star?"

"Up real shiny, last I saw. But heck, Mama probably never even looks at her star, because that plastic guy—"

"And Little Brother's star?"

"Humph, Little Brother! Beat his star up about a week after we put 'em up. Said it was just what he needed for the rear end of his space tube. You know how Little Brother is about space."

"And so yours is the only star that has fallen. Mother's is still up, though she doesn't have time to look at it, you think. Little Brother took his down in the interest of space. Yours just fell."

"Daddy, where is your star, Daddy?"

He looked at her, and he thought, Damn these little girls. Always so much sentiment. And so schemy, too. He said, "I had Nugall store my star away. It's somewhere with the tree, in a box. It interfered with my deep thinking. I've got to have entirely a bare room, so far as Xmas trees are concerned, for my deep thinking, if you don't mind."

For just a moment he thought she was going to get the sniffles. She looked at him, float-eyed, her face ready to buckle and twist into tearful complaint. But she held and stared at him more sternly, and he said, "Sure I'll fix the damned star for you. Drag me a chair over. And then I must rush right back to my place." (Dangerous, this being together so much. And so old-fashioned. And besides, he had been really cooking on a formula when she burst in.) So he stood on the chair she dragged to him, and he fixed the frosti-glass star to its hook in the iron ceiling and he adjusted the star until it was almost impossible to tell that it wasn't attached to the green plastic tree. Then he whistled at the door.

Just as he was passing through the opening, leaving, he felt something tug at a leg of the fire-red suit. Damn! It was she again. "What now?" he asked.

"Daddy!" she piped, "you know what, Daddy? I thought, what if we'd go over to Mother's and Little Brother's places, since it's Xmas. And you've got on your red suit. Isn't this a very special day? I've been hearing on the programs—"

"No," he said, "it isn't a very special day. But if you want to—and you'd probably do a fit about it if you didn't get to—come on." So after she had put on a green snow suit, they trudged across the white yard, a strange study in old Xmas colors, and they stopped first at Little Brother's place, who was just past five.

Dressed in a pressure suit and sturdy beyond all sense, from the weight lifting and the vitamin taking and the breakfast-of-champions eating, he wanted to know what the hell all the nonsense of a visit was about so early. And he let them know that Nogoff, his iron man, was taking care of everything at his place very well, thank you. Then he strode about in his muscles, sturdy beyond all meaning, and he showed them the new jet tube part he had hammered out of the star, and they left pretty soon from his surliness. On the way over to Mother's place Little Sister suggested that she thought Little Brother thought too much about rockets and jets and space. Didn't Father think so? Father agreed dully that maybe he did, he didn't know, but really, could one ever think too much about rockets and jets and space?

As they walked along, over the yard to Mother's place, she kicked up snow and chortled and laughed and told off-color jokes—she had heard them on the programs—almost like a normal little girl should. Father tracked dourly through the unmarked snow under the featureless gray sky and thought only how all this nonsense of walking so early was making the silver parts of his joints hurt, and before he'd had his morning bracer, too. Yes indeed, Father, for the *most* part, was flesh only in those portions that they had not yet found ways to replace safely. He held on grimly, walking hard, and wished he were back in his hip-snuggie thinking chair where he worked on Universal Deep Problems.

At Mother's place they found her having one of her plasto-rubs from the plastic man, who did truly act a little odd about Mother. Do you suppose he wasn't really all machine but was a man who had been replaced part by part until it was impossible now to tell where the man left off and the robot plastic began? Father worried about it for half a second and then dismissed it. So what if he was? What could he do to Mother? And what if he did, what would it matter? Mother—new alloys now in almost all the places.

Little Sister yelled MERRY XMAS! at the top of her good

flesh lungs, and Mother turned through the waist only, as though on a swivel in that portion, and Father coughed dry in the metal of his embarrassment.

"'Twas Little Sister's idea," he mumbled. "So sorry, Marblene. I guess Mox hasn't been watching her programs right, her insisting on Xmas trees and all this year, and now the idea of a visit among the folks of the family. I'm sorry, Marblene." He coughed again. "So out of date."

Mother blazed at him from her very plain blue eyes that were almost all 'replaced' now. It was clear that she wished to continue her rub with the plastic man as soon as possible. "Well?" she demanded.

"That's all," he mumbled, "if Little Sister's ready." Then for some silly reason—he couldn't explain it afterwards, unless it was because he wasn't all 'replaced' yet—he said a silly thing, something that would obligate him months hence. "Do you—I mean, would you—I mean, could I," he stammered, "could I see you a couple of minutes, maybe at Easter? Our places are just across the yard from each other, you know. Maybe when I'm all 'replaced' I won't be able to walk." He hated himself for pleading.

She airily tossed her left hand, and fluttered those fabulous 'replaced' plastic fingers, and great rays of light shot and quavered and streamed from rings of 'moderne' diamond. "Why not?" she said resignedly. "What's to lose? If Jon's through in time—" Jon was her plastic man—"we'll talk a bit on Easter."

And so it was done, and over, and soon they were again outside in the yard. "I guess I won't have to walk you back will I? You have your whistle, don't you?" he said.

"No," she said, "I dropped it in the red rug. I just remember I did. I heard it. It squished down in the wet. While the snowballs were melting. Maybe I could come to your place!"

Damn these little girls, he thought. So tricky. Always scheming. He'd have to start having her 'replaced' as soon as he could after Xmas.

"There's nothing of interest at my place," he hastened to say. "Just my hip seat and my thinking space and Nugall." He didn't see any use to tell her about Nig-Nag, the statue woman who wasn't quite all metal, that he kept under the bed until he needed her so much that he had to ... There were some things you just didn't tell a daughter, not until she was much older or well on the road toward being all 'replaced.' "Tell you what we'll do," he said. "I'll walk you back to your place and I'll whistle at the door and you can go in to Mox. Your star's all fixed and everything. You've had quite a Xmas!"

So they walked back through the iron-cold snow to her place, under a sky that was rapidly thickening in a day turning black. And as her door glided open he felt so relieved that he stooped and kissed her on top of the head, and he tapped her playfully a little on her good flesh buttocks as she passed through the plastic entrance. When she was gone he stood there thinking a little while outside her house. Like an old man in the starting third of good dreaming, he stood nodding, prompted perhaps by things from a time before the time of 'replacements,' wondering maybe if he had not paid some uncalculated and enormous price for his iron durability.

While he stood thus idly musing, a light high and wee came up suddenly—from eastward, from toward the coast airports—and moved fast down the murky sky toward him, gaining speed. Soon the countryside all around recoiled from a giant blow as the barrier burst. He heard Little Sister behind him scream and beg for him to come back, and he knew without looking that her star was off its iron hook again. Like some frightened monster eager to gain its lair he dug in harder with his metal feet and lumbered off across the yard to his place, anxious to rest again in his hip-snuggie chair, desirous to think further on Universal Deep Problems.

The light, unswerving, went on down the sky, high and wee, like a fleeing piece of star, like something for somewhere else in a great hurry.

A new carol for a future Christmas.

CHRISTMAS TROMBONE
Raymond E. Banks

IT WAS CHRISTMAS Eve and Shorty went into the closet and dug out his old trombone. He pumped it a couple of times and made a lip on it and let out a blast. It came out as two sour bleats.

"Hold the phone," he told himself. "You've dialed yourself a wrong number."

There came the insistent cracking of Mrs. Thompson's thimble on the radiator pipes. He had a very particular landlady, the toughest old gal in Blessington, and she didn't encourage her roomers in their self-expression.

Shorty made two soft, low mocking notes on the horn. Clean stuff that rolled off the ear. Too bad he didn't dare toot out loud what he thought of her.

He shoved his horn under his coat and went downstairs. Mrs. Thompson met him in the living room.

"You playing that old horn again, Shorty?" she said.

"Figure on a few carols," he said.

"The singing cones," she said firmly, "can do it better. If

you try to play carols, they'll run you out of town for peace-disturbing."

"I've lived in Blessington for 45 years," said Shorty, "man, boy and tadpole. I want to see them run me out of town."

"Chief Nelson said the next time you tried to play that horn he was going to take it from you," she said. "The singing cones do it better."

"Who's afraid of Chief Nelson?" he said.

She sniffed in reply and went to the end table and turned on her singing cone. She punched out a number—inside, the wafer-thin discs of Venusian heavy water responded with real, throbbing stuff. Quarter of a million earth musicians had played to make those discs. All dissonance matched out by the peculiar properties of the inch-wide Venusian solidified water discs. If you had a perfect recording material and knew what to expect from the organ of Corti in the human cochlear structure of the ear you could even write an equation for the cones' "perfect" music. Shorty grunted and went out into the cold night with his horn.

He listened. Moon was out; stars were out. A light, crusty snow covered the earth. He could see the lights of Blessington twinkling on the snow. He could hear the voices of far-off carolers. They were fewer every year. He could hear, most of all, the singing cones. From private homes, from the bars, from Salvation Army kettles, Christmas music hung heavy on the air.

Over on Grover Cleveland Street he could hear the dominating throb of the biggest singing cone in Blessington. It was going to be a big night at the Church of All-Comers, and the Rev. Dr. Blaine was warming them up with a candlelight service.

Straight out from Venus, that cone. Not a factory job stuffed with Venusian water discs, like Mrs. Thompson's, but a real Venusian cone. Eight feet high. Inside gallons and gallons of purest Venusian water, hungry for the sound of music. Once a clean pattern of sound was heard by that container, it solidified a portion of the water and remained in crystallized perfection, captured for the centuries-long life of the cone . . .

come midnight and Dr. Blaine would give the signal to the altar boy. Altar boy would play the exciter cone and the big cone would pour forth its tones throughout the Dominic Valley like an unearthly benediction and everybody would shudder in delight at the sound of the All-Comers cone—they would sure know it was Christmas!

Shorty's nose got cold and his feet went numb as he crunched through the snow. In one pocket bulged the package that he had for Dr. Blaine, in the other the one he had for Edith. After that, a quick cup of Christmas cheer at the Dogleg; then home and he'd be in bed by 10 o'clock. With his ears stuffed with cotton. He didn't want to hear the singing cones on Christmas Eve. He had always made his own music, always would. He wouldn't play for the singing cones like the other fools of earth musicians, giving up their souls to the gadgets. He had something better inside.

Hadn't come out yet, but someday he'd show them. When he was ready. None of this stuff of having the cones change around and delete like they did, because they'd heard the tune better somewhere else.

He walked resolutely past the Dogleg. Time for that later. A few citizens were just going in for Christmas cheer and one of them asked Shorty how soon his aircar would be repaired and out of Shorty's garage. Whenever Shorty had a particularly tough repair to do, like this job, he always mumbled something about getting parts "from upstate." The citizen rolled his eyes and shrugged while his companions laughed.

"When the singing cones came, we lost a good musician and gained a poor mechanic," said one. "That right, Shorty?"

"Don't talk to me about the singing cones. They hit me in my income."

"Where you going with that trombone, Shorty?" asked another. "Chief Nelson sees you with that old slush pump, he'll run you in."

"Let him try," said Shorty, passing on.

He ran into Chief Nelson just a block before he got to the church. The Chief stopped him.

"Now, look, Shorty. Last Fourth of July I told you that you couldn't be playing that horn and disturbing the peace."

"I'm not playing it, Chief. I'm carrying it."

The Chief blew on his cold hands and stamped his feet in the snow, his face red from the gleam of the Christmas lights strung overhead on the street lamps.

"Man carries a gun, he figures to use it," he said.

"It's my own personal, private property."

"I got rights too," said the Chief. "To protect the peace. That sour old horn of yours always makes trouble when you get a couple of Dogleg Specials in you. Hand it over."

"I won't."

"You can have it back tomorrow, Shorty. I'd rather put the horn in the jail safe than put you in the jail cell."

"Go to hell."

"May I be forgiven for preventive maintenance," said the Chief. His burly arms slapped at Shorty and he jerked the trombone from Shorty's grasp. Shorty shouted something incoherent and slugged at the Chief. But in the snow he missed his footing and slid to the ground.

"Stay with your repair business," said the Chief, marching off triumphantly with the horn.

The sharp wind stung his eyes and they filled with tears as he rose again, alone on the street. He felt a cold, unpleasant place where the snow clung to his clothes. Time was when he played for all their local affairs. Time was when he played the organ for weddings (including Chief Nelson's) and funerals (it'd be a pleasure to rumble that old boy down), led the choir and provided the hot music for local dances. That was before the singing cones.

A whiff of Christmas cooking fell on his nostrils as he went up the street to the church. Everybody was busy, happy, alert with Christmas, but it was agony for him.

Dr. Blaine smiled up at him as he entered the study, sniffing because the warm air made his nose run.

"It's good to see you on Christmas Eve," said the clergyman. "Just like the old days when we had the choir and organ."

Shorty handed over his gift and got one in return. "I sure do miss that midnight service," said Shorty. "Church crowded, the special feeling of importance in the decorations and the occasion, the choir all worried and nervous about the long, extra-special program they had to get through with perfection . . ."

"I'm afraid Christmas for you was waffles at 1 A.M. in the rectory," smiled Dr. Blaine. "It's more than just a show, Shorty. It has something to do with Christ, remember?"

He felt better at the scolding. Dr. Blaine was a real soul-chaser. Felt good to have somebody worry about you.

"Sure," he said.

"Coming to the midnight service tonight, Shorty?"

Shorty frowned. "You've got your singing cone," he said.

Dr. Blaine took him by the arm and led him into the nave. Across from them rested the only true singing cone in Blessington. It was almost eight feet high, a tapering mound of pure whiteness, just as it had been on Venus. It "lived" on sound, not talking voices, not explosions or discords. It "lived" on music adding every sweet sound it heard to its repertoire until all its water was solidified and it could no longer hear and remember.

Near it stood the exciter cone, an ordinary cone-shaped home recorder which gave off the first few notes of the required tune and then surrendered to the swelling grandeur of the big cone that picked up the tune and played it through in perfection—remembering all of the overtones of all the musicians or singers it had ever heard play or sing. One decibel for four, and if you turned up your little exciter cone high, the Venusian cone roared loud enough to shake the church and fling its quivering harmonies throughout the length of Dominic Valley.

"Here," said Dr. Blaine, "I've got all the great artists who ever recorded Christmas music, Shorty. The best voices, the best arrangements."

"I know."

"People need the solemn pageantry of the greatest church music to find the Christmas spirit in these commercial times."

"Yeah."

"This cone was a foot-high mound on Venus the night Christ was born in Bethlehem, Shorty. It's been on earth now for twenty years, adding only the purest and best church music to its being."

"It's only been in Blessington five years," said Shorty, "while I been here 45, man, boy and molecule."

Dr. Blaine sighed. "Nobody wants the old choir and organ any more, Shorty. When the cone plays we go back along the centuries to Bethlehem, we watch the miracles beside the Red Sea, we are in the room where the Last Supper was served and we walk with Christ up that final hill—"

"A couple of times I got 'em pretty excited with that old organ you got stashed in the basement."

"Then play for the cone, Shorty," said Dr. Blaine. "Play for the cone and make it hear and remember your notes alone with the world's best musicians."

Shorty cleared his throat. "I been meaning to tell you, Reverend. I took a look at your aircar today. You need a new rotor blade."

In the silence that followed, Dr. Blaine shrugged and then went across and opened the stained glass windows behind the cone. Shorty knew why he did that. In a few hours now it would be time for that cone to fill the valley with sound. Funny, nobody ever opened the windows to let the music out in the old days. Just as well, though. You take a choir singer with a cold, he gets mean.

"You've lost a lot of friends in these last years, Shorty," said Dr. Blaine. "Even Edith's been worrying about you lately. I think you need to come to church."

"That's a thought, Reverend," said Shorty without conviction. He turned to leave. "Merry Christmas."

"Merry Christmas," said Dr. Blaine sadly, watching him go.

❄   ❄   ❄

Edith wore bangs. Her round face was wrong for bangs, but Shorty had long ago given up worrying about her face because below the chin she was all woman. She had a bowl of Christmas punch and they had one. She looked pretty good, he thought, in her new Christmas dress.

"Thought I might go to the Church of All-Comers tonight," she said. "What're you going to do?"

"Thinking of breaking into jail."

"Why?"

"They went and arrested my trombone."

Her eyes mocked him. "Give it up, old boy. When the All-Comers cone gets rolling, nobody wants to hear your sour old horn."

"Time was—"

"Give it up, Shorty! In the old days you were something else beside the aircar repairman when you stood up before the people of this town and played your music. Now you're just Shorty from the aircar repair shop with a musician's pension."

Her face was incredibly soft in the dim, multi-colored glow of the Christmas tree lights. It was a good, factory tree with bulb-shaped projections that were part of the plant and yet gave off tender, colored lights, finer than the old-fashioned Christmas tree lights. And approved by Underwriters' Lab, of course, since the tree generated its own electricity and was shockproof.

"What're you trying to say?"

"Maybe I'm tried of waiting for you to snap out of it. Maybe I'm going to Church tonight anyway—with Del Gentry."

"I guess it's legal," he said, "as long as you save me New Year's for the jam session over in Kingsbury."

"New Year's I'm going to Del Gentry's party," she said. "I'm tired of a sour old aircar repairman for company."

He couldn't control himself. He sent the tree down with an angry flip of his hand. She sat with a set smile on her face, her Christmas cup before her face, both arms resting on the table. Like somebody who'd said something a long time coming.

"Phoney!" he shouted. "Like the singing cones. Everything phoney!"

"Sure," she said. "Everything that's been invented since you were twenty is phoney, Shorty. But the world moves on. That tree is better than the old ones. The singing cones make better music than the old music—"

He jerked the home-sized singing cone she had on the end table from its socket and smashed it at the wall. The wafer-discs raced over the floor in aimless circles.

Edith didn't move. "You can't go on being twenty and smelling the apple blossoms in the spring forever, Shorty—"

"I've got a soul!" he yelled at her. "I ain't no aircar repairman!"

"You've got an ego," she said.

Shorty wheeled and ran out, slamming the door.

"Merry C-Christmas," Edith whispered.

Chief Nelson was at the Dogleg. Shorty went to the jail instead and sat down at the desk with the extra man.

"Sure is cold out."

"Yeah." Shorty's hands had finally stopped trembling.

"Chief said you might be around," said the extra man. "I was to tell you—no playin' on trombones."

"Who wants to play on a trombone?" asked Shorty. "I got my musician's pension."

The man leaned forward. There wasn't anybody in the jail and he was bored. This was diversion. "How about that pension stuff?" he said. "How about that?"

Shorty shrugged. "When the singing cones idea was brought in from Venus, the music companies did a right noble thing. Gave everybody who held a card the amount of dough they could reasonably expect to make over a lifetime. They even subsidized schools for the kids—"

"Subsawhooed?"

"Gave dough," said Shorty shortly. "So the kids that're coming up would get a chance to play—for the singing cones. Then the cones gobble up *their* music too. Get fat offa the young talent. They still buy new tunes, even for the cones. But there ain't no real music any more."

"You ever played for the cones?"

"I been asked," said Shorty, "but I never have; I'm not ready. You stand up in front of a real one—the cones record you forever. But they only pick up your best stuff and delete the rest." He shuddered. "They suck up the soul you put in music. I still got self-respect, even if I only play for myself."

He eased open the bottom drawer of the man's desk with his toe, saw the glint of a bottle.

"I don't know," said the man. "Seems to me when my singing cone plays a sad tune I want to cry. Happy makes me laugh. I ain't much for music, but those cones sure make you wiggle better than the old music."

"Why not? They've got the souls of all the earth's best musicians." Shorty peered down into the drawer. "Looks like a bottle down there," he said.

The extra man peered down. "Say, you're right."

"Looks like whisky," said Shorty.

The extra man's face was almost angelic. "Say, it sure does," he said. "How'd a bottle of liquor get into this little, old jail?"

"It ain't too far to reach," hinted Shorty.

"By God, I bleeve I can make it," said the extra man, reaching for it.

Shorty clipped him on the neck. The man went "gawwwk!" and rolled over on the floor, unconscious. "Merry Christmas," Shorty muttered to him, digging for the keys to Chief Nelson's safe.

It was midnight. Shorty was pretty well away from town now. The moon was big in an amazingly clear sky. The powdery snow numbed his feet; the air stung his lungs. The horn felt cold even through his gloves. Down below he could see the lights from the windows and doors of the Church of All-Comers dancing on the snow.

Suddenly he wondered about himself. "What am I doing

out here all alone?" he asked himself. "Got to get out of town to even play my horn any more." His hands were trembling as he took off his gloves.

"Man likes to play a horn; man's gotta play a horn," he said, scowling at a jackrabbit that broke through the under-brush and then quickly retreated.

He looked over the silent, snow-covered empty hills and then back at the friendly lights of the All-Comers Church and then he knew that this would have to be the last time he ever played the horn. Otherwise you'd be going up the mountain for keeps, he told himself.

He blew a blast. It sounded real loud. He stirred in surprise when he heard an answering blast from the singing cone down in the Church.

Shorty pumped his chest full of the open valley air. He re-membered all the years he'd been in the center and how they were gone and felt sad—so he blew happy. He ran off "Joy to the World." He made a couple of sour notes, but it was loud and bold and joyful and he felt better. "How do you like that, cone?" he asked silently.

As if in response the singing cone down below in the Church gave it back to him—"Joy to the World." He stood still in shock, because it had picked up some of his own notes. He could see some of the people still outside the church, turning to stare at the hill where he stood. By gosh, they could hear him. Even the cone. Old Blaine must've turned the big cone around to those open windows when he heard that challenging blast.

He felt hot and cold inside. He thought how it was with people with everything changing and being different and nothing was really eternal, and pretty soon it was your last chance to toot your own horn. He felt lightheaded with anger and frustration and sadness and then suddenly he needed his own music real bad. Something to say everything he'd felt in a simple, dignified way.

Here goes.

Silent Night. Not too gooey, not too sweet. Firm and clear and certain. He began to cry at his own music; he couldn't help it. The tune was somber and great and all-embracing, and the occasional catch in his throat gave the old horn a tremolo he'd never had before.

> *Silent night, Holy night!*
> *All is calm, All is bright,*

The cone was silent, listening. He could feel its presence in the background. A moment before it had been scouring out the valley with its sound. Now it was comparing his notes with all the wonderful music stored in its memory.

Softly, you son-of-a-bitch, he told himself. This is final. Shorty, by God, now we've *got* to do the thing!

For 45 seconds he reached the great plane of art that he'd been trying to reach all his life. For 45 seconds he made music that no human or nonhuman agency had ever made before or would ever make again. It was one of those moments. It was clear and clean, human but not gooey. It was one tiny notch more than satisfactory.

> *Silent night, Holy night!*
> *All is calm, All is bright,*
> *Round yon Virgin Mother and Child,*
> *Holy Infant so tender and mild—*

After it was over, he had just enough left to start again and use his horn as an exciter cone to the big one. Then he stood there, silent, horn to his lips, unable to move.

Now they came back to him, those golden, unforgettable 45 seconds; solo, nothing added, nothing taken away. No other sound except his own horn and his own soul. The cone had listened and compared down through its centuries of experience. The cone had found it good—all of it—nothing deleted, nothing added.

In Bethlehem, on Venus and beyond to outer space it was a thing of perfect uniqueness.

Shorty drew back his horn and hurled it as far away from him as he could. It had been inside and he knew it, but nobody else did—now they did. There was no need to play any more.

If you've got influence or friends, you can attend the world-famous Christmas Trombone services at the Church of All-Comers in Blessington. But it's pretty hard to get in on Christmas Eve. When they do that original version of "Silent Night" on the Christmas Trombone, you'll be glad you came, though. It's solo stuff with a keen, cutting edge and you'll never forget it. They've made a million discs for the home recorders but it's not the same.

And if you take a look over to the right, you'll see a short, fat man sitting in a pew, nodding and smiling. When they play the Christmas Trombone, everybody in Blessington watches him with a little awe. And his wife, Edith, grins. She's got a right to grin. That's Shorty Williams, the best doggone aircar repairman in Dominic Valley, and the man who taught the singing cones how to handle Christmas carols.

A story of Christmas in the long, hot summer.

Dark Conception
Joe L. Hensley
& Alexei Panshin

Four blocks down the street, opposite the courthouse with the Confederate monument and the stack of cannonballs on the lawn, Grove Avenue was a row of antiseptic, air-conditioned storefronts. The windows looked like magazine ads. White faces moved here, in the store, in the courthouse—the black faces were hidden, in kitchens, in storerooms, or invisibly mowing the courthouse lawn. It was the way things were.

Four blocks in Mississippi can be a long way. On the other side of the overpass, Grove Avenue was peeling paint, chipped brick, and ten-year-old cars, a smashed bottle in the gutter, stores pinched together, two storefront churches. It was a darker world—here there were no white faces—and even the sun seemed duller and hotter. It was the way things were.

He looked out the window at the street below for a long time. He'd come a long way from New York, in years as well as distance. Sometimes he wondered why he'd come at all.

Doctor William Roosevelt Brown turned away from the

window that mirrored the Bington scene below feeling the sense of loss and futility that had gripped him for a long time. He looked around his neat, out-of-date examining room and brought his mind back to present time.

His nurse came in the door. She was a thin, brown girl, much lighter than his own color and she had worked for him for about a year. She was attractive in her white uniform and Brown had cat and moused her for a long time without real enthusiasm. He liked her and once he had kissed her in the darkness of the drug room, but they had broken quickly away, and that was all. Now it was strictly business.

"Eli Cadwell," she said.

"In the waiting room?" he asked, surprised.

She nodded.

Cadwell was among the people Brown had counted as least likely to show up in his office, although once they'd been friends. But that had been long ago, before Brown had gone north to med school, when Cadwell had been able to think of something other than his festering hate.

"He brought his wife in," the nurse said.

"Miss Emmet," he said formally, "are you telling me that Eli Cadwell is married?"

She nodded. "Since last month. I thought you knew. Mary Lou Shipman."

Brown picked at his neat mustache. "She's about fifteen, Eli's over fifty," he said with irritation.

"Yeah."

"All right—show them in."

At the door, Miss Emmet looked back, unsmiling. "She's pregnant, Doctor."

She ushered them in. Cadwell came first, then the girl. Cadwell's eyes darted here and there about the office, never resting. He was a lean man and once he had been tall, but now his height seemed an illusion and he walked bent, his body queerly out of focus. A group of white men, drunk on raw moonshine, larking, had caught him stealing chickens. They had lashed him between the front bumpers of two cars and backed away gently until his bones and joints had torn and cracked. That had been in the next county and a long time ago, before Brown had come here. Mostly they didn't do that sort of thing any more. They had other ways of dealing with you.

The girl, Mary Lou, was obviously pregnant. She was tiny and low breasted, her hands nervously carried over the hump of her stomach. She watched her husband like a silent wren and her eyes were fearful when she looked elsewhere in the room, more fearful when she looked at him.

"You want me to look at her, Eli?"

Cadwell nodded. "Just look," he said.

Brown pointed at his nurse, who waited at the door. "Go with her, Mary Lou. She'll show you what to do."

She looked at her husband, awaiting his nod. When it came she shuffled, head down, following Miss Emmet.

Cadwell limped around the room. Brown watched him study the signed picture of Thurgood Marshall and the Brotherhood of Man framed certificate.

"Is that baby yours?" he asked.

Cadwell turned back and his cold eyes came up and he smiled sourly. "You're a smart son of a bitch, Brown. You figure it out." Then his eyes went down and a look of secret triumph came in his smile. "You jus' examine her, *Doctor*." He sat down in a chair and got out a worn bible. "I'll read me a little of this hogwash while you're doing it."

"White men, black men, and God," Brown said, feeling the tiredness come. "All right, Eli."

He went into his tiny obstetrics room and examined the girl. She lay passively, without curiousity, under his hands.

When he was done he said: "Stay here with the nurse, Mary Lou. I'll be back in a few minutes." He closed the connecting door behind him.

"Eli," he said, "did you know your wife's a virgin?"

The old man nodded crookedly. "I want a paper sayin' it. I mean to get me papers from fo', maybe five doctors saying it."

"What for?"

Now the triumph came lashing through. "For the newspapers, man. To let 'em know jus' the way things is. I mean to let all them white bastards know that a virgin pregnant and she a black girl. They say here," he said pointing at the bible, "that it happen before, but they lie all the time with their Jesus Crise this and Jesus Crise that and they put us down with it and spit on us." His eyes were crafty and unsane. "Now I got us a God and now we rise up and grind them to blood." He pulped the world together by grinding his hands savagely. "And we'll kill all the rest, all of the ones that don't stay with us."

"That would mean me," Brown said.

"Sure, you." His lips made a vicious parody of a smile. "Bad as them. You try to live with them. You one of them tries to get us to march to the courthouse. You fooled some of them, but not me. All them big people you got here in town. What good that do? March a few times and they stick you in the gut with a club or hose you off and you noplace— nothing. You can't live with them—you got to kill . . ."

Brown held up his hands. "You're wrong, Eli."

"Don' you call me Eli! Call me Mr. Cadwell or don' call me. You're no white man to call me Eli or Boy." He moved up close and for the first time Doctor Brown could smell the corn whiskey on his breath, sour and strong. "I'm not wrong."

Brown shook his head and retreated behind his desk out of breathshot. He looked down the titles of his books, then took one down and thumbed until he found the right place.

"Here! Crumm, Weizmann and Evans, 'Heredity, Eugenics, and Human Biology.' See here—'Parthenogenesis.' Now read what it says. It says it's possible for a virgin to have a baby. It's extremely rare, but it's possible." He thrust the book at Cadwell. "Read!"

Cadwell took the book suspiciously. In a moment he thumped it with a finger. "I don' make out these words." But he went on reading.

After awhile he looked up. "It say a virgin can only have a girl baby, not a boy baby."

"Yes."

"Well, you been a big Jesus Chrise man. How you explain that?" Cadwell challenged triumphantly.

Doctor Brown kept the self-taught carefulness in his voice. You learned to be careful when you were a negro doctor in Bington.

"I'm not trying to explain Jesus. I didn't examine Jesus or his Mother. I'm only saying that your wife is pregnant with a fully intact and inelastic hymen and that medical science says it's possible, but the child born in such circumstances has to be a female."

"Why?" Cadwell almost shouted.

Brown controlled his exasperation. He said: "Every woman is a female because she has two X chromosomes. The male has one X and one Y. If the man gives an X, during intercourse, the woman gives another X, which is all she has, and the baby is a girl. If the man gives a Y the woman still gives an X and the baby is a boy. But a woman who conceives without a man has nothing but X chromosomes and so the baby *has* to be a girl."

"You mean it ain't a miracle?" Cadwell said uncertainly, partially beaten down by the flood of words.

"That's right."

Cadwell looked away and when he looked back there was a sign of craftiness in his eyes. He said slowly, as if to himself: "But mos' people, they don' know that. They think it's a miracle. It still mean somethin'."

"Not for what you want it for. You start giving stories out to the newspapers and it will come out just like another freak story. You tell anything else then maybe you'll get a few people lathered up and maybe some killed."

Cadwell said, very quietly: "They's more of us in this state than they is of them."

"Sure," Brown said desperately, "but you haven't got the answer to it there. Hate and bloodshed is no solution to hate and bloodshed. All of the things worth having are coming for us. All you'll do is set it back."

Cadwell's face tensed with lines of bitterness. "I don' want what you want, man. I want what they got and for them to be like me now. I want to lead a lynch mob and hang someone who look at one of *our* girls. I want to rent me some of my land to one of them and let them get one payment behind. I want them to try to sen' they kids to our school. I want 'em to give me back myself like I was before, when I didn't hurt so bad that I better off dead."

He held out his hands so Brown could see the pink, calloused palms. "I do it with these, Doctor. Now I want a paper from you sayin' nothin' but the hones' truth. I want you to write me a paper and say that you look at Mary Lou and that she a virgin and pregnant. You a black man and I'm a black man. You give that to me—that paper."

Brown looked at the old man steadily for a moment and then he said evenly: "I want to finish my examination. I'll be back."

The old man smiled and made his eyes go sleepy. "I'll wait," he said. He sat his crooked body in a chair and Brown felt the terrible weight of those eyes until he closed the door.

Brown looked down at the supine woman. "All right, Mary Lou. Just lay still and relax." He crossed over to the sideboard and picked up a sterile instrument pack lying there. Miss Emmet, the nurse, watched him with curious eyes.

"What you goin' to do?" Mary Lou asked, her eyes big and afraid.

"I won't hurt you," he said. He placed the towel around her legs and, with surgical care, slit the hymen.

She gave a cry of outrage and surprise and Brown heard the door to the room open with a whoosh of air.

"What you do to Mary Lou?" Eli Cadwell demanded.

Brown turned on the water tap at the sink and calmly scrubbed his hands. He watched the girl sit up on the table. There was a thin, red line of blood on the towel.

Cadwell saw it also. With a howl of rage that was also a sound of pain he stepped forward to the sink and swung his fist at Brown. Brown saw it coming, and tried to move away. He went down hard.

"Get out of here," he heard Miss Emmet say. "I'm going to call the police. You get out of here!"

Cadwell ignored her and looked down at Brown. He said: "Maybe I take that little knife and cut you so you never bother no one again. Maybe that the answer fo' you. But I think I let you stay like you is. You know it, too. Maybe you a doctor, but when the white boys see you then you jus' another nigger." Without turning his head he said to the sobbing, frightened girl on the table, "Mary Lou, you get your clothes on."

Brown came up to a sitting position and the old man kicked him hard. Brown felt the breath go out of his lungs and he slid back down, the hurt almost gone now in semiconsciousness.

He heard the old man say: "You an Uncle Tom. You eat their spit and you take their learnin'. White men wrote them books out there. White men can't change this baby. When this baby born I'm goin' to raise him up to hate the way I hate. They's goin' to be a line that baby draw someday and you goin' to be on the wrong side. Boy baby or girl baby— hate like I hate. We see what this virgin's baby be when it grow up."

He took Mary Lou's hand in his and they went on out the door.

When they were gone Brown let Miss Emmet help him to his feet. He looked at himself in the mirror. There was a large welt on his chin and his ribs were sore, but he felt no worse than he had when he had been hit by the firehose in the march on the courthouse. He would not allow Miss Emmet to call the police. He was not sure they would come anyway.

He sat down in his chair. Despite the pain in his face and chest he didn't feel bad, not bad at all.

Through the fall Brown heard almost nothing of Eli Cadwell. Sometimes on his rounds, he would hear a little of him as he heard of others, but the old man seemed peaceful and appeared to be working his tiny area of rented ground. It wasn't until the middle of December that he really heard anything of interest. One of his patients told him that Mary Lou had had her baby.

When they were back in the car after seeing that patient Brown told Miss Emmet, "I think we'd better go past Eli Cadwell's."

She shook her head. "Don't go. You'll only get in trouble."

He looked at her. "You want me to take you back to town before I go over?"

After a minute she said, "No" in a suddenly tired voice.

"Now that the little girl is here I want to try to help," he explained. "Maybe he'll let me check them over. I'd give a lot if some of these people would give up their midwives and come to me. There'd be fewer to bury."

The house was a small cabin, old and unpainted. On behind there was an outhouse. Both were in the state that comes shortly before total collapse. Brown pulled his car up into the rutted, red dirt drive and walked through the fireweed that winter had not quite killed.

No one answered his knock. He started back for the car, oddly relieved. He saw Miss Emmet watching him with frightened eyes.

A voice called to him from down the road and he recognized Mrs. Jackman. She was stout and old and she wore a tired red sweater over her dress. She waddled towards him.

"They gone off," she said breathlessly when she was close enough.

He went on up to her. She lived down the road and she was a part time midwife. He looked at her hands, the nails encrusted with dirt no soap would reach, and sighed to himself.

"Where?" he asked.

"I don' know," she said. "Eli never talk much. After the baby born, Eli pack that old car and they all leave."

"How soon after the baby was born?"

"Three, fo' days," she said. "I tol' him that was too soon, but he don't listen. He give me his mule fo' ten dollahs and helpin' with the baby like I done. He sold his tools, too. I don' think he comin' back."

"Thank you, Mrs. Jackman," Brown said and started to turn.

"Hol' on there," she said. "I s'pose to pass on a message to you."

"To me?" Brown said in surprise.

"Yeah, he said to tell you they named the boy Elijah after his pa."

Slowly Brown said, "It was a boy . . ."

"Oh, yeah. Real buster of a boy."

With her message delivered, she left and Brown watched her walk back down the road to her own place. He stood there for a minute just thinking and then he went back to the car.

"I feel like a drink," he said. "Doris, do you feel like having a drink?"

She looked at him. "All right," she said.

There wasn't any place to hide, really. In twenty years he might be dead, anyway. He thought about it for a minute, and then he reached across and opened the glove compartment. He took out a bottle and some Dixie cups.

"Merry Christmas," he said.

"It isn't Christmas yet," Doris said.

"Oh, yes," he said. "Oh, yes."

**A miniature sleigh and eight tiny reindeer?
Not this time!**

Cyber–Claus
William Gibson

In the night of 12/24/07, though sensors woven through the very fabric of the house had thus far registered a complete absence of sentient bio-activity, I found myself abruptly summoned from a rare, genuine, and very expensively induced example of that most priceless of states, sleep.

Even as I hurriedly dressed, I knew that dozens of telepresent armed-response drones would already be sweeping in from the District, skimming mere inches above the chill surface of the Potomac. Vicious tri-lobed aeroforms that they were, they resembled nothing more than the Martian war machines of George Pal's 1953 epic, *The War of the Worlds*.

And while, from somewhere far above, now, came that *sound*, that persistent *clatter*, as though gunships disgorged whole platoons of iron-shod mercenaries, I could only wonder: who? Was it my estranged wife, The Lady Betsy-Jayne Motel-6 Hyatt, Chief Eco-trustee of the Free Duchy of Wyoming? Or was it Cleatus "Mainframe" Sinyard himself, President of the United States and perpetual co-chairman of the

Concerned Smart People's Northern Hemisphere Co-prosperity Sphere?

"You're mumbling again, big guy," said Memory, shivering into hallucinatorily clear focus on the rumpled sheets, her thighs warm and golden against the Royal Stewart flannel. She adjusted the nosecones of her chrome bustier. "Also, you're on the verge of a major fashion crime."

I froze, the starched white tails of an Elmore of Shinjuku evening shirt half-tucked into the waistband of a favorite pair of lovingly-mended calfskin jodhpurs. She was right. Pearl buttons scattered like a flock of minuscule flying saucers as I tore myself out of the offending Elmore. I swiftly chose a classic Gap T-shirt and a Ralph Lauren overshirt in shotgun-distressed ochre corduroy. The Gap T's double-knit liquid crystal began to cycle sluggishly in response to body-heat, displaying crudely animated loops of once-famous tele-vangelists of the previous century, their pallid flanks streaked with the sweat of illicit sexual exertion. Now that literally *everything* was digital, History and Image were no more than Silly Putty in the hands of anyone with a BFA and a backer in Singapore. But that was just the nature of Postmodernity, and, frankly, it suited me right down to the ground.

"Visitors upstairs, chief," she reminded me pointlessly, causing me to regret not having invested in that last chip-upgrade. "Like on the roof."

"How many?" And this was Samsung-Sears's idea of an *expert* system?

"Seventeen, assuming we're talking bipeds."

"What's that supposed to mean?"

"That Nintendo-Dow micropore sensor-skin you had 'em stretch over the RealistiSlate? After those Colombian bush ninjas from the Slunk Cartel tried to get in through the toilet-ventilators? Well, that stuff's registering, like, *hooves*. Tiny ones. Unless this is some kinda major Jersey Devil infestation, I make it eight quadrupeds—plus one *definite* biped."

"It can't be Sinyard then." I holstered a 3mm Honda and pocketed half a dozen spare ampules of gel. "He'd never come alone."

"So maybe that's the good news, but I gotta tell you, this guy weighs in at close to one-forty kilos. And wears size eleven-and-a-half boots. As an expert system, I'd advise you to use the Mossad & Wesson bullpup, the one with the sub-sonic witness protection nozzles—" She broke off, as if listening to something only she could hear. "Uh-oh," she said, "I think he's coming down the *chimney* . . ."

Promises to Keep
Jack McDevitt

I received a Christmas card last week from Ed Iseminger. The illustration was a rendering of the celebrated Christmas Eve telecast from Callisto: a lander stands serenely on a rubble-strewn plain, spilling warm yellow light through its windows. Needle-point peaks rise behind it, and the rim of a crater curves across the foreground. An enormous belted crescent dominates the sky.

In one window, someone has hung a wreath.

It is a moment preserved, a tableau literally created by Cathie Perth, extracted from her prop bag. Somewhere here, locked away among insurance papers and the deed to the house, is the tape of the original telecast, but I've never played it. In fact, I've seen it only once, on the night of the transmission. But I know the words, Cathie's words, read by Victor Landolfi in his rich baritone, blending the timeless values of the season with the spectral snows of another world. They appear in schoolbooks now, and on marble.

Inside the card, in large, block, defiant letters, Iseminger had printed "SEPTEMBER!" It is a word with which he hopes to conquer a world. Sometimes, at night, when the snow sparkles under the hard cold stars (the way it did on Callisto), I think about him, and his quest. And I am very afraid.

I can almost see Cathie's footprints on the frozen surface. It was a good time, and I wish there were a way to step into the picture, to toast the holidays once more with Victor Landolfi, to hold onto Cathie Perth (and not let go!), and somehow to save us all. It was the end of innocence, a final meeting place for old friends.

We made the Christmas tape over a period of about five days. Cathie took literally hours of visuals, but Callisto is a place of rock and ice and deadening sameness: there is little to soften the effect of cosmic indifference. Which is why all those shots of towering peaks and tumbled boulders were taken at long range, and in half-light. Things not quite seen, she said, are always charming.

Her biggest problem had been persuading Landolfi to do the voice-over. Victor was tall, lean, ascetic. He was equipped with laser eyes and a huge black mustache. His world was built solely of subatomic particles, and driven by electromagnetics. Those who did not share his passions excited his contempt; which meant that he understood the utility of Cathie's public relations function at the same time that he deplored its necessity. To participate was to compromise one's integrity. His sense of delicacy, however, prevented his expressing that view to Cathie: he begged off rather on the press of time, winked apologetically, and straightened his mustache. "Sawyer will read it for you," he said, waving me impatiently into the conversation.

Cathie sneered, and stared irritably out a window (it was the one with the wreath) at Jupiter, heavy in the fragile sky. We knew, by then, that it had a definable surface, that the big planet was a world sea of liquid hydrogen, wrapped around a rocky core. "It must be frustrating," she said, "to know you'll never see it." Her tone was casual, almost frivolous, but Landolfi was not easily baited.

"Do you really think," he asked, with the patience of the

superior being (Landolfi had no illusions about his capabilities), "that these little pieces of theater will make any difference? Yes, Catherine, of course it's frustrating. Especially when one realizes that we have the technology to put vehicles down there. . . ."

"And scoop out some hydrogen," Cathie added.

He shrugged. "It may happen someday."

"Victor, it never will if we don't sell the Program. This is the last shot. These ships are old, and nobody's going to build any new ones. Unless things change radically at home."

Landolfi closed his eyes. I knew what he was thinking: Cathie Perth was an outsider, an ex-television journalist who had probably slept her way on board. She played bridge, knew the film library by heart, read John Donne (for style, she said), and showed no interest whatever in the scientific accomplishments of the mission. We'd made far-reaching discoveries in the fields of plate tectonics, planetary climatology, and a dozen other disciplines. We'd narrowed the creation date down inside a range of a few million years. And we finally understood how it had happened! But Cathie's televised reports had de-emphasized the implications, and virtually ignored the mechanics of such things. Instead, while a global audience watched, Marjorie Aubuchon peered inspirationally out of a cargo lock at Ganymede (much in the fashion that Cortez must have looked at the Pacific on that first bright morning), her shoulder flag patch resplendent in the sunlight. And while the camera moved in for a close-up (her features were illuminated by a lamp Cathie had placed for the occasion in her helmet), Herman Selma solemnly intoned Cathie's comments on breaking the umbilical.

That was her style: brooding alien vistas reduced to human terms. In one of her best-known sequences, there had been no narration whatever: two spacesuited figures, obviously male and female, stood together in the shadow of the monumental Cadmus Ice Fracture on Europa, beneath three moons.

"Cathie," Landolfi said, with his eyes still shut. "I don't wish to be offensive: but do you really care? For the Program, that is? When we get home, you will write a book, you will be famous, you will be at the top of your profession. Are you really concerned with where the Program will be in twenty years?"

It was a fair question: Cathie'd made no secret of her hopes for a Pulitzer. And she stood to get it, no matter what happened after this mission. Moreover, although she'd tried to conceal her opinions, we'd been together a long time by then, almost three years, and we could hardly misunderstand the dark view she took of people who voluntarily imprisoned themselves for substantial portions of their lives to go 'rock-collecting.'

"No," she said. "I'm not, because there won't be a Program in twenty years." She looked around at each of us, weighing the effect of her words. Iseminger, a blond giant with a reddish beard, allowed a smile of lazy tolerance to soften his granite features. "We're in the same class as the pyramids," she continued, in a tone that was unemotional and irritatingly condescending. "We're a hell of an expensive operation, and for what? Do you think the taxpayers give a good goddam about the weather on Jupiter? There's nothing out here but gas and boulders. Playthings for eggheads!"

I sat and thought about it while she smiled sweetly, and Victor smoldered. I had not heard the solar system ever before described in quite those terms; I'd heard people call it *vast, awesome, magnificent, serene,* stuff like that. But never *boring.*

In the end, Landolfi read his lines. He did it, he said, to end the distraction.

Cathie was clearly pleased with the result. She spent three days editing the tapes, commenting frequently (and with good-natured malice) on the *resonance* and *tonal qualities* of the voice-over. She finished on the morning of the 24th (ship time, of course), and transmitted the report to *Greenswallow* for relay to Houston. "It'll make the evening newscasts," she said with satisfaction.

It was our third Christmas out. Except for a couple of experiments-in-progress, we were finished on Callisto and, in fact, in the Jovian system. Everybody was feeling good about that, and we passed an uneventful afternoon, playing bridge and talking about what we'd do when we got back. (Cathie had described a deserted beach near Tillamook, Oregon, where she'd grown up. "It would be nice to walk on it again, under a *blue* sky," she said. Landolfi had startled everyone at that point: he looked up from the computer console at which he'd been working, and his eyes grew very distant. "I think," he said, "when the time comes, I would like very much to walk with you. . . .")

For the most part, Victor kept busy that afternoon with his hobby: he was designing a fusion engine that would be capable, he thought, of carrying ships to Jupiter within a few weeks, and, possibly, would eventually open the stars to direct exploration. But I watched him: he turned away periodically from the display screen, to glance at Cathie. Yes (I thought), she would indeed be lovely against the rocks and the spume, her black hair free in the wind.

Just before dinner, we watched the transmission of Cathie's tape. It was very strong, and when it was finished we sat silently looking at one another. By then, Herman Selma and Esther Crowley had joined us. (Although two landers were down, Cathie had been careful to give the impression in her report that there had only been one. When I asked why, she said, "In a place like this, one lander is the Spirit of Man. Two landers is just two landers.") We toasted Victor, and we toasted Cathie. Almost everyone, it turned out, had brought down a bottle for the occasion. We sang and laughed, and somebody turned up the music. We'd long since discovered the effect of low-gravity dancing in cramped quarters, and I guess we made the most of it.

Marj Aubuchon, overhead in the linkup, called to wish us season's greetings, and called again later to tell us that the telecast, according to Houston, had been "well-received." That was government talk, of course, and it meant only that no one in authority could find anything to object to. Actually, somebody high up had considerable confidence in her: in order to promote the illusion of spontaneity, the tapes were being broadcast directly to the commercial networks.

Cathie, who by then had had a little too much to drink, gloated openly. "It's the best we've done," she said. "Nobody'll ever do it better."

We shared that sentiment. Landolfi raised his glass, winked at Cathie, and drained it.

We had to cut the evening short, because a lander's life-support system isn't designed to handle six people. (For that matter, neither was an Athena's.) But before we broke it up, Cathie surprised us all by proposing a final toast: "To Frank Steinitz," she said quietly. "And his crew."

Steinitz: there was a name, as they say, to conjure with. He had led the first deep-space mission, five Athenas to Saturn, fifteen years before. It had been the first attempt to capture the public imagination for a dying program: an investigation of a peculiar object, filmed by a Voyager on Iapetus. But nothing much had come of it, and the mission had taken almost seven years. Steinitz and his people had begun as heroes, but in the end they'd become symbols of futility. The press had portrayed them mercilessly as personifications of outworn virtues. Someone had compared them to the Japanese soldiers found as late as the 1970s on Pacific islands, still defending a world long since vanished.

The Steinitz group bore permanent reminders of their folly: prolonged weightlessness had loosened ligaments and tendons, and weakened muscles. Several had developed heart problems, and all suffered from assorted neuroses. As one syndicated columnist had observed, they walked like a bunch of retired big-league catchers.

"That's a good way to end the evening," said Selma, beaming benevolently.

Landolfi looked puzzled. "Cathie," he rumbled, "you've questioned Steinitz's good sense any number of times. And ours, by the way. Isn't it a little hypocritical to drink to him?"

"I'm not impressed by his intelligence," she said, ignoring the obvious parallel. "But he and his people went all the way out to Saturn in those damned things—" she waved in the general direction of the three Athenas orbiting overhead in linkup "—hanging onto baling wire and wing struts. I have to admire that."

"Hell," I said, feeling the effects a little myself, "we've got the same ships he had."

"Yes, you do," said Cathie pointedly.

I had trouble sleeping that night. For a long time, I lay listening to Landolfi's soft snore, and the electronic fidgeting of the operations computer. Cathie was bundled inside a gray blanket, barely visible in her padded chair.

She was right, of course. I knew that rubber boots would never again cross that white landscape, which had waited a billion years for us. The peaks glowed in the reflection of the giant planet: fragile crystalline beauty, on a world of terrifying stillness. Except for an occasional incoming rock, nothing more would ever happen here. Callisto's entire history was encapsuled within twelve days.

Pity there hadn't been something to those early notions about Venusian rain forests and canals on Mars. The Program might have had easier going had Burroughs or Bradbury been right. My God: how many grim surprises had disrupted fictional voyages to Mars? But the truth had been far worse than anything Welles or the others had ever committed to paper; the red planet was so dull that we hadn't even gone there.

Instead, we'd lumbered out to the giants. In ships that drained our lives and our health.

We could have done better; our ships could have *been* better. The computer beside which Landolfi slept contained his design for the fusion engine. And at JPL, an Army team had demonstrated that artificial gravity was possible: a *real* gravity field, not the pathetic fraction created on the Athenas by spinning the inner hull. There were other possibilities as well: infrared ranging could be adapted to replace our elderly scanning system; new alloys were under development. But it would cost billions to build a second-generation vehicle. And unless there were an incentive, unless Cathie Perth carried off a miracle, it would not happen.

Immediately overhead, a bright new star glittered, moving visibly (though slowly) from west to east. That was the linkup, three ships connected nose to nose by umbilicals and a magnetic docking system. Like the Saturn mission, we were a multiple vehicle operation. We were more flexible that way, and we had a safety factor: two ships would be adequate to get the nine-man mission home. Conditions might become a little stuffy, but we'd make it.

I watched it drift through the icy starfield.

Cathie had pulled the plug on the Christmas lights. But it struck me that Callisto would only have one Christmas, so I put them back on.

Victor was on board *Tolstoi* when we lost it. No one ever really knew precisely what happened. We'd begun our long fall toward Jupiter, gaining the acceleration which we'd need on the flight home. Cathie, Herman Selma (the mission commander), and I were riding *Greenswallow*. The ships had separated, and would not rejoin until we'd rounded Jupiter, and settled into our course for home. (The Athenas are really individually-powered modular units which travel, except when maneuvering, as a single vessel. They're connected bow-to-bow by electromagnets. Coils of segmented tubing, called 'umbilicals' even though the term does not accurately describe their function, provide ready access among the forward areas of the ships. As many as six Athenas can be linked in this fashion, although only five have ever been built. The resulting structure would resemble a wheel.)

Between Callisto and Ganymede, we hit something: a drifting cloud of fine particles, a belt of granular material stretched so thin it never appeared on the LGD, before or after. Cathie later called it a cosmic sandbar; Iseminger thought it an unformed moon. It didn't matter: whatever it was, the mission plowed into it at almost 50,000 kilometers per hour. Alarms clattered, and red lamps blinked on.

In those first moments, I thought the ship was going to come apart. Herman was thrown across a bank of consoles and through an open hatch. I couldn't see Cathie, but a quick burst of profanity came from her direction. Things were being ripped off the hull. Deep within her walls, *Greenswallow* sighed. The lights dipped, came back, and went out. Emergency lamps cut in, and something big glanced off the side of the ship. More alarms howled, and I waited for the clamor of the throaty klaxon which would warn of a holing, and which consequently would be the last sound I could expect to hear in this life.

The sudden deceleration snapped my head back on the pads. (The collision had occurred at the worst possible time: *Greenswallow* was caught in the middle of an attitude alignment. We were flying backwards.)

The exterior monitors were blank: that meant the cameras were gone.

Cathie's voice: "Rob, you okay?"

"Yes."

"Can you see Herman?"

My angle was bad, and I was pinned in my chair. "No. He's back in cargo."

"Is there any way you can close the hatch?"

"Herman's in there," I protested, thinking she'd misunderstood.

"If something tears a hole out back there, we're all going to go. Keeping the door open won't help him."

I hesitated. Sealing up seemed to be the wrong thing to do. (Of course, the fact that the hatch had been open in the first place constituted a safety violation.) "It's on your console," I told her. "Hit the numerics on your upper right."

"Which one?"

"Hit them all." She was seated at the status board, and I could see a row of red lights: several other hatches were open. They should have closed automatically when the first alarms sounded.

We got hit again, this time in front. *Greenswallow* trembled, and loose pieces of metal rattled around inside the walls like broken teeth.

"Rob," she said. "I don't think it's working."

The baleful lights still glowed across the top of her board.

❄   ❄   ❄

It lasted about three minutes.

When it was over, we hurried back to look at Herman. We were no longer rotating, and gravity had consequently dropped to zero. Selma, gasping, pale, his skin damp, was floating grotesquely over a pallet of ore-sample cannisters. We got him to a couch and applied compresses. His eyes rolled shut, opened, closed again. "Inside," he said, gently fingering an area just off his sternum. "I think I've been chewed up a little." He raised his head slightly. "What kind of shape are we in?"

I left Cathie with him. Then I restored power, put on a suit and went outside.

The hull was a disaster: antennas were down, housings scored, lenses shattered. The lander was gone, ripped from its web. The port cargo area had buckled, and an auxiliary hatch was sprung. On the bow, the magnetic dock was hammered into slag. Travel between the ships was going to be a little tougher.

Greenswallow looked as if she had been sandblasted. I scraped particles out of her jet nozzles, replaced cable, and bolted down mounts. I caught a glimpse of *Amity*'s lights, sliding diagonally across the sky. As were the constellations.

"Cathie," I said. "I see Mac. But I think we're tumbling."

"Okay."

Iseminger was also on board *Amity*. And, fortunately, Marj Aubuchon, our surgeon. Herman's voice broke in, thick with effort. "Rob, we got no radio contact with anyone. Any sign of Victor?"

Ganymede was close enough that its craters lay exposed in harsh solar light. Halfway round the sky, the Pleiades glittered. *Tolstoi*'s green and red running lights should have been visible among, or near, the six silver stars. But the sky was empty. I stood a long time and looked, wondering how many other navigators on other oceans had sought lost friends in that constellation. What had they called it in antiquity? The rainy Pleiades. . . ." Only *Amity*," I said.

I tore out some cable and lobbed it in the general direction of Ganymede. Jupiter's enormous arc was pushing above the maintenance pods, spraying October light across the wreckage. I improvised a couple of antennas, replaced some black boxes, and then decided to correct the tumble, if I could.

"Try it now," I said.

Cathie acknowledged.

Two of the jets were useless. I went inside for spares, and replaced the faulty units. While I was finishing up, Cathie came back on. "Rob," she said, "radio's working, more or less. We have no long-range transmit, though."

"Okay. I'm not going to try to do anything about that right now."

"Are you almost finished?"

"Why?"

"Something occurred to me. Maybe the cloud, whatever that damned thing was that we passed through: maybe it's U-shaped."

"Thanks," I said. "I needed something to worry about."

"Maybe you should come back inside."

"Soon as I can. How's the patient doing?"

"Out," she said. "He was a little delirious when he was talking to you. Anyhow, I'm worried: I think something's broken internally. He never got his color back, and he's beginning to bring up blood. Rob, we need Marj."

"You hear anything from *Amity* yet?"

"Just a carrier wave." She did not mention *Tolstoi*. "How bad is it out there?"

From where I was tethered, about halfway back on the buckled beam, I could see a crack in the main plates that appeared to run the length of the port tube. I climbed out onto the exhaust assembly, and pointed my flashlight into the combustion chamber. Something glittered where the reflection should have been subdued. I got in and looked: silicon. Sand, and steel, had fused in the white heat of passage. The exhaust was blocked.

Cathie came back on. "What about it, Rob?" she asked. "Any serious problems?"

"Cathie," I said, "*Greenswallow*'s going to Pluto."

❅   ❅   ❅

Herman thought I was Landolfi: he kept assuring me that everything was going to be okay. His pulse was weak and rapid, and he alternated between sweating and shivering. Cathie had got a blanket under him and buckled him down so he wouldn't hurt himself. She bunched some pillows under his feet, and held a damp compress to his head.

"That's not going to help much. Raising his legs, I mean."

She looked at me, momentarily puzzled. "Oh," she said. "Not enough gravity."

I nodded.

"Oh, Rob." Her eyes swept the cases and cannisters, all neatly tagged, silicates from Pasiphae, sulfur from Himalia, assorted carbon compounds from Callisto. We had evidence now that Io had formed elsewhere in the solar system, and been well along in middle age when it was captured. We'd all but eliminated the possibility that life existed in Jupiter's atmosphere. We understood why rings formed around gas giants, and we had a new clue to the cause of terrestrial ice ages. And I could see that Cathie was thinking about trading lives to satisfy the curiosity of a few academics. "We don't belong out here," she said, softly. "Not in these primitive shells."

I said nothing.

"I got a question for you," she continued. "We're not going to find *Tolstoi*, right?"

"Is that your question?"

"No. I wish it were. But the LGD can't see them. That means they're just not there." Her eyes filled with tears, but she shook her head impatiently. "And we can't steer this thing. Can *Amity* carry six people?"

"It might have to."

"That wasn't what I asked."

"Food and water would be tight. Especially since we're running out of time, and wouldn't be able to transfer much over. If any. So we'd all be a little thinner when we got back. But yes, I think we could survive."

We stared at one another, and then she turned away. I became conscious of the ship: the throb of power deep in her bulkheads (power now permanently bridled by conditions in the combustion chambers), the soft amber glow of the navigation lamps in the cockpit.

McGuire's nasal voice, from *Amity*, broke the uneasy silence. "Herman, you okay?"

Cathie looked at me, and I nodded. "Mac," she said, "this is Perth. Herman's hurt. We need Marj."

"Okay," he said. "How bad?"

"We don't know. Internal injuries, looks like. He appears to be in shock."

We heard him talking to someone else. Then he came back. "We're on our way. I'll put Marj on in a minute; maybe she can help from here. How's the ship?"

"Not good: the dock's gone, and the engine might as well be."

He asked me to be specific. "If we try a burn, the rear end'll fall off."

McGuire delivered a soft, venomous epithet. And then: "Do what you can for Herman. Marj'll be right here."

Cathie was looking at me strangely. "He's worried," she said.

"Yes. He's in charge now. . . ."

"Rob, you say you *think* we'll be okay. What's the problem?"

"We might," I said, "run a little short of air."

Greenswallow continued her plunge toward Jupiter at a steadily increasing rate and a sharp angle of approach: we would pass within about 60,000 kilometers, and then drop completely out of the plane of the solar system. We appeared to be heading in the general direction of the Southern Cross.

Cathie worked on Herman. His breathing steadied, and he slipped in and out of his delirium. We sat beside him, not talking much. After awhile, Cathie asked, "What happens now?"

"In a few hours," I said, "we'll reach our insertion point. By then, we have to be ready to change course." She frowned,

and I shrugged. "That's it," I said. "It's all the time we have
to get over to *Amity*. If we don't make the insertion on time,
Amity won't have the fuel to throw a U-turn later."

"Rob, how are we going to get Herman over there?"

That was an uncomfortable question. The prospect of jamming him down into a suit was less than appealing, but there
was no other way. "We'll just have to float him over," I said.
"Marj won't like it much."

"Neither will Herman."

"You wanted a little high drama," I said, unnecessarily.
"The next show should be a barnburner."

Her mouth tightened, and she turned away from me.

One of the TV cameras had picked up the approach of *Amity*. Some of her lights were out, and she too looked a bit
bent. The Athena is a homely vessel in the best of times,
whale-shaped and snub-nosed, with a midship flare that suggests middle-age spread. But I was glad to see her.

Cathie snuffled at the monitor, and blew her nose. "Your
Program's dead, Rob." Her eyes blazed momentarily, like a
dying fire into which one has flung a few drops of water.
"We're leaving three of our people out here; and if you're
right about the air, we'll get home with a shipload of defec-
tives, or worse. Won't that look good on the six o'clock
news?" She gazed vacantly at *Amity*'s image. "I'd hoped,"
she said, "that if things went well, Victor would have lived to
see a ship carry his fusion engine. And maybe his name, as
well. Ain't gonna happen, though. Not ever."

I had not allowed myself to think about the oxygen problem we were going to face. The Athenas recycle their air supply: the converters in a single ship can maintain a crew of
three, or even four, indefinitely. But six?

I was not looking forward to the ride home.

A few minutes later, a tiny figure detached itself from the
shadow of the Athena and started across: Marj Aubuchon on
a maintenance sled. McGuire's voice erupted from the ship's
speakers. "Rob, we've taken a long look at your engines, and
we agree with your assessment. The damage complicates
things." Mac had a talent for understatement. It derived, not

from a sophisticated sense of humor, but from a genuine conviction of his own inferiority. He preferred to solve problems by denying their existence. He was the only one of the original nine who could have been accurately described as passive: other people's opinions carried great weight with him. His prime value to the mission was his grasp of Athena systems. But he'd been a reluctant crewman, a man who periodically reminded us that he wanted only to retire to his farm in Indiana. He wouldn't have been along at all except that one guy died and somebody else came down with an unexpected (but thoroughly earned) disease. Now, with Selma incapacitated and Landolfi gone, McGuire was in command. It must have been disconcerting for him. "We've got about five hours," he continued. "Don't let Marj get involved in major surgery. She's already been complaining to me that it doesn't sound as if it'll be possible to move him. *We have no alternative.* She knows that, but you know how she is. Okay?"

One of the monitors had picked him up. He looked rumpled, and nervous. Not an attitude to elicit confidence. "Mac," said Cathie, "we may kill him trying to get him over there."

"You'll kill him if you don't," he snapped. "Get your personal stuff together, and bring it with you. You won't be going back."

"What about trying to transfer some food?" I asked.

"We can't dock," he said. "And there isn't time to float it across."

"Mac," said Cathie, "is *Amity* going to be able to support six people?"

I listened to McGuire breathing. He turned away to issue some trivial instructions to Iseminger. When he came back he said, simply and tonelessly, "Probably not." And then, cold-bloodedly (I thought), "How's Herman doing?"

Maybe it was my imagination. Certainly there was nothing malicious in his tone, but Cathie caught it too, and turned sharply round. "McGuire is a son-of-a-bitch," she hissed. I don't know whether Mac heard it.

✲   ✲   ✲

Marjorie Aubuchon was short, blond, and irritable. When I relayed McGuire's concerns about time, she said, "God knows, that's all I've heard for the last half-hour." She observed that McGuire was a jerk, and bent over Herman. The blood was pink and frothy on his lips. After a few minutes she said, to no one in particular, "Probably a punctured lung." She waved Cathie over, and began filling a hypo; I went for a walk.

At sea, there's a long tradition of sentiment between mariners and their ships. Enlisted men identify with them, engineers baby them, and captains go down with them. No similar attitude has developed in space flight. We've never had an *Endeavour*, or a *Golden Hind*. Always, off Earth, it has been the mission, rather than the ship. *Friendship VII* and *Apollo XI* were far more than vehicles. I'm not sure why that is; maybe it reflects Cathie's view that travel between the worlds is still in its *Kon-Tiki* phase: the voyage itself is of such epic proportions that everything else is overwhelmed.

But I'd lived almost three years on *Greenswallow*. It was a long time to be confined to her narrow spaces. Nevertheless, she was shield and provider against that enormous abyss, and I discovered (while standing in the doorway of my cabin) a previously unfelt affection for her.

A few clothes were scattered round the room, a shirt was hung over my terminal, and two pictures were mounted on the plastic wall. One was a Casnavan print of a covered bridge in New Hampshire; the other was a telecopy of an editorial cartoon that had appeared in the *Washington Post*. The biggest human problem we had, of course, was sheer boredom. And Cathie had tried to capture the dimensions of the difficulty by showing crewmembers filling the long days on the outbound journey with bridge. ("It would be nice," Cathie's narrator had said at one point, "if we could take everybody out to an Italian restaurant now and then.") The *Post* cartoon had appeared several days later: it depicted four astronauts holding cards. (We could recognize Selma, Landolfi, and Marj. The fourth, whose back was turned, was exceedingly feminine, and appeared to be Esther Crowley.) An en-

ormous bloodshot eye is looking in through one window; a
tentacle and a UFO are visible through another. The "Selma"
character, his glasses characteristically down on his nose, is
examining his hand, and delivering the caption: *Dummy looks
out the window and checks the alien.*

I packed the New Hampshire bridge, and left the cartoon.
If someone comes by, in 20 million years or so, he might
need a laugh. I went up to the cockpit with my bag.

McGuire checked with me to see how we were progress-
ing. "Fine," I told him. I was still sitting there four hours
later when Cathie appeared behind me.

"Rob," she said, "we're ready to move him." She smiled
wearily. "Marj says he should be okay if we can get him over
there without breaking anything else."

We cut the spin on the inner module to about point-oh-five.
Then we lifted Herman onto a stretcher, and carried him carefully down to the airlock.

Cathie stared straight ahead, saying nothing. Her fine-
boned cheeks were pale, and her eyes seemed focused far
away. These, I thought, were her first moments to herself, un-
hampered by other duties. The impact of events was taking
hold.

Marj called McGuire and told him we were starting over,
and that she would need a sizable pair of shears when we got
there to cut Herman's suit open. "Please have them ready,"
she said. "We may be in a hurry."

I had laid out his suit earlier: we pulled it up over his legs.
That was easy, but the rest of it was slow, frustrating work.
"We need a special kind of unit for this," Marj said. "Probably a large bag, without arms or legs. If we're ever dumb
enough to do anything like this again, I'll recommend it."

McGuire urged us to hurry.

Once or twice, Cathie's eyes met mine. Something passed
between us, but I was too distracted to define it. Then we
were securing his helmet, and adjusting the oxygen mixture.

"I think we're okay," Marj observed, her hand pressed
against Selma's chest. "Let's get him over there. . . ."

I opened the inner airlock, and pulled my own helmet into

place. Then we guided Herman in, and secured him to *Greenswallow*'s maintenance sled. (The sled was little more than a toolshed with jet nozzles.) I recovered my bag and stowed it on board.

"I'd better get my stuff," Cathie said. "You can get Herman over all right?"

"Of course," said Marj. "*Amity*'s sled is secured outside the lock. Use that."

She hesitated in the open hatchway, raised her left hand, and spread the fingers wide. Her eyes grew very round, and she formed two syllables that I was desperately slow to understand: in fact, I don't think I translated the gesture, the word, until we were halfway across to *Amity*, and the lock was irrevocably closed behind us.

"Good-bye."

Cathie's green eyes sparkled with barely controlled emotion across a dozen or so monitors. Her black hair, which had been tied back earlier, now framed her angular features and fell to her shoulders. It was precisely in that partial state of disarray that tends to be most appealing. She looked as if she'd been crying, but her jaw was set, and she stood erect. Beneath the gray tunic, her breast rose and fell.

"What the hell are you doing, Perth?" demanded McGuire. He looked tired, almost ill. He'd gained weight since we'd left the Cape, his hair had whitened and retreated, his flesh had grown blotchy, and he'd developed jowls. The contrast with his dapper image in the mission photo was sobering. "Get moving!" he said, striving to keep his voice from rising. "We're not going to make our burn!"

"I'm staying where I am," she said. "I couldn't make it over there now anyway. I wouldn't even have time to put on the suit."

McGuire's puffy eyelids slid slowly closed. "Why?" he asked.

She looked out of the cluster of screens, a segmented Cathie, a group-Cathie. "Your ship won't support six people, Mac."

"Dammit!" His voice was a harsh rasp. "It would have just meant we'd cut down activity. Sleep a lot." He waved a hand in front of his eyes, as though his vision were blurred. "Cathie, we've lost you. There's no way we can get you back!"

"I know."

No one said anything. Iseminger stared at her.

"Is Herman okay?" she asked.

"Marj is still working on him," I said. "She thinks we got him across okay."

"Good."

A series of yellow lamps blinked on across the pilot's console. We had two minutes. "Damn," I said, suddenly aware of another danger: *Amity* was rotating, turning toward its new course. Would *Greenswallow* even survive the ignition? I looked at McGuire, who understood. His fingers flicked over press pads, and rows of numbers flashed across the navigation monitor. I could see muscles working in Cathie's jaws; she looked down at Mac's station as though she could read the result.

"It's all right," he said. "She'll be clear."

"Cathie . . ." Iseminger's voice was almost strangled. "If I'd known you intended anything like this. . . ."

"I know, Ed." Her tone was gentle, a lover's voice, perhaps. Her eyes were wet: she smiled anyway, full face, up close.

Deep in the systems, pumps began to whine. "I wish," said Iseminger, absolutely without expression, "that we could do something."

She turned her back, strode with unbearable grace across the command center, away from us, and passed into the shadowy interior of the cockpit. Another camera picked her up there, and we got a profile: she was achingly lovely in the soft glow of the navigation lamps.

"There is something . . . you can do," she said. "Build Landolfi's engine. And come back for me."

❄   ❄   ❄

For a brief moment, I thought Mac was going to abort the burn. But he sat frozen, fists clenched, and did the right thing, which is to say, nothing. It struck me that McGuire was incapable of intervening. ·

And I knew also that the woman in the cockpit was terrified of what she had done. It had been a good performance, but she'd utterly failed to conceal the fear that looked out of her eyes. And I realized with shock that she'd acted, not to prolong her life, but to save the Program. I watched her face as *Amity's* engines ignited, and we began to draw away. Like McGuire, she seemed paralyzed, as though the nature of the calamity which she'd embraced was just becoming clear to her. Then it—she—was gone.

"What happened to the picture?" snapped Iseminger.

"She turned it off," I said. "I don't think she wants us to see her just now."

He glared at me, and spoke to Mac. "Why the hell," he demanded, "couldn't he have brought her back with him?" His fists were knotted.

"I didn't know," I said. "How could I know?" And I wondered, how could I not?

When the burn ended, the distance between the two ships had opened to only a few kilometers. But it was a gulf, I thought, wider than any across which men had before looked at each other.

Iseminger called her name relentlessly. (We knew she could hear us.) But we got only the carrier wave.

Then her voice crackled across the command center. "Good," she said. "Excellent. Check the recorders: make sure you got everything on tape." Her image was back. She was in full light again, tying up her hair. Her eyes were hooded, and her lips pursed thoughtfully. "Rob," she continued, "fade it out during Ed's response, when he's calling my name. Probably, you'll want to reduce the background noise at that point. Cut all the business about who's responsible. We want a sacrifice, not an oversight."

"My God, Cathie," I said. I stared at her, trying to understand. "What have you done?"

She took a deep breath. "I meant what I said. I have enough food to get by here for eight years or so. More if I stretch it. *And plenty of fresh air.* Well, relatively fresh. I'm better off than any of us would be if six people were trying to survive on *Amity.*"

"Cathie!" howled McGuire. He sounded in physical agony. "Cathie, we didn't know for sure about life support. The converters might have kept up. There might have been enough air! It was just an estimate!"

"This is a hell of a time to tell me," she said. "Well, it doesn't matter now. Listen, I'll be fine. I've got books to read, and maybe one to write. My long-range communications are *kaput*, Rob knows that, so you'll have to come back for the book, too." She smiled. "You'll like it, Mac." The command center got very still. "And on nights when things really get boring, I can play bridge with the computer."

McGuire shook his head. "You're sure you'll be all right? You seemed pretty upset a few minutes ago."

She looked at me and winked.

"The first Cathie was staged, Mac," I said.

"I give up," McGuire sighed. "Why?" He swiveled round to face the image on his screen. "Why would you do that?"

"That young woman," she replied, "was committing an act of uncommon valor, as they say in the Marines. And she had to be vulnerable." And compelling lovely, I thought. In those last moments, I was realizing what it might mean to love Cathie Perth. "This Cathie," she grinned, "is doing the only sensible thing. And taking a sabbatical as well. Do what you can to get the ship built. I'll be waiting. Come if you can." She paused. "Somebody should suggest they name it after Victor."

This is the fifth Christmas since that one on Callisto. It's a long time by any human measure. We drifted out of radio contact during the first week. There was some talk of broadcasting instructions to her for repairing her long-range transmission equipment. But she'd have to go outside to do it, so the idea was prudently tabled.

She was right about that tape. In my lifetime, I've never seen people so singlemindedly aroused. It created a global surge of sympathy and demands for action that seem to grow in intensity with each passing year. Funded partially by contributions and technical assistance from abroad, NASA has been pushing the construction of the fusion vessel that Victor Landolfi dreamed of.

Iseminger was assigned to help with the computer systems, and he's kept me informed of progress. The most recent public estimates had anticipated a spring launch. But that single word *September* in Iseminger's card suggests that one more obstacle has been encountered; and it means still another year before we can hope to reach her.

We broadcast to her on a regular basis. I volunteered to help, and I sit sometimes and talk to her for hours. She gets a regular schedule of news, entertainment, sports, whatever. And, if she's listening, she knows that we're coming.

And she also knows that her wish that the fusion ship be named for Victor Landolfi has been disregarded. The rescue vehicle will be the *Catherine Perth*.

If she's listening: we have no way of knowing. And I worry a lot. Can a human being survive six years of absolute solitude? Iseminger was here for a few days last summer, and he tells me he is confident. "She's a tough lady," he said, any number of times. "Nothing bothers her. She even gave us a little theater at the end."

And that's what scares me: Cathie's theatrical technique. I've thought about it, on the long ride home, and here. I kept a copy of the complete tape of that final conversation, despite McGuire's instructions to the contrary, and I've watched it a few times. It's locked downstairs in a file cabinet now, and I don't look at it anymore. I'm afraid to. There are two Cathie Perths on the recording: the frightened, courageous one who galvanized a global public; and our Cathie, preoccupied with her job, flexible, almost indifferent to her situation. A survivor.

And, God help me, I can't tell which one was staged.

Leaving earth at Christmas has its rewards

THE GIFT
Ray Bradbury

TOMORROW WOULD BE Christmas, and even while the three of them rode to the rocket port the mother and father were worried. It was the boy's first flight into space, his very first time in a rocket, and they wanted everything to be perfect. So when, at the custom's table, they were forced to leave behind his gift which exceeded the weight limit by no more than a few ounces and the little tree with the lovely white candles, they felt themselves deprived of the season and their love.

The boy was waiting for them in the Terminal room. Walking toward him, after their unsuccessful clash with the Interplanetary officials, the mother and father whispered to each other.

"What shall we do?"

"Nothing, nothing. What *can* we do?"

"Silly rules!"

"And he so wanted the tree!"

The siren gave a great howl and people pressed forward into the Mars Rocket. The mother and father walked at the very last, their small pale son between them, silent.

"I'll think of something," said the father.

"What . . .?" asked the boy.

And the rocket took off and they were flung headlong into dark space.

The rocket moved and left fire behind and left Earth behind on which the date was December 24, 2052, heading out into a place where there was no time at all, no month, no year, no hour. They slept away the rest of the first "day." Near midnight, by their Earth-time New York watches, the boy awoke and said, "I want to go look out the porthole."

There was only one port, a "window" of immensely thick glass of some size, up on the next deck.

"Not quite yet," said the father. "I'll take you up later."

"I want to see where we are and where we're going."

"I want you to wait for a reason," said the father.

He had been lying awake, turning this way and that, thinking of the abandoned gift, the problem of the season, the lost tree and the white candles. And at last, sitting up, no more than five minutes ago, he believed he had found a plan. He need only carry it out and this journey would be fine and joyous indeed.

"Son," he said, "in exactly one half hour it will be Christmas."

"Oh," said the mother, dismayed that he had mentioned it. Somehow she had rather hoped that the boy would forget.

The boy's face grew feverish and his lips trembled. "I know, I know. Will I get a present, will I? Will I have a tree? You promised—"

"Yes, yes, all that, and more," said the father.

The mother started. "But—"

"I mean it," said the father. "I really mean it. All and more, much more. Excuse me, now. I'll be back."

He left them for about twenty minutes. When he came back he was smiling. "Almost time."

"Can I hold your watch?" asked the boy, and the watch was handed over and he held it ticking in his fingers as the rest of the hour drifted by in fire and silence and unfelt motion.

"It's Christmas *now*! Christmas! Where's my present?"

"Here we go," said the father and took his boy by the shoulder and led him from the room, down the hall, up a rampway, his wife following.

"I don't understand," she kept saying.

"You will. Here we are," said the father.

They had stopped at the closed door of a large cabin. The father tapped three times and then twice in a code. The door opened and the light in the cabin went out and there was a whisper of voices.

"Go on in, son," said the father.

"It's dark."

"I'll hold your hand. Come on, Mama."

They stepped into the room and the door shut, and the room was very dark indeed. And before them loomed a great glass eye, the porthole, a window four feet high and six feet wide, from which they could look out into space.

The boy gasped.

Behind him, the father and the mother gasped with him, and then in the dark room some people began to sing.

"Merry Christmas, son," said the father.

And the voices in the room sang the old, the familiar carols, and the boy moved forward slowly until his face was pressed against the cool glass of the port. And he stood there for a long long time, just looking and looking out into space and the deep night at the burning and the burning of ten billion billion white and lovely candles. . . .

The train pulls in.

Winter Solstice, Camelot Station
John M. Ford

Camelot is served
By a sixteen-track stub terminal done in High Gothick Style,
The tracks covered by a single great barrel-vaulted glass roof
    framed upon iron,
At once looking back to the Romans and ahead to the
    Brunels.
Beneath its rotunda, just to the left of the ticket windows,
Is a mosaic floor depicting the Round Table
(Where all knights, regardless of their station of origin
Or class of accommodation, are equal),
And around it murals of knightly deeds in action
(Slaying dragons, righting wrongs, rescuing maidens tied to
    the tracks).
It is the only terminal, other than Gare d'Avalon in Paris,
To be hung with original tapestries,
And its lavatories rival those at Great Gate of Kiev Central.
During a peak season such as this, some eighty trains a day
    pass through,
Five times the frequency at the old Londinium Terminus,

Ten times the number the Druid towermen knew.
(The Official Court Christmas Card this year displays
A crisp black-and-white Charles Clegg photograph from the
    King's own collection,
Showing a woad-blued hogger at the throttle of "Old
    XCVII,"
The Fast Mail overnight to Eboracum. Those were the days.)
The first of a line of wagons has arrived,
Spilling footmen and pages in Court livery,
And old thick Kay, stepping down from his Range Rover,
Tricked out in a bush coat from Swaine, Adeney, Brigg,
Leaning on his shooting stick as he marshalls his company,
Instructing the youngest how to behave in the station,
To help mature women that they may encounter,
Report pickpockets, gather up litter,
And of course no true Knight of the Table Round (even in
    training)
Would do a station porter out of Christmas tips.
He checks his list of arrival times, then his watch
(A moon-phase Breguet, gift from Merlin):
The seneschal is a practical man, who knows trains do run
    late,
And a stolid one, who sees no reason to be glad about it.
He dispatches pages to posts at the tracks,
Doling out pennies for platform tickets,
Then walks past the station buffet with a dyspeptic snort,
Goes into the bar, checks the time again, orders a pint.
The patrons half-turn—it's the fella from Camelot, innit?
And Kay chuckles soft to himself, and the Court buys a
    round.
He's barely halfway when a page tumbles in,
Seems the knights are arriving, on time after all,
So he tips the glass back (people stare as he guzzles),
Then plonks it down hard with five quid for the barman,
And strides for the doorway (half Falstaff, half Hotspur)
To summon his liveried army of lads.
Bors arrives behind steam, riding the cab of a heavy Mikado.
He shakes the driver's hand, swings down from the footplate,

And is like a locomotive himself, his breath clouding white,
Dark oil sheen on his black iron mail,
Sword on his hip swinging like siderods at speed.
He stamps back to the baggage car, slams mailed fist on steel
     door
With a clang like jousters colliding.
The handler opens up and goes to rouse another knight.
Old Pellinore has been dozing with his back against a crate,
A cubical chain-bound thing with FRAGILE tags and air
     holes,
BEAST says the label, *Questing, 1* the bill of lading.
The porters look doubtful but ease the thing down.
It grumbles. It shifts. Someone shouts, and they drop it.
It cracks like an egg. There is nothing within.
Elayne embraces Bors on the platform, a pelican on a rock,
Silently they watch as Pelly shifts the splinters,
Supposing aloud that Gutman and Cairo have swindled him.

A high-drivered engine in Northern Lines green
Draws in with a string of side-corridor coaches,
All honey-toned wood with stained glass on their windows.
Gareth steps down from a compartment, then Gaheris and
     Agravaine,
All warmly tucked up in Orkney sweaters;
Gawaine comes after in Shetland tweed.
Their Gladstones and steamers are neatly arranged,
With never a worry—their Mum does the packing.
A redcap brings forth a curious bundle, a rude shape in red
     paper—
The boys did that themselves, you see, and how *does* one
     wrap a unicorn's head?
They bustle down the platform, past a chap all in green.
He hasn't the look of a trainman, but only Gawaine turns to
     look at his eyes,
And sees written there *Sir, I shall speak with you later.*

Over on the first track, surrounded by reporters,
All glossy dark iron and brass-bound mystery,

The Direct-Orient Express, ferried in from Calais and Points
     East.
Palomides appears. Smelling of patchouli and Russian leather,
Dripping Soubranie ash on his astrakhan collar,
Worry darkening his dark face, though his damascene armor
     shows no tarnish,
He pushes past the press like a broad-hulled icebreaker.
Flashbulbs pop. Heads turn. There's a woman in Chanel
     black,
A glint of diamonds, liquid movements, liquid eyes.
The newshawks converge, but suddenly there appears
A sharp young man in a crisp blue suit
From the Compagnie Internationale des Wagons-Lits,
That elegant, comfortable, decorous, close-mouthed firm;
He's good at his job, and they get not so much as a snapshot.
Tomorrow's editions will ask who she was, and whom
     with. . . .
Now here's a silver train, stainless steel, Vista-Domed,
White-lighted grails on the engine (running no extra sections)
The *Logres Limited*, extra fare, extra fine,
(Stops on signal at Carbonek to receive passengers only).
She glides to a Timken-borne halt (even her grease is clean),
Galahad already on the steps, flashing that winning smile,
Breeze mussing his golden hair, but not his Armani tailoring,
Just the sort of man you'd want finding your chalice.
He signs an autograph, he strikes a pose.
Someone says, loudly, "Gal! Who serves the Grail?"
He looks—no one he knows—and there's a silence,
A space in which he shifts like sun on water;
Look quick and you may see a different knight,
A knight who knows that meanings can be lies,
That things are done not knowing why they're done,
That bearings fail, and stainless steel corrodes.
A whistle blows. Snow shifts on the glass shed roof. That
     knight is gone.
This one remaining tosses his briefcase to one of Kay's
     pages,
And, golden, silken, careless, exits left.

Behind the carsheds, on the business car track, alongside the
    private varnish
Of dukes and smallholders, Persian potentates and Cathay
    princes
(James J. Hill is here, invited to bid on a tunnel through the
    Pennines),
Waits a sleek car in royal blue, ex-B&O, its trucks and
    fittings chromed,
A black-gloved hand gripping its silver platform rail;
Mordred and his car are both upholstered in blue velvet and
    black leather.
He prefers to fly, but the weather was against it.
His DC-9, with its video system and Quotron and waterbed,
    sits grounded at Gatwick.
The premature lines in his face are a map of a hostile country,
The redness in his eyes a reminder that hollyberries are
    poison.
He goes inside to put on a look acceptable for Christmas
    Court;
As he slams the door it rattles like strafing jets.

Outside the Station proper, in the snow,
On a through track that's used for milk and mail,
A wheezing saddle-tanker stops for breath;
A way-freight mixed, eight freight cars and caboose,
Two great ugly men on the back platform, talking with a third
    on the ballast.
One, the conductor, parcels out the last of the coffee;
They drink. A joke about grails. They laugh.
When it's gone, the trainman pretends to kick the big hobo
    off,
But the farewell hug spoils the act.
Now two men stand on the dirty snow,
The conductor waves a lantern and the train grinds on.
The ugly men start walking, the new arrival behind,
Singing "Wenceslas" off-key till the other says stop.
There are two horses waiting for them. Rather plain horses,

Considering. The men mount up.
By the roundhouse, they pause,
And look at the locos, the water, the sand, and the coal,
They look for a long time at the turntable,
Until the one who is King says "It all seemed so simple,
    once,"
And the best knight in the world says "It is. We make it
    hard."
They ride on, toward Camelot by the service road.
The sun is winter-low. Kay's caravan is rolling.
He may not run a railroad, but he runs a tight ship;
By the time they unload in the Camelot courtyard,
The wassail will be hot and the goose will be crackling,
Banners snapping from the towers, fir logs on the fire,
    drawbridge down,
And all that sackbut and psaltery stuff.
Blanchefleur is taking the children caroling tonight,
Percivale will lose to Merlin at chess,
The young knights will dally and the damsels dally back,
The old knights will play poker at a smaller Table Round.
And at the great glass station, motion goes on,
The extras, the milk trains, the varnish, the limiteds,
The *Pindar of Wakefield*, the *Lady of the Lake*,
The *Broceliande Local*, the *Fast Flying Briton*,
The nerves of the kingdom, the lines of exchange,
Running to schedule as the world ought,
Ticking like a hot-fired hand-stoked heart,
The metal expression of the breaking of boundaries,
The boilers that turn raw fire into power,
The driving rods that put the power to use,
The turning wheels that make all places equal,
The knowledge that the train may stop but the line goes on;
The train may stop
But the line goes on.

The myths arrive for Christmas.

A Holiday
in the Park
John M. Ford

The sign above the ticket booths reads KING ARTHUR'S
    WORLD OF CAMELOT.
The Wizard holds the Child's hand tight as they approach,
Casting the glamour so the attendant sees
Coats not robes, money pushed his way, nothing fairy or
    luminous.
This is magic. This is what magic is:
Making people see what you would have them see.
The pair goes in. One admission covers all.
The park is all color and music and motion,
Shoving back winter as actually Camelot did,
By denying it a place to settle.
There's Sir Bors's Joust-a-Thon, Ride the Dragon, Table-Go-
    Round,
Battle of Badon Theatre (film produced by ITV),
Duck Sir Kay for Charity, three balls fifty pence,
Ceridwen's Happy Cauldron Restaurant, Elayne's Hot Tubs,
Something with Robin Hood, whoever he was,
Pennons a-snap from Merlin's Tower,

(The Wizard, whose place was the forest, chuckles at that),
The Green Chapel Duel, every hour on the hour,
And wouldn't the folks turn pale if they knew the truth.
There are stones in a ring. Everyone loves hanging stones,
So much that the Ministry has middle-range plans
To reconstruct Stonehenge in the same resin as these,
Then alter the maps to hide the original.
A crude but effective ruse, thinks the Wizard,
Having done it himself when the Romans passed through.
As Camelot, it's woeful, as a vision of Camelot, not bad:
There are too many peacocks, not enough geese, not nearly
    enough dogs,
(And no vermin at all, but they really aren't missed)
The lutenists are okay, but the mimes are right out.
But crass, cheap, calculated as it all may be, this is magic,
This is what magic is: shaping things to fit the vision.

Child and Wizard visit Arthur's Castle, which is full to the
    crenellations
With warlike hardware and dungeon accessories that never
    knew hate or pain,
Tapestries untouched by human hands,
220-volt cressets, flush privies, direct-dial pages,
A table shaped like you know what.
There's a twenty-minute wait to view the Grail,
With a printed disclaimer framed on the wall
That no medical or therapeutic benefits are claimed or should
    be implied.
The British Medical Association is not mocked.
Another turn brings them to a crowded desk,
RESERVATIONS spelled out above it in Celtic half-uncial.
For an additional fee, chargeable to all major cards,
One can experience (not merely buy)
The Night at the Palace Adventure Package,
Including dinner and minstrelsy, costumes and pageantry,
(Lovely word, pageantry, wonder what it means?)
Double occupancy accomodation in a room with a four-poster
    (nudge nudge) bed,

And for a limited time only,
You will witness the surprise raid by Mordred's knights on
    Gwyn's bedchamber.
You will believe Lancelot can kill.
The Wizard hugs the Child. He cannot take this.
He was there (an Adeptus is everywhere) and—and he
    couldn't—
Damn Lerner and Loewe anyway.
The Child reminds him that this is magic, this is what magic
    is,
Vision sometimes too clear to be borne.

They go outside, Child leading Man, and they ride the
    Dragon.
It sweeps on rails, breathing acetylene fire,
Arching over the pavilions and wimpled towers and
    snackbars,
Suspended above the whole absurdity,
And then the Wizard laughs out loud:
This is exactly how he showed it to Arthur (they were geese
    then),
And the boy saw,
Understood with the casual epiphany of youth
That the only borders there are on the earth
Are those chanted into being by the fearful tribes,
Reinforced with bricks and spears;
A few miles up even those are invisible. This is magic,
This is what magic is, showing things as they might actually
    be.

They arrive, finally
(And there is nothing accidental in that Finally,
It has been guaranteed by the lines and arcs of the park's
    design,
The asymptote of a curve that begins with the Druid circles
    and peaks here)
At the Ever-Changing Seasonal Special Exhibits Pavilion:

Animated shepherds, robot magi, fiberglass mangerstraw and
    electric sheep.
Clockwork angels sing *gloria in excelsis*,
Gloria manifest in a tin plate bolted to the Childroid's head.
The gifts of the Three (who were sorcerers, not just Wise,
They were much more casual about it then)
Are wrapped in foily paper with neat shop bows.
The living Child is not revolted.
He knew when he drove the yuppies from the Temple
That they would only relocate on the Temple steps.
And he knows that this dumbshow, this parable of
    incorporations,
Is in one sense truly an attempt at veneration,
Conducted by people who have simply lost the power to
    venerate.
Minds and times slip (to when that power was only fading):
To a Solstice night when the Wizard stood in a cold wood,
Not far from the place this place thinks it is,
Where once they danced, in masks and horns, the Sun to life
    again.
The King never knew what took place on his grounds,
He was raised in the shade of a different tree,
Out of touch with those things, as a dweller by ocean
Who cannot swim.
Arthur thought the birthday was the Child's (it was Mithras's)
That the halo was pure glory (it was the Unconquered Sun)
That the gifts came from the East (and not Saturnal)
The carols liturgical (they were sung round the stones)
Didn't know that the Cup his knights sought was once
    Ceridwen's,
Though several of them could have told him so.
The Wizard asks the Child if He is pleased with His gifts,
The Child nods, accepting, comprehending,
(As men do not) the magnitude of the offering.
The Wizard kept Arthur from the old world
That he might draw the sword and bring the new. So with all
    of them,
Mithras, Magi, pagans, prophets,

Giving the best they had to a world
That would go on without them.
Zealots burn what they would deny,
Reformers destroy what they must deny,
But the Child (who gave Himself) knows no jealousy. This is
      magic,
This is what magic is:
To alter the perception of the world,
To bring it in accordance with the will.

It is full night now, the park closing, though it still,
Throws up enough light to be seen clear across Broceliande,
And probably by any magi who care to look,
(Though most of them now watch by radio or infrared,
The gold of their gifts a data plaque on a long-duration
      probe).
The Wizard looks up at the pink-shot clouds,
Moves his hand, says a word, and the sky sifts snow.
Water spell, air and a wish, scarcely a novice's trick:
This is Britain, after all.
He takes the Child's hand once more, and they drift toward
      the gates,
Out through the crowd enchanted by light and snow.
The Wizard shoulders the Child, as in that other carol,
And before they return into night and Time,
They watch the flickering hearts around them,
Knowing:
Though most will go home clutching ad-copy mystery,
Synthesized chivalry,
Low-resolution faith,
Some few will follow the star for themselves,
Some few will quest for the Grail for themselves,
And from them, true wonder will radiate,
Light to the many.
This is the way it has always been.
This is magic.
This is what magic is.

Not a creature was stirring, except ...

THE NEW
FATHER CHRISTMAS
Brian W. Aldiss

LITTLE OLD ROBERTA took the clock down off the shelf and put it on the Hotpoint; then she picked up the kettle and tried to wind it. The clock was almost on the boil before she realised what she had done. Shrieking quietly, so as not to wake old Robin, she snatched up the clock with a duster and dropped it onto the table. It ticked furiously. She looked at it.

Although Roberta wound the clock every morning when she got up, she had neglected to look at it for months. Now she looked and saw it was 7.30 on Christmas Day, 2388.

"Oh dear," she exclaimed. "It's Christmas Day already! It seems to have come very soon after Lent this year."

She had not even realised it was 2388. She and Robin had lived in the factory so long. The idea of Christmas excited her, for she liked surprises—but it also frightened her, because she thought about the New Father Christmas and that was something she preferred not to think about. The New Father Christmas was reputed to make his rounds on Christmas morning.

"I must tell Robin," she said. But poor Robin had been

very touchy lately; it was conceivable that having Christmas suddenly forced upon him would make him cross. Roberta was unable to keep anything to herself, so she would have to go down and tell the tramps. Apart from Robin, there were only the tramps.

Putting the kettle on to the stove, she left her living-quarters and went into the factory, like a little mouse emerging from its mincepie-smelling nest. Roberta and Robin lived right at the top of the factory and the tramps had their illegal home right at the bottom. Roberta began tiptoeing down many, many steel stairs.

The factory was full of the sort of sounds Robin called "silent noise." It continued day and night, and the two humans had long ago ceased to hear it; it would continue when they had become incapable of hearing anything. This morning, the machines were as busy as ever, and looked not at all Christmassy. Roberta noticed in particular the two machines she hated most: the one with loomlike movements which packed impossibly thin wire into impossibly small boxes, and the one which threshed about as if it were struggling with an invisble enemy and did not seem to be producing anything.

The old lady walked delicately past them and down into the basement. She came to a grey door and knocked at it. At once she heard the three tramps fling themselves against the inside of the door and press against it, shouting hoarsely across to each other.

Roberta was unable to shout, but she waited until they were silent and then called through the door as loudly as she could, "It's only me, boys."

After a moment's hush, the door opened a crack. Then it opened wide. Three seedy figures stood there, their faces anguished: Jerry, the ex-writer, and Tony and Dusty, who had never been and never would be anything but tramps. Jerry, the youngest, was forty, and so still had half his life to drowse through, Tony was fifty-five and Dusty had sweat rash.

"We thought you was the Terrible Sweeper!" Tony exclaimed.

The Terrible Sweeper swept right through the factory every morning. Every morning, the tramps had to barricade themselves in their room, or the sweeper would have bundled them and all their tawdry belongings into the disposal chutes.

"You'd better come in," Jerry said. "Excuse the muddle."

Roberta entered and sat down on a crate, tired after her journey. The tramps' room made her uneasy, for she suspected them of bringing Women in here occasionally; also, there were pants hanging in one corner.

"I had something to tell you all," she said. They waited politely, expectantly. Jerry cleaned out his nails with a tack.

"I've forgotten just now what it is," she confessed.

The tramps sighed noisily with relief. They feared anything which threatened to disturb their tranquility. Tony became communicative.

"It's Christmas Day," he said, looking round furtively.

"Is it really!" Roberta exclaimed. "So soon after Lent?"

"Allow us," Jerry said, "to wish you a safe Christmas and a persecution-free New Year."

This courtesy brought Roberta's latent fears to the surface at once.

"You—you don't believe in the New Father Christmas, do you?" she asked them. They made no answer, but Dusty's face went the colour of lemon peel and she knew they did believe. So did she.

"You'd better all come up to the flat and celebrate this happy day," Roberta said. "After all, there's safety in numbers."

"I can't go through the factory: the machines bring on my sweat rash," Dusty said, "It's a sort of allergy."

"Nevertheless, we will go," Jerry said. "Never pass a kind offer by."

Like heavy mice, the four of them crept up the stairs and through the engrossed factory. The machines pretended to ignore them.

In the flat, they found pandemonium loose. The kettle was boiling over and Robin was squeaking for help. Officially bed-ridden, Robin could get up in times of crisis; he stood now just inside the bedroom door, and Roberta had to remove the kettle before going to placate him.

"And why have you brought those creatures up here?" he demanded in a loud whisper.

"Because they are our friends, Robin," Roberta said, struggling to get him back to bed.

"They are no friends of mine!" he said. He thought of something really terrible to say to her; he trembled and wrestled with it and did not say it. The effort left him weak and irritable. How he loathed being in her power! As caretaker of the vast factory, it was his duty to see that no undesirables entered, but as matters were at present he could not evict the tramps while his wife took their part. Life really was exasperating.

"We came to wish you a safe Christmas, Mr. Proctor," Jerry said, sliding into the bedroom with his two companions.

"Christmas, and I got sweat rash!" Dusty said.

"It isn't Christmas," Robin whined as Roberta pushed his feet under the sheets. "You're just saying it to annoy me." If they could only know or guess the anger that stormed like illness through his veins.

At that moment, the delivery chute pinged and an envelope catapulted into the room. Robin took it from Roberta, opening it with trembling hands. Inside was a Christmas card from the Minister of Automatic Factories.

"This proves there are other people still alive in the world," Robin said. These other fools were not important enough to receive Christmas cards.

His wife peered short-sightedly at the Minister's signature.

"This is done by a rubber stamp, Robin," she said. "It doesn't prove anything."

Now he was really enraged. To be contradicted in front of these scum! And Roberta's cheeks had grown more wrinkled since last Christmas, which also annoyed him. As he was about to flay her, however, his glance fell on the address on the envelope; it read, *"Robin Proctor, A.F.X10."*

"But this factory isn't X10!" he protested aloud. "It's SC541."

"Perhaps we've been in the wrong factory for thirty-five years," Roberta said. "Does it matter at all?"

The question was so senseless that the old man pulled the bedclothes out of the bottom of the bed.

"Well, go and find out, you silly old woman!" he shrieked. "The factory number is engraved over the output exit. Go and see what it says. If it does not say SC541, we must leave here at once. Quickly!"

"I'll come with you," Jerry told the old lady.

"You'll all go with her," Robin said. "I'm not having you stay here with me. You'd murder me in my bed!"

Without any particular surprise—although Tony glanced regretfully at the empty teapot as he passed it—they found themselves again in the pregnant layers of factory, making their way down to the output exit. Here, conveyor belts transported the factory's finished product outside to waiting vehicles.

"I don't like it much here," Roberta said uneasily. "Even a glimpse of outside aggravates my agoraphobia."

Nevertheless, she looked where Robin had instructed her. Above the exit, a sign said "X10."

"Robin will never believe me when I tell him," she wailed.

"My guess is that the factory changed its own name," Jerry said calmly. "Probably it has changed its product as well. After all, there's nobody in control; it can do what it likes. Has it always been making these eggs?"

They stared silently at the endless, moving line of steel eggs. The eggs were smooth and as big as ostrich eggs; they sailed into the open, where robots piled them into vans and drove away with them.

"Never heard of a factory laying eggs before," Dusty laughed, scratching his shoulder. "Now we'd better get back before the Terrible Sweeper catches up with us."

Slowly they made their way back up the many, many steps.

"I think it used to be television sets the factory made," Roberta said once.

"If there are no more men—there'd be no more need for television sets," Jerry said grimly.

"I can't remember for sure. . . ."

Robin, when they told him, was ill with irritation, rolling out of bed in his wrath. He threatened to go down and look at the name of the factory himself, only refraining because he had a private theory that the factory itself was merely one of Roberta's hallucinations.

"And as for *eggs* . . ." he stuttered.

Jerry dipped into a torn pocket, produced one of the eggs, and laid it on the floor. In the silence that followed, they could all hear the egg ticking.

"You didn't oughta done that, Jerry," Dusty said hoarsely. "That's . . . interfering." They all stared at Jerry, the more frightened because they did not entirely know what they were frightened about.

"I brought it because I thought the factory ought to give us a Christmas present," Jerry told them dreamily, squatting down to look at the egg. "You see, a long time ago, before the machines declared all writers like me redundant, I met an old robot writer. And this old robot writer had been put out to scrap, but he told me a thing or two. And he told me that as machines took over man's duties, so they took over his myths too. Of course, they adapt the myths to their own beliefs, but I think they'd like the idea of handing out Christmas presents."

Dusty gave Jerry a kick which sent him sprawling.

"That's for your idea!" he said. "You're mad, Jerry boy! The machine'll come up here to get that egg back. I don't know what we ought to do."

"I'll put the tea on for some kettle," Roberta said brightly.

The stupid remark made Robin explode.

"Take the egg back, all of you!" he shrieked. "It's stealing, that's what it is, and I won't be responsible. And then you tramps must leave the factory!"

Dusty and Tony looked at him helplessly, and Tony said, "But we got nowhere to go."

Jerry, who had made himself comfortable on the floor, said without looking up, "I don't want to frighten you, but the New Father Christmas will come for you, Mr. Proctor, if you aren't careful. That old Christmas myth was one of the ones the machines took over and changed; the New Father Christmas is all metal and glass, and instead of leaving new toys he takes away old people and machines."

Roberta, listening at the door, went as white as a sheet. "Perhaps that's how the world has grown so depopulated recently," she said. "I'd better get us some tea."

Robin had managed to shuffle out of bed, a ghastly irritation goading him on. As he staggered towards Jerry, the egg hatched.

It broke cleanly into two halves, revealing a pack of neat machinery. Four tiny, busy mannikins jumped out and leapt into action. In no time, using minute welders, they had forged the shell into a double dome; sounds of hammering came from underneath.

"They're going to build another factory right in here, the saucy things!" Roberta exclaimed. She brought the kettle crashing down on the dome and failed even to dent it. At once a thin chirp filled the room.

"My heavens, they are wirelessing for help!" Jerry exclaimed. "We've got to get out of here at once!"

They got out, Robin twittering with rage, and the New Father Christmas caught them all on the stairs.

The future brings new gifts at Christmas.

STARS OVER
SANTA CLAUS
William Morrison

HURLEY PAUSED IN his shaving and asked almost casually, as if it didn't matter to him in the least, "Anything materialize in the past half hour?"

"Only this, sir," said Alfven respectfully, and held up a feathery body for him to see. By the light of the blue sun overhead it was a ghastly sight.

"What in space is that?"

"It started out as a turkey, Captain Hurley. They thought it would make a nice gift for the season. But the head and one wing were lost, and the body was twisted in transit, and it doesn't look so appetizing. All the same, it's still edible—I think."

"If you think so, you'll have a chance to eat it," grunted Hurley. "Or else feed it to the Domes. Those creatures will swallow anything. By the way, you haven't been using my blowtorch, have you?"

"I always shave with my own."

Hurley rubbed his face thoughtfully. "This one feels a little hot. By Pluto, that's the last straw. When men a hundred light years from home start sneaking in the use of their captain's blowtorch, and don't have the common decency to tell him they need another, an expedition's really demoralized."

"Shall I have them materialize a replacement for you, sir?"

"This one's still good enough to use. Just doesn't keep to the right wavelength and give a cool enough shave anymore. And I think we have better work for our materializer to do."

"Frankly, I think so too, Captain."

Hurley gave him a sour look. "Then why make a fool suggestion like the one for a replacement? Trying to please me? Alfven, you're a good kid, but you've been spoiled by that blasted Politeness course they give nowadays. Respect your captain and obey his orders—I go along with that. But only up to a certain point. Only up to the point where you still treat him as a human being, and not as a tin god. The trouble with you, sonny boy, is that you respect me too much."

"Yes, sir," said Alfven respectfully.

Hurley snorted. "I should have taken my wife along. Regulations or no regulations, I should have brought Clara with me. She'd have put an end to this confounded formality around here."

"I hear that Mrs. Hurley has great talents along that line, sir."

"You've heard right. Too bad she was tied up taking care of a sick kid. She's a lot better captain than I am. She's the best captain I ever heard of, bar none."

So even the captain was homesick. Alfven kept a discreet silence. He was younger than anyone had a right to be on an expedition of this kind, a mere twenty-five, and he looked practically infantile. His face was so pink and smooth that sometimes Hurley wondered whether he really used his blowtorch to shave or just pretended to. But it wasn't his youth that Hurley held against him. It was, as he said, that blasted Politeness, which was drilled into them in school, and served as a barrier against laxness of all kinds.

It was an old tradition, and even young Alfven admitted secretly that it was a stupid one. Back in the old days, it had been customary to dress for dinner in the fever-infested jungles of both Earth and Venus, to shave every day, and to maintain a pose of all-powerful majesty, both in order to awe supposedly inferior peoples and to keep a grip on a possibly rebellious crew. But the supposed inferiors had taken the absurdly formal behavior as a sign of insanity more than anything else, and the old crews had bitterly resented the airs that their captains gave themselves. The old tradition had not exactly been a success.

So it had been modified. Part of it, the old custom of shaving every day, had been kept. Now, of course, instead of sharp-edged razors, they used tiny induction heaters, tuned to the proper frequency for human hair. These efficient little gadgets, popularly known as blowtorches, burned the beard off a face smoothly and coolly, leaving it with a faint non-irritating tan. The part of the tradition that had to do with formal dress, on the other hand, had been discarded as too inconvenient. And the relationship of captain to crew had been changed. No longer was it one of master and near-slave. Now it was more like that of a group of gentlemen, among whom one happened to be First among Equals.

According to regulations, the captain no longer gave orders, he merely addressed Requests. But on trips too far from home, some of the older captains, like Hurley, had a tendency to forget themselves and, especially in emergencies, to tell their men what to do. Once in a while they might even curse mildly. But not much. They too had been subjected to a course in Politeness during their refresher training periods, and they couldn't quite break the shackles.

Alfven turned to his materializer, which had begun to work again, and made a slight adjustment of the tuning dial. He himself had begun to realize the disadvantages of the official Politeness some months back. It set a wall between officer and men, prevented them from sharing their hopes and fears. The intensity of Hurley's feelings had led him to talk of his wife, Clara. But Alfven felt slightly embarrassed as he listened, and he showed no inclination to encourage further discussion of the lady on Hurley's part.

Yes, the old reticences persisted, despite what they had gone through together. And they had gone through plenty. They had swept through a hundred light years of stellar space, they had narrowly by-passed a dark high-frequency emitting star, and they had finally come to rest on this bare and rocky planet in a crash landing that had killed half of their crew.

Fortunately, they had saved most of their instruments, particularly the materializers. It was these alone that permitted them to survive. It was too bad that the apparatus didn't work as well as it should have.

Another battered turkey was materializing, and Alfven looked at it in amused disgust. The intentions of Contact back home were undoubtedly good. But Contact's intelligence was nothing to brag about. It might better have used the apparatus to transmit more spare parts.

Rayton came in, a tired old man of thirty-five, stared at the turkey, and wonder of wonders, recognized what it was. "Why send us that?" he said in amazement. "We have enough to eat."

"Contact is being thoughtful. Christmas is coming."

"Pluto, you're right. Another month, isn't it?"

"Twenty-nine days."

"I wonder if we'll last that long."

"Of course we will. We're going to set up a colony here."

Rayton laughed, somewhat bitterly. "We're setting up a cemetery. Do you know how many men we've got left unhurt? Ten. At the present rate, they won't last another two weeks. Why don't they send us more weapons?"

"They can't. As you know, the materializer doesn't work right."

"Is it the distance? I thought there was supposed to be no trouble up to a thousand light years."

"There usually isn't. But in our case there are interfering stresses in the transit path. The transmitting waves are distorted most of the time, and the major part of what they send us is ruined. The result is that Contact has to use at least half our transmission time merely to send repair parts for the purpose of keeping the materializer in working condition. And it spends most of the other time sending indispensable supplies. Weapons are in last place."

"And half of them, when they do come over, are useless. Frankly, Alfven, I think that this new-fangled method of establishing an advanced base and sending supplies by means of materializers is stupid. Space ships may be slower, but they're sure."

"Accidents happen to space ships too. And materializers do work most of the time. We happen to have picked a planet in a bad part of space."

Rayton looked at him as if it were the fault of his youth and inexperience that the apparatus didn't work. "Have you tried using different sorts of equipment?"

Alfven nodded. "I've tried all the standard circuits. And I've varied the size of the materializer, using parts they managed to get to me. Big ones are even worse. I'm working now on a small model that I hope will be less subject to distortion."

"Send a letter to Santa Claus," said Rayton cynically, "and maybe he'll tell you what to do."

"It won't exactly be a Merry Christmas," admitted Alfven. "But I think that we'll be able to stick it out."

"If your mind can't turn out anything more brilliant than that, you'd better stop thinking," snarled Rayton, forgetting his own course in Politeness. "Personally, I can think of nothing better than to be out of here."

"The Domes make you nervous?"

"They certainly do. They keep reminding me of those imaginative pictures of men of the future—great brain-packed skulls, with wonderful minds that can probe yours at a glance. It doesn't do any good to tell myself that appearances are deceiving, that their heads are packed not with brains, but with complicated digestive organs, and that there's hardly a thought in a carload. They just make me feel uneasy."

"I sometimes feel the same way. I suppose we'd both get over it if we understood what made them tick."

"Not much chance of that," said Rayton. "If we had a

psych expert as good as Franelli . . . But there's no use wishing. I could write a letter to Santa Claus too, asking him to cure Franelli, but I'm afraid it wouldn't do much good."

"Yes, it's too bad that he was so badly hurt in the crash."

"Which brings up another thing," Rayton went on. "Our injured are never going to get well here. Either we haven't got the proper means of treatment, or there's something in the air that prevents cure."

"It's the captured Domes," said Alfven thoughtfully. "Our men can see them across a partition, and the sight isn't reassuring. The creatures sit there motionless, and our invalids wonder what's going on in those impressive heads. We should get rid of them."

"We ought to blast them."

"We can't do that. The other Domes would hear of it and probably launch an all-out attack."

"That's just a guess."

"We can't take a chance. We'll have to find another way to handle them."

"Let them go free," suggested Rayton.

"After they've had a chance to fight against us, and have acquired a taste for it?"

Rayton gritted his teeth and stared at the materializer, where another turkey was slowly making its appearance, this one stripped of its feathers.

"Look at that, will you. We face insoluble problems on all sides—and they send us mangled turkeys."

"They try," said Alfven defensively. "Their intentions are good."

"Intentions, my eye. Is the communicator working without distortion?"

"Perfectly."

"Then send Contact a message from me, personally. I'll tell you what to say."

"Whatever you wish. Within the limits of Politeness, of course."

Rayton made a disrespectful comment about Politeness,

and turned away. Young Alfven sighed. The man was obviously badly demoralized. He wondered if it were Rayton who had used the captain's blowtorch.

While waiting for the next object to materialize—fortunately, it was a spare part for the materializer itself, and not another turkey—Alfven thought of that letter to Santa Claus, alias Home Contact. In a way, he would have to send one, for Contact would certainly expect a message of thanks and good wishes for its thoughtfulness in sending the turkeys. Politeness called for at least that.

He considered, too, the things he would ask for, the things the expedition needed if they were to live to eat those turkeys. They could all have been accommodated within the confines of a single space ship. A wife for Captain Hurley, new materializer supplies with innumerable spare parts, weapons, doctors, psych experts, and possibly one or two other specialists. And on the trip home, the ship would take back the sick and wounded, the captured Domes, and the demoralized. That wouldn't leave much of an expedition, but at least it would leave a happier one.

From outside came the hoarse and impolite call, "Alfven!"

"Yes, Captain?"

"Get out of your cell fast and give us a hand. We need you."

It was the first time he had been called from his important station at the materializer to assist in repelling the Domes. It made him realize exactly how serious the situation was. He set the instruments for automatic control, hoping that the tuning wouldn't shift, and hurried out.

In front of the expedition's camp, set at the top of a high hill, a long thin line of Domes advanced. They looked slow and topheavy, but they were quick to utilize every bit of cover on the steep slope, and as they darted from behind one rock to the next, they let loose with their slingshots, sending an endless shower of small and medium-sized stones at the defenders. The latter hugged the ground, and tried to laugh off the occasional hit that couldn't be avoided.

"They're in large numbers this time, aren't they, sir?" said Alfven.

"It's the biggest crowd we've seen yet. That's why I needed you. Next thing you know, I'll be putting the injured in the ranks to help fight them off."

"Would it be worth while to increase the deadliness of our weapons?"

The captain shook his head. "From the point of view of putting them out of commission, it's just as good to wound them as to kill them. From the point of view of saving ammunition, it's better to keep our weapons at low potential, and shock instead of kill."

"Contact really could have supplied us with more effective weapons, sir."

"I don't know what Contact could have done," said Hurley wearily. "The more effective the weapons, and the more damage we do, the more they counter-attack, and the worse it is for us. We could have taken along atomics that would have enabled us to blast half the planet, but then the other half would have ganged up on us and wiped us out in no time. Our only hope is to fight them off without doing enough damage to get them angry. And we can't do that for too long."

"Yes, it's a difficult spot," agreed Alfven, and with his blaster caught a Dome sprinting from one rock to the next. The creature fell down rubbing its thin legs, waved its arms unhappily for a moment, and then subsided.

The Domes seemed to be putting on speed, as if determined to get them for good this time. Stones fell around them faster than ever, and here and there Alfven saw one of the defenders stepping up the power on his blaster, forgetting common sense in the desire for revenge, the desire to hurt as badly as their comrades were hurt. That too was a sign of demoralization, and it worried him.

Half an hour later, when the Domes had finally been beaten off, and teams went out to bring in the wounded as prisoners, Alfven returned to his materializer. Several more spare parts had arrived, one of them so badly twisted that it was useless, and another turkey was in process of solidification. He turned his eyes away from it, and thought of a name for the Polite idiots at Contact. Then, suddenly, a low humming noise came to his ears, so faint that at first he could hardly be sure he was hearing it.

He got up and turned down the corridor where the sick and wounded were cared for, whenever the camp was not under attack, and the defenders could spare them some attention. From the left, the imprisoned Domes glared at him from behind transparent sheets of thin neometal. At the right, a man was sitting up in bed, giving himself a shave.

"Hello, Dr. Franelli," said Alfven casually. "Feeling better?"

"I'm not sick." He spoke with the stubborn aggressiveness of a man who has received a severe blow on the head and never recovered.

"Glad to hear it. By the way, that's the captain's blowtorch. It's good to know that you can walk far enough to get it. Does the wavelength suit you?"

"Not quite. But a man has to shave. First rule of Politeness."

"Of course. Where's your own?"

"They tell me that the ship crashed. It disappeared then."

"Too bad. You know, the captain's been wondering who used his blowtorch. He's very touchy these days, too. Perhaps I'd better return it before he finds out that you've used it."

The sick man shook his head. "I like this one. I've decided to keep it."

"Come now, you know that's against all the rules of Politeness. You can't take away a man's personal property."

"A blowtorch isn't as personal as that. He can materialize another one for himself."

Alfven sighed. The man was a little out of his head or he wouldn't have acted that way, but there was no denying that from the point of view of common sense, he was right. All the same, the captain wouldn't like it. He might even try to remove his property from the sick man with polite force. The expedition had reached the point where tensions smoldered behind the Politeness, and even an incident as trivial as that could cause a blow-up.

"I'll tell him what you suggest," said Alfven. And then, for the first time, a warning yell came as a welcome relief. The Domes were attacking again, and he was needed to repel them.

This time, when he joined the defense line, he was not as lucky as before. A stone, descending in a swift parabola, caught him on the shoulder and left a bruise that would last for days. He felt a momentary impulse to step up the power of his own blaster and get the so-and-so who had hit him, but he resisted it. Later, however, when he felt how stiff his arm became, he was almost sorry he hadn't.

That night there was something new. Screaming awoke him, and he leaped from his soft plastic cot near the materializer, to find himself one of a dozen men rushing down the corridor. The invalids were awake too, and it took no more than a glance to see how frightened they were. They were staring through the transparent neometal at the Domes who were making the racket.

The noise died down, and Hurley said, "Now, what on earth—or on this blasted planet—set them off?"

"Might be a psychological attack to disturb our sleep," suggested Rayton.

"Don't be absurd, Rayton. They don't know that there is such a thing as psychology."

"I'm not being absurd, sir. And that's hardly Polite language."

"It may not be Polite, but it fits what you said. You talk like an idiot."

Rayton flushed. Alfven said hastily, "It sounded as if they were terrified, Captain."

"They were. Look at the tears rolling down their heads."

"But if their heads contain digestive organs, those may not be ordinary tears. They may be what we might call tears of laughter, and their howling might actually be laughing."

"Could be," admitted Hurley. "We can't tell without knowing what set them off. Anybody been down this corridor?"

No one answered. After a while Rayton said, "Perhaps they scented an attempt to rescue them."

"We haven't seen any signs of it outside. All right, men, let's get back to sleep and do some resting. Those of you on guard stay at your posts."

Alfven returned to his own cot, but he did not sleep. Something that had happened on the other side of the corridor had set off the Domes. And of all the invalids, only Franelli had shown enough energy to wander about. Also, Franelli had the captain's blowtorch, and a passion for using it.

He thought that over, then got up and went down the corridor again. Franelli was sitting up in bed, trying to give himself another shave, which he obviously didn't need. The thing was becoming an obsession with him, and Alfven pushed him back into place, turned on a sleeping ray, and took away the blowtorch.

There was no more screaming in the night, but when morning arrived, Alfven directed the captain's blowtorch at one of the Domes. A yell immediately burst forth from its lips, and its arms began to move convulsively. At the same time, the muscles around the lips began to quiver in the same way as when the creature scented food.

Hurley and others were running toward him. Alfven turned to meet them, saw the angry looks on their faces.

"I've learned what makes them scream, sir," he said hurriedly.

"I can hear that you have. What is it?"

"I found Franelli using your blaster yesterday. He's rather shaky, and did not adjust it properly. That's why it's a little out of tune. And sometimes he didn't direct it straight at his face. I think he managed to hit the Domes with a few accidental blasts. That's what set them to screaming."

"And the wave-lengths we use for shaving have an effect on the internal digestive organs in their heads?"

"That's what I think, sir."

"Pleasant or painful?"

"I think both, sir. They laugh and try to get away at the same time."

"That doesn't make sense."

"Perhaps not, sir. But have you ever been tickled, sir?"

Hurley said thoughtfully, "I see what you mean. What do you suggest, Alfven?"

"That we set our blowtorches for distance, Captain, and use them as mass weapons. They're not at all deadly, and they won't arouse the resentment of a whole planetful of Domes. But they should be very effective."

Later, he discovered that they were. Once a Dome had tasted the effect of a blowtorch, he wanted no more of it, and ran as fast as his slender legs would take him. For the first time in weeks, Hurley smiled.

"It's more blessed to give than to receive," he said. "Let's give it to them, boys."

Alfven's eyes narrowed thoughtfully in his boyish face. "You have an idea there, Captain Hurley."

"I should say I have. Look at them run!"

After that, the news spread, and the number of attackers fell off. On the fourth day, there were none at all. On the fifth, they lined up the captive Domes, gave them a good taste of vibrations, and sent them running wildly out into freedom.

From then on, Alfven was able to work at his materializer without the previous sense of impending doom. Now they were sure that they would live until Christmas—at least that most of them would live, and there was a good chance even for the more severely injured among the invalids.

Contact kept sending turkeys which it managed to squeeze into a crowded materialization schedule, and soon they had enough for two Christmas dinners. The one on Christmas Eve wasn't bad, but none the less, the celebration was rather tame. Contact had been inspired enough to try to send a couple of bottles of ethanolic stimulant, but these had broken in transit, and their contents spilled somewhere over a distance of a hundred light years.

The invalids remained with the expedition, almost as sick as before, while homesickness tore both at them and at the men who still managed to go about their duties. They had won a reprieve, but they were still doomed. It was the glummest holiday celebration that Alfven or the captain had ever known. Some of the men didn't even make a pretense that they had enjoyed it, and went to bed early. Alfven was the last one to remain up.

In the morning, Captain Hurley had what began as a dream. He dreamed that he was back on the farm where he had spent his childhood, and that he was being awakened by the crowing of a rooster. When he started up, the dream turned into a hallucination. The rooster was standing on his stomach, crowing right into his face.

He threw off the covers and the rooster with them, and was just about to lift himself from the pillow when a hearty voice roared in his ears.

"Get out of bed, you pot-bellied spacewart, before I dump you out! A fine sample of a ship captain you are!"

Hurley leaped, hit the floor, and bounced forward. "Clara!"

"It's me, all right," said Mrs. Hurley, as he grabbed her and gave her a squeeze that would have cracked the bones of any other woman. "But I've taken a look at that sheepish hangdog face of yours, and by Pluto, I wonder if what I see is my husband."

"I'll prove my identity," beamed Hurley. "You can take my fingerprints. . . . So they finally sent a space ship."

"Space ship, your foot," said Clara, speaking with all the freedom of a skipper who had never taken a course in Politeness. "That young fellow you've got working for you brought me over a lot quicker than that."

Hurley turned toward the doorway and saw Alfven standing there, smiling, but obviously tired and sleepy. "That's right, sir," agreed Alfven. "I used the materializer."

Captain Hurley blanched. "But I saw what happened to those turkeys! And they were dead to start with, Clara, you might have—you're strong, but you might have been twisted into—"

❆   ❆   ❆

No danger, sir," said Alfven. "I wouldn't take the chance of getting you angry by killing your wife. I made perfectly sure it would be safe before asking Contact to get in touch with Mrs. Hurley and see if she'd want to be transported here."

"You worked on it all last night?"

"Last night was merely the climax, sir. I've been working at improving the materializer for almost a month now—ever since you made that remark about it being more blessed to give than to receive."

"I made that remark?"

"It was when we gave the Domes a touch of our blow-torches. And then it suddenly struck me that was what was wrong with our materializers. We received, but we didn't give."

"Am I stupid, or is it just that you don't know how to explain things?"

Clara laughed uproariously. "Why don't you come right out and admit it, son? You think we're all stupid."

"Not all, ma'am. It's simply that you lack scientific training. You see, when we were merely receiving, there was a one-way transmission of a high material-current density through space. Slight distortions mounted up and badly twisted everything from turkeys to spare parts. But when we gave things back to Contact, we sent a strong material-current in the other direction. In other words, we balanced a strong positive current with a strong negative one."

"I get it. When Contact sent you a new part, you returned an old one at the same time. You worked the materialization both ways."

"Exactly, sir. First I built up a return materializer with special parts I asked Contact to send, and then I started experimenting. I had a little trouble the first two weeks, but then things began to work well."

"It was almost like transforming the bad part at this end into a good one, and the good part at Contact into a bad one," Hurley said.

"A little oversimplified, sir, but the general idea is correct. After I had acquired some experience with inanimate objects, I went on to small animate ones. Several of our turkeys came over alive."

"I didn't know that."

"I meant it to be a surprise, sir, and refrigerated them as soon as they arrived. Last night, however, when I knew that things were working perfectly, I started to materialize things in earnest. First I brought over that rooster, merely as a test run, to be sure that my apparatus was in perfect order. I shipped a specimen of native fauna back to balance. When I saw that things were going well, I had Contact materialize Mrs. Hurley."

"He sent an invalid back to balance me," said Clara.

Alfven nodded. "We'll need psych experts, physicians, and possibly other assistants. We can send the most badly injured back to balance them. And for those men who are going to remain here, we can bring their wives over too."

"Son," said Captain Hurley, "I thought at first that you were one of those impractical young squirts who know formulas and nothing else. I take that thought back. You're a genius."

Alfven didn't deny it. He merely blushed and said, "Thank you, sir."

"Young and foolish sometimes, but a genius none the less," said the captain. "You deserve a reward."

"No, sir, in this case I think that virtue, so to speak, is its own reward."

"You don't even want to go back for a vacation on Earth?"

"Not at all. From now on, Captain, I think I'm going to enjoy it here." And then, to the captain's surprise, a new face appeared in the doorway. It was a young girl, a *very* young girl in the captain's eyes, and a pretty one by his or any man's standards. She was flushing prettily as Alfven said, "This is Ellen, sir. Mrs. Hurley has already made her acquaintance."

"Huh?" exclaimed the captain brightly.

"They want to get married," said Clara. "You ought to be

able to understand that, you old space-bum. They've brought a license, and it'll be perfectly legal. Legal, but funny. They're going to have *you* perform the ceremony."

Hurley gulped. "Of course I'll do it. With pleasure. But I'm kind of overwhelmed, young fellow. I never suspected—"

"I don't like to talk about my own affairs, sir. Politeness rather forbids it. But you didn't think I could go on experimenting night after night and losing sleep without an incentive, did you, sir?"

"You've got one of the nicest incentives I've ever seen. But I'm surprised. I thought you just loved science—"

Clara nudged him, and he stopped. There was nothing scientific in the look young Alfven was giving his Incentive. And suddenly it struck Captain Hurley that a great many things were going to materialize on this planet, including a young generation that would get here without benefit of the ingenious apparatus that had brought his wife.

"We have a few things to talk over, my good man," Clara said. "Let's leave these young people alone."

"Thank you, ma'am," said Alfven respectfully. "I've already sent a message of thanks to Santa Claus—that is, Home Contact. And I've received a return message. It says simply, 'You're Welcome. Merry Christmas.' "

"That's the spirit. Merry Christmas!" said Hurley, and walked off with his gift.

Strange gifts arrive in the spirit of Christmas.

THE GIFTS
OF THE MAGISTRATE
Spider Robinson

"MERRY CHRISTMAS, MR. Chief Justice," the Captain of the Guard said; but his subsequent behavior scarcely reflected the holiday spirit.

Wolfgang Jannike submitted philosophically to the finger-printing, retina scan, and close body search which were his Christmas presents from his subordinate. Jannike could hardly protest an order he had written himself. Nor would any conceivable protest have made the slightest difference; all the human guards at this stronghold were—again, by his own direction—Gurkhas, the deadliest humans alive.

Scanners had shown him unarmed, and the ID signal broadcast by the chip in his skull had been confirmed as legitimate and valid, else he would not have lived to reach Captain Lal. But even after Jannike had been positively identified as the person described by that ID chip, and therefore as the Chief Justice of the Solar High Court—nominal master of this prison—Captain Lal remained vigilant.

That was understandable. Of the four assassins who had come here to date, two had gotten this far; one of them so recently that Jannike could still see the stains on the wall. That one, he knew, had been a friend of the Captain's.

"How may I help Your Honor?" Lal asked when the ritual was done.

"I will speak with the prisoner alone for a time," Jannike replied firmly. He was committed now; at least three microphones had recorded those words.

There was a long pause, during which Captain Lal's eyes made all the responses his lips dared not—even a Gurkha must sometimes tread cautiously—and at last his lips made the only reply they could. "Yes, sir."

"Have you ever read the works of Clement Samuels, Captain?" the Chief Justice was moved to ask then.

"No sir," Lal replied, doubtless baffled but showing nothing. He spun smartly in place and headed for the door, motioning to two of his men. They fell in behind Jannike in antiterrorist mode, one facing forward and one facing back, weapons out and ready. Somehow, he noted over his shoulder, they contrived to make it seem merely ceremonial. Then he faced forward and followed the Captain, to the cell which held the Vandal, the worst vandal of all time.

"Cell," it was in a legal and actual sense, but most of the humans alive in the Solar System in 2061 occupied meaner quarters. The Chief Justice himself owned slightly more cubic, and more flexible hedonics therein—but not by much. It was odd. The whole System was angry at the Vandal, murderously angry, but it seemed to be a kind of anger that precluded cruelty. The execution would be retribution, but not vengeance. Revenge was not possible, and the crime was so numbingly enormous and senseless that deterrence could have no meaning. Nonetheless society would do what it could to redress the balance.

The Vandal was in an odd and striking position, both legally and morally, and—Jannike saw as Captain Lal waved him into the cell—physically as well. Virtually all humans in free fall are uncomfortable if they can not align themselves with an arbitrary "up" and "down"; since the earliest days of spaceflight men have built rooms with an assumed local vertical, and the occupants have oriented themselves accordingly. This occupant was crouched upside down and tilted slightly leftward with respect to the Chief Justice, drifting slightly in the eddy of the airflow.

The prisoner was studying the display wall: the cell had a better computer and much greater data storage capacity than Jannike's own home. (On the other hand, Jannike's computer was plugged into the Net, could send and receive data; the prisoner's could only manipulate it. And Jannike's door unlocked from the inside. . . .) Most of the datawindows that were open on the wall displayed scrolling text or columns of changing figures, which must have been hard to read upside down. So the Vandal's attention must have been chiefly devoted to the central and largest window, which showed a detailed three-dimensional model of the Solar System as seen from above the plane of the ecliptic.

She rotated slowly to face Jannike. Recognizing him, she starfished her body until it precessed around to his local vertical, a polite gesture that touched him. "Clear sky, Chief Justice," she said.

"And delta vee to you, Citizen," he responded automatically.

Behind him, Captain Lal made a frown Jannike could actually hear, over the muffled pounding in his own ears, and left them alone; there was an audible click just after the door had irised shut.

Vonda McLisle (ironic that her name should look and sound so much like the word Vandal) almost smiled at her judge. "May I offer you refreshment?"

"I'd be pleased to share tobacco with you."

Her eyebrows rose. "You're a user, too?"

Automatically he gave his stock reply. "It gives solace. And costs hours of life, but I don't expect to run short."

"And I won't live long enough to pay the bill," she agreed. He winced. She struck two cigarettes and floated one toward him; a bearing hummed as the room turned up its airflow to compensate. "Have you come to deliver a hangman's apology?"

"No." He picked his cigarette out of the air and took a deep drag. "It is Christmas Eve on Terra. I've brought you three gifts."

"But we don't even know each other."

"On the contrary, we've slept together for weeks."

"I beg your pardon?"

"You and I have both dozed through most of the trial so far, like most of those who've watched it. You're very good, but one of your eyelids flutters when you're deep under."

Again she nearly smiled. "With you it's the nostrils. You're right: as the old joke goes, it's been the equivalent of a formal introduction. But I'm afraid I have nothing to give you in return."

"I think you are wrong."

She pursed her lips quizzically. "Why would you want to give me presents, if deciding whether I live or die isn't enough to keep you awake?"

"Oh, it does keep me awake, Ms. McLisle—at night. But why *not* sleep through the trial itself? It's merely the formal public recitation of facts we both know already, that *everyone* knows already. You nap because my court has nothing to say to you. I nap because you have something to say to me, and will not."

She let smoke drift from her mouth, hiding her face. "The trial told you everything you need to know. The prosecution's case was exhaustive."

"But the defense stood mute. I am so constructed that I cannot condemn a woman to death without knowing the motive for her crime. Even if I cannot understand it, I must know what it is, what she at least conceives it to be."

"I will not tell you my motive."

"You do not have to."

She nodded, taking his statement only at face value, and he let her. "That's right, and I don't want to. So if that's the gift you wanted, I'm afraid—"

"Not at all. The gift I want is a much smaller thing. But before we get to that, here is the first of my gifts." He took an item from a pocket and sent it to her.

Her eyes widened when she recognized the gift.

"A modem! I can find out *what's going on*, get the latest figures, find out how bad I—" Her voice trailed off as she turned it over in her hands, tracing its design with sure slender fingers. She looked up at him, and the raw gratitude in her eyes seared his heart. "Have you ever been cut off from the Net? Thank you, *Herr* Jannike."

"You are welcome, Ms. McLisle."

"Vonda."

"Wolf. My second gift, Vonda, may seem disappointing; I ask that you wait until it is completely unwrapped before judging. It is a short speech, entitled, 'How I Spent My Christmas Vacation.' "

She must have been desperately eager to interface her first gift with her computer, but she made herself display polite interest. It faded fast.

"The holiday season was a perfect excuse for a short recess, and I needed one. What you did was perfectly clear and indisputable. You misappropriated the *Tom Swift*, the electrical drive unit your firm owns. Abrogating your contract with Systel S.A., you abandoned their o'neill in mid-deceleration, leaving several thousand colonists in an orbit that caused them to overshoot the Asteroid Belt by a wide margin. You used the *Tom Swift*'s enormous delta vee to intercept Halley's Comet, beyond the orbit of Mars. And then you stole the comet, and threw it away.

"Clear, indisputable—and inexplicable. The experts say you're sane. Your record is admirable. Yet you endangered thousands of innocents, and committed the greatest act of vandalism ever. The Comet that led William to Hastings in 1066 and appears in the Bayeux Tapestry, that inspired Newton to write the *Principia*, the greatest scientific book ever, that inspired the first cooperative international space expedition in human history—kicked out of the ecliptic for good, never again to be seen in the sky of Terra after two millenia of faithful punctuality.

"I *had* to know why. I had to understand you, to imagine

why you might do the inexplicable. So I went to your apartment."

The modem floated unheeded a meter from her hand. There was no other indication that she was still listening to him; her gaze had drifted away and her body was starting to do the same.

"A thousand reporters must have swarmed over that place, but none did what I did. I sat in it, for two entire days. I was trying to become you.

"I noticed the books at once; I share your fetish. Actual books, bound hardcopy on acid-free paper. Naturally I was not surprised to find the complete works of Clement Samuels. He is surely the greatest writer still using that old-fashioned medium, and has millions of subscribers, myself among them. I *was* surprised to find the complete works of Mark Twain. Even though Samuels makes no secret of his debt to his palindromic namesake, few of his readers bother to go back to the source any more."

"Of all the arts," she said softly, "humor travels worst through time."

"I sat there for hours," he went on, "thinking of odd things. The comet, of course. Tom Sawyer. The food riots in New York. Clement Samuels, inexplicably wasting away in his seventies, when most citizens expect to see their hundredth birthday. The way the chief prosecutor sprays spittle when he's especially angry. The color of . . . no matter.

"I felt awful, inexpressibly sad. Samuel's work has always consoled me—but I've memorized everything he wrote, and I couldn't think of one I wanted to reread. So I took a Twain at random from your shelves.

"The first thing I noticed was the letter that acted as a bookmark. I read it without hesitation when I saw the return address. I never knew you and Samuels were lovers; I don't know how the media missed it."

"It was very brief," she whispered, "and a long time ago. His marriage was too good to risk, and I had a career in space, where he cannot live."

"So I gathered. When I had digested the letter, I finally noticed the passage it marked—and everything fell into place at once."

She was looking at him again now, eyes tracking him as she drifted. "The last eighty years have brought more technological change than the previous two hundred," she said. "That implies an immense amount of pain, Mr. Chief Justice, as you know better than most. One of the things that got us through it, as a society, as a species, was the humor of Clem Samuels. It was gentle humor, humor with no cruelty in it, humor that didn't make you want to curl up and die with the hilarity of it all. Humor that helped you to go on, to endure, to enjoy. Maybe he didn't save us single handed, but we might not have made it without him. I know I wouldn't have; I wouldn't have kept on wanting to. A few hours of stolen passion fifty years ago had nothing to do with it."

"I know," The Chief Justice murmured.

"But he had to identify so damned strongly with Mark Twain. He rarely talked about it, but it tickled him to death that he'd been born at the beginning of 1986, with Halley's Comet at perihelion, just like Twain."

" 'Now the Almighty must have said, "Here are these two unaccountable freaks," ' Jannike quoted from memory. " 'They came in together, and so they must go out together.' And Twain died on schedule."

"So of course Samuels insisted that he'd go the same way. It was funny—when he was twenty-six."

"And a little pretentious," Jannike said, "so he never mentioned it in interviews. It's not in his authorized biography."

"And then it was 2061 and he was *dying* and nobody knew why," she burst out. *"I knew why!"*

"So you took the most powerful tug in space and hijacked Halley's Comet, flung it out of human space. And now Clement Samuels is said to be recovering. And every astronomer in the System wants a recording of your death-agonies, and the rest of the Federation just wants you gone."

She had been ready to die calmly; now she was white with fear. "You mustn't tell anyone, Wolf! *He mustn't know!*"

"That was my first question to myself: why would you

conceal your motive? I concluded that you did not want to damage Samuel's marriage by announcing what must have been his first and only infidelity.

"So then I wondered why you had come back, why you did not simply stay with the comet when you knew your life was finished. I decided it was to return the *Tom Swift*, so that the colonists of Systel 2 could be rescued and towed to their proper orbit."

She was calming down as she persuaded herself that he meant to keep her secret. "That's only part of it. I . . . things went out of control out there. I landed on the nucleus, put down the hoses, filled her tanks, lit the fusion torch—and all hell broke loose. The hydrogen I got from the nucleus was even dirtier than I expected, so the drive burned wrong, and the second ion tail I made interacted weirdly with the comet's own and gave me more thrust than I wanted, in an uncontrollable direction. I meant to see that the Comet never appeared in Terra's sky again, but I didn't mean to kick it out of the System completely. I had to cut loose, come back and get access to better computer power, and see if there wasn't any way to partially undo the damage. And you let me have this computer—but without the Net, without the precise up-to-the-minute observations of the entire System network, I didn't have the numbers to crunch."

"And because the rest of the System doesn't have your special empirical knowledge of what happens when you set a comet on fire, and is too angry to ask for it, any answers they get will be wrong," Jannike said. "That's why I brought you the modem. Please use it now."

She leaped to obey. It took her almost fifteen minutes to interface, access, download, integrate, and get a trial answer.

"There's a chance," she announced. "If I've understood and correctly described all the anomalies I witnessed—if there are no new anomalies waiting to be discovered—there's a chance to keep Halley in the system. But the window closes in a matter of days, and I wouldn't sell insurance to whoever goes. Oh, Wolf, see that they examine this data—make them send someone! She's so . . . she's so *beautiful* I nearly changed my mind. It made me crazy when I saw how badly I'd miscalculated. I hate to think of her alone out there in the cold dark. Make them send someone!"

"I will," he promised. "Vonda, I said I had three presents for you. May I give you the third now? It's a letter from a friend."

"Oh. Okay, tell me the code and I'll access it."

He shook his head. "No. The friend wanted you to have hard copy, for some reason." He passed it across, an old-fashioned letter in an actual envelope, and politely rotated himself to let her read it in privacy.

It read:

"My dear Vonda,

The bearer of this letter is more arrogant than you are, more arrogant even than myself, and that much arrogance takes my breath away. You were arrogant enough to maim the Solar System to suit yourself. I was arrogant enough to liken myself to Mark Twain, to think that the stars were placed in their courses to enhance the ego of Clement Samuels. Between us we cost mankind one of its favorite comets. But Wolf Jannike makes us look silly. He was arrogant enough to risk the destruction of two human beings and their marriage—and unlike us, he got away with it.

Did you really think you could anger or hurt my wife, by acting to extend my life with her? Yes, I am recovering, slowly but unmistakably, as you knew I would. Dorothy says she remembers you, always liked you, and wishes you to know that you are always welcome in our home.

Perhaps the purpose for your silence was to spare me the humiliation and guilt of knowing what destruction my folly inspired. I don't think I was meant to be spared that humiliation and guilt, Vonda; I think I needed it badly. I've been too successful for too long.

Now that—thanks to you!—I am no longer voodooing myself to death, I intend, in the words of the philosopher Callahan, to live forever or die in the attempt. I don't know if I will survive long enough to assuage my guilt, and I know I'll never live long enough to thank you for what you did, but I promise you I will live long enough to write a book about what you did, a book so funny and so sad that people will stop hating you and start laughing at me.

You took a comet the size of a city, and made it a City of Two Tails. That is a far, far better thing than I for one have ever done, and I'm damned if I'll see you lose your head over it.

Meanwhile, my wife and I thank you with all our hearts. There was never any danger of my forgetting you, Vonda my dear, and now I owe you my life. I'll try not to waste the balance of it.

> *Very truly yours,*
> *Clement Samuels*

Jannike knew when she was done digesting it, because she stopped crying and started trying to thank him. He interrupted her.

"I told you that I brought three gifts, Vonda McLisle," he said formally. "I've also brought you something else, which it would be inappropriate to call a gift. As your magistrate, I bring you your sentence. Are you ready to hear it?"

She shook her tears from her head like a horse tossing off flies, and nodded gravely. "Yes, Chief Justice."

"When Mr. Samuels's book is released and understood, I believe you will be considerably less unpopular than you are now. But that will take time. For now, there is only one sentence other than death which I feel the public might accept without rioting. Therefore I condemn you—"

—so this was what Scrooge felt like on Christmas morning!—

"—to fuel and refit the *Tom Swift* at once, and repair your

vandalism as completely and as soon as possible. Charge the
fuel to my personal account; I have reason to believe the System Federation will one day reimburse me. And may God
have affection for your soul, Vonda my friend."

And he got the gift he had wanted in return: the first smile
he had seen upon her face.

Salvation comes, around the world,
at Christmas.

Peace On Earth,
Good Will To Men
Rick Shelley

James August Solomon

The weather was as horrible as it can get in Chicago just days before Christmas. The sky was banded in a dozen ugly shades of gray. The wind that was officially clocked at twenty-seven miles per hour by the National Weather Service at O'Hare International topped forty miles per hour through the open-topped tunnels of the city's streets. The temperature hadn't climbed above twenty-five degrees in a week. Nighttime lows had been consistently below zero. There were patches of ice on streets and sidewalks. New snow was falling—blustery, hitting unprotected skin with the force of blasted sand. The only good thing about the weather was that it had driven the young toughs indoors. The streets were as safe as they ever got.

Jim Solomon got off the CTA bus on Halsted and walked the last dozen blocks home rather than pay for a transfer that would take him almost to his front door. As the wind started to penetrate his clothing, Jim tried to huddle deeper into his coat. The miserable weather accentuated his already depressed mood. A black Santa Claus next to a Salvation Army pot rang his bell perfunctorily, keeping his back to the wind. In the middle of the next block, a store door opened and a few bars of Christmas elevator music came wafting out before the door closed again. One of the elderly nuns who worked at the parish daycare center smiled and wished Jim a Merry Christmas. Jim had to force a polite response, and that was rare for him. But the nun, braving the cold, was too preoccupied to notice.

It was a long walk home in bitter weather for Jim. He didn't get any relief from the odd thought that yesterday had been the shortest day of the year, that every day would be a little longer than the one before now.

"Hey, bro! Got a smoke?"

Jim stopped to look at the boy who darted out from between two buildings. He looked maybe eleven or twelve years old, dressed even less warmly than Jim.

"Smokin's no good for you," Jim said, frowning.

"So what I got to look to?" the kid challenged.

It was too cold to stand there and lecture, even if Jim had been in the mood. He shook his head and said, "Forget it," then walked on. The kid shouted a few emotionless obscenities, then ducked back between the buildings, out of the wind, to wait for a more willing mark.

And what do I have to look forward to? Jim asked himself, mocking. *Some Christmas this is going to be.*

The cold made his face feel brittle, as if pieces of his dark brown skin might crack and fall off long before he reached the red brick house in the middle of a block of identical red brick houses. Home. Urban homesteading. Take an old house in a dilapidated, mostly abandoned neighborhood. Buy it from the city for a dollar. Agree to bring the house up to standard. Live in it. Work with other people who are out for similar bargains, get the neighborhood back on its feet. *The pride of home ownership*, that's what everybody talked about.

"Bills, nothing but bills," Jim muttered.

He climbed the five steps to the small front porch and door. Alice must have swept the new snow from the porch and steps within the last hour, Jim thought. There was barely a dusting of snow on the gray-painted wood. He shook his head while he fumbled at his keys with long fingers that were stiff and almost numb from the cold. When he got the door open, he went inside, stomping his feet on the papers in the little entryway to get rid of the snow he had brought in and to get his circulation going again. His toes tingled from the cold walk.

"That you, Jim?" Alice called from the kitchen.

"It's me," he said, too softly for her to hear, as he stripped off his coat and brushed snow from his hair. His ear hurt when he touched it. Louder, he said, "What were you doing outside sweeping the porch? You know you're not supposed to be doing stuff like that now."

They met in the hallway leading back to the kitchen.

"I was only out five minutes," Alice said. "I have to get a little air now and then, and it's dry snow, not heavy at all."

"You can't get sick now. The baby's due next week."

Alice tilted her head back, ready for a normal greeting kiss. Then she noticed how upset he looked.

"I'm fine, Jim, really. I didn't work hard at all."

He shook his head, almost violently. "It's not that, dear."

"What's wrong?" She reached up and touched his cold face.

"They're shutting down two lines at the factory. I'm the black foreman with the least seniority."

"Jim!"

"All right, I'm the foreman with the least seniority, black or white. What difference does it make? I'm still out of a job."

"When?" She grasped his arms.

"Today. I'm out of work right now." He put his arms around Alice and held her as tight as he dared with her so far along in her third pregnancy. "It couldn't have happened at a worse time."

"We'll manage," Alice said. "I can go back to my job as soon as the baby's three weeks old, and you'll find another job fast. Right after Christmas. You're good, Jim. You've got a good work record."

"Huh. This time of year, I'll be lucky to land a job bagging burgers at McDonalds. That won't pay enough to help. All the bills will eat through what we've got saved in a hurry."

"We'll manage," Alice repeated, more firmly. "You know that. If nothing else, we can get a home-equity loan to get through any rough spots."

Jim sighed. "Yeah, and get even deeper in debt. Where are the kids?"

"At my sister's. Rae will bring them home in time for supper."

"We're going to have to put off buying that car again."

"So we take the bus a while longer. That doesn't matter."

"And Christmas will be pretty lousy for the kids."

"Don't get so melodramatic. We've been buying their presents for two months now. And anyway, I've got a surprise for you.

"You win the lottery?"

"You know I don't play that. We got a big package in the mail today."

"Package? Who from?"

"I'm not sure. But it's really something. Come on. I've got it in the kitchen."

The package was large, eight inches high and two foot by three.

"What the hell is that?" Jim asked.

"A letter came with it," Alice said. She picked it off the table and handed it to Jim.

Merry Christmas,
We are delighted to present you with a free INSTANT CHRISTMAS KIT in order to help you celebrate this most joyous holiday. There is no charge. No salesman will call. No one will attempt to sell you anything. We only ask that you enjoy your INSTANT CHRISTMAS and pass the bonus pack on to someone close to you.

Complete instructions on how to activate your IN-STANT CHRISTMAS are on a separate sheet.

"This is crazy," Jim said, looking from the letter to the open package on the kitchen table.

"I know it sounds crazy, but there must be *something* to it," Alice said. She had the instruction sheet. "There's a large aluminum roaster pan—big enough for a twenty-five-pound turkey and then some, a smaller pan like for a sheet cake, five pounds of sugar, two quarts of motor oil, two smaller bags labeled simply *A* and *B*. According to the instructions, the only other ingredient is water."

"What's it supposed to do?" Jim poked suspiciously through the items.

"The big roaster pan is supposed to provide a full Christmas dinner for six people. The other pan is supposed to provide 'Christmas surprises,' also for six people."

"This has to be somebody's idea of a sick joke," Jim said.

"Well, we've got nothing to lose by trying it," Alice told him.

Suzette Ann Carrera

"The Red Sea really does look as brilliant as it does in those pictures from space," Suzy Carrera said. This wasn't her first time across the Red Sea by airplane, but she had her face almost against the tiny window on the side of the military transport. Travel by air didn't normally impress her, but this one route, over terrain shown from space so often, was different.

"What, you thought they faked all those shots?" Jeff Senna asked. Jeff was a new volunteer on the project, a college student taking a year off from his studies. In the week Suzy had known him, Jeff had seemed unwilling to take anything very seriously.

If you can get through the next twenty-four hours and still be like that, you're not even human, Suzy thought, glancing at him briefly. Jeff Senna dwarfed her, and Suzy was no small woman at five feet, ten inches.

"We're coming up to the Ethiopian coast now," the pilot said over the PA system. "If we're going to run into any trouble, it will probably be in the next few minutes."

"Hey, I thought this flight was cleared," Jeff said.

"It has been cleared," Suzy replied. "That doesn't mean much though. We wouldn't be the first cleared relief flight to be shot down by one side or the other." She quit looking at the sparkling water and looked toward land, wondering if she would see any sign of a missile coming toward the plane—or toward one of the other two cargo planes following them. Parched ground flashed beneath the plane almost immediately after it crossed the shoreline. Suzy looked, but there didn't seem to be any significant areas of green in sight.

"Mars couldn't look any more desolate than this," she said.

"Well, what do you expect—drought year after year, senseless chopping of the forests, all the rest? They haven't had four good years' worth of rain all told in the last thirty. Total. The way things are going, all of Africa will be a desert from the Mediterranean to Angola."

"You one of those young hotshots who thinks that since we can't stop the hell here we should stop prolonging people's agony by bringing in food year after year?"

"I wouldn't be here if I felt that way. We can't just let tens of millions of people die without trying to help. But unless somebody makes them stop cutting down the forests—hell, the whole continent could be as barren as Antarctica in another twenty years."

"Maybe we can do something permanent to help now," Suzy said softly, holding back her sense of amusement at the way the young man was lecturing her.

"I've heard *that* number before," Jeff replied, turning away from her.

"Are you in for a surprise," Suzy whispered. Jeff either didn't hear or chose to ignore it.

"We're starting our landing pattern," the pilot announced. "Remember, I warned you that the landing might be rough. All we've got is a dusty plain to set down on, not a finished runway. Strap in tight."

Suzy adjusted her safety harness. The small passenger cabin in the military cargo plane didn't have the simple lap straps of a commercial passenger liner. Jeff didn't seem inclined to follow her example.

"Buckle up," Suzy said sharply. "We've got a lot of work to do when we land. I can't afford to have you all banged up if this gets rough."

Jeff stared at her for a moment, started to say something, then held back. He fastened his straps.

As the plane glided in toward the landing strip, Suzy gripped the armrests of her seat with all her strength. Before leaving the United States five days before, she had seen the latest intelligence estimates for the region. The fighting between rebels and government forces was near an all-time high, and both sides had declared open season on neutral relief efforts. Both sides had the weapons to knock the planes out of the sky. And any landing was hazardous enough in the rough country they were descending toward even without the threat of missiles up the kazoo.

Occasional dead trees marked the dusty plain. The lines of long-dry watercourses were clearly visible. The plane chased its shadow to the ground, over a cluster of buildings, past acres of rough tents, wattle and thatch huts, and thousands of refugees. The landing gear touched down and bounced the plane back into the air for an instant before they finally settled into the dirt. Clouds of dust plumed out, leaving a thick trail behind the plane. Braking started the transport skewing from side to side. The near wing dipped perilously near the ground once. Even Jeff Senna grabbed his armrests and held on.

"Just be glad we're the first plane in," Suzy said through almost-clenched teeth. "The others will be landing through our dust."

"What's the big rush?" Jeff asked. "Planes don't land that close together even at O'Hare."

"Nobody's ever shot down a plane landing in Chicago," Suzy said. "It's happened three different times here."

The cargo plane finally stopped moving forward. The pilot didn't wait for anything more than that. He turned left and moved off to the side—over to a seldom-used roadway—and reversed course to taxi back toward the cluster of buildings and tents they had flown over on final approach. The second plane was already braking on the dirt landing strip, and Suzy and Jeff saw the third plane touch down.

"That's too damn close," Jeff said.

"Just be glad we got all three planes down safely," Suzy told him. "We'd be in a royal mess if we lost even one."

"What's so special about these particular planes?" Jeff asked. "There are loads of relief supplies coming in every week or two."

"Not like we're carrying. You'll learn more when we show the people here what we've got."

"We unload by hand?" Jeff asked as the plane turned and stopped. The engines were shut off. The dust didn't show any immediate tendency to settle.

"Every bit of it," Suzy said. "But we'll have help. Some of the refugees here are still strong enough to do a little work, and there are several dozen workers brought in from outside, volunteers like us."

The cargo doors at the rear of the plane opened with a mechanical whine and a ramp extended itself as Suzy and Jeff made their way back through the pallets of cardboard boxes toward the exit. Heat and dust found their way inside the plane quickly.

"Is it this hot here all the time?" Jeff asked.

That was a question Suzy had heard before. She had asked it herself the first time she flew in. "This is the cool season," she replied. The joke wasn't even worth an interior chuckle any longer.

A thin sunburned man, whose glasses had slid to the end of his nose, met them on the ramp.

"Reverend Abernathy, this is Jeff Senna, one of my new volunteers," Suzy said. Abernathy and Senna shook hands.

"We can use all the helpers we can get," the Anglican priest said. "Glad to have you, young man. And good to see you again, Suzy."

"You'll be even happier when you see what we've got for

you this time, Reggie," Suzy said, smiling broadly as she first shook hands with and then embraced the clergyman who looked much older than his forty years.

"Oh, you brought me a genie in a lamp?" They started down the ramp together. "I wondered how we rated three planes at once."

"Genie in a lamp is pretty close, Reggie," Suzy said, laughing openly. "Pretty close indeed."

He stopped and put out a hand to stop Suzy at the bottom of the ramp. "You wouldn't be having sport with the old vicar, would you?" He wiped at the bald top of his head with a handkerchief. The fringe of hair around his crown seemed to be a mirror image of his sideburns and the thin line of beard that followed his jawline. Reggie Abernathy had been bald since divinity school.

"I wouldn't joke about this, Reggie," Suzy said. "We're turning the corner with these loads. Once I show you the cargo, you might think it's manna from heaven and water from rocks."

"I pray that you're telling the truth, Suzy, but *please*, don't talk like that around my people here. Some of them might think you were mocking God, and they don't have much more than their faith left." Hundreds of people were approaching the plane on foot—tired faces, filled more with resignation than hope. A few children came on ahead of the crowd, but not even the youngsters had the strength to hurry.

"I won't, Reggie, but I am telling you the exact truth. You're getting the first shipment of . . . well, just let me show you." She turned to Jeff. "Grab one of the cases marked A-7 and bring it along, would you?"

"This is a whole new technology," Suzy said when she started to open the crate in Reggie's office. "We're moving far beyond simply hauling in food to get each group of refugees through the next few days. We've finally got a way to start making the region self-supporting again."

Abernathy stared at her for a moment, squinting—as if that might help him see inside her. "You *are* serious," he said.

When Suzy nodded, the priest said, "Then you can only be talking about molecular engineering, factory bugs, right?"

"You might say that," Suzy said.

"There've been rumors for so many years, but nothing's ever come of them," Abernathy said.

"This is only a guess," Suzy lied, "but I'd say that security concerns outweighed everything else for a long time. But the situation here—and in a few other critical areas—has become so desperate that humanity finally won out." She pulled three small packages from the crate, glancing briefly at Jeff. He was on a camp stool at the side of the office, his face drained of color after walking past a sampling of the emaciated residents of the refugee camp.

"Once this gets going, it will be virtually self-sustaining," Suzy said, turning her attention to the vicar again. "Each of these packets will produce a day's food for four people, plus a starter kit for the next day's food. Horn of plenty. Genie's lamp. The initial packet merely requires three liters of water and two hours. After that, the following days' packets will need the water and certain organic materials."

"Water is a problem, as you know," Abernathy said, his voice sounding tired suddenly. "And just what do you mean by 'certain organic materials'?"

"Don't look so dour, Reggie," Suzy said. "We have the situation well in hand, as you might say. These molecular replicators can take carbon, oxygen, hydrogen, and nitrogen—basically in any available form—and construct the food. The air alone can provide a lot of the necessary raw material. The rest can come from virtually any organic matter—trees, bushes, inedible portions of grain and other crops, weeds, scraps. It can also come from organic material locked up in the soil, or from human and animal wastes. Recycling."

Reggie nodded. "But that still leaves the problem of water. And some very serious religious concerns about using wastes, especially human, as anything more than fertilizer."

"The water is simpler than you might think," Suzy said. "All the oxygen is in the air. And there's more than enough hydrogen to be had in surface and subsurface compounds, and again in waste products. Scavenging." Suzy dragged the word out. "Hydrogen can be liberated from a lot of different sources around here." She pulled a small notebook from her hip pocket. "I didn't want to trust all this to memory. Chemistry's not my strong suit."

"Mine either," Reggie said with a smile.

"The major surface sources here are clay, gypsum, shale, and mica. The Danakil is lousy with gypsum. The plateau and the Rift Valley have shale and mica, and there's clay all over. There are deposits of oil and natural gas that offer hydrocarbons for the taking. The desert areas, even where there's no real gypsum, have quite a number of hydrides and hydroxides available."

"I'll have to take your word for it," Reggie said when Suzy looked at him.

"And there are sources people can help provide. Plastics, wood ash, organic waste. This system can liberate hydrogen and turn it into water from all of those. Our planes are going to start bringing in bales of discarded plastics once the food packets get going around the area. We're going to start a self-sustaining water cycle, Reggie, really we are." She paused to give him a chance to say something, but he kept quiet.

"We start by digging a shallow hole and dumping 100 gallons of water in—water we've brought along that has been seeded with the assemblers to obtain the oxygen and hydrogen and combine them into water. We've brought enough to start a dozen of these breeder ponds to get the program off to a flying start. After a week, we figure that each site should have accumulated a decent small pond, close to 1,000 gallons under local conditions. And 100 gallons of *that* can be removed to start the next pond. Every week, each existing pond can start another similar pond. And the sludge at the bottom of each pond can be dredged daily to support three dozen food packets—about 200 people—and the waste the people generate will keep the process from slowing down markedly once the most-easily reachable levels of the soil are leached of their hydrogen."

Abernathy sat heavily, making his folding chair creak. His mouth fell open. He stared at Suzy but didn't seem to see her. Suzy watched him for a moment, then continued.

"The molecular assemblers that grab oxygen from the air to make the water will also help minimize evaporation—almost like a sheet of plastic wrap across the surface. We can't eliminate evaporation completely, but we don't want to. Seepage will be held to a minimum by the sludge that will line each pond. The seepage and evaporation that *do* occur will help make the ground fertile again and put needed water vapor back into the air. Once the region is thoroughly seeded with breeder ponds, we hope—we *expect*—to see a shift in the climate again to get a decent rain cycle established. Well, before the ponds have extracted the last available hydrogen from the soils and rocks. Careful planting around the ponds will help maintain the new balance."

Suzy had to shake Jeff's shoulder to get his attention. He was as mesmerized by the recitation as Reggie. Suzy sent Jeff out to get water for her first demonstration.

"The further along we get with the ponds," Suzy said while Jeff was gone, "the less hydrogen we'll need from the ground. There'll be more organics available from the recycling, from the inedible parts of the new crops and so forth. And once the system is fully operational, we'll be back to almost entirely natural means, with the odds and ends added just to keep us on the plus side."

"It's a miracle," Abernathy whispered two hours later when he saw the result of Suzy's tinkering with the food packet—food, hot and ready to eat. He started praying, more fervently than he had in years.

Edward Henryk Witans

It was nearly midnight in Warsaw. The sky was clear, each star sharply etched against the black of space. There was a half meter of snow on the ground, but the streets and sidewalks had been cleared. The temperature was just below freezing. There was little wind. A pleasant winter night. Ed Witans got out of his car and crossed the street to the church his grandparents had attended before leaving Poland eighty years before. Since being posted to the United States Embassy in Warsaw, Ed had attended the church himself—at least once a month when his other duties permitted. After three years, the priests and most of the parishioners knew him at least casually. Ed had a fluent, colloquial command of the language, and he recalled many of the stories has grandparents told him when he was young. Some of the same families still belonged to the parish.

There was little traffic on the street, and people came along the sidewalks singly or in small family groups, but there would be a full house for Midnight Mass. Christmas Eve was about to become Christmas Day. Ed went inside the church, exchanged Christmas greetings with some of the people lingering in the narthex, then went through to the nave, knelt by the font of holy water, dipped his fingers, crossed himself, and went down the aisle to the pew his family had occupied generations before.

Ed was comfortable in the church. The service reminded him of his childhood in Detroit. There was no Latin here, but much of the services back then had been in Polish—the sermon and lesson, all the little odds and ends, the announcements at the end. And in the parish hall in Detroit there had been more Polish than English spoken. Ed hid the smile that came when he pictured himself as a young boy, back when he believed every word that the priests—and the nuns who taught at and ruled the parochial schools he attended—said. And the almost inevitable period in his childhood (it may have lasted for nearly two years) when he thought he might like to be a priest himself someday.

This is almost enough to make me believe it all again, he thought.

At the end of Mass, there was the special announcement that Ed had come to hear, about the Christmas presents sent from a group of Polish congregations in the United States. "Enjoy the Christmas dinner," the priest said. "Keep one of the two packets that are left. Give the other to a friend or relative who hasn't received one already." The priest spoke with a passion that was more than faith. He had witnessed a demonstration.

And outside, the parishioners went home with their presents, the new Christmas miracle that they were about to be astounded by. Many stopped to thank Ed or to ask him to pass on their thanks to the donating parishes in America. Ed wished every one of them a Merry Christmas and tried to imagine how they would react when they learned just what kind of present they had.

He couldn't suppress the upwelling of hope and joy in himself.

Alice Kersey Solomon

"Go on now. You just stay in the living room with the children while I do this," Alice told her husband, lightly pushing him away from the kitchen door. "You don't believe. You think this is a waste of time, so you get out there and watch 'How the Grinch Stole Christmas,' or whatever you've got on now."

"I thought this was for Christmas Day, not Christmas Eve," Jim said. He moved slowly, "letting" her push him. He tried to hide his smile.

"It's for Christmas, period. And we'll be at my mother's tomorrow, so we've got to have *our* Christmas here tonight."

"Or an early April Fool's Day," Jim said, teasing. He had set aside the worst of his depression over losing his job, at least for the moment. The children were too happy, too excited about Christmas, for him to remain blue. Alice was excited about the strange package they had received in the mail. And there had been an unexpected bonus from the factory, a small check, along with a letter suggesting that there was a possibility that the layoff would only last three or four months.

That hope was enough to get Jim through Christmas. There was a chance. It would be tight; Jim had spent much of the day figuring up bills, trying to see where they could cut expenses. *If it is just three months, I think we can do it*, he had decided. Unemployment benefits. Alice should be able to re-

turn to her teacher's-assistant job by February first. Jim's op-
timism might evaporate on December 26, but it would hold
until then.

Alice shook her head at Jim and went back to the kitchen.
She already had the two pans set out. The instructions were
on the table. Everything was in the proper pan except the liq-
uids. Pour in the water and oil, cover both pans with generous
sheets of waxed paper, and wait for two hours. Simple.

"I think I'm gonna sit here and watch you," she whispered
as she poured the water into the larger pan. "I'd hate for Jim
to be right about this all being a crazy joke." She covered the
pans and pulled up a chair.

Nothing seemed to be happening at first. Alice read the instructions again. There was nothing about stirring. After a
few minutes, Alice mumbled, "I could fall asleep like this."
She got up, set the wind-up kitchen timer at its maximum—
one hour—and went to the living room. She chuckled before
she left the kitchen though. She knew she would never manage to wait the whole hour before she came back to peek.

"Is it soup yet?" Jim asked when Alice reached the living
room.

"Takes two hours now, the instructions say," she replied,
sticking her tongue out at him. "What's on TV?"

When Alice returned to the kitchen after thirty minutes, the
waxed paper was fogged over both pans. She stood over them
for a couple of minutes, fighting the itch to peek. The instructions had cautioned against that. "I don't want to goof it up,
give Jim a chance to laugh at me 'cause of that," she told herself.

After an hour, the paper on both pans had formed bulges.
Alice could smell enticing aromas. When she went back to
the living room that time, she was wearing a wide grin.
"Looks like you're gonna have to eat your words, and then
some, Mister Smartypants," she told Jim.

"The thing's actually working?" he asked, surprised, skeptical.

"It's doing something." Then, when Jim started to get up

to look for himself, she said, "You just plant your pants back on that sofa and wait."

After another half hour, Alice went to the kitchen again, and turned around almost as soon as she reached the door. She brought Jim and their two daughters back with her.

"What's that?" seven-year-old Abby asked.

"Our Christmas surprise," Alice said.

"Smells good," five-year-old Debbie decided.

"Sure does," Jim said, unable to contain his surprise. "Can I peek?"

"No, sir!" Alice said. "We've got another . . ." She stopped and pressed a hand against her side, where her waist used to be.

"Alice?" Jim asked, noticing the way her eyes had widened.

"I think we may have an extra Christmas surprise," she said after a moment. She relaxed a little. "Strong contraction."

"Just the one?" Jim asked.

"I've been having little ones most of the day," Alice confessed.

"You call the doctor?"

"Not yet. There's plenty of time," Alice said.

"This is why we need a car," Jim said, remembering the earlier, forced decision to postpone that purchase again.

"Don't start now, Jim," Alice said. "Jess knows it's coming. He and Rae have a telephone right next to their bed."

"Shouldn't have to call a brother-in-law for this."

"Now hush!" Alice said. "It's Christmas Eve." She sniffed theatrically over the larger pan. "Abby, you want to help your father set the dining room table?"

All four Solomons were standing at the kitchen table when the two hours were up. The food smells were enough to start all their stomachs growling, and Mama had to watch her daughters—and husband—closely to keep them from peeking under the waxed paper too soon. Alice had only turned away once, to hide the fleeting grimace that came with another strong contraction. Twenty minutes after the last.

I don't care how close it is, I'm gonna eat tonight, she told herself. The *Instant Christmas* food smelled too good to pass up or just sample.

The dinger on the timer went off. Alice peeled the waxed paper off the larger pan . . . and gasped. There was steaming turkey and dressing, mashed potatoes and gravy, corn and peas, and a whole pumpkin pie, each in separate open containers. There were also celery stalks, green onions, and cole slaw.

"There's enough food here for *two* meals," Jim said, staring at it. He shook his head, trying to dislodge a sense of unreality about it all. His words felt disjointed, abstract things to him. He had trouble believing his eyes and nose.

"And here's the starter for another meal," Alice said, lifting a compressed block the size of a meat loaf pan from another corner.

"What's in the other pan?" Jim asked.

"We'll have to look and see," Alice said, reaching for that waxed paper.

"Christmas presents!" Debbie said when she saw the brightly-wrapped packages in the other pan. "Where's mine?"

"We'll just have to open them all and see who gets what," Alice said. "There are no name tags on them." Alice closed her eyes for a moment. Personalized tags on the presents would have been one miracle too many. "After dinner," she said when both girls started reaching. "We've got to eat before the food gets cold."

"I'll carry it," Jim said. The pan with the food in it was far heavier than Alice was allowed to carry. Abby and Debbie ran ahead. "Afterwards," Jim whispered to Alice, "I think we should go to the midnight service at church."

Alice smiled. It was the first time Jim had ever suggested going to church. He would go with Alice and the children when he couldn't get out of it, but *this* was a first.

"That would be nice," she said, "but I don't think I can make it. I think I'll have to call Rae long before midnight."

❊   ❊   ❊

Howard McMichaels Dawson

There were no Christmas decorations in the room, nothing more than a page-a-day calendar showing December 25 in red with *Christmas* in black block letters below, and a thin green and red wreath around the entire page. The one clock in the room was a 24-hour dial showing 0700. A map of the world covered one wall. Time zones were marked across the top. A large desk in the center of the gray-walled room faced the map. Behind the desk in place of a credenza there was a table with computer terminals, radios, printers, and a fax machine. The desk held only a lamp, an 8½″ by 11″ lined yellow pad, and three telephones.

Howard Dawson stretched and yawned. His chair creaked softly as he moved. He reached to the corner of his desk, picked up a telephone, and pressed the intercom button. "How we fixed for coffee?" he asked.

"I'll bring you a cup right away, sir," the clerk outside said. "Just brewed up a fresh pot." He didn't have to ask how Dawson wanted his coffee. He knew. They worked together often enough.

"Thanks, Bill," Dawson said. "And check to see if Matt Thomson's in the building yet. I want him down here as soon as he arrives."

"He signed in at the entrance three minutes ago, sir," Bill replied. "he should be down any minute now."

"Have coffee ready for him when he arrives. Black with three teaspoons of sugar."

"Yes, sir."

Howard stood and stretched again. He walked to the map and back, trying to get his blood flowing, trying to get alert again. The situation room—one of several in the lower reaches of the building—was silent. Calling the level *The Tombs* was an old joke, stale but appropriate. Dawson was deep below the agency's most recent headquarters building at Langley, Virginia. No one really believed that the deep level was safe against nuclear attack, but it was—mostly—proof against casual eavesdropping. Howard flexed his shoulders, thinking of the many nights and days he had spent in this room or one of the others, where no trace of the outside was visible or audible.

"Almost over," he whispered. Not just this operation, but his career, all the years of service—covert and overt. He scratched his head with both hands. His hair was short and white—whiter than it deserved to be, he thought. Thirty-plus years of intelligence work, of every possible kind of operation and administrative nightmare.

"But never anything like this," he mumbled. *This is a good one to be going out on.*

Bill Kent came in with both cups of coffee. "Mr. Thomson's in the elevator coming down, sir."

Dawson nodded. "Show him right in, Bill."

Matt Thomson was twenty years younger than Howard's sixty-seven. Matt combed his black hair straight back, accentuating a high forehead. He had a deep suntan, a reminder that he had been spending his time in places where December was a lot kinder.

"Morning, sir," Matt said, taking the hand Howard offered.

"You can knock off the *sir* crap," Howard said amiably. "A week from today, you'll have my job. That's punishment enough for anyone."

"I was a little surprised that you called me in so early this morning," Matt said, not mentioning that he hadn't anticipated coming in to Langley at all on Christmas Day. Working for the agency was guaranteed to bring surprises like that. "Is something wrong?" Matt asked the question hesitantly. Howard seemed much too relaxed for a crisis.

Howard's laugh threatened to get out of control before he reined it in. Matt looked at him with one eyebrow raised, and more questions springing to mind. "No, Matt," Howard said. "For one of the few times in the agency's history, nothing at all is wrong. Maybe nothing's ever been so right. Have a seat, and coffee. I trust Bill got it the way you like it."

"Fine," Matt said after he had taken the chair at the side of Howard's desk and sampled the coffee. He looked carefully at Howard's face. The air of joviality was ... out of place. "So what's up?"

"Operation Santa Claus," Howard said, holding back another laugh, enjoying the consternation he saw on Matt's face.

"Sir?" Matt said. Howard's laugh came out.

"Sorry, Matt," Howard said. He took a deep breath. "You'll understand in a few minutes. Operation Santa Claus. It's probably the only ongoing operation you haven't been briefed on yet in our piece of the pie. Up to this minute, only three people in the country have known the full scope of it—the president, the director, and me. It's that tight. Now it's your turn."

Matt settled back in the chair and took another sip of coffee to cover any other reaction he might show. Howard's introduction hinted strongly at trouble, *somewhere* down the line.

"That's right," Howard said. He had been in the business too long to miss the concern in his successor's face and actions. "We bypassed the National Security Council, the Joint Committee on Intelligence, and the Congressional Oversight Committee. We had no choice at all. You'll know that once you know what Operation Santa Claus is all about. You'll have the complete file, but I want to give you an overview personally. Then you can study all the data and I'll answer any questions you still have."

Matt nodded. He had known that there would be problems when he became head of Covert Operations. He simply hadn't expected anything quite so major going in. And withholding an entire operation from the oversight apparatus—in American intelligence, that sin was even more deadly than failure.

"It has to be something of, ah, unprecedented importance to take that kind of risk," Matt said.

"It is," Howard said, nodding soberly. "*Unprecedented* is a very good word in this case. You know the way we've been sitting on molecular replicators so long?"

"I know," Matt said quietly. The knot that had been threatening his stomach grew more convoluted. "We've never been able to find a foolproof security system for the little buggers so we've held back any real applications here and sabotaged every foreign project." Matt had been control officer for several of those operations.

"We're not sitting on them any longer," Howard said. The lines of mirth had quietly disappeared from his face. He leaned toward Matt. "Maybe the security angle still isn't fool-proof, but it's probably as close as we'll ever be able to manage. It came down to what most of us thought when we first started looking at the technology closely. Whoever is first to use the full potential of the technology will control . . . *it*." Howard and Matt both leaned back in their chairs at the same time. Matt allowed himself a long, slow blink.

"So," Howard said, drawing out the word, "in the last four days, we've distributed eight million food factories around the world—several different versions, tailored to specific needs—to needy people of all sorts, here and abroad." He paused for a few seconds. "And some people who aren't so needy. From the inner cities of the U.S. to the capitals of all the Communist bloc countries, on to the famine centers of the southern hemisphere and Asia and even into the centers of our staunchest allies. By the end of today, at least some people in virtually every country in the world will have sampled our molecular-factory food, with kits that'll keep right on providing food, and duplicate factories to pass on to others."

"We're going back to the Uncle Sugar image?" Matt asked. He knew that the answer had to be no, and he could already make a good guess as to what the real answer was. . . . But this was no time for guesses, no matter how well-informed.

"Well, we expect to receive some initial benefits along those lines." Howard said, smiling as he nodded, "but this time, we're not counting on free goodwill. We've had to wipe *that* off our faces too many times before."

"What *are* we counting on then?" Matt asked, determined to get a straight answer from Howard.

"Technology," Howard said, spreading his hands in an open gesture. "Little computers, to be exact. In a space the size of a sugar cube, we can pack more computing power than the human brain has—faster, smarter, more durable. And it will use all of its potential, not just the small fraction that people use.

With very precise programming. In six months, half the people in the world will have our custom-designed molecular computers in their systems, interacting strongly with their own brains—informing, improving, *guiding*. The computer systems are self-replicating and able to spread very quickly through almost any casual contact—easier to catch than a cold. Inside eighteen months, the spread should be complete, worldwide. Put together your own dreams, Matt—universal peace, prosperity, no more hunger or disease, people reaching out to the stars. Your dreams can't be any more glowing than the reality will be." Howard couldn't repress a sign of satisfaction. Many of his own dreams had gone into the programming.

Matt shook his head very slowly. "I've seen all the theories, of course, but it still sounds impossible, totally impossible."

"But it isn't," Howard said, tapping the desk in front of him. He leaned toward Matt. "This time, the *Pax Americana* won't be a joke."

"You're talking about mind control," Matt said. Then he turned to look at the map on the wall to escape the look he saw on Howard's face.

"I'm talking mind control," Howard said, evenly, emphasizing each word. "And there is no antidote, no immunity. We had no choice, Matt. Sooner or later, *someone* would develop this technology. And there is no room for a second-place finisher. It had to be either us or somebody else. And there is no 'somebody else' who would be acceptable." He leaned back and drew his hands down over the sides of his nose and across his mouth before he continued. "Utopia has a price, Matt."

There was complete silence in the room then, for far more than a minute. Howard stared at Matt. Matt stared at the map on the wall, not ready to face the man he was scheduled to replace at the end of the year.

"But, *Congress*," Matt started lamely. He didn't finish the thought.

"There is no immunity, Matt," Howard said softly.

Matt felt a pressure at the sides of his neck, as if the arteries carrying blood to his brain had suddenly constricted. *I can't faint*, he thought. *That would be ridiculous.*

"Our preparations were very thorough, Matt. Every representative and senator received a box of Christmas candy from the White House. We catered the dinner the president hosted for Congress just before the holiday adjournment—*and* the meals for the last two days in the restaurants that most of our congressmen use around Capitol Hill."

The silence returned. Matt continued to stare at the map on the wall. *What am I walking into?* he asked himself. He looked for flaws, for escapes. He didn't see any. "Can it really work?" he asked.

Howard's emphatic affirmative was preempted by a buzz from the intercom. He picked up the telephone receiver.

"We have a call coming in from Buenos Aires, sir," Bill Kent said from the outer office.

"Put it through," Howard said, switching the phone to its speaker so Matt could hear. He gestured to Matt. "This will be another mission-accomplished call. I've been getting them for the last sixteen hours."

"Mister Dawson? This is Carl Alvarez." The name was phony, but both Matt and Howard recognized the voice of the Buenos Aires station chief.

"Go ahead, Carl."

"We just received a holiday wire. It reads, 'Yes, Virginia, there is a Santa Claus.' "

"Good work, Carl. Merry Christmas." Howard turned off the phone and looked straight at Matt. "There's no way it can fail to work."

THE GREATEST GIFT
Philip Van Doren Stern

THE LITTLE TOWN straggling up the hill was bright with colored Christmas lights. But George Pratt did not see them. He was leaning over the railing of the iron bridge, staring down moodily at the black water. The current eddied and swirled like liquid glass, and occasionally a bit of ice, detached from the shore, would go gliding downstream to be swallowed up in the shadows.

The water looked paralyzingly cold. George wondered how long a man could stay alive in it. The glassy blackness had a strange, hypnotic effect on him. He leaned still farther over the railing . . .

"I wouldn't do that if I were you," a quiet voice beside him said.

George turned resentfully to a man he had never seen before. He was stout, well past middle age, and his round cheeks were pink in the winter air, as though they had just been shaved.

"Wouldn't do what?" George asked sullenly.

"What you were thinking of doing."

"How do you know what I was thinking?"

"Oh, we make it our business to know a lot of things," the stranger said easily.

George wondered what the man's business was. He was a most unremarkable person, the sort you would pass in a crowd and never notice. Unless you saw his bright blue eyes, that is. You couldn't forget them, for they were the kindest, sharpest eyes you ever saw. Nothing else about him was noteworthy. He wore a moth-eaten fur cap and a shabby overcoat. He was carrying a small black satchel. A salesman's sample kit, George decided.

"Looks like snow, doesn't it?" the stranger said, glancing up appraisingly at the overcast sky. "It'll be nice to have a white Christmas. They're getting scarce these days—but so are a lot of things." He turned to face George squarely. "You all right now?"

"Of course I'm all right. What made you think I wasn't?"

George fell silent before the stranger's quiet gaze.

The man shook his head. "You know you shouldn't think of such things—and on Christmas Eve of all times! You've got to consider Mary—and your mother, too."

George opened his mouth to ask how this stranger could know his wife's name, but the fellow anticipated him. "Don't ask me how I know such things. It's my business. That's why I came along this way tonight. Lucky I did, too." He glanced down at the dark water and shuddered.

"Well, if you know so much about me," George said, "give me just one good reason why I should be alive."

"Come, come, it can't be that bad. You've got your job at the bank. And Mary and the kids. You're healthy, young and—"

"And sick of everything!" George cried. "I'm stuck here in this mudhole for life, doing the same dull work day after day. Other men are leading exciting lives, but I—well, I'm just a small-town bank clerk. I never did anything really useful or interesting, and it looks as if I never will. I might just as well be dead. Sometimes I wish I were. In fact, I wish I had never been born!"

The man stood looking at him in the growing darkness. "What was that you said?" he asked softly.

"I said I wish I'd never been born," George repeated firmly.

The stranger's pink cheeks glowed with excitement. "Why, that's wonderful! You've solved everything. I was afraid you were going to give me some trouble. But now you've got the solution yourself. You wish you'd never been born. All right! Okay! You haven't!"

"What do you mean?"

"You haven't been born. Just that. No one here knows you. You have no responsibilities—no job—no wife—no children. Why, you haven't even a mother. You couldn't have, of course. All your troubles are over. Your wish, I am happy to say, has been granted—officially."

"Nuts!" George snorted and turned away.

The stranger caught him by the arm.

"You'd better take this with you," he said, holding out his satchel. "It'll open a lot of doors that might otherwise be slammed in your face."

"What doors in whose face? I know everybody in this town."

"Yes, I know," the man said patiently. "But take this anyway. It can't do any harm, and it may help." He opened the satchel and displayed a number of brushes. "You'd be surprised how useful these brushes can be as introduction—especially the free ones." He hauled out a plain little hand brush. "I'll show you how to use it." He thrust the satchel into George's reluctant hands and began: "When the lady of the house comes to the door, you give her this and then talk fast. You say, 'Good evening, madam, I'm from the World Cleaning Company, and I want to present you with this handsome and useful brush absolutely free—no obligation to purchase anything at all.' After that, of course, it's a cinch. Now you try it." He forced the brush into George's hand.

George promptly dropped the brush into the satchel and closed it with an angry snap. "Here," he said, and then stopped abruptly, for there was no one in sight.

The stranger must have slipped away into the bushes growing along the riverbank, George thought. He certainly wasn't going to play hide-and-seek with him. It was nearly dark and getting colder. He shivered and turned up his coat collar.

The street lights had been turned on, and Christmas candles in the windows glowed softly. The little town looked remarkably cheerful. After all, the place you grew up in was the one spot on earth where you could really feel at home. George felt a sudden burst of affection even for crotchety old Hank Biddle, whose house he was passing. He remembered the quarrel he had had when his car had scraped a piece of bark out of Hank's big maple tree. George looked up at the vast spread of leafless branches towering over him in the darkness. He felt a sudden twinge of guilt for the damage he had done. He had never stopped to inspect the wound—he was afraid to have Hank catch him even looking at the tree. Now he stepped out boldly into the roadway to examine the huge trunk.

Hank must have repaired the scar or painted it over, for there was no sign of it. George struck a match and bent down to look more closely. He straightened up with an odd, sinking feeling in his stomach. There wasn't any scar. The bark was smooth and undamaged.

He remembered what the man at the bridge had said. It was all nonsense, of course, but the nonexistent scar bothered him.

When he reached the bank, he saw that something was wrong. The building was dark, and he knew he had turned the vault light on. He noticed, too, that someone had left the window shades up. He ran around to the front. There was a battered old sign fastened on the door. George could just make out the words:

FOR RENT OR SALE
Apply JAMES SILVA, Real Estate

Perhaps it was some boys' trick, he thought wildly. Then he saw a pile of ancient leaves and tattered newspapers in the

bank's ordinarily immaculate doorway. A light was still burning across the street in Jim Silva's office. George dashed over
and tore the door open.

Jim looked up in surprise. "What can I do for you?" he
said in the polite voice he reserved for potential customers.

"The bank," George said breathlessly. "What's the matter
with it?"

"The old bank building?" Jim Silva turned around and
looked out of the window. "Nothing that I can see. Wouldn't
like to rent or buy it, would you?"

"You mean—it's out of business?"

"For a good ten years. Went bust. Stranger 'round these
parts, ain't you?"

George sagged against the wall. "I was here some time
ago," he said weakly. "The bank was all right then. I even
knew some of the people who worked there."

"Didn't know a feller named Marty Jenkins, did you?"

"Marty Jenkins! Why, he—" George was about to say that
Marty had never worked at the bank—couldn't have, in fact,
for when they had both left school they had applied for a job
there and George had gotten it. But now, of course, things
were different. He would have to be careful. "No, I didn't
know him," he said slowly. "Not really, that is. I'd heard of
him."

"Then maybe you heard how he skipped out with fifty
thousand dollars. That's why the bank went broke. Pretty near
ruined everybody around here." Silva was looking at him
sharply. "I was hoping for a minute maybe you'd know
where he is. We'd like to get our hands on Marty Jenkins."

"Didn't he have a brother named Arthur?"

"Art? Oh, sure. But he don't know where his brother went.
It's had a terrible effect on him, too. Took to drink, he did.
It's too bad—and hard on his wife. He married a nice girl."

George felt the sinking feeling in his stomach again. "Who
did he marry?" he demanded hoarsely. Both he and Art had
courted Mary.

"Girl named Mary Thatcher," Silva said. "She lives up on

the hill just this side of the church—Hey! Where are you going?"

But George had bolted out of the office. He ran past the empty bank building and turned up the hill. For a moment he thought of going straight to Mary. The house next to the church had been given to them by her father as a wedding present. Naturally Art Jenkins would have gotten it if he had married Mary. George wondered whether they had any children. Then he knew he couldn't face Mary—not yet, anyway. He decided to visit his parents and find out more about her.

There were candles burning in the windows of the little weather-beaten house on the side street, and a Christmas wreath was hanging on the glass panel of the front door. George raised the gate latch with a loud click. A dark shape on the porch hurled itself down the steps, barking ferociously.

"Brownie!" George shouted. "Brownie, stop that! Don't you know me?" But the dog advanced menacingly. The porch light snapped on, and George's father stepped outside to call the dog off. He held the dog by the collar while George cautiously walked past. He could see that his father did not know him. "Is the lady of the house in?" he asked.

His father waved toward the door. "Go on in," he said cordially. "I'll chain the dog up. She can be mean with strangers."

His mother, who was waiting in the hallway, obviously did not recognize him. George opened his sample kit and grabbed the first brush that came to hand. "Good evening, ma'am," he said politely. "I'm from the World Cleaning Company. We're giving out a free sample brush. No obligation. No obligation at all . . ." His voice faltered.

His mother smiled at his awkwardness. "I suppose you'll want to sell me something. I'm not really sure I need any brushes."

"I'm not selling anything," he assured her. "This is just— well, it's just a Christmas present from the company."

His father entered the hall and closed the door.

"Won't you come in for a while and sit down?" his mother said. "You must be tired, walking so much."

"Thank you, ma'am. I don't mind if I do." He entered the parlor and put his bag down on the floor. The room looked different somehow, although he could not figure out why.

"I used to know this town pretty well," he said. "I remember a girl named Mary Thatcher. She married Art Jenkins, I heard. You must know them."

"Of course," his mother said. "We know Mary well."

"Any children?" he asked casually.

"Two—a boy and a girl."

George sighed. He looked around the little parlor, trying to find out why it looked different. Over the mantelpiece hung a framed photograph which had been taken on his kid brother Harry's sixteenth birthday. He remembered how they had gone to Potter's studio to be photographed together. There was something queer about the picture. It showed only one figure—Harry's.

"That your son?" he asked.

His mother's face clouded. She nodded but said nothing.

"I think I met him, too," George said hesitantly. "His name's Harry, isn't it?"

His mother turned away, making a strange choking noise. Her husband put his arm clumsily around her shoulder. His voice, which was always mild and gentle, suddenly became harsh. "You couldn't have met him," he said. "He's been dead a long while. He was drowned the day that picture was taken."

George's mind flew back to the long-ago August afternoon when he and Harry had visited Potter's studio. On their way home they had gone swimming. Harry had been seized with a cramp, he remembered. He had pulled him out of the water and had thought nothing of it. But suppose he hadn't been there!

"I'm sorry," he said miserably. "I guess I'd better go. I hope you like the brush. And I wish you both a very Merry Christmas." There, he had put his foot in it again, wishing them a Merry Christmas when they were thinking about their dead son.

Brownie tugged fiercely at her chain as George went down

the porch steps and accompanied his departure with a rolling
growl.

He wanted desperately now to see Mary. He wasn't sure he
could stand not being recognized by her, but he had to see
her.

The lights were on in the church, and the choir was making
last-minute preparations for Christmas vespers. The organist
had been practicing "O Holy Night" evening after evening
until George had become thoroughly sick of it. But now the
music almost tore his heart out. He stumbled blindly up the
path to his own house.

When he knocked at the door, there was a long silence, followed by the shout of a child. Then Mary came to the door.

At the sight of her, George's voice almost failed him.
"Merry Christmas, ma'am," he managed to say at last. His
hand shook as he tried to open the satchel.

When George entered the living room, unhappy as he was,
he could not help noticing with a secret grin that the too-
high-priced blue sofa they often had quarreled over was there.
Evidently Mary had gone through the same thing with Art
Jenkins and had won the argument with him, too.

George got his satchel open. One of the brushes had a
bright-blue handle and varicolored bristles. It was obviously
a brush not intended to be given away, but George handed it
to Mary. "This would be fine for your sofa," he said.

"My, that's a pretty brush," she exclaimed. "You're giving
it away?"

He nodded solemnly. "Special introductory offer."

She stroked the sofa gently with the brush, smoothing out
the velvety nap. "It is a *nice* brush. Thank you. I—" There
was a sudden scream from the kitchen, and two small children rushed in. A little, homely-faced girl flung herself into
her mother's arms, sobbing loudly, as a boy of seven came
running after her, snapping a toy pistol at her head. "Mommy,
she won't die," he yelled. "I shot her a hunnert times, but she
won't die."

He looks just like Art Jenkins, George thought. Acts like
him, too.

The boy suddenly turned his attention to George. "Who're you?" he demanded belligerently. He pointed his pistol at him and pulled the trigger. "You're dead!" he cried. "You're dead. Why don't you fall down and die?"

There was a heavy step on the porch. The boy looked frightened and backed away. George saw Mary glance apprehensively at the door.

Art Jenkins came in. He stood for a moment in the doorway, clinging to the knob for support. His eyes were glazed. "Who's this?" he demanded thickly.

"He's a brush salesman," Mary tried to explain. "He gave me this brush."

"Brush salesman!" Art sneered. "Well, tell him we don't want no brushes." Art lurched across the room to the sofa, where he sat down suddenly.

George looked despairingly at Mary. Her eyes were begging him to go. He went to the door, followed by Art's son, who kept snapping his pistol at him and saying, "You're dead—dead—dead!"

Perhaps the boy was right, George thought when he reached the porch. Maybe he was dead, or maybe this was all a bad dream from which he might eventually awake. He wanted to find the man on the bridge again and try to persuade him to cancel the whole deal.

He hurried down the hill and broke into a run when he neared the river. George was relieved to see the stranger standing on the bridge. "I've had enough," he gasped. "Get me out of this—you got me into it."

The stranger raised his eyebrows. "I got you into it! You were granted your wish. You got everything you asked for. You're the freest man on earth now. You have no ties. You can go anywhere—do anything. What more can you possibly want?"

"Change me back," George pleaded. "Change me back—please. Not just for my sake but for others, too. You don't understand. I've got to get back. They need me here."

"I understand," the stranger said slowly. "I just wanted to make sure *you* did. You had the greatest gift of all conferred upon you—the gift of life, of being a part of this world and taking a part in it. Yet you denied that gift." As the stranger spoke, the church bell high up on the hill sounded, calling the townspeople to Christmas vespers. Then the downtown church bell started ringing.

"I've got to get back," George said desperately. "You can't cut me off like this. Why, it's murder!"

"Suicide rather, wouldn't you say?" the stranger murmured. "You brought it on yourself. However, since it's Christmas Eve—well, anyway, close your eyes and keep listening to the bells." His voice sank lower. "Keep listening to the bells . . ."

George did as he was told. He felt a snowdrop touch his cheek—and then another and another. When he opened his eyes, the snow was falling fast, so fast that it obscured everything around him. The stranger could not be seen, but then neither could anything else. The snow was so thick that George had to grope for the bridge railing.

As he started toward the village, he thought he heard someone saying "Merry Christmas," but the bells were drowning out all rival sounds, so he could not be sure.

When he reached Hank Biddle's house he stopped and walked out into the roadway, peering down anxiously at the base of the big maple tree. The scar was there, thank heaven! He touched the tree affectionately. He'd have to do something about the wound—get a tree surgeon or something. Anyway, he'd evidently been changed back. He was himself again. Maybe it was all a dream, or perhaps he had been hypnotized by the smooth-flowing black water.

At the corner of Main and Bridge Streets he almost collided with a hurrying figure. It was Jim Silva. "Hello, George," Jim said cheerfully. "Late tonight, ain't you? I should think you'd want to be home early on Christmas Eve."

George drew a long breath. "I just wanted to see if the bank is all right. I've got to make sure the vault light is on."

"Sure it's on. I saw it as I went past."

"Let's look, huh?" George said, pulling at Silva's sleeve. He wanted the assurance of a witness. He dragged the surprised real-estate dealer around to the front of the bank, where the light was gleaming through the falling snow. "I told you it was on," Silva said with some irritation.

"I had to make sure," George mumbled. "Thanks—and Merry Christmas!" Then he was off, running up the hill.

He was in a hurry to get home, but not in such a hurry that he couldn't stop for a moment at his parents' house, where he wrestled with Brownie until the friendly old bulldog waggled all over with delight. He grasped his startled brother's hand and wrung it frantically, wishing him an almost hysterical Merry Christmas. Then he dashed across the parlor to examine a certain photograph. He kissed his mother, joked with his father and was out of the house a few seconds later, slipping on the newly fallen snow as he ran on up the hill.

The church was bright with light, and the choir and the organ were going full tilt. George flung the door to his house open and called out at the top of his voice: "Mary! Where are you? Mary! Kids!"

His wife came toward him, dressed for church and making gestures to silence him. "I've just put the children to bed," she protested. "Now they'll—" but not another word could she get out of her mouth, for he smothered it with kisses, and then he dragged her up to the children's room, where he violated every tenet of parental behavior by madly embracing his son and his daughter and waking them up thoroughly.

It was not until Mary got him downstairs that he began to be coherent. "I thought I'd lost you. Oh, Mary, I thought I'd lost you!"

"What's the matter, darling?" she asked in bewilderment.

He pulled her down on the sofa and kissed her again. And then, just as he was about to tell her about his queer dream, his finger came in contact with something lying on the seat of the sofa. His voice froze.

He did not even have to pick the thing up, for he knew what it was. And he knew that it would have a blue handle and varicolored bristles.

The alien and the very old
meet at Christmas.

LA BEFANA
Gene Wolfe

WHEN ZOZZ, HOME from the pit, had licked his fur clean, he howled before John Bannano's door. John's wife, Teresa, opened it and let him in. She was a thin, stooped woman of thirty or thirty-five, her black hair shot with gray; she did not smile, but he felt somehow that she was glad to see him. She said, "He's not home yet. If you want to come in we've got a fire."

Zozz said, "I'll wait for him," and, six-legging politely across the threshold, sat down over the stone Bananas had rolled in for him when they were new friends. Maria and Mark, playing some sort of game with beer-bottle caps on squares scratched on the floor dirt said, "Hi, Uncle Zozz," and Zozz said, "Hi," in return. Bananas' old mother, whom Zozz had brought here from the pads in his rusty powerwagon the day before, looked at him with piercing eyes, then fled into the other room. He could hear Teresa relax, the wheezing outpuffed breath.

He said, half humorously, "I think she thinks I bumped her on purpose yesterday."

"She's not used to you yet."

"I know," Zozz said.

"I told her, Mother Bannano, it's their world, and they're not used to *you*."

"Sure," Zozz said. A gust of wind outside brought the cold in to replace the odor of the gog-hutch on the other side of the left wall.

"I tell you it's hell to have your husband's mother with you in a place as small as this."

"Sure," Zozz said again.

Maria announced, "Daddy's home!" The door rattled open and Bananas came in looking tired and cheerful. Bananas worked in the slaughtering market, and though his cheeks were blue with cold, the cuffs of his trousers were red with blood. He kissed Teresa and tousled the hair of both children, and said, "Hi, Zozzy."

Zozz said, "Hi. How does it roll?" And moved over so Bananas could warm his back. Someone groaned, and Bananas asked a little anxiously, "What's that?"

Teresa said, "Next door."

"Huh?"

"Next door. Some woman."

"Oh. I thought it might be Mom."

"She's fine."

"Where is she?"

"In back."

Bananas frowned. "There's no fire in there; she'll freeze to death."

"I didn't tell her to go back there. She can wrap a blanket around her."

Zozz said, "It's me—I bother her." He got up. Bananas said, "Sit down."

"I can go. I just came to say hi."

"Sit down." Bananas turned to his wife. "Honey, you shouldn't leave her in there alone. See if you can't get her to come out."

"Johnny—"

"Teresa, dammit!"

"Okay, Johnny."

Bananas took off his coat and sat down in front of the fire. Maria and Mark had gone back to their game. In a voice too low to attract their attention Bananas said, "Nice thing, huh?"

Zozz said, "I think your mother makes her nervous."

Bananas said, "Sure."

Zozz said, "This isn't an easy world."

"You mean for us. No it ain't, but you don't see me moving."

Zozz said, "That's good. I mean, here you've got a job anyway. There's work."

"That's right."

Unexpectedly Maria said: "We get enough to eat here, and me and Mark can find wood for the fire. Where we used to be there wasn't anything to eat."

Bananas said, "You remember, honey?"

"A little."

Zozz said, "People are poor here."

Bananas was taking off his shoes, scraping the street mud from them and tossing it into the fire. He said, "If you mean us, us people are poor everyplace." He jerked his head in the direction of the back room. "You ought to hear her tell about our world."

"Your mother?"

Bananas nodded. Maria said, "Daddy, how did Grandmother come here?"

"Same way we did."

Mark said, "You mean she signed a thing?"

"A labor contract? No, she's too old. She bought a ticket—you know, like you would buy something in a store."

Maria said, "That's what I mean."

"Shut up and play. Don't bother us."

Zozz said, "How'd things go at work?"

"So-so." Bananas looked toward the back room again. "She came into some money, but that's her business—I didn't want to talk to the kids about it."

"Sure."

"She says she spent every dollar to get here—you know,

they haven't used dollars even on Earth for fifty, sixty years, but she still says it, how do you like that?" He laughed, and Zozz laughed too. "I asked how she was going to get back, and she said she's not going back, she's going to die right here with us. What could I say?"

"I don't know." Zozz waited for Bananas to say something, and when he did not he added, "I mean, she's your mother."

"Yeah."

Through the thin wall they heard the sick woman groan again, and someone moving about. Zozz said, "I guess it's been a long time since you saw her last."

"Yeah—twenty-two years Newtonian. Listen, Zozzy . . ."

"Uh-huh."

"You know something? I wish I had never set eyes on her again."

Zozz said nothing, rubbing his hands, hands, hands.

"That sounds lousy I guess."

"I know what you mean."

"She could have lived good for the rest of her life on what that ticket cost her." Bananas was silent for a moment. "She used to be a big, fat woman when I was a kid, you know? A great big woman with a loud voice. Look at her now—dried up and bent over; it's like she wasn't my mother at all. You know the only thing that's the same about her? That black dress. That's the only thing I recognize, the only thing that hasn't changed. She could be a stranger—she tells stories about me I don't remember at all."

Maria said, "She told us a story today."

Mark added: "Before you came home. About this witch."

Maria said: "That brings the presents to children. Her name is La Befana the Christmas Witch."

Zozz drew his lips back from his double canines and jiggled his head. "I like stories."

"She says it's almost Christmas, and on Christmas three wise men went looking for the Baby, and they stopped at the old witch's door, and they asked which way it was and she told them and they said come with us."

The door to the other room opened, and Teresa and Ba-

nanas' mother came out. Bananas' mother was holding a tea-
kettle; she edged around Zozz to put it on the hook and swing
it out over the fire.

"And she was sweeping and she wouldn't come."

Mark said: "She said she'd come when she was finished.
She was a real old, real ugly woman. Watch, I'll show you
how she walked." He jumped up and began to hobble around
the room.

Bananas looked at his wife and indicated the wall. "What's
this?"

"In there?"

"The charity place—they said she could stay there. She
couldn't stay in the house because all the rooms are full of
men."

Maria was saying, "So when she was all done she went
looking for Him only she couldn't find Him and she never
did."

"She's sick?"

"She's knocked up, Johnny, that's all. Don't worry about
her. She's got some guy in there with her."

Mark asked, "Do you know about the baby Jesus, Uncle
Zozz?"

Zozz groped for words.

"Giovanni, my son . . ."

"Yes, Mama."

"Your friend . . . Do they have the faith, Giovanni?"

Apropos of nothing, Teresa said, "They're Jews, next
door."

Zozz told Mark, "You see, the baby Jesus has never come
to my world."

Maria said: "And so she goes all over everyplace looking
for him with her presents, and she leaves some with every kid
she finds, but she says it's not because she thinks they might
be him like some people think, but just a substitute. She can't
never die. She has to do it forever, doesn't she, Grandma?"

The bent old woman said, "Not forever, dearest; only until
tomorrow night."

There was an old woman
who lived in a capsule ...

TRACK OF A LEGEND
Cynthia Felice

CHRISTMAS STARTED AT school right after we returned from
Thanksgiving holiday and took down the paper turkeys and
pilgrims from the windows. The teacher sang "Jingle bells,
Santa smells, Rudolph laid an egg" all the while that he was
supposed to be reprogramming my December reading assignment, and the computer printed out MERRY CHRISTMAS every
time I matched a vowel sound with the right word, and BAH,
HUMBUG whenever I was wrong. And it said BAH, HUMBUG a
lot and didn't light up the observation board. We used the
gold math beads as garlands for the tree because we ate most
of the popcorn, and paper chains were for kindergarteners
who weren't smart enough to scheme to get out of lessons.
Still, we had to listen to civic cassettes so that we would
know it was also the anniversary of the Christmas Treaty of
'55 that brought peace to all the world again. And to top it
off, on the very last day before Christmas our teacher improvised a lecture about how whole stations full of people had
nowhere to go but back to Earth, their way of life taken from
them by the stroke of a pen. The cassettes didn't mention that

part. I didn't think Earth was such a bad place to go, but I didn't speak up because I was eager to cut out prancing, round-humped reindeer with great racks of antlers from colored construction paper. I put glitter that was supposed to be used on the bells on the antlers and hooves, and the racks were so heavy that my reindeer's heads tore off when I hung them up. After lunch the teacher said he didn't know why we were sitting around school on Christmas Eve day when it was snowing, and he told us to go build snowmen, and he swept up the scraps of construction paper and celluloid and glitter alone while we put our Christmas stars in plastic sacks and tucked them into our jackets so that our hands would be free to make snowballs.

My best friend, Timothy, and I took some of the gingerbread cookies sprinkled with red sugar to leave in the woods for Bigfoot, then ran out the door and got pelted with snowballs by upper-graders who must have sneaked out earlier.

Timothy and I ran over the new-fallen snow in the playground to duck behind the farthest fence, where we scooped up snow and fired back. We were evenly matched for a while, snowballs flying thick and heavy. Then the little kids came out of school and betrayed us by striking our flanks.

"The little brats," Timothy muttered, throwing down a slushball. I suspect he was less upset that the little ones had decided to team up with the big kids than that one of them was crying and making his way to the school building, and someone was sure to come checking to see who was making ice balls. "Come on," he said, still feigning disgust. "Let's go build our own fort and get ready for Bigfoot."

The creature of yore was not so legendary in our parts, where we kids often found footprints in mud after rainstorms and in the snows of winter, especially in the woods surrounding the school. The grown-ups just shook their heads and said someone was playing a joke, that nobody wore shoes that big and that a real Bigfoot would be barefoot, like in the video show. But no one really knew what Bigfoot's toes looked like. My dad said even the video maker just guessed. We kids figured Bigfoot's foot was full of matted hair or lumpy skin that left those strange-looking ridges. And we just knew that Bigfoot came out in the dark storms looking for a stray child to eat, and that gingerbread cookies merely whetted the creature's appetite.

Leaving the school behind us, we made our way toward the greenway along the hoverpath, where the freighters sprayed us with a blizzard of snow when they whooshed by.

"Look here," Timothy shouted, tugging at something he'd stepped on in the snow. Both of us scratched at the snow and pulled until we freed a great piece of cardboard. It was frozen stiff.

"Let's go to the hill," I said.

Dragging our cardboard sled behind us, we trudged along Bigfoot's own trail through the woods. You could tell the creature had passed here from time to time because branches were broken back wider than any kid could cause, and the path circled the hill outside a wire-and-picket fence, and the gate was always locked to keep Bigfoot and everyone else out. The hill was treeless, acres of grass manicured by robots with great rotary blades in summer and smooth as a cue ball in winter. Perfect for sledding. The only trouble with the hill was that Timothy's aunt lived in the shiny tin-can-lying-on-its-side house at the top. I knew she was weird because Timothy said she never came outside or went anywhere, and my parents would shake their heads when they talked about her. But we had the cardboard sled in our hands, and he was pulling strongly; so I guess he didn't care about his weird aunt.

The fence might keep clumsy Bigfoot out but delayed us only a few seconds when we snagged a ragged edge of the cardboard on it and had to stop to free it. Then we climbed what seemed to be fourteen thousand one hundred ten meters of elevation to a place a little below the odd house, where we finally rested, breathing as hard as ancient warriors who'd just dragged their elephant up the Alps.

Timothy's aunt's house whirred and clicked, and I looked up. There were no windows, but it had a thousand eyes hidden in the silver rivets that held the metal skin over tungsten bones.

In the white snow it looked desolate, save for a trickle of smoke.

"Hey, your aunt's house is on fire," I said.

Timothy gave me a look that always made me feel stupid. "Her heat exchanger's broken. She's burning gas," he said. "I know because she asked my dad to get her a new one before Christmas."

"Does she come to your house for Christmas?"

"Nah. Sometimes she comes video, just like she used to when she lived up there." He gestured skyward, where snow-flakes were crystallizing and falling on us, but I knew he meant higher, one of the space stations or orbiting cities. "It's better now because there's no delay when we talk. It's like she was in Portland or something."

"What's she like?" I said, suddenly wondering about this peculiar person who had been a fixture in my community since I was little, yet whom I'd never seen.

Timothy shrugged. "Like an aunt ... always wanting to know if I ate my peas." Warrior Timothy was patting the cardboard elephant sled, making ready to resume our journey in the Alps.

"Why doesn't she come out of there?"

"My dad says she's got a complex or something from when she lived up there." He gestured skyward again.

"What's a complex?"

For a moment Timothy looked blank, then he said, "It's like what Joan-John and Lester-Linda Johnson have."

"You mean she goes to the clinic and comes back something else?" I said, wondering if his aunt used to be his uncle.

"I mean she doesn't go anywhere."

"But like to the consumer showcases down in the mall and the restaurant. She goes there, doesn't she?"

"Nope. Last year when her mux cable got cut and her video wasn't working she practically starved to death."

"But why? Is she crippled or something?" The teacher had said he knew a spacer who spent most of his time in a swim-ming pool, and when he did come out he had to use a wheel-chair because he was too old to get used to gravity again.

"No, she's not crippled."

"What's she look like?"

"My mother."

Timothy's mother was regular looking; so whatever a complex was, it had nothing to do with getting ugly. The Johnsons weren't ugly either, but they went through what my dad called phases, which he said was all in their heads. Maybe Timothy's aunt's complex was like Lester Johnson's Linda phase, but that didn't seem right because Lester-Linda came outside all the time and Timothy's aunt never did.

"What does she do inside all the time?"

"Works."

I nodded, considerably wiser. The old public buildings were down in the woods with the school, mostly monuments to waste of space ever since we got our mux cable that fed into every building in the community. Most of the grown-ups stopped *going* to work, and they stopped coming to school on voting day, but we still had to go, and not just on voting day.

"Come on," Timothy said.

But the smoke fascinated me. It puffed out of a silver pipe and skittered down the side of the house as if the fluffy falling snow was pushing it down. It smelled strange. I formed a snowball, a good solid one, took aim at the silver pipe, and let it fly.

"Missed by at least a kilometer," Timothy said, scowling.

Undaunted I tried another, missed the pipe, but struck the house, which resounded with a metallic thud. I'd closed one of the house's eyes with a white patch of snow. Timothy grinned at me, his mind tracking with mine. She'd have to come out to get the snow off the sensors. Soon we had pasted a wavy line of white spots about midway up the silver wall.

"One more on the right," commanded Timothy. But he stopped midswing when we heard a loud whirring noise. Around the hill came a grass cutter, furiously churning snow with its blades.

"Retreat!" shouted Attila the Hun. Timothy grabbed the frozen cardboard sled.

We leaped aboard and the elephant sank to its knees. I didn't need Timothy to tell me to run.

At the fence we threw ourselves over the frozen pickets, miraculously not getting our clothes hung up in the wires. The grass cutter whirred along the fenced perimeter, frustrated, thank goodness, by the limits of its oxide-on-sand mind.

"Ever seen what one of those things does to a rabbit?" he asked me.

"No."

"Cuts them up into bits of fur and guts," Timothy said solemnly.

"Your aunt's weird," I said, grateful to be on the right side of the fence.

"Uh oh. You lost a glove," Timothy said.

I nodded unhappily and turned to look over at the wrong side of the fence. Shreds of felt and wire and red nylon lay in the grass cutter's swath.

We walked on, feeling like two dejected warriors in the Alpine woods without our elephant and minus one almost-new battery-operated glove until we spied Bigfoot's tracks in the snow—big, round splots leading up the side of the wash. Heartened by our discovery, we armed ourselves properly with snowballs and told each other this was the genuine article. The snowfall was heavier now, really Bigfoot weather, and we knew how much Bigfoot liked storms, or we'd find tracks all the time.

We followed the footprints all the way to the Wigginses' house, only to find little Bobby Wiggles in them, hand-me-down boots overheating and making great puddles with each step.

Bobby stood looking at us, cheeks flushed from heat or stinging wind. Then he or she—I couldn't tell if Bobby Wiggles was a boy or a girl—giggled and went running into the house.

Timothy and I stayed out in the snow searching for Bigfoot tracks but found only rabbit tracks, which we followed in hopes that Bigfoot might do likewise, since aside from children there was nothing else for it to eat in our neighborhood, and no children had ever been reported eaten. Bigfoot may not have been hungry, but we had had only a few gingerbread cookies since noon; so when the rabbit tracks zagged near my house, we didn't turn again. We forgot the rabbit and Bigfoot and walked the rest of the way through the ghost-white woods to my front door, where we kicked off our boots and threw down our jackets and gloves. Mom and Dad were in the media room in front of the kitchen monitor, checking the Christmas menu.

"Go back and plug your gloves into the recharger," Dad said without glancing up.

But Mom must have looked up because she said right away, "Both of them."

"I lost one," I said.

"Go back out and find it."

Timothy and I looked at each other.

Mom was still watching me. "It won't do any good," I said finally. "We were up on the hill, and Timothy's aunt sicced the grass cutter on us."

"Why would she do a thing like that?"

Timothy and I shrugged.

"Well, I'll call her and ask her to let you get your glove," Dad said, rolling his chair to the comm console.

"The grass cutter got it," I said, more willing to face punishment for losing a glove than what might happen if Dad found out the day before Christmas that we'd closed her house's eyes.

"I told you she was getting crazier by the minute," Dad said.

"She isn't dangerous."

"How do you know that? The grass cutter, of all things."

"She has too much dread to be deliberately mean. I don't doubt for a second that she knew a couple of kids could outrun the grass cutter, and what else could she do? Go outside and ask them to go away?" Mom shook her head. "Her heart would stop from the anxiety of leaving her little sanctuary."

"She left the clinic fast enough when it caught on fire, and when she first came back that was as much her sanctuary as her spaceship house is now."

"You can't expect her to have enough energy to treat every minor day-to-day incident like an emergency."

"I think she should go back where she came from."

"Hush, dear. We voted for the treaty."

"They ought to have sent them to L-5."

"Couldn't, and you know—"

Timothy and I left them talking about his aunt, but I knew I'd probably not heard the end of the glove. That was the problem with sexagenarian parents; they knew all the tricks from the first set of kids, and they had very good memories.

In the kitchen we had hot chocolate, slopping some on the puzzle my big sister had broken back into a thousand pieces before she gave it to me.

"What are you getting for Christmas?" Timothy asked me, his cheeks still pink from being outdoors and his eyes as bright as tinsel fluttering in the warm convection currents of the house.

I shrugged. My parents were firm about keeping the Christmas list up-to-date, and that started every year on December twenty-sixth. I still wanted the fighting kite I'd keyed into the list last March, and the bicycle sail and the knife and the Adventure Station with vitalized figures and voice control. I also wanted the two hundred and eighty other items on my list and knew I'd be lucky if ten were under the tree tomorrow morning and that some of them would be clothes, which I never asked for but always received. "An Adventure Station," I finally said, more hopeful than certain. It was the one thing I'd talked about a lot, but Dad kept saying it was too much like the Hovercraft Depot set I'd gotten last year.

"Me too," Timothy said, "and a sled. Which should we play with first?"

A sled! I didn't have to go to the terminal and ask for a display of my Christmas list to know that a sled was not on it. My old one had worked just fine all last winter, but I'd used it in June to dam up Cotton Creek to make a pond for my race boats, and a flood had swelled the creek waters and carried it off and busted the runners. Too late to be remembering on Christmas Eve, because I didn't believe in Santa Claus or Kriss Kringle. Only in Bigfoot, because I had seen the footprints with my own eyes.

"We should play with the sleds first," Timothy said, "before the other kids come out and ruin the snow."

"I'm going to get a knife with a real L-5 crystal handle."

Timothy shrugged. "My aunt's going to give me one of hers someday. She has lots of stuff from when she was a spacer."

"Yeah, but my knife will be new. Then I'd like to see Bigfoot get away from me!"

"We can bring Bigfoot back on my sled," Timothy said excitedly. He chugalugged the rest of his chocolate. "Early, right after presents. Meet me at the hill."

"Why at the hill?" I said suspiciously. But Timothy was already heading for the door and pulling on his boots.

"Best place for sledding."

"But what about your aunt's mower?" I said, whispering now.

"Early," he reminded me as he stepped out into the snow. I followed him, holding the door open. "And bring your sled."

"What time do you open presents?" I said. But if Timothy answered, I didn't hear.

The snow was falling in fat flakes, and the wind had come up and the snow was starting to drift over the hedges. Funny how it wasn't really dark with all that white around, and funny, too, how I wasn't so glad that it was coming down. What good was it without a sled? I could use the cardboard if I could find it again, which I doubted, for I could tell that if it kept snowing at the rate I was seeing from my doorway, there would be half a meter or more by morning, which also meant the grass cutter would get clogged before it got five meters from Timothy's crazy aunt's house. Timothy would let me try his sled if I pulled it up the hill, 'cause if he didn't I wouldn't let him hold my L-5 crystal-handled knife . . . if I got one.

"Close the door!" my father shouted, and I closed it and went to bed early, knowing I couldn't sleep but wanting to because morning would come sooner if I did, and when it did I would not have a sled—maybe not even an L-5 crystal-handled knife—only an old Adventure Station that Timothy didn't want to play until after lunch, and who cared about snow anyhow, even if it did come down so fast and hard that it was catching on my bedroom window like a blanket before my sleepy eyes.

I woke to silence and the sure knowledge that it was Christmas morning. I didn't know whether to look out the window or check under the tree first, until I heard my sister in the hall and made a dash to beat her to the living room, where my parents had piled all the packages, with their red bows and wrappings, under the tree.

The big one wrapped in red plastic had to be the Adventure Station, though my parents were famous for putting little items like L-5 crystal-handled knives in packages the size of CRTs, complete with rocks to weigh it down so you couldn't tell. I couldn't wait to find out for sure what was in it, but I had to because my parents came in muttering about coffee and asking if it was even dawn and not caring that it wasn't when they had their coffee and I put their first presents to open in their laps. I wanted to open the red plastic-covered package, but I couldn't tear the plastic, and my big sister was hogging the slitter; so I opened a smaller one with my name on it. A shiny blue crystal that was almost mirror bright but not quite, so I could see the steel blade was in the package, and suddenly I felt good about the snow, too, and about looking for Bigfoot even if we did have to carry it back on Timothy's sled. I got the slitter away from my sister and sliced open the Adventure Station, only it wasn't. I looked at my parents in complete amazement and saw that they both had that special knowing twinkle in their eyes that parents get when they've done something you don't expect them to do. In the packing popcorn was a new sled, the collapsible kind with a handle for carrying it back up the hill and a retractable towing cord and three runner configurations so that it could be used on hard-packed snow or powder. I extended it to its full length right there in the living room, awed by its metallic gleam and classy black racing stripes.

And then with my knife strapped around the outside of my jacket and my sled in hand, I was off to meet Timothy, determined to have Bigfoot in tow before lunchtime. The going was slow because the drifts were tall and I loved to break their peaks and feel the stuff collapse beneath my feet and to stand under the tallest pines and shake the snow off the branches, as if I were in a blizzard and not in the first sparkling rays of sunshine. I went the long way to the hill, sure I would find traces of Bigfoot so early in the morning, and I did. Huge prints that were bigger than I could make, even though they were filled in with new snow, and the stride sure wasn't kid-size. Besides, what grown-up would walk through the woods on Christmas Eve during a snowstorm? I'd follow them, I decided, until I had to turn off for the hill, then Timothy and I would come back and follow the tracks to Bigfoot's lair. But I didn't have to turn off. The fat tracks headed right off through the woods along the same shortcut Timothy and I had used yesterday.

Timothy wasn't there yet, and because I couldn't wait to try my sled on the hill and not because I was afraid to follow the tracks alone, I stopped at the place we'd climbed over yesterday. The snow had drifted along the inside of the fence, almost hiding the pickets from view. I figured that with just a little more accumulation it would have covered the top, then my silver sled could carry me all the way from the top of the hill, over the fence, and deep into the woods, where the trees would provide a test of steering skill or a fast stop. I climbed the fence, sled in hand, then carried armfuls of snow to the highest drift, scooping and shoving until the tops of the pickets were covered. When I was satisfied the sled would glide over, I looked around for Timothy, who might still be opening his presents for all I knew, then I started to the top of the hill. I was only a little bit wary about the grass cutter, for I figured it would get clogged if it came out in the snow, but you never know what else a crazy lady who sent out grass cutters to hack up kids might have. But the little house at the top was almost completely snow covered, and there was no sign of smoke. Either Timothy's father got her that new heat exchanger or she froze.

At the top of the hill, not too close to the house in case she was just sleeping and not dead, I extended the sled, putting the runners in their widest configuration to keep me atop the deep snow. I climbed on and took off, the Teflon bottom gliding like ice on ice, and the wind stinging my face, and my heart beating with joy at the sled's speed on its very first trial run. Only trouble was that the wide runners didn't steer very well as I picked up speed, and there being no beaten path in the snow, I wasn't completely certain I'd be on target to make my fence jump. I pulled hard to the right, and the sled came with it sluggishly, but enough so I started to think again that I would make the jump. I could see the pickets on either side, and those would make a painful stop, but I was going to make it and know what it was like to fly on a sled for a few meters, or I would have known if I hadn't overcorrected just before hitting the big drift. The sled skidded along the downside of the drift and into a hole. I hit on something that sent me flying. I came down hard, hurt and crying, upside down.

It took me a minute to realize that I wasn't badly hurt, just scraped and bumped here and there, and stuck. My head felt funny, almost like someone was choking me and pressing against my skull, but it wasn't so bad that I couldn't see once I stopped crying. But I couldn't get loose. I could get hold of the fence and turn a bit but not enough to unhook my foot, which was firmly wedged between two pickets as far as it could go. Try as I would, as nimble as I was, and as desperate in knowing that I was quite alone and there was no one to send for help, I could not get loose. I shouted for Timothy, prayed he would come out of the woods and get me loose, but he never came. I cried again, and my tears froze, and the plug in my mitten power pack must have come loose, because my fingers were cold, too. The woods were things with icy tentacles frozen to the sky, and the sun reflected brightly off the snow-topped world and made me cry again. The wide expanse of sky looked vast and forbidding and somehow confirmed my worst fears that there was no one but me within a million klicks. And I wondered how long a person could live upside down. Didn't they do that all the time out in space? It had made Timothy's aunt weird but, oh, Timothy's aunt! Maybe her house had ears as well as eyes, and I shouted and shouted, promising I'd never throw snowballs at her house again. I thought that all the blood in my body was pooled behind my eyeballs, and if I cried again my tears would be blood, and I wanted to cry again because I knew that Timothy's aunt never would come because she never went anywhere.

And then in the stillness of the morning, when there was nothing to hear in the snow-packed world but my crying, I heard what sounded like an animal breathing into a microphone—a very powerful microphone or a very big animal.

I held my breath and listened carefully, watching the woods, terrified that the creature was lurking there behind the snow-covered bushes. But I was hanging upside down, and it took me a moment to realize that the sound was coming from behind me, closer now, hissing. I turned wildly and pressed my face against the pickets to see what was on the other side.

A towering hulk.

Shoulders like a gorilla.

White as the snow.

Breath making great clouds.

Feet leaving massive tracks.

There wasn't a doubt at all in my mind that I'd finally found Bigfoot, and it was more awful than anything I had imagined.

I screamed and struggled, quite willing to leave my foot behind in the fence, if only that were possible. I tried to unsheathe my knife, and I dropped it in the snow. It was within reach, and I might have retrieved it, but the massive creature grabbed me by my coattails and hefted me up. With my foot free I kicked blindly, and I must have hurt it because it finally put me down. The fence was between us, but its hands still gripped me by the shoulders—smooth hands without fur, white and slightly slick looking, except there were wrinkles where the joints ought to have been, and those were like gray accordion pleats. I stood, dazed and dizzy from being on my head so long, staring up at Bigfoot's shiny eye. Her face was featureless but for the eye, and she still hissed angrily, and she had a vapor trail drifting out from her backside.

She let go of me, reached over to pick up the L-5 knife, and twirled it between her thumb and forefinger. The crystal flashed in the sunlight, just like the ads they'd filmed on L-5. She flipped it, and I caught it two-handed. I backed away toward where my sled lay, didn't bother to collapse it, but grabbed the cord. I ran for the woods.

When I looked back, Bigfoot was gone, but her tracks left a clear trail to the desolate little house at the top of the hill, where Christmas was wholly a video event, where Timothy's crazy aunt would rather starve to death than come out for food.

And sometimes when it snowed, especially when it snowed on Christmas Day, I climbed over the fence of her universe to wipe the drifts of snow off the eyes of her house. It fell like glittering Christmas stars, peaceful again for all the world.

THE BEST IN
SCIENCE FICTION

☐	54310-6	A FOR ANYTHING	$3.95
☐	54311-4	*Damon Knight*	Canada $4.95
☐	55625-9	BRIGHTNESS FALLS FROM THE AIR	$3.50
☐	55626-7	*James Tiptree, Jr.*	Canada $3.95
☐	53815-3	CASTING FORTUNE	$3.95
☐	53816-1	*John M. Ford*	Canada $4.95
☐	50554-9	THE ENCHANTMENTS OF FLESH & SPIRIT	$3.95
☐	50555-7	*Storm Constantine*	Canada $4.95
☐	55413-2	HERITAGE OF FLIGHT	$3.95
☐	55414-0	*Susan Shwartz*	Canada $4.95
☐	54293-2	LOOK INTO THE SUN	$3.95
☐	54294-0	*James Patrick Kelly*	Canada $4.95
☐	54925-2	MIDAS WORLD	$2.95
☐	54926-0	*Frederik Pohl*	Canada $3.50
☐	53157-4	THE SECRET ASCENSION	$4.50
☐	53158-2	*Michael Bishop*	Canada $5.50
☐	55627-5	THE STARRY RIFT	$4.50
☐	55628-3	*James Tiptree, Jr.*	Canada $5.50
☐	50623-5	TERRAPLANE	$3.95
☐		*Jack Womack*	Canada $4.95
☐	50369-4	WHEEL OF THE WINDS	$3.95
☐	50370-8	*M.J. Engh*	Canada $4.95

Buy them at your local bookstore or use this handy coupon:
Clip and mail this page with your order.

Publishers Book and Audio Mailing Service
P.O. Box 120159, Staten Island, NY 10312-0004

Please send me the book(s) I have checked above. I am enclosing $ _____
(Please add $1.25 for the first book, and $.25 for each additional book to cover postage and handling.
Send check or money order only—no CODs.)

Name _____
Address _____
City _____ State/Zip _____
Please allow six weeks for delivery. Prices subject to change without notice.